KEEP QUIET

Also by Lisa Scottoline

KEEP QUIET

Lisa Scottoline

ST. MARTIN'S PRESS NEW YORK

This is a work of fiction. All of the characters, organizations, and events portrayed in this novel are either products of the author's imagination or are used fictitiously.

www.stmartins.com

The Library of Congress Cataloging-in-Publication Data is available upon request.

ISBN 978-1-250-01009-4 (hardcover)
ISBN 978-1-4668-4204-5 (e-book)

St. Martin's Press books may be purchased for educational, business, or promotional use. For information on bulk purchases, please contact Macmillan Corporate and Premium Sales Department at 1-800-221-7945, extension 5442, or write specialmarkets@macmillan.com.

First Edition: April 2014

10 9 8 7 6 5 4 3 2 1

Dedicated to the memory of the incomparable Matthew Shear, brilliant publisher, beloved friend, warmest heart

Making the decision to have a child—it is momentous.
It is to decide forever to have your heart go
walking around outside your body.

—Elizabeth Stone

KEEP QUIET

Chapter One

Jake Buckman knew his son had a secret, because his wife told him so. They didn't know what it was but they suspected it was about a girl, since Ryan had been texting non-stop and dressing better for school, which meant he actually cared if his jeans were clean. Jake wished he and his son were closer, but it was probably too late to turn it around. Ryan was sixteen years old, and Jake couldn't compete with girls, friends, the basketball team, Facebook, Call of Duty, Xbox, Jay-Z, Instagram, and pepperoni pizza. No father could, least of all an accountant.

Jake drummed his fingers on the steering wheel, waiting in front of the multiplex for Ryan, who'd gone to the movies with his teammates. The rift between father and son began five years ago, when Jake lost his job. The accounting firm he'd worked for had gone bankrupt in the recession, and he'd been out of a job for almost a year. They'd lived on his unemployment, his wife's salary, and savings, but he felt ashamed at the brave smile on Pam's face, the snow globe of bills on the kitchen table, and the endless rejection from jobs for which he was overqualified.

He shuddered, thinking back. Since he hadn't been able to

get a job, he'd done something he'd always wanted to do, start his own financial-planning business. He named it Gardenia Trust for Pam's favorite perfume and he'd dedicated himself to getting it off the ground. He'd worked days and nights at a rented cubicle, cold-calling everyone he knew to drum up clients. He'd said yes to every speaking engagement, keynote or not. He'd given seminars at retirement villages, Rotary Clubs, and libraries. In time he became one of the top-ten ranked financial planners in southeastern Pennsylvania, but it had taken a toll on his family. He and Pam had fixed their marriage with counseling, but in the meantime, Ryan had grown up. Only Pam believed Jake could still fix his relationship with Ryan before their son left for college. She'd encouraged him, even tonight.

Go pick him up at the movie, she'd said. *He's expecting me, but you go instead.*

The movie theater was wedged between Best Buy and Nordstrom, and cars idled out front, their exhausts making chalky plumes. Jake wondered if some of the other parents were in the cars, but he wouldn't recognize them anyway. He'd only attended one or two parents' nights, a National Honor Society induction, and assorted basketball finals, because Ryan played varsity. Pam went to all of Ryan's games, having more flexibility in her work schedule, and Jake had told himself that her being there was the same as his being there, as if he could parent by proxy. He'd been wrong. He'd made himself superfluous in his own son's life. His wife was the keynote.

A crowd flowed from the multiplex, lighting cigarettes, checking phones, and chatting as they passed in front of his headlights. Jake looked over to see Ryan push open the exit door with his shoulder and roll out of the theater with his teammates, whose names Jake had made a point to memorize: Caleb, Benjamin, and Raj. They were all tall, but Ryan was the biggest at six foot five and 225 pounds, the scruffy tentpole of a shuffling group of shaggy haircuts, black North Face jackets, and saggy pants—except for the two girls.

Jake shifted upward in the driver's seat, surprised. He hadn't known Ryan and his buddies were going to the movies with any girls and he was pretty sure Pam didn't, either. One girl was a redhead and the other a long-haired blonde, who stood near Ryan. Jake wondered if the blonde was the mystery girl and if he could get a conversation going about it with Ryan on the way home. Pam always said her best conversations with him happened spontaneously, while they were driving around. If so, Jake would plan his spontaneity.

The girls waved good-bye, and he waited for Ryan to notice the Audi. He'd texted to say he was coming, but Ryan hadn't replied, so he couldn't be sure the text got delivered. Jake didn't honk, wave, or do something else dorky, so as not to embarrass himself or suburban fathers in general.

Jake saw Ryan slide his iPhone from his pocket and flick his bangs back, so that the phone illuminated his son's face. Ryan had large, warm brown eyes, a long, thin nose and largish mouth, his handsome features framed by wavy, chestnut-brown hair, which he kept longish. Everybody said Ryan was the spitting image of his father, but Jake knew that was true too many years and twenty-five pounds ago. Jake was forty-six years old, with crow's-feet, graying temples, and a starter paunch to prove it. He always said that Ryan got his size from his father, but his brains from his mother, which was the best of both.

Jake watched as Ryan looked up from his iPhone, spotted the Audi, and jerked his chin up in acknowledgment, then slapped Caleb's palm and came toward the car. Jake unlocked the passenger door, and Ryan opened it and slid inside, his jacket sliding against the leather seat.

"Where's Mom?" he asked, eyebrows lifting.

"She was busy, so I figured I'd come. How was the movie?"

"Okay. You left Moose home?" Ryan kept an eye on his iPhone screen.

"Oops, yeah." Jake hadn't thought to take the dog, though Pam carted him everywhere. He disengaged the brake, fed the car gas, and headed for the exit.

"I get you didn't want him to come. This car is too awesome." Ryan kept his head down, his thumbs flying as he texted, growing the blue electronic bubble on the phone screen.

"No, it's not that. I forgot. I'll bring him next time."

"Don't. He'll drool on the seats. We must keep the machine pristine." Ryan paused as he read the screen. "You mind if I keep texting? I want to stay with this convo."

"It's okay, do your thing." Jake steered around the back of the King of Prussia mall, where the lights of JCPenney, Macy's, and Neiman Marcus brightened a cloudy night sky. Cars were rushing everywhere; it was Friday night, the busy beginning to the weekend. It should have been colder for February, but it wasn't. A light fog thickened the air, and Jake remembered something he had learned tonight from the pretty weathergirl on TV.

Fog is a cloud on the ground.

He turned the defrost to maximum and accelerated toward Route 202, heading for open road. Ryan texted away, his hip-hop ringtone going off at regular intervals, punctuated by the Apple-generated swoosh. Jake wondered if his son was talking to the mystery girl. He himself remembered racking up huge phone bills when he first dated Pam, at college. He'd fallen for her their freshman year at Pitt and felt unbelievably lucky when she married him. She was a great wife, and he gave her total credit for Ryan being so well-adjusted and popular, despite his naturally reserved manner. He was earning A's in AP courses, got solid SAT scores, and was already being recruited by college basketball programs, some Division I.

Jake switched into the slow lane, heading for the exit. He

wanted to ask Ryan about the girls, but he'd warm up first. "So, how was the movie?"

"Good. Like I said."

"Oh, right." Jake forgot, he had asked that already. "How's Caleb? And Raj and Benjamin?" He wanted to show he remembered the names.

"Fine."

"Everybody ready for the finals?"

"Yep."

Jake was getting nowhere fast. He still wanted to know about the girls, and according to Pam, the trick with Ryan was to act like you didn't care about the answer to the question you'd asked, or you'd never get an answer. So he said, offhandedly, "By the way, who were those girls at the movie?"

Ryan didn't look up from his phone, his thumbs in overdrive. Pink and green bubbles popped onto his phone screen, so he was texting with more than one person, like a conference call for teenagers.

"Ryan?" Jake tried again. "The girls at the movie, who were they?"

"Girls from school."

"Oh. Friends?"

"Yeah." Ryan still didn't look up.

"Nice." Jake let it go, an epic fail, in the vernacular. He pressed a button to lower the window, breathing in the moist, cool air. The fog was thickening, softening the blackness of the night, and the traffic dropped off as they approached the Concordia Corporate Center. They passed glowing signs for SMS and Microsoft, then turned onto Concordia Boulevard, which was lined with longer-stay hotels. He'd eaten enough of their reception-desk chocolate chip cookies to last a lifetime, because even his out-of-town clients were in the suburbs, the new home of American business.

Jake returned to his thoughts. His own office was in a nearby corporate center, and he spent his days ping-ponging between his corporate center and his clients' corporate centers, after which he drove home to his housing development. Some days the only trees he saw were builder's-grade evergreens, planted in zigzag patterns. Lately he felt as if his life were developed, rather than lived. He was a financial planner, but he was coming to believe that too much planning wasn't natural for trees or accountants.

Fog misted the windshield, and the wipers went on to clear his view, and Ryan chuckled softly. "Dad, this car is *sick*. I love how it wipes the windshield automatically."

"Me, too." Jake grinned, feeling the spark of a reconnection. They both liked cars, and last year, when Jake's old Tahoe hit 132,000 miles, he'd bought the Audi, mainly because Ryan had lobbied for one. Jake was a born Chevy guy, but Ryan had built umpteen online versions of the flashy Audi on the company web-site and designed what he called a "dream machine"—an A6 sedan with a 3.0 liter engine, Brilliant Black exterior, Black leather interior, and Brushed Aluminum inlay on the dashboard. They'd gone together to pick it up, and Jake had given Ryan a few driving lessons in it, when Ryan had the time.

"Dude." Ryan shifted forward, sliding the phone into his jacket pocket. "We're coming up on Pike Road. Can I drive?"

Jake checked the dashboard clock, which read 11:15. "You're not supposed to drive after eleven o'clock. You only have a learner's permit."

"But Dad, I've had it for five months already. I only have one month left before I can get my license. I did fifty-five out of the sixty-five hours, and all the nighttime driving hours and bad-weather hours. And you're with me, you're an adult."

"It doesn't matter, technically."

Ryan deflated. "Oh, come on, there's never traffic on Pike, not on the weekends. I can do it, Dad. You know I'm an excellent driver."

"We'll see when we get to Pike. If there's people around,

no." Jake wanted to keep the conversational momentum going, especially when Ryan's ringtone started up again. "So. It sounds like you're in demand tonight."

"I'm blowing up." Ryan smiled.

"Is something going on, or is it just the usual women beating down your door?"

Ryan snorted. "Yeah, right. I'm a chick magnet."

"Nobody's a chick magnet, buddy. That's why God invented cars."

"Ha!" Ryan slapped his hands together. "*That's* what I'm talking about! Agree!"

Yes! Jake realized he'd said the exact right thing, and Ryan shifted around to face him, with a new grin.

"When I get my license, you'll lend me the machine, right? I won't have to drive the Tahoe all the time."

"I will." Jake smiled.

"Awesome! Dad, guess what, I'm so stoked. I might have a date tomorrow night."

Bingo! "Really? Who?"

"Wait. Whoa. Hold on, it's Pike Road, we're here. Please, please, pull over." Ryan gestured to the right side of Pike, where the asphalt ended without a curb. "Right over there."

"Relax, remain calm." Jake braked as he approached the street.

"Please let me drive. We're almost home. Look, the place is dead." Ryan waved toward the corporate center. The follow-up ringtone sounded in his pocket. "Can I drive?"

"We'll see." Jake cruised to a stop, letting an oncoming truck pass, then made a left and pulled over, so he could scope out the scene. Pike Road was a long street that ran between the woods on its right and the Concordia Corporate Center, on its left. It was used mainly as a shortcut to the corporate-center parking lots, and during the week, corporate running teams and athletic teams from Jake's high school used it to train. There was no traffic on the weekends.

"Dad, *please.*" Ryan leaned over, his eyes pleading, and Jake didn't want to ruin the mood.

"Okay, let's do it."

"Sweet!" Ryan threw open the door and jumped out of the car. Jake engaged the parking brake, opened the door, and straightened up, but Ryan was already running around the front, slapping him a strong high-five. "Thanks, dude!"

Jake laughed, delighted. "Speed limit is forty, but watch out for deer."

"Gotcha!" Ryan plopped into the driver's seat, and Jake walked to the passenger seat, got in, and closed the door behind him. He didn't have to adjust the seat because they were the same size.

"Now. Hold on. Before you go anywhere, adjust the mirrors, outside and in."

"On it." Ryan pushed the button to rotate the outside mirror, then reached for the rearview, and Jake watched him line it up, with approval. His son was careful and methodical, a perfectionist like him. Ryan even enjoyed practicing, especially basketball. Once he had told Jake that it took two-and-a-half hours to shoot a thousand foul shots, and Jake didn't have to ask Ryan how he knew.

"Don't forget your harness."

"I wasn't going to." Ryan fastened himself into the seat with a *click.*

"I have the low beams on. For this street, with no lights, I recommend the high beams."

"Agree." Ryan peered at the dashboard and switched them on.

"Take a second and look around." Jake looked down the street with Ryan, the high beams cutting the light fog. Pike Road was a straight shot the length of the corporate center, then took a sharp curve to the right. Tall trees lined the road, their branches jagged and bare.

"Good to go." Ryan released the emergency brake as his phone signaled an incoming text.

"Don't even think about getting that text. No texting while driving." Jake himself had stopped texting while he drove unless he was at a stoplight, and he talked on the phone only if he had the Bluetooth.

"I know." Ryan fed the car gas. The follow-up ringtone played but he stayed focused on his driving. "That's just Caleb, anyway. He's hyper tonight. He likes one of those girls we were with, the redhead with the white coat."

"I saw her." Jake relaxed in the seat, since Ryan had everything in control.

"Anyway, this girl I might go out with tomorrow night? She's new." Ryan smiled as he drove, warming to the topic. "Her family moved here over the summer from Texas. She rides horses. Barrel-racing. How baller is *that*?"

"Baller." Jake knew *baller* meant good. They passed Dolomite Road on their left, which ran behind the corporate center. "Was she the other girl at the movie? The blonde?"

"Yes." Ryan burst into an excited grin. "Did you see her? Isn't she *mad* cute?"

"I did see her. She's very cute."

"Yo, I'd be so lucky to be with this girl! She's short, but it works on her, you know?"

"Sure. Short is good. I like short. Your mom is short." Jake smiled. Pam was only five foot three, and his mother had called them Mutt and Jeff, back in the days when people knew who Mutt and Jeff were. Jake's mother had died ten years ago of blood cancer, and he still missed her every day. He didn't miss his father at all, though his father had outlived his mother by six years, which proved that not only was life unfair but death was, too.

"Her name's kinda weird, not gonna lie. Janine Mae Lamb.

Janine Mae is her first name. You have to say both names." Ryan maintained his speed as they approached the curve, marked by a caution sign with an arrow pointing right.

"I don't think that's a weird name. I think it's pretty. Feminine." Jake made approving noises to keep up the good vibe. The car's headlights illuminated the caution sign, setting its fluorescence aglow. "Lower your speed. It's a blind curve."

"On it." Ryan slowed down.

"So what's she like, personality-wise?"

"She's funny. She has a Texas accent. She says pin when she means pen."

"Accents are good. Accents can be adorable."

"Agree!" Ryan beamed as they reached the curve, and Jake felt happy for him.

"So you're going out with her tomorrow night? Why don't you take her someplace nice, on me, like a restaurant?"

"A *restaurant*? Dude, we're not *olds* like you!" Ryan looked over in disbelief as he steered around the curve, and Jake met his eye, bursting into laughter.

But in that split second, there was a sickening *thump*.

They jolted as if they'd hit something, and Ryan slammed on the brakes, cranking the wheel to the left. The right side of the car bumped up and down, fishtailed wildly, and skidded to a stop.

And then everything went quiet.

Chapter Two

"What was *that*?" Jake threw an arm across Ryan, but the accident was over as suddenly as it had begun. The noise had come from the passenger side of the car, toward the front.

"Dad, I'm sorry, I hit something, I think it was a deer." Ryan shook his head, upset. "I didn't see it, I was looking at you. I hope I didn't hurt it or the car."

"It's okay. Don't worry about the car." Jake hadn't seen anything because he'd been looking at Ryan. The car sat perpendicular on the street, its headlights blasting the trees. The airbags hadn't gone off. The windshield was intact. The engine was still running.

"If it's a deer, maybe it's not dead. Maybe we can call the vet. Dr. Rowan is a good guy. He'd come, wouldn't he?"

"Hmm, I don't know. It's kind of late to call him." Jake twisted around and checked behind them. The back of the car had stopped short of a tree and a yellow stanchion sticking out of the ground with a sign that read GAS PIPELINE. He shuddered to think how much worse it could have been.

"Maybe the emergency vet then? Can we call them?"

"Let me go see. You stay here." Jake patted Ryan's arm, opened the car door, and got out, steeling himself for the sight. He'd hit a deer two years ago and still felt guilty. He looked to the right, where the sound had come from. Something dark and lumpy lay off the road, in the raggedy fringe of brush bordering the woods, bathed in the red glow of their taillights.

Oh my God.

Jake knew what he was seeing, in his heart, before his brain let him accept the reality. He found himself racing toward the dark and fallen form. It wasn't a deer. It was a human being, on its side, facing away from him. It couldn't be anything else from the shape. And it was lying still, so still.

Jake threw himself on the ground beside the body. A woman runner in a black jersey and black running tights lay motionless on her side, her skinny body like a limp stick figure.

"Miss, Miss!" Jake called out, frantic. She didn't reply or moan. He pressed her neck to see if she had a pulse, but didn't feel anything. He couldn't see much in the dim light. The woman was petite. She had long hair. Dark blood flowed from a wound near her hairline. Her features glistened, abraded by the asphalt. Road dirt pitted her nose and cheek.

"Miss!" Jake leaned over her chest, trying to hear a heartbeat, but he couldn't hear anything. He turned the woman over on her back to begin CPR and put an arm under her neck to open her airway. Her head dropped backwards. He realized with horror that she was dead.

"Ryan! Help! Call 911!" Jake shouted, horrified. He'd left his phone in the car. He knew CPR. He'd been an Eagle Scout. He prayed the protocol hadn't changed. He bent over and began CPR, breathing into her mouth, willing oxygen into her lungs, counting off breaths in his head. Her lips were still warm, but she didn't respond.

"Dad! Oh my God, oh my God!" Ryan came running up, his

hands on his head, doubled over in shock. "It's a *lady*! *I hit a lady*?"

"Call 911!" Jake stopped breathing for her, shifted position, linked his fingers, and pumped the woman's chest, counting off in his head, praying to God he could resuscitate her. He had to bring her back. She couldn't be dead. This couldn't be happening.

"What are you doing? Tell me she's alive! She's alive, isn't she? No, this can't be! She has to be alive! I'm calling 911!" Ryan shook his head, edging backwards. His breaths came in ragged bursts. He pulled his phone from his pocket, but dropped it, agitated. "Dad, she . . . doesn't look like she's alive! She's alive . . . isn't she? She can't be . . . *dead*!"

"Stay calm, pick up your phone, and call 911." Jake pumped her chest, counting off the beats, trying to stay in emotional control. The woman still didn't respond. He kept pumping.

"Dad . . . no it *can't* be true!" Ryan cried out, bursting into an anguished sob. "I have to call . . . my phone! They can help her!" He dropped to his knees, frantically looking in the dark for his phone, crying and crawling around the street. "She can't be dead . . . where's my phone? I can't find my phone!"

Jake kept pumping on the woman's chest. His efforts became futile, grotesque. He was abusing her body. She had become a corpse. He couldn't believe it. He didn't understand. It was inconceivable. She had been alive a minute ago, running around the curve. Now she was dead. They had killed her.

God, no.

Jake stopped pumping and leaned back on his haunches. Tears came to his eyes. His hand went to his mouth, reflexively stifling himself. He looked down at the woman in the dim light. The sight broke his heart, and he knew it would be seared into his brain for the rest of his life. He bent his head and sent up a silent prayer on her behalf.

"No, no! Where's my . . . *phone*?" Ryan sobbed, scrambling

for his phone on all fours. "I *killed* . . . a lady, I *killed* . . . a lady, I wasn't looking . . . it's all my fault!"

"Ryan, she's gone," Jake whispered, his throat thick with emotion.

"No, no, no, no, she's not *gone* . . . she's not gone . . . what did I *do*?" Ryan fell over, collapsing into tears, his forehead on the asphalt. "Dad, I killed her . . . no, no, no!"

Jake rubbed his eyes, dragged himself to his feet, and half-walked and half-stumbled to Ryan.

"No, no, no!" Ryan cried, his big body folded onto itself, racked with sobs. "I can't . . . believe this. I . . . *killed* someone, I *killed* that . . . lady!"

"We'll get through this, Ryan." Jake gathered him up and hugged him tight, and they clung to each other in a devastated embrace.

"I *killed* . . . that lady . . . *I killed* . . . *that lady!* I wasn't . . . *looking*!"

"I didn't see her either. I'm at fault too, we both are." Jake held him close, then spotted Ryan's phone glinting in the light, by the side of the road.

"*I killed her!* Oh no oh no . . . what did I do?" Ryan wept and permitted himself to be held, and Jake's thoughts raced ahead. He'd call 911, but if he told the police that Ryan had been at the wheel, Ryan could get a criminal record, since he'd been driving after hours on a learner's permit. It would jeopardize his college admissions, basketball scholarships, everything. And Pam would never forgive him for letting Ryan drive or letting this happen. The open secret of their marriage was that his wife loved their son more than she loved him. Jake reached a decision.

"Ryan, listen to me. We need to call the police, but we can't tell them the truth. We're going to tell them that I was driving, not you. Got it? We'll say I was the driver, and you were the passenger."

"No, no . . . *I did it* . . . *I killed that lady* . . . she's *dead*!" Ryan sobbed harder, his broad chest heaving. Tears poured down his cheeks. His nose ran freely, his mucus streaming.

"Ryan, look at me. Look at me." Jake put his hands on his son's tearstained face. They had to get the story straight before they called the police. They had no time to lose. A car could come along any minute. "I need you to listen to me."

"I killed her!" Ryan kept shaking his head, hiccuping with sobs. "Dad—"

"Ryan, listen, try to calm down—"

"I can't, I can't!" Ryan shook his head back and forth, almost manically, out of control. "I killed her, I killed her!"

"Ryan, listen!" Jake shouted, only because Ryan was becoming hysterical. "We're going to tell the police I was driving the car, do you understand? I was driving the car and you were the passenger. Got it? I'll do all the talking, you keep quiet. You can do that, can't you?"

"No, no, no, I . . . *killed her*!" Ryan shouted back, his words indistinct, his tears and mucus flowing.

"Ryan, stop. We're going to tell the cops *I* killed her. Do you hear me? You *cannot* contradict me, no matter what they ask you. I'll do the talking, you keep your mouth shut."

"Dad . . . no!" Ryan lurched out of his arms, scrambled backwards, and staggered to his feet, shaking his head. "No, no, Dad. No!"

"Yes, do what I say, it's the only way." Jake got to his feet, hustled to the phone, and picked it up to call 911.

"No, no, wait . . . look. Wait." Ryan plunged his hand into his pocket, pulled out a plastic Ziploc bag, and showed it to Jake, sobbing. "Dad . . . I . . . bought this . . . today. What do I do with it . . . when the cops come?"

"What is it?"

"I'm sorry . . . it's weed . . . I'm sorry—"

"*What?*" Jake asked, aghast.

"I smoked up . . . with Caleb . . . after practice." Ryan wept, his hand flying to his hair, rubbing it back and forth. "But I'm not . . . high now, I swear it . . . I'm not, I'm not."

"You *smoke dope*? Since *when*?"

"I don't do a lot . . . I swear. I did it today . . . but I'm fine now . . . that's not why I hit the lady—"

"Give me that!" Jake grabbed the bag from Ryan's hand. It was a quarter full of marijuana.

"I killed that lady . . . she's dead!" Ryan dissolved into tears, holding his head, falling to his knees. He rocked on his haunches, back and forth, becoming hysterical. "She's dead . . . because of me . . . Dad, what do we do? I killed her . . . I killed her . . . I killed her!"

Jake had to make a split-second decision, wrestling with his conscience. A woman was dead, horribly, but that couldn't be changed. If Jake called the police and told them the truth, then two lives would be destroyed—hers and Ryan's. And Ryan was too distraught to maintain any lie to the police. Even if Jake tried to claim that he himself had been driving the car, the cops would question them both. He couldn't be sure Ryan wouldn't blurt out the truth about who was driving, and if Ryan did, the cops would test him and find marijuana in his blood. They would convict him of driving under the influence and vehicular homicide. He would go to jail. There would be no college, no future, no nothing. Ryan's entire life would be ruined—and all because Jake had let him drive.

Jake's mouth went dry. He couldn't bring himself to look back at the poor woman lying off the road, lifeless. He had no more time to ponder. He was a family man, and he'd lived his whole life being good, moral, and honest. He'd never broken the law in any way. So he knew he was making the absolute worst decision of his life when he stuffed the cell phone and Ziploc bag into his pocket, grabbed Ryan by his coat, and pulled him to his feet.

"Get back in the car, son," Jake said, grimly. "Hurry."

Chapter Three

Jake entered the kitchen to face his wife ahead of Ryan, according to plan. He felt sick to his stomach with guilt and horrified at what they had done. All he could think about was the dead woman, but he had to keep it together for Ryan's sake, to get past Pam. He'd been able to wipe the blood off his face and hands in the car, and he'd hidden his blood-stained parka in the garage. Pam wouldn't think it was strange that he didn't have a coat on because he often left it in the car, since their garage was attached. On the way home, Jake had pulled over and quieted his weeping son, even as he'd laid down the law.

Ryan, don't tell Mom. Never, ever.

I . . . never ever would. Are you . . . insane?

I mean it. No matter what. You know what she'd do. She'd have to.

I swear . . . I won't tell Mom . . . I won't tell anybody.

"Jake, what took you so long?" Pam was standing at the sink and turned toward him, a petite, naturally pretty woman with intelligent blue eyes, an upturned nose, and a small mouth with a perfect smile. She had her horn-rimmed glasses on, and with her long brown ponytail, gray hoodie, and jeans, she looked exactly like what she was, the smartest girl in the class, his vale-dictorian wife.

"Ryan was starving, and we stopped at the diner." Jake tried to mask his emotions and avoided her eye, while Moose trotted over and began sniffing him, wagging his feathery tail harder than usual. The golden retriever must have been smelling the blood he hadn't been able to wipe off his jeans, because it had seeped too quickly into the fabric. He hoped Pam wouldn't notice, since there wasn't much and the denim was dark blue, but Jake felt repulsed at the very thought. He never would have imagined himself being responsible for the death of an inno-cent woman, much less leaving her body by the side of a road.

"Why didn't you call?" Pam shut the dishwasher door with a solid *clunk,* then looked past him for Ryan, as if she was already sensing something amiss.

"Sorry, I should have." Jake put his hands on her shoulders and gave her a quick kiss on the lips, feeling like Judas himself. He had never lied to her, except to tell her that he liked all the wacky things she did to her hair. Highlights, lowlights, whatever, she was beautiful to him. He loved her.

"So why didn't you call?" Pam pulled away, with a slight frown.

"Fill you in later," Jake whispered quickly, as if he were try-ing to say it before Ryan came in. He pressed Moose's muzzle away from his jeans, but the dog wasn't giving up, so he reached down and scratched the dog's head, as if he wanted him close.

"Okay." Pam's forehead relaxed, and Jake could see that she had put a wifely checkmark in the box next to Explanation Pending. He glanced at the TV, which showed the local news, playing on low volume. He couldn't bear it if a breaking news report about the accident on Pike Road came on, with a lurid HIT AND RUN banner. Every time he'd seen a hit-and-run report on the news, he'd wondered to himself what kind of person would do such a hateful thing. And now he knew. He'd just become the guy he hated. In fact, he'd just become the guy everybody hated. He turned off the TV, his hand shaking slightly.

Pam looked over when Ryan entered the kitchen and she flashed him a warm grin. "Hey honey, how was the movie?"

"Okay," Ryan answered, his voice sounding almost normal.

Jake turned around to see what his son looked like in the bright lights of the kitchen, and his eyes were predictably reddish and puffy, his fair skin mottled. Jake's heart broke for him, because he knew how guilty and anguished Ryan was feeling. Yet at the same time, Jake was relieved that they had their story in place, because any mother could tell that the boy had been crying, especially as good a mother as the Honorable Judge Pamela A. Buckman, of the Superior Court of Pennsylvania.

"Only 'okay'? The reviews were excellent." Pam folded her arms and leaned a slim hip against the kitchen island, getting ready for a conversation, but Ryan kept walking through the kitchen to the hallway, precluding any question-and-answer, as planned.

"Mom, I'm going up, I'm beat," Ryan called out, tugging Moose away by the collar, on the fly. "See you in the morning. Good night, guys."

"Oh, okay, sleep tight, honey." Pam shifted her gaze to Jake, lifting an eyebrow.

Jake called out, "Good night, Ryan!"

They both watched as Ryan crossed the entrance hall and climbed the stairs, followed by Moose, wagging his fluffy tail. As soon as their son was out of sight and Jake was alone with Pam, he felt the tension level rise, as if their kitchen had a barometric pressure of its own. He had to tell Pam a convincing lie, but all he could think of was the woman he'd left dead, in the darkness. He'd driven away, too appalled and disgusted with himself to look in the rearview mirror. Her face had glistened with dark blood, slick and black as tar, covering her features so completely that he couldn't see what she looked like or how old she was.

"So what's going on?" Pam asked, mystified. "Was he crying? It looked like he was crying."

"He was, but he'll be okay, you'll see." Jake crossed to the sink and turned on the faucet, thinking about the dead woman. He felt stricken, knowing that she had been somebody's mother, wife, or even daughter.

"Why was he crying?" Pam followed him, tucking a strand of hair into her ponytail.

"We had a fight after the movie, but we worked it out." Jake pumped overpriced hand soap into his palm, lathered up, and began washing his hands of the poor woman's blood. He didn't see any telltale pink water going down the drain, and the very notion made his stomach turn. He felt as if he were in a waking nightmare, walking in the shoes of someone else entirely. A murderer, a criminal, a liar, or all three.

"But you guys don't fight. You don't talk enough to fight."

Jake reddened, but it gave him an idea for a better story. He'd been about to tell the story they'd made up in the car, involving Ryan getting mad at Caleb, but his new idea didn't involve a third party. He kept rinsing his hands, as if it would cleanse him of his guilt, like some villain in Shakespeare, he couldn't remember which. "Well, we fought this time, a bad one."

"Really."

"Yes, believe it or not." Jake kept his head down and his eyes on the water. The image of the woman's face reappeared. He could feel the warmth of her lips, when he was trying to get her breathing again. Maybe he shouldn't have given up so soon. Maybe he should have kept trying. He couldn't bring her back to life. She was really gone, and they had killed her.

"So what was it you fought about?" Pam folded her arms. "And why do I have to take your deposition? Tell me already."

"I am telling you." Jake realized she was right. He was stalling. He didn't want to lie to her. Once he did, the nightmare would become real, and there would be no going back. He didn't know if he could lie to her anyway. He hated lying to her, and he hated telling her the truth. It was a night of no-win decisions.

"Jake, you're beating around the bush."

"No, I'm not."

"Yes, you are. Honey, what is *going on*?"

Man up! Jake willed himself to get a grip. There'd been no going back the moment he'd left the scene. He twisted off the faucet, reached for the dishcloth, and started drying his hands, but he still couldn't make eye contact with her. "Okay, you're right, maybe I am. I don't feel that great about it, is all." He thought fast, realizing that his obvious discomfort could serve his story. "I mean, think about it from my point of view. I go to pick him up at the movies to get closer to him, and we fight and I make him cry, pushing him further away. I tried to do a good thing, but it turned out wrong." His throat caught when he realized that he was telling the truth, in a way. All of the emotions were real, if not the facts. "So now I'm home, and I have to tell you what happened."

"Aw, honey." Pam's voice softened, and she rubbed his back lightly. "I didn't mean to be sharp. I'm so tired. The weeks we sit *en banc* are a bitch. I'm sorry."

"No need to apologize." Jake knew that when the Superior Court sat *en banc,* the entire court would come to Philadelphia to hear oral arguments. There was a lot of preparation, and Pam worked extra hard, drafting opinions into the night to keep up with her regular caseload. Still, she wasn't so tired that she wasn't peering at him, intently.

"So tell me what happened."

"Okay, but it won't be easy for you to understand, because you guys have such a good relationship." Jake folded the dishcloth and set it in its pile by the paper towels, more deliberately than necessary. "Plus I'm worried that, the way I handled it tonight, I blew it. I'll never get in sync with him now, not before he goes to college."

"Aw, yes you will." Pam rubbed his back again. "So what happened already, ya big lug?"

Jake cringed inwardly, because he loved when she called him that. Pam liked his size because she said it made her feel safe, and he always thought he could protect her and Ryan—until tonight. He never would have guessed there'd be a jogger around the curve. He never would have foreseen they'd hit her. He told himself to get back on track and tell the story. He said, "It was silly, a little thing that got to be a big thing."

"That happens." Pam nodded in an encouraging way. He'd seen her do the same thing in the courtroom, trying to put a lawyer at ease during oral arguments. *Counsel, don't let us intimidate you,* she'd say. *Judges are people too. Just smarter.*

"Well, we were driving home from the movie, and I was trying to have a conversation with him, but he was texting the whole time."

"I don't let him do that in the car." Pam's lips pursed. "It's the same rule as at mealtimes. The principle is the same, whatever the location. He doesn't get to ignore his parents or people around him. It's just plain rude."

"Right, I think so, too, but I didn't want to lower the hammer—"

"Oh, be honest."

She knows. Jake reddened, stricken. "What do you mean? Honest about what?"

"You wanted to be Fun Dad." Pam snorted. "That's why you didn't lower the hammer."

Jake tried to recover, but she was right. That was exactly what had happened. He never should have let Ryan drive. He'd made the classic mistake. He'd acted like a friend, not a parent. Pam would never have made such a terrible decision. He sighed heavily, feeling the weight of his conscience. "I know, you're right. I know, I know, I know."

"Honey, enough. Don't beat yourself up."

Jake couldn't help it. If she only knew. He tried to return to the story, to spit it out. "So anyway, I didn't tell him to stop texting. My plan was to win him over, to see if I could engage him on my own. Make it volitional, not a rule."

"I hear you." Pam regarded him impatiently behind her glasses. "And so . . ."

"And then, well, to go back a minute, when I picked him up at the movie, I noticed that there were two girls they were talking to."

"Girls?" Pam lifted an eyebrow.

"Yeah, so while he was texting, I started to ask him about them, who they were and how they came to be at the movie. I was trying to make conversation, to get something going." Jake was making it up as he went along, but Pam's manner had changed from impatient to intrigued.

"So what did he say? I didn't know there were girls going to the movie, or that they were meeting girls there."

"I didn't get an answer. But wait"—Jake caught himself—"if I tell you what happened, you can't talk to him about it."

"Why not?"

"If you say anything, he'll never confide in me again, and that would defeat the purpose of my going to pick him up in the first place." Jake realized suddenly that if he could get Pam not to bring up the subject with Ryan, then the boy wouldn't have to lie to her. "Let us work it out, him and me. I think we did by the end, so let me keep at it."

"Okay, Coach." Pam rolled her eyes, amused. Her hands went to her ears, fingering the diamond studs he had given her, checking the backs to make sure they stayed on, a nervous habit. "So, as you were saying . . ."

"Well, all he would tell me about the girls was that they were from school and . . ." Jake stopped short, not wanting to tell her about the girl from Texas that Ryan had asked out. "Anyway, when I asked him another question, he kept texting, and I heard him mutter under his breath, 'It's none of your business.'"

"That is so disrespectful!" Pam's mouth dropped open. "He gets that from Caleb, you know. I *hate* that kid. He's a bad influence."

Jake bit his tongue. Pam was more right than she knew. "Ryan says he didn't say it, but I swear he did, and we got in a fight. I told him I thought he was being fresh and entitled—"

"Hoo boy." Pam's eyes flared.

"—and he told me that he was too old to be reporting his personal life to his father, and he shouldn't have to account for everything he did, and we yelled at each other."

"And he *cried*? He *never* cries."

Jake told himself to remain calm. Pam may have been a Ryan expert, but she didn't know he smoked marijuana and she would disapprove heartily. He had tried pot in college, and she hadn't even tried it. His wife took seriously the fact that she was a judge and had sworn an oath to uphold the law. Plus she believed marijuana turned kids into underachievers, which in her mind, was practically criminal. Jake reminded himself to get back on track with the story. "He cried from the stress, I guess. I shouted at him. I lost my temper."

"*You?*" Pam blinked. "You never lose your temper."

"I do sometimes."

"Okay, whatever." Pam shrugged, but Jake didn't want to remind her of the night he'd lost his job, when he'd thrown his laptop across the kitchen and cracked the screen. It wasn't even under warranty.

"Anyway, he pushed my buttons."

"Did you call him names? Remember, you're not supposed to call names."

"Of course not, I don't call names." Jake knew from therapy that name-calling was against the rules, like the Geneva Convention of marriage.

"I don't understand something. Was this in the car or the diner?"

"Was what?" Jake lost his train of thought again. He kept thinking of the woman, how horrible she had looked, lying there.

"The fight," Pam was saying. "Did you have it in the car or the diner?"

What diner? "In the car."

"After a fight like this, you went to the diner?"

Jake realized it sounded implausible. "Yes," he answered anyway.

"He went along with that?" Pam recoiled, surprised. "I would think he'd be embarrassed. He'd been crying. What if he ran into someone he knew? Everybody knows who he is, from the team. You can't miss him, he's built like a lighthouse."

"That's what he said, but I insisted on it. He cleaned himself up in the car. I always have those Wet Wipes in the console, for when I eat in the car." In truth, Jake was the one who cleaned up using the Wet Wipes. There had been blood on his face and hands. He'd driven away from a hit-and-run, thrown away the Wet Wipes and the marijuana in a Dumpster, and taught their son that dishonesty was the best policy. Jake didn't know himself anymore. This wasn't him.

"Why'd you want to go to the diner? You mean Mason's?"

"Yes, Mason's." Jake realized he'd just trapped himself. He was a terrible liar. His heart beat wildly in his chest, as if it wanted to escape his very body.

"But you hate Mason's. Every time I ask you to go, you say no."

"I know, but you and Ryan love it, and I thought we could sort things out better there."

"In public?" Pam didn't look suspicious, merely critical. "Why didn't you come home? I could've helped."

Think! "I know, that's the problem. If we came home, we would have looked to you to settle it, like Judge Mom. I didn't want that. We had to do this on our own, just the two of us."

"Really." Pam nodded, with a new half smile. "So you went to Mason's because I wasn't there?"

"Honestly, yes. I have to find my own way with him. That's the goal, right?" Jake felt he had turned a corner, inadvertently saying something that made complete sense, however false. Still it brought him no satisfaction or relief.

"Exactly."

"You keep saying you can't *facilitate* my relationship to him. The therapist said that too."

"True."

"So I tempted him with a cheeseburger, and we got over it."

"Wow." Pam brightened, genuinely happy, which only made Jake feel horrible.

"So it's over. We solved it."

"You *resolved* it."

"Whatever, I'll take it." Jake managed a shaky smile, and Pam patted him on the back.

"You're a good guy, Jake. That's why I knew we'd be fine. Back when, you know."

Jake's throat caught. She meant when he'd lost his job and they had their rough patch. She'd dragged him into marriage counseling. It wasn't his way, with his old-school, close-mouthed, working-class Scottish upbringing, from the other side of town. But like everything else he'd learned growing up, it had been 180 degrees wrong. Pam had taught him that, and now he was lying to her face.

"You're reliable, and kind, and you try. You really do." Pam smiled, sweetly. "You know what my mom always said about you."

Jake couldn't even fake a smile back. It was something they always said, a marital call-and-response, but the words soured on his tongue. "I'm Husband Material?"

"Ha! Don't say it that way. Yes, you are." Pam gave his back a final pat, like a period at the end of the sentence, then turned to go upstairs. "Okay, let's go up. This week needs to end."

"Right behind you." Jake followed her from the kitchen, flicking off the lights. He should be relieved that he'd gotten away with lying to Pam, but it made him sick to his stomach.

He trudged upstairs behind Pam, leaning on the banister and hanging his head. He tried to unravel the night in his mind, to unspool the hours, to undo all the times it had gone wrong. He wished he had told Pam the truth. He wished he'd called the cops at the scene. He wished he hadn't distracted Ryan while he was driving. He wished he hadn't let Ryan drive in the first place. He wished he'd never even gone to pick Ryan up. Most of all, he wished that that poor woman was alive and well, back from her run, happy and at home, with her family.

But she wasn't.

Jake had committed himself and his son to a course, and he had to see it through. Even though the notion filled him with dread.

And the deepest, deepest shame.

Chapter Four

Jake turned over, facing away from his sleeping wife, and opened his eyes. The bedroom was pitch dark because Pam liked to keep the blackout shades down, and it made the green digital numerals in his alarm clock glow even brighter. It was 2:45 A.M., and he'd been tossing and turning since he'd showered and gone to bed. He knew he would never fall asleep, replaying the night in his head, starting with him being parked outside the movie theater and ending with his avoiding his rearview mirror, so he couldn't see the broken corpse of the woman vanish into blackness.

Jake tugged the covers up over his shoulder. In his mind, he went over everything he did and everything he said, then everything Ryan did and said, again and again, trying to see how it could have come out differently, or how he could've reached a different decision. But he kept coming out in the same horrendous place, reaching the same unthinkable conclusion.

Anguished, Jake felt like it was a no-win situation from the moment they hit the runner, or maybe from the moment he found out about the marijuana, or maybe from the moment he let

Ryan drive. His guilt and remorse drove him to keep trying to parse his decisions and sent him into another spiral of what-if reasoning, *what if I hadn't gone to pick him up, what if I hadn't let him drive, what if I had paid attention to the road, what if, what if, what if.*

Jake squeezed his eyes shut, keeping tears at bay. He slept on the side of the bed closer to the door, because he was supposed to protect everybody, the Daddy-dragon guarding the Dutch Colonial. The thought made him cringe, after what had happened. He'd protected his son into a nightmare. And if he was having a sleepless night, he could only imagine that Ryan had it worse.

He eased off the covers, got up quietly, and padded down the hallway to Ryan's room. He turned the knob carefully, opened the door, slipped inside, and closed the door behind him. The bedroom was dark, and moonlight came through the striped curtains. Ryan made a large mound under his comforter, and Jake could see his head on the pillow, but couldn't make out his face. Moose was curled up on the bed, his head resting on Ryan's feet, and the golden retriever didn't stir.

"Dad?" Ryan whispered, and Jake crossed to the bed and sat down on the edge.

"How are you doing?"

"Horrible. How are you?"

"Horrible, and worried about my boy." Jake's eyes were adjusting to the light level, and he could see the shadows of Ryan's young features, the hollows of his eyes and cheeks, and the dark waves in his hair. "Are you getting any sleep?"

"No."

Jake sighed heavily. "I know, I'm sorry. I'm so sorry that it happened."

"Me, too, I'm sorry, so sorry. Everything is my fault, all of it."

"That's not true."

"It is, you know it is. I was the driver. I'm the one responsible."

"No, it was an accident. That's why they call it an accident. Accidents happen." Jake had been giving himself the same speech for the past hour. "We weren't doing anything really wrong, it just happened."

"Come on. I *was* doing something wrong. I wasn't watching the road."

"You happened to look over for a minute, a second, even a split second. You were having a conversation with me, and that happens every day, in cars all across this country."

"But, Dad—"

"You weren't texting or talking on the phone. In the fraction of a second you looked away, we hit a blind curve, and a runner was in the street. Who knew that she would be running that time of night? And she didn't have any reflective gear on, either."

"It's not her fault she got hit."

"I didn't mean that." Jake realized he was lying then, too. He did mean that. He had just blamed an innocent victim for getting herself killed. He must be losing his mind. A wave of guilt washed over him, so profound he had to close his eyes until it passed.

"Lots of people run late at night."

"I know, but it's not your fault that you hit her. That *we* hit her."

Ryan moaned. "No, *I* hit her, you just said it."

"Ryan, we're in this together, and we will get through this together." Jake stroked Ryan's hair back from his face, a gesture he did without thinking, then realized that he couldn't remember the last time he'd done it. He felt his throat thicken. "I love you, do you know that?"

"I love you too."

"You're a smart and able kid, and you're stronger than you think." Jake swallowed hard, not really knowing what to say. "By the way, everything went okay with Mom. But I didn't tell her the story about Caleb and you getting in a fight. I told her that you and I got in a fight about texting in the car."

"What?" Ryan asked, a new note of anxiety in his voice.

"I changed the story."

"Why did you do that? We decided on the Caleb story."

"I know, but this is better."

"No it isn't."

"I think it is." Jake hated himself, fussing with his son over which lie was better. "It makes more sense because it keeps everything between us and doesn't involve Caleb. We don't want her to start talking to Caleb's mom, do we?"

"Oh, no, because of the weed," Ryan answered sadly.

"That wasn't what I meant. I was just saying that I don't want any chatter between the moms about tonight, and also I told her that she shouldn't bring it up with you. If she does, just say you don't want to talk about it."

"You think that'll work?"

"For you, it'll work. For me, no chance in hell."

"That's a random thing to say, Dad." Ryan fell silent, then pulled out his iPhone. Its home screen glowed in the dark, showing a funny photo of Moose rolling on his back, his four big paws in the air. Ryan started to scroll to the Internet. "I looked online, but the news doesn't have anything about the lady. Does that mean they didn't . . . find her yet? Does that mean she's . . . still lying there?"

"Not necessarily. Maybe they found her but haven't released it to the public yet. They have to inform the next of kin."

"That means her family, right?"

"Yes."

"But she must live with her family. They would know that she didn't come home from her run."

"Maybe she lives alone."

"Do you think she does? Could you tell . . . how old she was?"

"No, I couldn't." Jake shuddered, flashing on the woman's abraded face.

"Also it's going to rain all night. Do you think she's out there . . . in the rain?"

Jake hadn't known it was raining. Pam's blackout shades muffled sound, too. "I don't want you to think about that anymore. What's done is done. These first few days are going to be hard, I know, because you're a good kid and you feel terrible."

"I do, I feel *terrible*. I keep wondering who she was. I keep thinking about her."

Jake squeezed his shoulder. "I know, but we need to stay the course. Keep it to yourself, and obviously, don't say anything to any of your friends or anyone on the team."

"I wouldn't, Dad. I'm not stupid."

"I know, but you're feeling bad and you could open up to people"—Jake didn't know where he was going with this, so he let it go—"anyway, enough said. We did the right thing, in the circumstances."

"*What?* You really think we did the right thing? I don't."

"Listen, I'm your father and my job is to protect you. I feel horrible about what we did and if I could bring her back, I would. I tried to. I made the best decision I could on the spot, and in that moment, my first concern is always you."

Jake's chest tightened as he tried to explain the inexplicable.

"Look. If there were any chance of saving her life, I never would've left. But she was gone. It was an accident, I don't know what purpose would have been served by your going to jail for a long, long time. Then two lives would have been destroyed, instead of one."

"So you think it was the wrong thing, too."

"Okay, yes, right."

"It was the wrong thing. We did the wrong thing."

"Yes, we did. Well, I did the wrong thing, for a good reason."

"What does *that* mean?"

"Forget it." Jake raked his hand through his hair. He had done the wrong thing. He had acted too fast. He should have called the cops and taken the blame himself. Maybe Ryan could have held it together under questioning. Maybe Ryan could have run home, though it was miles away. Or hid in the woods. Or whatever. He hadn't had time to think, on the scene. Either way, it was too late now.

"So then, maybe, we could change our minds. Could we do that?"

"No, we can't," Jake answered, more sharply than he intended. Moose lifted his head, then thumped his tail on the comforter, *whomp whomp whomp.*

"No, Dad, listen to me. I was thinking, couldn't we go to the police now and tell them that we left, but we're sorry we left . . . and tell them all about what happened?"

"No, we couldn't, no." Jake had been second-guessing himself, too, but he kept coming out in the same place. "Once we left the scene, we left the scene, and if they were to test you, they would find marijuana in your system. I think that stays in your system for days."

"I know, they give us random drug tests on the team. They just tested us yesterday for the playoffs. That's why we figured it was okay to smoke."

"It ends now, Ryan. No more smoking."

"Yes, agreed, of course, but maybe if we explained to them that I wasn't high when I hit her, that it was a blind curve, they would—"

"Understand? Let it go? It doesn't work that way, buddy."

"No, I know they wouldn't let me off or anything, but maybe I would get probation, or I wouldn't go to prison for that long—"

"No, this was the right thing."

Ryan scoffed. "Dad, it's *not* the right thing. Stop saying that."

Jake cringed. "Fair enough. But it's the only thing we could do, and if it makes you feel any better, please remember it wasn't your decision. It was my decision, and I think the thing to do, from here on out, is for you to live your life. It's going to be hard in the beginning, but then it will get easier, I promise."

"Why will it get easier?" Ryan asked, incredulous.

"Time changes things. It makes things easier."

"Dad, I *killed* that lady. That's wrong, like, forever. Time doesn't change *that*."

Jake felt a stab of sympathy for him, so deep it felt like a knife wound. He had no immediate reply, because Ryan's reasoning was logical, and in fact, he sounded just like his mother. Meantime, Moose had awakened and was stutter-stepping to them on the bed, then he plopped his feathery butt down and opened his mouth, so that his tongue lolled out. Jake decided to change tacks with Ryan. "So what are you doing tomorrow?"

"I don't know. After this, I feel—"

"No, what were you going to do tomorrow, before this happened?"

"Well, it's Saturday. Chemistry, Algebra. You know, homework." Ryan shrugged, and Moose lay down, tucking his muzzle between his meaty front paws.

"Okay, so do your homework. Do everything you would do. Go out on that date, with that blonde, Janine Mae—"

"Dad, are you serious right now? That's not possible."

"I know it's not easy, but it's the only way, and we did this so you can have a life. So live your life."

"Is that why we did it? For me?"

"No, well, for us both."

"No, for me." Ryan's voice softened, pained. "Tell the truth, Dad. You did it for me. You were going to tell the cops that you were driving, for me, before you even knew about the weed."

Jake waited, not understanding or not wanting to answer, or both. "Is that a question?"

"Yes."

"Then yes."

"That's, like, so unselfish of you."

Jake felt a surge of emotion that constricted his chest. "Son, I love you and I'd do anything for you. It's as simple as that."

"I love you, too." Ryan paused. "Dad, what are you doing tomorrow? Are you going to the office?"

"No, I'm—" Jake caught himself. "I told your mother I'm going in early, but I have to take care of the car."

Ryan gasped. "Oh no, I forgot! What about the car? Is there blood on it? Is it dented?"

"I'll handle it." Jake had found a dent on the front bumper and on the undercarriage. "I don't want you to think about this anymore. Let me handle everything. These are my decisions, not yours. The less you know the better, as a general matter."

"Can I go with you?"

"Where?"

"To the body shop."

"No. Now lie back, and go to sleep. In fact, make sure you sleep in. You always sleep in on Saturday mornings, and your mother expects that, so don't change anything." Jake sensed it would be safer if Ryan wasn't alone with his mother, in the short run. The boy was too fragile right now, and Pam could cross-examine a rock.

"Dad, how am I gonna sleep late? I can't sleep now."

"Stay in bed anyway. I'll be back before noon, and I'll come get you. Okay? Don't worry, let me handle everything. Now lie down and try to rest." Jake gave him a final pat on his shoulder, then rose to go. "I'll be down the hall in my office."

"Why?"

"I have some work to do." Jake realized he'd just told his third lie of the night and resolved to stop counting. "Try to get some sleep. I love you."

"Love you, too."

Jake went to the door, taking one last look at Ryan, who was hugging the dog in the dark. He flashed on his son as a child, cradling Moose as a fuzzy puppy, just brought home from the shelter. The memory was completely fresh, and for a moment, Jake felt stunned by its appearance, the sweetness of the past clashing so horribly with the anguish of the present.

Jake thanked God he had a son to put to bed when he knew somewhere there was a family, right now, waiting for someone who would never come home. Jake felt a wave of new shame. Then he slipped out of the bedroom, closed the door behind him, and padded down the hall to his office.

He was a planner, and he needed a plan.

Chapter Five

Jake slipped into his office, flicked on the overhead light, and closed the door behind him, so he didn't wake Pam up. He blinked while his eyes adjusted to the brightness and crossed the room, making a beeline for his desk, a cherrywood computer table facing the wall between two windows. He moved the mouse to wake up the computer, then sat down while it fired up. He wanted to know the penalty for vehicular homicide in Pennsylvania.

The large monitor came to life, and onto the screen popped his screensaver, which was their official family portrait, posed for his firm's website and brochure, to show that he was a good family man. Jake felt his chest constrict at the sight. The photograph was taken when Ryan was only in middle school, and both father and son were wearing identical blue oxford shirts that emphasized how much they looked alike, except that Ryan was all unruly hair and big goofy grin, with orthodonture for miles. His son said the same thing, every time he saw the photo:

Quite the grille.

In the picture, Jake stood beaming next to Ryan, and in front of them, seated on some ridiculously ornate chair, was Pam, who wore a light blue shirtdress, her legs crossed demurely at her ankles. She'd chosen the color to complement their outfits and the cerulean backdrop, which was meant to be clear blue sky but came off like a Tiffany's box, more upscale than anybody intended. Pam had been running for judge at the time and had made her unhappiness known to the photographer.

Don't you have a different backdrop? We elect judges in this state, and I have to get votes from normal people. I'm not running for Queen.

Jake went online and typed his search request into Google. He clicked through the first few websites and found himself reading one DUI site after another, featuring the crassest sort of brochureware with glossy photos of grave-faced lawyers in three-piece suits, troubled kids in handcuffs, and a six-pack of beer, with one spilled out. He'd wanted to read the actual law, but the DUI bar had evidently bought the neutral-sounding website names. One DUI firm had a pop-up showing a smiling man on the telephone, **NEED A DUI LAWYER?** above **Click Here!** or **No, Thanks!**

Jake kept searching and finally found a website that cited Pennsylvania statutes regarding the juvenile system. He read that if Ryan were charged as a juvenile, he'd go before a judge and there would be a trial that would send him to a juvenile facility for six months, then he'd be under court supervision until he was twenty-one. It was lighter punishment than Jake had thought, but then he saw a sentence that chilled him to the bone: **Call now to avoid serious ramifications, such as your child being charged and tried as an adult!**

He knew vaguely that the district attorney had discretion in deciding whether to charge a juvenile as an adult, and it could go either way with Ryan. It was certainly possible that Ryan could be tried as an adult, because the crime was serious enough, resulting in death. And Pam's status as a judge could cut either way. Either the district attorney would do her a favor and keep Ryan in the juvenile system or he might want to make an example of him, showing that Ryan didn't receive preferential treatment.

Jake didn't know the penalties if Ryan was tried as an adult, so he went back to the search engine, plugged in **Pennsylvania vehicular homicide DUI,** and got his answer in a nanosecond:

> **Under 75 Pa. Cons. Stat. § 3735, the criminal offense of homicide by vehicle while driving under the influence (DUI) is punishable as a second degree felony. A conviction for this offense can result in a prison sentence from three to ten years and/or a fine up to $25,000.**

Jake felt his gut clench. A three-year sentence would derail Ryan's future, and a ten-year sentence would obliterate it. If they hadn't left the scene, Ryan would've ended up a convicted felon. It was the worst-case scenario, and as a financial planner, Jake was supposed to make a living out of estimating the downside risk and preventing worst-case scenarios. He felt heartsick thinking about it now, too late. If he'd been considering the worst-case scenario on Pike Road, he never would have let Ryan drive and that woman would still be alive. He'd underestimated the downside risk, and a human being had lost her life.

He leaned back in the chair, his stomach in a knot. A woman was dead, and he was responsible, as surely as if he had been driving. He was the adult, and he should have known better. He would carry his remorse with him forever; he felt it to the marrow, as if guilt were seeping into his very cells. He never should have left the scene, but that wouldn't bring the woman back. He wished he had called the cops, but that wouldn't bring her back either. He hadn't wanted to destroy two lives, one of them his own beloved son's. It would kill Pam.

Jake swallowed hard, thinking of his wife, sleeping down the hall. She would know DUI law, because as an appellate judge, she had a general overview of all state law, which governed the nuts and bolts of real-life, from premeditated murder to employees who stole trade secrets. He tried to remember if Pam had written any significant opinions in any DUI cases, but couldn't. He was too distraught and exhausted to think clearly, and his heart kept returning to the dead woman.

He palmed the mouse again and navigated to the local news site to see if her body had been found. He scanned the front page, then the next few, but there was nothing except an upcoming snowstorm and articles about budget cutbacks in the township. He was surprised that the police still hadn't found her, and he wondered if she didn't have any family or if it just hadn't found its way into the news yet.

Jake rubbed his cheek, slumping back in his chair. His gaze traveled around his plush home office, taking in the beige sofa, matching chairs, and tasteful cherrywood shelves filled with books and awards. He didn't deserve an office like this, he was every inch a fraud. He found himself looking out the window, framed by beige curtains handpicked by his discerning wife.

This is the perfect color, see how it picks up the sisal rug?

Jake had laughed. *Is sisal the same as straw? Because to me, this rug is straw.*

Outside the window, a steady rain came down, running in rivulets on the windows and graying out the houses across the street, identical to his own. It was raining hard, and Jake knew it would be turning cold, with the snowstorm coming. He couldn't bear to think that the woman was still lying on the street and wondered why it was taking the police so long to find her.

He turned back to the computer, palmed the mouse, and clicked REFRESH, but nothing had changed on the news page. Still he refreshed another time, and the only sound in the quiet office was the *click* of the mouse and the thrumming of the rain outside the window. He and Ryan were the only people who knew that the woman was dead, and as far as the world was concerned, no crime had occurred and she was alive and well.

Jake wished he and Ryan could live inside that reality, in the very interstices of time, tucked under the comforter of not-knowing, sleeping as soundly as they used to, the Before the same as the After. But even so, he couldn't wait another second for the woman to be found, gathered up, lifted onto a gurney, and taken from the horrific scene, out of the rain, away from him and Ryan, and finally safe.

The horror of what he had done brought new tears to Jake's eyes. He clicked REFRESH again and again. He wanted to know the precise moment that After began.

But by morning, when it still hadn't happened, he got dressed and left by the kitchen door.

Chapter Six

Jake hurried into the chilly garage, holding his jacket over his arm and carrying his empty traveler's mug. He was dressed for work in an old wool sweater, jeans and sneakers, the way he always did on a Saturday; he'd worked at least one day of the weekend for as long as he could remember, because it was the quiet time he needed, to think without phones and interruptions.

He checked his watch—6:15 in the morning, which was when he usually left. He'd gotten ready quietly enough for Pam to remain asleep and he was doing everything the way he always did, just in case she woke up. He hadn't checked on Ryan because that would've been out of the ordinary; the Saturday routine was for Jake to go to work early, Pam to get up around eight o'clock, let the dog out, and leave for the gym around nine thirty. Ryan would stay in bed until eleven o'clock or so, if he didn't have a game or practice.

Jake hustled to the car, stopping to double-check the damage to the front bumper. It was too dark to see well because the only illumination came from three small windows in the garage door, but he wouldn't normally turn on a light, so he didn't now. He straightened up, chirped the car unlocked, opened the door, and jumped inside, throwing his coat on the passenger seat and screwing his travel mug into the console.

He buckled into his harness, hit a button on the rearview mirror to open the garage door, and while he waited for it to *ca-chunck* upward, he surveyed the front seat and floor of the car, scanning for any errant napkin, sign of blood, or anything from the accident scene or his efforts to clean up. Everything looked in order, and there wasn't any sign of blood or anything else on the front seat, dashboard, console, or steering wheel.

He twisted on the ignition, reversed out of the garage, and cruised down the street. It was too early for any of the neighbors to be out starting their Saturday errands, and he cruised past the darkened houses that sat silently behind the blue recycling bins and rolling trash cans. He fed the car some gas, switched on the heat, and turned right, heading for the office. He didn't breathe any easier once he left their street, but on the contrary, felt more nervous, either because he was leaving Ryan alone with Pam or because of what he had to do next.

What about the car?

Jake tried not to think about it as he drove through their development, the only car on the curvy, man-made streets with their oddly high curbs, taking the perimeter road, past the mandatory forestation and specimen plantings required by the township zoning board. The trees in the front row were the builder's-grade evergreens, planted in that telltale zigzag for maximum privacy, and though they'd grown and filled out, Jake remembered when they'd been only four feet tall, shaped like gumdrops the same height as Ryan. He'd taken a photo of Ryan with one of the trees, and they had the picture in the house somewhere, Pam would know where.

Jake steered past the Chetwynd Springs sign at the grandiose entrance/exit of the development and flipped on the radio. It was tuned to the local news channel from last night, but it was weather on the nines. He didn't need a meteorologist to tell him it was a crummy day, under a sky opaque with thick gray clouds.

Fog is a cloud on the ground.

Jake hit the open road and joined the line of sparse traffic, his thoughts shifting into gear at the task that lay ahead. He had a plan and he knew where he was going. He knew what he had to do and what he had to say. He had done the research he needed on the computer. He told himself to stay calm, and that he had to see his plan through, as dreadful as his purpose was, it was the only way to protect Ryan. He drove on autopilot, listening to the radio and waiting for the news as traffic got heavier, with people getting the jump on the day, ready to check off items on their things-to-do list. They'd run to Acme and Whole Foods in pre-snowstorm panic, stocking up on salt.

Suddenly, he heard the announcer change on the radio, and the news began, "In headline news, the victim of a hit-and-run driver in Concord Chase last night has been identified as sixteen-year-old Kathleen Lindstrom. A junior at Concord Chase High School, she was struck while jogging. Police are asking anyone with information regarding this incident to please call the main tipline, at number . . ."

Oh my God, no.

Jake gasped aloud, in horror. His fingers clenched the steering wheel. He almost ran into the maroon Subaru in front of him. He slammed on the brakes, setting his ABS system shuddering.

No, no.

Jake shook his head, shocked. He clung to the wheel as if it were a life raft and he a drowning man. His heart thundered. He broke a sweat under his shirt. He couldn't believe it was possible. The revelation stunned him.

I killed a kid. Kathleen Lindstrom.

Jake didn't recognize the name, but now it was a part of his DNA. It would echo in his head for the rest of his life. New tears brimmed in his eyes. He couldn't fathom that she was so young. He'd thought she was petite but she was just a *girl*. A teenager, only sixteen years old. Her life was just beginning, and now she was gone.

God, forgive me.

Jake flashed on her face, covered with blood. She had been somebody's daughter. She had parents, waiting for her to come home from her run. They would wait and wait, until they got the call that every parent dreads. They would never see her alive again. Their daughter, their child. His heart broke for them.

Jake felt shaken to his very foundations. Kathleen was the same age as Ryan. She was a student at the same high school. Jake realized, aghast, that Ryan probably knew her. Concord Chase High wasn't that large, only about a thousand students.

He killed his classmate.

Jake found himself reeling, stopped at a red light. This news would kill Ryan. His son wouldn't be able to bear the guilt; it would be unsupportable. He didn't know how Ryan could go to school, ever again. Ryan's classmates, and all of the faculty and staff would be mourning a girl that he knew he had *killed*. It would be impossible, untenable. Ryan was too sensitive a kid to get past this, ever. Jake feared for his son's sanity, maybe even his very life.

The horn of a car behind him blared, startling Jake out of his reverie. The traffic light had turned green, and he fed the car some gas, following the Subaru mechanically. He felt sick to his stomach and fought the impulse to call Ryan, but it was too risky, with Pam at home. Then he had another, darker thought. What if the news would send Ryan to Pam, to spill his guts?

Dad, I swear, I won't tell Mom. I won't tell anybody.

Jake couldn't process the information. He wanted to pull over but there wasn't time. He felt his gorge rising, but swallowed hard. He had to stay on plan. He blinked his tears away and tried vainly to ignore the pain in his chest. He drove ahead, past clapboard Cape Cods, new brick split levels, and a Dutch Colonial with white stucco, wondering if Kathleen Lindstrom lived with her family in a house like one of these. Pike Road was only ten minutes away.

Jake gritted his teeth, trying to recover. The stretch of road he was looking for lay just ahead, a two-lane street lined with houses, trees, and a strip mall that held a Chinese restaurant, a Wawa convenience market where he always stopped for coffee on the way to work, and the auto body shop he'd used for years. He'd given plenty of free financial advice to its owner Mike Ayanna, and Mike owed him a favor, but Jake wasn't about to depend on Mike, favor or no. The police would undoubtedly be investigating the local body shops, and Mike would be compelled to turn over his records.

Jake put on his right blinker when he spotted the Wawa sign, glowing a corporate red, and slowed as he approached its parking lot. It was the side entrance to the store, with a line of parking spaces under a white sign, NO IDLING—DIESEL POW-ERED VEHICLES OVER FIVE TONS. The parking spaces ended next to a bundle of cardboard recycling, a stack of flat boxes, and a green metal Dumpster. The side lot was completely empty, which is what Jake would've expected this early in the morning.

He turned into the parking lot and aimed at the Dumpster. He hit the gas, steering slightly to the right, knowing that the damage would obliterate the dents from last night. The Dump-ster raced forward to meet him.

Jake braced himself for impact, feeling that if anything went wrong, he deserved to die.

Kathleen, I am so very sorry.

Chapter Seven

The Audi slammed into the Dumpster, and Jake jolted forward, caught by his shoulder harness. His airbag exploded, hit him in the face, and pushed him backwards. The odor of plastic and a chemical powder filled his nostrils.

Abruptly the airbag deflated, imploding in a pile on his lap and draping over the steering wheel. The engine was still running, and the windshield was cracked but intact. The hood had buckled and his right front bumper crumpled into the Dumpster. No one would ever see the dent again.

Jake realized he'd succeeded, but he still felt sick to his stomach. The collision reminded him of last night, a memory embedded in his very body. He moved the airbag from his lap, his muscles stiff from shock, not of the accident, but of the revelation.

I killed a kid and left her dead. To save my own kid.

Jake was alive, but he didn't deserve to be.

"Jake, Jake!" someone called out, near the car. It was Christopher, a Wawa clerk, hurrying toward him. They knew each other because Jake always stopped here on the way to work.

Christopher appeared at the driver's-side window, his young face creased with concern. "Jake! Are you okay?"

Jake nodded, collected his phone and jacket, opened the door, and got out of the car, his knees suddenly wobbly. "Christopher, My God—"

"You look white as a ghost, Jake. Stay still, I'll call 911. My phone's in my locker, 'cause we have to lock it up during work." Christopher turned to hurry off, but Jake touched his arm.

"No, no, stay. I'm fine."

"For real?"

"Yes." Jake tried to recover. "I'm just a little . . . upset is all. I surprised myself. It's kind of a shock."

"Sure, I get it. You gonna toss 'em? You look it."

"No, I'm fine. Don't call."

"You sure you don't wanna go to a hospital? My manager might want you to." Christopher frowned, scanning him with worried eyes.

"Nah. I'm fine, thanks."

"Coulda been worse, I guess, huh?"

"Right." Jake dusted the airbag powder off his clothes. "I thought I hit the brake, but I must've hit the gas instead."

Christopher shrugged sympathetically. "You didn't have your coffee yet."

"Right." Jake walked to the front of the car, leaned on the hood, and surveyed the damage. He was thinking of Kathleen, her body broken in her running gear. It was too awful to comprehend. There was so much death and destruction, all of a sudden. He shuddered to his very bones, eyeing the car. "Damn, I really messed up, didn't I?"

"You never know. Mike next door can fix it."

"I'll let him take it, it's not drivable with that windshield anyway. My wife will pick me up." Jake slipped into his jacket, put his cell phone in his pocket, and gestured at the Dumpster, which had a large dent in its middle. "It looks like I did a number on your Dumpster, too. Sorry about that."

"Oh, forget about it." Christopher waved him off, but that was the wrong answer for Jake. He felt bad manipulating the kid, but it couldn't be helped. That was why he'd damaged their property. They would be required to make a police report for liability purposes, and he needed everything to be documented, so there would be no questions later.

"No, make a report, so my insurance will pay."

"But it's just a trash can. Who cares?"

"The store doesn't own the Dumpster, the hauling company does. See?" Jake gestured at the Waste Control logo on its lid. "The store will have to pay for the damage, and you shouldn't be in that position. I'll put in a claim, but we'll have to call the police."

"Let's see what Donna says. She's my manager." Christopher turned toward the store just as a ponytailed employee came hustling around the corner. She was heavyset and wore wire-rimmed glasses, her face a mask of worry.

"What happened? Are you hurt, sir?"

"I'm fine, thanks." Jake had seen her before but he didn't know her, and he could tell from her expression that she was thinking the same thing about him. "I'm Jake Buckman, I always stop in here before work. I hit the gas instead of the brake and crashed into the Dumpster."

Beside him, Christopher nodded. "He says he doesn't need to go to the hospital."

"That's lucky. The police will be here any minute, I already called them." Donna's forehead relaxed, and she eyed the car and Dumpster. "Any accidents on our property need to be reported. I hope you understand, sir."

"Yes, of course, please call me Jake."

"Jake, are you sure you weren't injured in any way?"

"I'm fine, thanks."

"Okay then. I'll have you sign some paperwork, if that's okay. Come with me. I have the file in the office." Donna started walking to the front of the store, and Jake and Christopher fell into step beside her.

Christopher looked over with a smile. "How about we treat you to a cup of coffee?"

"No thanks," Jake answered, with a twinge. Donna went to the door, yanked it open, and led them inside the store.

Christopher split off. "Okay, Jake, see you later. I gotta get back to the register. Let me know what Mike says about the car."

"Will do, Christopher. Thanks for the assist. I owe you one." Jake followed Donna past stacks of bound newspapers, shelves of blue antifreeze jugs, and a refrigerated case of prepared salads and hard-boiled eggs. A customer in a down jacket and sweatpants stood at the lineup of bronze plastic coffee canisters, where the air smelled of hazelnut flavoring and Lysol.

"This way," Donna called over her shoulder, leading him around the hoagie counter, down a short hallway, and into a cramped office that contained a box of paper towels, a cluttered gray desk, and a cheap black chair. A bulletin board held shift schedules, OSHA notices, and a cluster of kids' school pictures, next to a black metal shelf with a trio of security monitors, one of which had a red Phillies cap sitting on top.

"Go Phils," Jake said, nervous. He hadn't counted on the security monitors, and he could see that the one in the middle overlooked the side parking lot.

"Are you a baseball fan?" Donna fetched a manila folder from a tan file cabinet against the wall.

"Who isn't?" Jake couldn't stop looking at the security monitor. Its resolution was remarkably good, in full color, and he could clearly see the Audi's far side embedded in the Dumpster. He'd caught a lucky break in that the view of the camera was on the driver's side of the car, so it wouldn't have picked up the dent on the passenger side when he'd pulled in. Still, he wondered if Donna had seen the accident as it occurred or if there was a digital copy or videotape.

"Here we go." Donna set a few forms in front of him. "These say that you had an accident here and that you declined to go to the hospital. Would you sign them? We have to have it for the lawyers."

"I understand." Jake picked up a pen and started signing the forms, preoccupied with the security camera. He gestured to the monitor. "Look at that. My God, it looks like the car is growing out of the Dumpster."

"It kinda does, doesn't it?" Donna eyed the screen. "I'm sorry for you. That's a really sweet car."

"Thanks." Jake flipped to the next page of forms. "That monitor is good quality. Do you get a lot of detail?"

"Yes. We have it in case we get held up, but that hasn't happened yet. Knock wood." Donna rapped her knuckles on her head. "I tell my mom, it's Concord Chase. The worst thing that happens here is minors trying to buy cigarettes. Still, she hates my working the night shift. She worries."

"That's what parents are for, to worry about their kids." Jake cringed inwardly. He finished signing the forms and pushed them across the desk to her. "Here we go. Do you ever watch the monitor?"

"Mostly I'm busy on the floor."

"So you didn't see my accident?"

"No, sorry. I just heard the noise and covered the floor while Christopher ran out."

"Of course." Jake let it go. He didn't want to arouse her suspicion or provoke her into playing the video. "When do you think the police will get here? I should call my wife and give her the heads-up that I'll need a ride later."

"They said they had a car nearby."

Suddenly the door opened, and Christopher stuck his head inside the office. A tall, middle-aged police officer stood behind him, and Jake's mouth went dry. Christopher said, "Donna, look who's here, Officer John!"

"Yo, Officer John!" Donna burst into a grin, went to the door, and threw her arms around the policeman, who hugged her back.

"Hey, good to see you, girl!" he boomed, releasing her. He had a broad smile and friendly blue eyes under a black CTPD knit cap. A silver badge gleamed from his black nylon jacket, and embroidered white block letters over his right breast, which read MCMULLEN.

"You, too! When did you get back?"

"Yesterday." Officer McMullen grinned back at Donna. "I'm back in the pink and all healed up. I have rehab for a coupla weeks, but I'm good. How have you been?"

"Fine, thanks." Donna's gaze shifted to Jake. "Mr. Buckman, Officer John just recovered from hip replacement. Don't think it was anything cool like a gunshot wound."

"Oh." Jake managed a smile.

"Donna, I got a metal hip, I'm Robocop!" Officer McMullen shot back, and the others laughed, then the policeman faced Jake and extended a hand. "Sir, are you the gentleman who had the accident?"

"Yes. Jake Buckman." Jake prayed his palm wasn't sweaty and shook the officer's hand. "Thanks for coming out."

"It's no bother, sir. First things first. I understand you declined medical treatment?"

"Yes, I'm fine, really. I want to do whatever needs to be done for you and for the insurance company, then my wife will come pick me up."

"I'll need to take a statement and I won't keep you too long. Where do you live?"

"The Chetwynd development."

"Sure, I know it, about fifteen minutes away. I'll give you a lift home."

"No, that's okay. I'll call her, I hate to put you out." Jake hid his alarm. The last thing he wanted was to ride home with a cop, and God forbid that Ryan saw him pull up in a police cruiser.

"It's no trouble. I'm happy to do it."

Donna burst into laughter. "Of course he's happy to do it! Officer John gets lonely tooling around in his copmobile, since his partner got reassigned. He'll talk your ear off. The siren's the only thing that shuts him up."

"Ha! Very funny, Donna." Officer McMullen laughed again, then motioned Jake forward in a way that was suddenly authoritative. "Come with me, sir. I'll make an incident report, then I'll give you a lift home. I insist."

Chapter Eight

Jake followed Officer McMullen to his cruiser, a black-and-white muscle car with a massive chrome grille and a sleek modern lightbar on the roof. CHETWYND POLICE, read gold reflective letters on its jet-black door. Jake had managed not to be nervous when he'd given Officer McMullen his statement about the Dumpster accident because Donna had stayed with them, interrupting with chatter. But now that Jake was alone with the cop, he felt anxious about the ride home. He could have handled it before the news about Kathleen Lindstrom, but not now. It was as if he had too many emotions to hide.

"Mr. Buckman, there is no room for you up front. Don't take it personally. My duty bag takes up the whole damn passenger seat. See?" Officer McMullen motioned to the front seat of the cruiser, where a gray nylon messenger bag filled the passenger seat next to a laptop mounted over the console, tilted toward the driver's seat. A large black AK-47 was mounted upright between the two front seats, its butt down and its lethal muzzle facing up.

"I see," Jake said, trying to get his act together.

"There's not much room in this car, that's the problem. We got these new Dodge Chargers with a hemi. We love 'em because they're so fast. But they're not that comfortable and the seats are small. Sometimes I miss the old Crown Vics." Officer Mc-Mullen opened the back door. "Here you go, sir."

"Thank you." Jake climbed into the backseat, which had no cushioning, but was made of molded gray plastic and separated from the front seat by a metal barrier and a thick plastic panel, with a sliding window in the middle.

"Buckle up, sir." Officer McMullen shut the heavy door, which made a solid sound.

"Thanks." Jake reached for the shoulder harness, buckling himself in. He felt as if he deserved to be where he was, in the backseat of a cruiser. He should be under arrest, brought to justice to pay for the death of Kathleen Lindstrom.

"How you doing back there, sir? Could you be any less comfortable?" Officer McMullen climbed in the front seat, slammed his door closed, and buckled in his shoulder harness. He reached back and slid aside the window between the front seat and back-seat, making a foot-wide opening.

"It's fine, thanks," Jake called back, miserably.

"Let's roll." Officer McMullen started the ignition, reversed out of the lot, and headed for the exit. "It's a shame about your car."

"It sure is." Jake pulled out his iPhone and checked the time. It was almost nine o'clock, so Pam would be up. He prayed Ryan would still be in his room asleep, so he didn't know about Kathleen yet.

"My brother-in-law has an Audi. They're fast, aren't they?"

"Yes. Excuse me, I'll just text my wife and tell her we're on the way." Jake composed a text to Pam. **Had a minor fender bender. Cop giving me a ride home.**

"Good call." Officer McMullen cruised ahead, talking idly over his shoulder. "I'm married twenty-six years. My wife likes it when she knows what's going on. Women, they like to know things."

"Right." Jake added, **See you soon.** He hit SEND and held the phone. He looked out the window at the passing scenery, his heart aching.

"Kind of a busy morning, this one. Everybody's over at a scene on Pike Road, a hit-and-run. That's where I was when the property-damage call came in, for you. My supervisor told me to go."

Oh God. Jake kept his expression calm, so he didn't look suspicious in the rearview mirror. He hadn't anticipated that McMullen would've been at the scene, but Pike Road and the Wawa were both in Whiteland Township, which was small. It wasn't unlikely that the cop who came to the Wawa would also have been on Pike Road.

"I'll tell you this, it wasn't pretty." Officer McMullen slowed the cruiser to a stop at a red light. "The victim was a high-school kid, a jogger. Female."

"What a shame." Jake swallowed hard, feeling a wave of regret so powerful he almost confessed. Then it could all be over. He would be punished, he would pay. But so would Ryan.

"They were gathering evidence when I left. No suspects yet, in case you were wondering."

Jake should have been wondering, but he was still thinking about Kathleen. He flashed on her bloodied face, for the umpteenth time.

"We got a crack team on the case. We call in a team of accident-reconstruction officers who are specially trained to investigate a hit-and-run. We share them. We don't have the payroll to justify them, or the need, but we borrow them from Pikeland Township."

Jake nodded, but Officer McMullen didn't require encouragement to keep talking.

"They're crackerjack, five full-fledged accident-reconstruction specialists. Most of our guys were active-duty law enforcement, so they have a lot of experience too. We call it the total station."

"I see." Jake had to get it together. As anguished as he felt about Kathleen, it worried him to think of how expert the police could be. He felt his gut wrench, caught between feeling guilty and not wanting to get caught, for Ryan's sake.

"They go out there with equipment, like surveyor's equipment with the scope, and they triangulate the scene. They measure everything. They look for skidmarks, any damage, any trace evidence or other physical evidence, like pieces of the headlamp or any part that came off the car." Officer McMullen kept his eyes on the road, and they looked flinty in the glare from the bright gray sky. "They collect that evidence, log it in, and bag it, and they can run down exactly what car it was, make and model, the whole nine."

Jake's phone signaled an incoming text, and he looked down. It was Pam, saying, **Oh no, are you okay?**

"It's all up-to-the-minute technology, those guys are something else. They come back and upload all the data into the computer and they can completely rebuild the accident. They can tell you exactly how it happened."

Jake texted back, **I'm fine, don't worry. Go to the gym if you want to. Don't wait for me.**

"This poor kid was knocked out of her shoes, her sneakers. Most pedestrians who get hit, they get knocked out of their shoes. I bagged her sneaker myself."

Jake couldn't hide the revulsion he felt inside and he didn't try. He was the lowest form of life on the planet.

"A few months ago, I worked a scene, this is kind of gory, but we got body parts, like the skull. We put that in these cans, looks just like a regular paint can, gallon size. That's for evidence that can decompose. We get all the evidence we can and we comb the area for debris. You never know what'll pay off."

Jake's phone signaled a text. Pam replied, **Not going to the gym. Ryan's sick.**

"And that's only the beginning. We knock on doors, we ask the neighbors what did you see."

Jake guessed Ryan must have found out that their victim was his classmate. He texted quickly, **what's the matter?**

"Plus normally we can usually get good tapes from the cameras on the street, like the red-light cameras and such. They're usually a real help."

Jake felt panic tightening his chest. He hadn't thought that street cameras or red-light cameras could have spotted them the night of the accident, and evidently, Ryan was awake and talking to Pam.

"Unfortunately, we got no red-light cameras on Pike Road. There's nothing on that street. You know where else we get good evidence, usually?" Officer McMullen glanced in the rearview, waiting for an answer.

"No, where?" Jake asked, lightly. The text alert sounded on his phone, and Pam responded, **God only knows. Ttyl.** ☹

"The Wawa, like where you were. They have the best cameras around. The resolution is awesome. Any hit-and-run, we check the local Wawas for their cameras. We get lucky about half the time."

Jake realized he could've made a colossal blunder, going to the Wawa.

"You want my opinion, the driver was probably drunk. That's why people hit and run. To avoid detection because they're drunk."

Jake nodded, texting to Pam, **hang in, home soon**.

"Drunks usually stop for a hoagie or something to eat. They've been drinking and they get hungry. Wawa has cameras in the parking lot out front, too, so we can see the cars pull up. We even get a good view of their license plates. It's unreal how often we luck out." Officer McMullen snorted.

"Anyway, I'll go back to the scene after I drop you off. The rest of my platoon is still there, and I bet the body will be, too."

"Really?" Jake blurted out, appalled.

"Yep. I've had bodies lie for a while in this county." Officer McMullen's upper lip curled with distaste. "You have no idea. I've had bodies lie bleeding through the blanket and I had to change the blanket."

Jake flashed on Kathleen, bloodied in his arms last night.

"Problem is the coroner is in East Chester and he's not always in his office, because he doesn't have to be, and he's the only one who's allowed to pick up the body. He makes the declaration, then he takes the body to the hospital for the post. Postmortem, that is." Officer McMullen steered the cruiser onto the road leading to the Chetwynd development. "People think the coroner does the post, but he doesn't. He's an elected official, and so's the deputy coroner. They're not even doctors. They could even be dentists. That's why he's not in the office half the time. Between you and me, it's political." Officer McMullen shook his head. "I guarantee the body's still there."

Jake's stomach did a backflip, and another wave of guilt engulfed him. He knew he couldn't hide it, so he turned his face to the window, where the police officer couldn't see.

"So anyway, the post gets done at Paoli Hospital by a forensic pathologist, and unlike the coroner, he's the real deal. He gets the trace evidence off the body, like hair, fiber, any prints, evidence like that. Between what he finds and what we find, we'll get him."

Jake spotted his house at the end of the street, not a moment too soon.

"It could be a woman, too. Remember last year, that socialite who hit that kid on a skateboard?" Officer McMullen eyed him in the rearview mirror. "Did you read about that case?"

"Yes, I did." Jake edged forward, hoping that Ryan was nowhere near a window to see a police car pulling up.

"We caught her in the end, and we'll catch this one, too. It might take us a week, a couple of months, or even a year, but we'll get him. It's only a matter of time." Officer McMullen glanced over his shoulder. "What number did you say it was again?"

"My house? Two thirty-six, with the black shutters." Jake scanned the façade of his house, relieved nobody was at the windows. "Officer, thanks so much for the lift."

"No problem, sir." Officer McMullen steered the cruiser to the curb, slowed to a stop, and got out to open the back door. "Good luck with your car."

"Thanks," Jake said, fleeing the cruiser.

Chapter Nine

"What happened, honey?" Pam asked, meeting him in the entrance hall. Obviously, Ryan hadn't confessed to her, because she looked like her normal self—sweet, loving, and concerned about him. But she must already have been in Ryan's room, because Moose trotted up behind her.

"It was nothing, really. I hit the Dumpster at the Wawa. I clipped the edge." Jake gave her a brief hug, so he didn't get any residual airbag powder on her clothes. She was dressed for the gym, in glasses, ponytail, and a long T-shirt over her black yoga pants, but worry was etched into the lines of her lovely face.

"How did you do that? You weren't on the phone, were you?"

"No, I hit the gas instead of the brake."

"Really?" Pam recoiled, puzzled. "You're a better driver than that."

"I know."

"So how did it happen?"

"God knows. I needed my coffee." Jake let her go and shrugged it off, or tried to. He'd been too preoccupied on the ride home to make up a detailed story about the accident. "Mike's is right there, and I don't think it's totaled, so it's a nuisance, but that's all."

"Thank God." Pam's intelligent blue eyes searched his face from behind her glasses. "What's that powder on your sweater?"

"From the airbag." Jake brushed it away, but Pam lifted her eyebrow.

"The airbag went off? How fast were you going?"

"Not that fast."

"But you have to be going a certain miles an hour for the airbag to go off. You must've been going kind of fast."

"I didn't think I was, but whatever. We're insured, and I'm not going to sweat it. I have to rent a car." Jake looked around for Ryan, masking his anxiety. "So what's up with Ryan?"

"I don't know, he seems really sick." Pam raked her nails through her hair, which had a ridge from her ponytail. "He's thrown up twice and he looks terrible."

"Oh no." Jake let his concern show.

"And he hardly slept last night. He didn't want to tell me because he knows he can't be sick now. The game's Sunday. It's the playoffs, remember?"

"Right." Jake had forgotten. He didn't know how Ryan would bear up under the pressure. It was getting worse and worse.

"He could have something, like a bug, but he was hiding it from me. I heard him in the bathroom and went in. He's miserable, but there's no fever. It could be the flu, there's something going around."

"That's probably what it is. The flu." Jake's heart went out to his son. It sounded as if Ryan was distraught over the news about Kathleen, which was just what Jake would have expected. Ryan had to have known Kathleen, at least to say hello. And she had died at his hands.

"Wait a minute." Pam frowned. "Did you tell me he had a

hamburger last night, at the diner? I should call Sal right now and make a complaint."

Think fast. "No, he didn't have the burger. He only had ice cream." Jake had to prevent her from calling Sal, who would tell her that he and Ryan hadn't even been in last night.

"But you said he had a burger." Pam frowned, more deeply. "I remember because I was surprised. He'd been saying he wants to eat less meat."

"He ordered the burger, and I ordered a sundae, but when the food came, he thought mine looked better and we ended up switching." Jake knew this was believable because everybody coveted his ice-cream sundaes, but he was the only one who ever ordered them.

"Oh, okay. Then it wasn't the meat. Good." Pam cocked her head. "Hmmm. It could've been that cheesy crap with the nachos, at the movie."

"Right." Jake wanted to talk with Ryan alone, which would be a problem now that Pam wasn't going to the gym. But he knew how to make that happen. "Meanwhile, I didn't get any breakfast. I didn't even get my coffee yet."

"I can fix you some eggs, if you want."

"I'd love that, thanks. I'll change and stop in and see him." Jake went to the stairwell.

"Okay, I'll call you when they're ready." Pam went to the kitchen with Moose following her, his toenails clicking on the hardwood. Jake hustled upstairs, knocked on Ryan's door, then slipped inside his room.

"Dad!" Ryan looked pale and drawn, and there were dark circles under his eyes. His hair was a rumpled mess, and he was sitting up in bed in his sweats. His laptop, notebooks, and an open textbook lay scattered around him. "Did you hear? It was *Kathleen Lindstrom.* She's in my *class.* She goes to my *school.*"

"I know." Jake hurried over, scooped Ryan up, and hugged

him close. He could feel his son slump against his chest, as if there were no strength at all in his young, athletic body.

"She's *my age*." Ryan's voice sounded hoarse, about to give way to tears. "I didn't know her, but a lot of my friends did."

"I know, I know." Jake held him closer, rocking him a little, reflexively. For a second, he didn't know who was comforting whom, because they both felt so guilty and heartsick, bound by remorse.

"Janine Mae, that girl, the one I was going to go out with tonight, they were *best friends*. They both ran track. Dad, she even has MacCabe for homeroom. Remember Mrs. MacCabe?"

"Yes, of course, I'm so sorry."

"God, it's so horrible." Ryan pulled away, his face a tormented mask and his weary eyes glistening. He yanked his laptop over, his movements suddenly frantic. "Look, you should see on her Facebook page, they already made it a memorial and everybody's posting how they're so sorry and how could somebody do such a thing, to leave her to die in the street, and she was so nice, she had to work after school—"

"Oh, this is just awful." Jake glanced at the memorial Facebook page, which showed a photo of a grinning Kathleen Lindstrom, but he didn't have the heart to read the posts. He realized he'd have to set aside his own anguish to help his son, and be strong for him.

"I told Mom I was sick, but it's just that I feel so terrible, and you should see, everybody's posting about it, how sad it is, and it made me throw up, and the only reason I stopped was there was nothing left. Dad, I already got a text from Janine Mae saying she's so upset, and like, she was so cute, everyone on the boys team wanted to take her out." Ryan's words sped up, and he started scrolling through Facebook, tapping the trackpad. "Look, Dad, I think her mom and dad are divorced, and look at this, the track coach said on our Facebook page that nobody's allowed to run on Pike Road anymore. Caleb says on his page the school is going to stop all the teams from running there—"

"Ryan, please, I know how you feel, but maybe you shouldn't look at the computer anymore." Jake kept his hand on Ryan's shoulder. "It's making it worse—"

"But I killed Kathleen, I killed her—"

"Lower your voice, please." Jake glanced toward the door, though Pam couldn't hear from the kitchen. "Son, I'm worried about you—"

"Dad"—Ryan interrupted, tapping the trackpad in an agitated way—"they're all talking and texting and posting about her, and how could this horrible person kill her and leave her, and they all mean *me,* but they don't even know—"

"Ryan, we did it, we're both responsible, but you need to try and not get too focused on this." Jake tried to calm him down, but he could see that Ryan was hardly listening.

"Dad, no, you know what, I was thinking, if we tell them how it happened, we could explain that I wasn't high at the time—"

"Tell who?"

"The police."

"No, we couldn't," Jake said firmly. "If they test you and find out you smoked, you would be guilty of a DUI and vehicular homicide. If you got tried as an adult, which is distinctly possible, that could be a ten-year prison term. We can't go to the police. Don't even think about that. I know we did the wrong thing—"

"No, it was all my fault. *I* hit her—"

"Ryan, we can't keep going over and over this, around and around in circles." Jake had to tell him about the car accident at the Wawa, because it would look strange to Pam if he didn't. "Listen, I just had a fender bender that will cover the damage in the car."

"*What?* How?" Ryan's eyes widened, glistening and bloodshot.

"I don't have time to give you the details, and it doesn't matter."

"Don't forget your coat in the garage—"

"I'll take care of it, and I didn't forget." Jake knew what to do with the coat, but the car had taken priority. "I knew as soon as I heard that it was Kathleen, how you would feel, but you need to let me handle—"

"I just can't believe it. I hate myself, I hate this—"

"I know how you feel, but we have to keep it together." Jake squeezed his shoulder. "This is the time to stay calm. Let me handle everything. I know what's best for you, I really do. I love you."

"You said that I could get ten years in jail if they charge me as an adult, but what if they don't?" Ryan began to calm down and met his gaze evenly. His bloodshot eyes were still wet, but he was no longer on the verge of tears. "What if they decide I'm a kid, a juvenile? I went online and did the research—"

"You can't find an answer like that online." Jake didn't add that he'd tried.

"But I found these websites for lawyers, and if I go in the juvenile system, it looks like a lot less time—"

"No website can tell you whether you'll be tried as an adult. Considering who your mother is, they might want to make an example of you."

"But you don't know that, you can't tell that for sure. What if we went to a lawyer?"

"No, we need to keep it to ourselves—"

"We could go to a lawyer together and tell him what happened, and see what he said." Ryan seemed to recover, sitting up straighter, his voice strengthening. "Maybe there's a way we can still make it come out right. We could go to the police and make them understand."

"No." Jake stiffened. "There's no way."

"But if we could get, like, an expert opinion—"

"I know what I'm doing, son."

Ryan blinked, and Jake knew he was remembering the year that his dear old dad got laid off, rejected for every job he applied to, dressed up for interviews that got canceled. Pam and Ryan had seen him every morning, leaving the house for his rented cubicle, wearing a tie and jacket like a costume. It had been the year that his family had learned Dad wasn't infallible. Jake felt as if he could never live it down, but he had to try.

"Ryan, I do know what I'm doing. You have to believe me."

"But the lawyer on one of the sites said that anything clients tell him is confidential. Is that right, that he can't tell anybody?"

"Yes."

"So then why can't we go?"

"How are we going to go see a lawyer together? What do we tell your mother?"

"She doesn't have to know. She has that dinner tonight, remember, for whatever? She has to go, she's supposed to give a speech."

Jake had forgotten that, too. He was so preoccupied with Kathleen and Ryan.

"Dad, what if she goes to the dinner, and you say you have to stay home with me because I'm sick, then you and me can go to a lawyer?"

"No, I don't want to do that." Jake's every instinct told him to contain the information. Any lie he told, like the one about the hamburger, not only led to other lies, but greater exposure. "I'm not even sure you should go with me if I see a lawyer. Then we can't tell him that I was driving."

"Why not?"

"Because if we tell him that I was driving and it's not the truth, he can't represent to the court that it is."

"How do you know that? You're not a lawyer."

"I know a few things, Ryan."

"That makes no sense." Ryan frowned in confusion. "You

mean it's okay if he keeps it secret that we committed a crime, but it's not okay if he keeps the details secret, like who was driving?"

"Yes." Jake realized it didn't make sense, either. "Look, I admit, I don't know the niceties, but I don't like the idea and I doubt that we could get a lawyer that quick anyway."

"What if I already got us one?"

"*What?*" Jake asked, dismayed. He could see Ryan's life exploding, flying into a million pieces, right before his eyes. "What did you *do?*"

"Don't be mad—"

"I'm not mad, I'm *scared,* for you! What did you do?" Jake tried not to raise his voice. Panic gripped his heart. "Ryan, this is a secret. Once it's out, it's out, and you can't put it back."

"Don't worry—"

"Ryan, did you call? Did you use your cell phone?"

"No, I sent an email, but I made up a second new Gmail account under a fake name, John Kane. I didn't use my own name. It's safe."

"Ryan, they can still find out it's from your computer, if they trace that. You know every computer has its own ISP address."

"The lawyer's not going to look it up, and nobody else is either. You don't have to go if you don't want to, but I want to."

"Wait, hold on." Jake had to slow him down. "Tell me what you did. What did you tell him?"

"Nothing. All I said was that I needed to talk to an expert."

"You didn't tell any of your friends, did you?"

"No."

"You swear?" Jake's fears started to run away with him. "You didn't tell anybody on the team, or this girl you're supposed to go out with?"

"No, Dad, I swear, I didn't, I only emailed the lawyer and he emailed back."

"What were you thinking?" Jake reached for Ryan's arm.

"Don't you realize how serious this is? You can't tell anybody what happened! You can't play games with this!"

"I'm not playing games. I want to see if there's another way—"

"You can lose your whole life over this, Ryan. I'm not going to let that happen, and we're not going to see any lawyer."

Ryan pursed his lips. "Dad, I want to see a lawyer. All I did was write an email."

"Show it to me."

"Here." Ryan grabbed his laptop, hit a button, and swiveled it around, and Jake read the lawyer's response, which came up first:

Dear Mr. Kane, I am available for a confidential consultation entirely free of charge, anytime this evening starting at seven o'clock. I look forward to hearing from you. Sincerely, Morris

Jake read down to see Ryan's email. He felt himself losing control of the situation, which terrified him.

Dear Sir, I have a confidential question about a DUI law. Are you available tonight? Sincerely, John Kane

Jake looked up, stricken. "Who is this lawyer? Where is his office?"

"Westtown, but he could meet us wherever we wanted. It doesn't have to be his office. I bet it could even be in a car."

"Ryan, this guy can put two and two together. If he gets an email like that and he's in Westtown, he'll know there was a hit-and-run sometime last night, and that you're probably—"

"Dad, don't be mad, please, don't be mad." Ryan's brow furrowed deeply under his messy hair. "I'm just trying to do the right thing."

"I'm not mad at you, I'm worried for you. Worried sick."

"But I would feel better if I knew it was the only thing left to do, like, we really tried to see if we could do the right thing, but we just couldn't, in the end." Ryan's voice turned pleading, his eyebrows sloping down plaintively. "I'm just trying to deal with it, and if the lawyer says this is the right thing, the only way, then I think I would feel better."

"You're being naïve, son. You don't know how bad this can get, and I'll be damned if I'll put your life into the hands of some second-rate DUI lawyer."

"He went to Yale."

"He's a stranger. He doesn't know you or care about you, or love you like I do." Jake had to get Ryan in control. "We already decided. There's no going back. What's done is done. It's *done*."

"Can't we just go, to make sure? For me?"

Suddenly, there was a commotion in the hallway, and Moose burst through the door, bounded into the room, and jumped on the bed, landing in the middle of Ryan's worksheets and knocking into the laptop.

"No, buddy!" Jake faked a laugh, grabbing the dog by the collar.

"Whoa, Moosie!" Ryan moved the laptop out of harm's way and closed the lawyer email.

"What are you two up to?" Pam entered the room, puzzled. "Jake, I called you twice. Your eggs are ready."

"Sorry, babe. We've been solving a mystery. You were right. He had the cheese nachos."

"I knew it!" Pam smiled in triumph, then looked at Ryan. "Honey, nachos in a movie theater? Really?"

"Sorry, Mom," Ryan said, with a sigh.

Chapter Ten

Jake climbed into the passenger seat next to Pam, for the trip to pick up the rental car. He'd changed his clothes and eaten, only so Pam wouldn't get suspicious. It had taken everything in him to swallow each bite, because he'd felt so terrible, thinking about Kathleen. His gaze strayed to the metal shelves along the garage wall and the white jugs of Roundup weed killer that hid the nondescript brown bag with his parka, covered with Kathleen's blood. The lifeblood of a young girl was on his hands.

"You and Ryan looked like you were having quite the bonding session." Pam set her purse on the console, disengaged the emergency brake, and twisted the key in the ignition.

"We were just talking." Jake tore his gaze away from the hidden parka, for fear of tipping off his wife. He tried to put on a calm expression but he couldn't. He'd known Ryan would be devastated when he heard about Kathleen, but he hadn't foreseen that his son would start contacting random DUI lawyers. Jake hated leaving him alone, not knowing what his son would do next.

"What were you guys talking about?" Pam glanced behind

her before she put the car into reverse. She drove a black Mer-
cedes SUV, which had a camera in the dashboard that showed
a full view behind the car, but she never trusted it. She wasn't
the kind of woman who delegated the important things in life.
She wouldn't have made any of the decisions he'd made. She
never would have let Ryan drive. She never would have left the
scene. She believed in the law, in what was right and moral. So
did Jake, but that was Before. Now, in the After, he was a hypocrite. He turned to the window, instinctively hiding his face,
ashamed of himself.

"Jake?" Pam asked. "Did you hear me?"

"I'm sorry." Jake had let his thoughts get away from him. "We
talked about how he was feeling, like that."

"He seems kind of upset, don't you think?"

"Throwing up will do that to you."

"But it's more than that." Pam frowned as she put the car in
forward gear and gave it some gas. She steered down the street,
flipping down her visor against the glare of the cloudy sky. "It
could be the playoffs, you know. There's a lot of pressure on
him. His job is to make a three, and he knows that Coach
Marsh and Dr. Dave count on him."

"I think I know what's on his mind, and it's not the playoffs."
Jake suppressed a twinge of annoyance. Coach Marsh ran the
basketball program at school, and Dr. Dave Tolliver was Ryan's
shooting coach, a parent volunteer on the team whose son had
graduated a while ago. Jake felt that both men had too much
influence over Ryan's life, or maybe he was just jealous that they
saw him so much.

"What do you think it is?" Pam glanced over, her blue eyes
frank. They drove through their development, where neighbors
were unpacking groceries, heavy bags of salt, and new Back-
saver snow shovels from their SUVs, their hatchbacks open like
so many gaping maws.

"I think it's about that girl. This is only a guess, but I think he was supposed to go out with her tonight. He was just start-ing to tell me when you came in, this morning."

"Damn!" Pam hit the steering wheel with her palm. "I wonder who she is."

"I'm not sure, but I think he asked her out on a date."

"My God, that would be his first real date! Our baby's grow-ing up." Pam puckered her lower lip, mock comically, but Jake knew she wasn't kidding. He'd inadvertently stumbled onto a good way to change the subject.

"We're going to have to cut the cord sometime."

"I know, I know." Pam let her voice trail off. "I don't know what I'm going to do when he goes to college."

"What am I, chopped liver?" Jake managed a smile.

"You know it's nothing against you, right? It's just that as a mother, it's hard to let him go."

"I understand," Jake said, meaning it.

"Cheryl and Jamie say the same thing, we all do. If you have a great kid, it's hard to let them go. The world is a dangerous, dangerous place. Anything can happen."

"I know." Jake was thinking of Kathleen, with a new wave of guilt. He turned toward the window, again.

"I mean, it's not easy being an empty-nester. Jamie's already on antidepressants. It's just sad. It's a loss. I know you feel the same way, honey."

"I do." Jake knew she said it out of a sense of parity. "Any-way, as far as this alleged date goes, I got the impression that something about it bummed him out."

"What?"

"Two possibilities. Either he asked her out and she said no, or she said yes, but now he can't go because he's sick."

"Oh no." Pam's shoulders fell. "That sucks. I hope she didn't reject him, but either way, he can't go out tonight."

"Agree."

Pam shook her head. "What a shame."

"The course of true love never did run smooth."

"Was he studying when you went up there?"

"I think he was trying to, but cut him a break, he's sick."

"That reminds me." Pam looked over, suddenly businesslike. "You know we have that Eldercare Services dinner tonight, that benefit? I have to go. I can't get out of it, they're giving me some kind of award. Can you stay home with him?"

Jake hesitated, for show. "Sure."

"I think you should. If he keeps throwing up, he's going to get dehydrated, and I think we need to keep an eye on him."

"Fine, right. What time do you think you'll be home?"

"Late. I speak after dinner, and that's when they present the award, so I'll be there 'til the bitter end. Probably be home around midnight. Call me if he takes a bad turn, so will you?"

"Of course. Hopefully, he can get some sleep. I wouldn't mind taking it easy tonight, myself. I started the day off with a bang, after all."

Pam looked over. "So you have a good excuse for missing the rubber chicken."

"I don't mind the rubber chicken. It's the weird black rice I hate."

"That's wild rice, and it's classy."

"Rice gone wild?"

Pam smiled. "Exactly."

"Yuck. I like my girls wild and my rice tame. Is that so much to ask?"

Pam laughed, and Jake felt his heart lift. She had a great laugh, and he loved to make her laugh. He loved her, and he would lose her if she knew what he had done to Kathleen, and their son.

"So fill me in on the schedule," Jake said, because he had some planning to do. "What time do you have to leave for your gig?"

"It's at the Wyndham downtown, but there's a VIP reception

before the dinner, so I have to be there by five." Pam glanced at the dashboard clock, which read 11:15. "I have to leave the house by three thirty, just to be sure. What are you going to do today?"

Jake had to think of a lie, because the truth was appalling. "Work."

"You're not going into the office, I hope?"

"No."

"You're not feeling too good, are you?" Pam patted his leg, and though Jake felt the softness of her touch, it gave him no comfort. He turned back to the window. After putting on a false front for the Wawa employees, the cop, and Ryan, he was running out of energy to put one on for Pam. He couldn't wait to be alone, apart from her and anybody else, so he didn't have to pretend anything anymore, so he could let the grief and guilt come.

"I'm just tired, is all," Jake told her.

"Could you be having a delayed reaction to the crash?"

"No, really."

"Should we go to the emergency room?"

"No, no." Jake eased his head onto the headrest and closed his eyes.

"Did you get whiplash or anything like that?"

"Honestly, no." Jake turned to her, trying to smile. "What kind of idiot has a car accident when there's nobody around to sue?"

"An honest one," Pam answered, smiling back at him, with love.

Chapter Eleven

Jake went about his task with grim purpose and he didn't have much time. Ryan was sleeping in his bedroom, and Pam had just left for her benefit dinner, made up, perfumed, and sparkly in a slim black dress with sequins at the neckline. She'd come to his office to say good-bye, her face alive with excitement and a black lace shawl over her arm, which matched her lacy black high heels. Jake knew his wife well enough to guess that she had coordinated even that subtle touch.

Pretty damn sexy for a member of the judiciary, he had told her, kissing her on the cheek.

Don't be silly, she had said, but he knew she was pleased when she kissed him on the lips, then hurried off.

Jake had made sure Pam was gone, when he'd locked the dog in the house, hurried out to the garage, and started looking for bits of plywood. He'd muddled his way through his share of home projects and had plenty of random lumber around, for when the table leg needed shimming or the window air conditioners had to be braced on the windowsill.

He collected a few pieces of wood, then rooted through the

storage shelves and found some old soiled towels and rags. He grabbed some to-be-recycled newspapers, his bloody jeans, and the brown bag that held the bloody parka, then hustled out of the garage, glancing around to see if any of his neighbors were watching. Only his neighbor across the street, Sherry Kelly, was out, but she was already walking up her front walk, her back to him, so the coast was clear. Even so, Jake was about to do what plenty of suburban daddies did on a Saturday, which was burn some trash in a burn pile. Technically, he needed a permit, but the law was honored only in the breach.

He went down the side of the property, then let himself past their gate and into their yard, screened from view by their privacy fence. It was six feet tall, and it enclosed their backyard on the east and west sides, but left it open in back to the woods that surrounded the development. They owned a two-acre parcel, and neither he nor Pam had seen any reason to cut themselves off from the forest, a decision that would work to his benefit right now.

He hurried past their swimming pool, covered with a stretched green tarp for the winter, to the back where he kept his burn pile. He worried about a neighbor's wandering by, or the off-chance that the police decided to start enforcing the law, or Pam's having forgotten something, but he had prepared for all of those eventualities as best he could, using the other trash for cover.

Jake dumped the brown bag, rags, and wood on the cold ashes of the burn pile, where the lumber landed with a clatter. He bunched up the newspapers, reached into his pocket, pulled out the pack of matches, then struck the match. The newspaper began to burn, smoldering at the ragged corner at first, then catching fire gradually, curling the front-page headline BUDGET DEFICIT WIDENS before it burst into flames.

He glanced reflexively over his shoulder, but no one could see, and he reminded himself again that even if they could, nothing would look amiss. He burned trash all the time, probably once a month, and gray smoke rose from the burn pile like it always did. It didn't even smell funny. A sharp-eyed neighbor might have noticed that he was standing closer to the pile than usual, but no one was watching.

Jake grabbed a stick and stirred the pile, encouraging the flames to creep over the plywood, and when it began to catch, he tossed the stick aside, bent over the paper bag, and rolled out his jeans and balled-up parka. He fed the parka to the fire, starting with the front, where the blood had been. He couldn't get close enough to see the stains, but he knew they were there. The black nylon was stiff where the blood had dried, making shapes that reminded him of a map of the continents, so when the jacket finally caught fire, the entire globe was aflame.

He stood there, watching, waiting, and tending the fire, then threw in the bloody jeans and burned them, too, until wood, rags, newspaper, and incriminating evidence had been consumed, and all that remained were chunks of charred wood and the melted plastic zipper of his jacket, lying on the glowing ashes like the molted black skin of a snake.

Jake turned back to get the hose. Luckily, it was getting dark out and the risk of detection was miniscule, if not nil. Still, he wasn't about to take any chances. He planned to put out the fire, gather the ashes, and dump them. Oddly, he felt no relief now that the jacket had been destroyed, and if anything, he felt worse than before. Now, if all went right, or dreadfully wrong, neither he nor his son would ever pay for the young life they had taken.

Smoke clung to his sweater and filled his nostrils, and he took a few deep breaths as he strode toward the house. He reached the hose and was about to turn on the faucet, but he looked around, yet again, to make sure no one was watching. But this time, there was a silhouette in the window on his own second floor, at the back of the house. It was Ryan, motionless, then he vanished.

Fifteen minutes later, Jake was driving a white Toyota Corolla, the "intermediate" rental car. He was hoping to make quick work of disposing of the soggy ashes and melted zipper, which he had scooped into a large coffee can and stowed in the trunk. He cruised through his development, avoiding his neighbors' eyes, even as he scanned their trash cans. He couldn't take a chance of being seen disposing of the ashes. It was dark, but there were still too many people around, unloading their cars.

He hit the road, heading for the first gas station, but bypassed it when there were too many people in line waiting to fill up. He cruised ahead and figured he'd stop at the Wegman's, but as he steered into the landscaped entrance, he spotted the boxy security cameras on the stores. He decided against, curved around the turnaround, and navigated out the exit.

He hit the gas and found himself surveying every stoplight for a camera meant to catch traffic violations, but which could also catch him. He tried to think where he could dispose of the ashes. He needed a place where there was no development, but developments surrounded him, commercial and residential. There was only one place he could think of that would have no cameras, because it was still natural. He'd grown up here and always thought he'd move away, but when he met Pam, she liked the hominess of the area, so they'd stayed.

Jake pulled up to the quarry and parked next to a lighted sign that must've been new. **FUTURE SITE OF LIMEKILN CORPO-RATE MEWS**, it read, and underneath that, **BURNER CONSTRUC-TION COMPANY, WILL BUILD TO SUIT**. He got out of the car, not completely surprised. It was the site of an abandoned limestone quarry, typical of the kind that pockmarked the Lehigh Valley. He and his family used to picnic on its far side, the three of them spreading raggedy bathtowels on the hard rock, with only one beach chair, a faded plastic lattice affair that his father commandeered as the head of the family, if not its bread-winner.

Jake shook off the memory, which wasn't a good one. William "Bucky" Buckman couldn't hold a steady job but he'd acted like a king on a throne, placing the plastic chair on the flattest rock he could find, where it would nevertheless wobble uncertainly, representing one of the many trials his father had to endure. The open secret of the Buckman household was that his mother's secretarial job was the one that put food on the table. Still, Jake and his mother would be relegated to the rocky ground, while his father would sit in the chair and complain about how unappreciated he was by his family, his various bosses, and the universe in general.

Story of my life, his father would always say, in his sad-sack way. Or, *just my luck.*

Jake hurried around the car in the light from the sign, popped the trunk, grabbed the can with the ashes. He hustled through the rubble and overgrowth toward the quarry, then slowed his step out of caution. He could barely see where he was going because the lighted sign was behind him and the night was moonless. He wasn't sure where the edge of the quarry was, but it was several hundred feet down to the water and the last thing he needed was to fall in.

Story of my life.

Jake tried to ignore his father's voice. He and Pam had come here once or twice when Ryan was little, but by then, swimming had been prohibited, for which Jake was grateful. He had too many bad associations with the quarry and had vowed long ago never to become his father, which was only one of the reasons why he'd taken losing his job so hard.

Just my luck.

Jake almost tripped on some black netting on wooden stakes, but stepped over it, guessing he was approaching the edge. The underbrush reached to his knees, scratching his jeans, but he took a few more steps and stopped. He was close enough, and the undergrowth anchored his feet. He took a deep breath, and the air smelled the way it used to, fishy and vaguely gritty, as if it were still leavened with limestone silt.

Construction of the new corporate center must have begun, because klieglights glowed on the opposite side of the quarry, and Jake could make out job trailers and the hulking outlines of backhoes, dump trucks, and Dumpsters behind cyclone fencing. He couldn't see anyone walking around, and it was too great a distance for anyone there to see what he was up to. He gazed into the massive crater, dark as night, with the water below glinting like pooled ink.

The sky above him was black, the water below him was black, and he stood at the edge of an abyss that he tried not to see as metaphorical. He couldn't fathom how he had fallen so low, so fast. He had killed a young girl, left her in the street, and counseled his son into a nightmare. He was no better a man than his father; on the contrary, he was far worse.

He raised the can and dumped the ashes and melted zipper into the quarry. It was too dark to see if it all came out, so he tossed the entire can into the water.

Then he turned around and hurried back to the car.

Chapter Twelve

Jake showered and came out of the bathroom, a towel around his waist, surprised to find Ryan waiting for him in his bedroom, fully dressed in a white polo shirt, jeans, and sneakers, and sitting in one of the chairs. He had a good guess about why Ryan was dressed up, but he wasn't sure.

"Ryan, feeling better?" Jake asked, concerned.

"Not really. Where were you?"

"Out."

"Did you burn the jacket?"

"The less you know the better." Ryan's eyes were puffy, but his mouth a firm line.

"Don't treat me like a baby, Dad."

"I'm not, I don't mean to, but we had this conversation already." Jake padded to the dresser, leaving wet footprints on the rug. He pulled open the drawer and grabbed a fresh pair of boxers. He usually felt so good after a shower, but not tonight. He felt miserable, depressed, and guilt-stricken. He couldn't come to terms with the notion that they'd hit Kathleen. A classmate of Ryan's and so young. Her life had been cut short before it had even begun. In the shower, he kept thinking about her mother and her father. They would never see their daughter again. They would know she had died alone, and violently. That knowledge and burden would be with them every minute, every day they woke up and every night they went to sleep. It had to be hell on earth.

"Are you not telling me to protect me?"

"Exactly." Jake went to his bottom drawer, pulled out a pair of jeans, then closed it and went over to the bed to put them on. The room was warmly lit by crystal lamps on their night tables.

Ryan fell silent, then asked, "Do you guys ever even use these chairs?"

"Not really." Jake slid off the towel and into his boxers, even though he was still a little wet.

"Then why do you have them?"

"Your mom likes them. Sometimes, she uses them." Jake stood up and put on his pants quickly, feeling strange being naked in front of Ryan, oddly vulnerable and exposed.

"What for?"

"To sit down, when she puts on her shoes." Jake sensed that Ryan was trying to pick a fight, but he didn't take the bait. He went back to his dresser, opened a middle drawer, and pulled out a plain blue T-shirt. He slipped it on, standing there. He was getting dressed for staying home, not going to any lawyer's office.

"I don't know why you need chairs and a table in the bedroom. Like, what exactly is the purpose of this?" Ryan gestured to the sitting area that Pam had created in front of the fireplace, a decorative upgrade that didn't work. She'd covered its surround with Delft tile and bought a soft chair and a reclining couch in a yellow-and-blue flowered pattern, for either side. She'd finished it off with an antique pine table, its surface only large enough to hold another small crystal lamp and a stack of hardback books.

"I think your mom wanted it to be a reading area."

"Does she ever use it for that?"

"No." Jake finger-combed his wet hair into place, eyeing himself briefly in the dresser mirror. He had to bend at the knees to see his face, which didn't look good. His eyes were bloodshot, and his expression showed the strain. He could still smell traces of smoke on his skin and hair. "You must be hungry. Why don't we get some dinner?"

"Dad, I really want to go see this lawyer."

"I said no."

"I want to, I have to. Kathleen was in my class, Dad. I want to know if there's anything we can do, and what my options are—"

"No, it's too risky." Jake palmed his wallet on the dresser and tucked it into his back pocket.

"Dad, please."

"Tell you what." Jake sighed. He knew how Ryan felt but he couldn't let this happen. "Let's go downstairs and talk about it over dinner. We'll feel better when we've had something to eat."

"We don't have time." Ryan stood up. "I already wrote him back. He's expecting us to meet him at his office at seven o'clock."

"Are you *kidding me*?" Jake turned in disbelief, and Ryan drew himself up to his full height.

"I'm going, whether you go with me or not."

"What are you *talking* about?"

"I need to see a lawyer," Ryan answered, almost preternaturally calm. "I did something horrible, something criminal. I need a criminal lawyer, so I can decide what to do."

"We already *decided* what to do." Jake started to lose his temper, more out of fright for Ryan than anger. "We already did what we did. There's no decisions left. There's no going back."

"Maybe there is."

"There isn't!" Jake grabbed Ryan's arm, more roughly than he needed to, but he had to shake some sense into the kid. "I'm trying to keep you out of prison. I'm trying to save your life, your future."

"I know, you're trying to protect me." Ryan's eyes filmed, but he didn't cry. "But I want to know my rights."

"You don't have any!"

"Yes, I do. I'm going to see the lawyer, whether you come with me or not."

"How are you going to get there?" Jake stopped just short of saying, *You gonna drive?*

Ryan blinked, hearing the words that Jake didn't say, and for a split second, father and son eyed each other, wounded and hurting in front of the pretend fireplace.

"I'm sorry." Jake grabbed Ryan, just as his son pulled away.

"No, no, I'm sorry, it's all my fault."

"Ryan, come here!"

"No!" Ryan jumped aside and batted Jake's hands away, but Jake went after him, grabbed him, and struggled mightily to muscle him closer, into an embrace. The days were over when he was stronger than Ryan, and Jake didn't know if he could still take him. He flashed suddenly on Ryan as a little boy and remembered that they used to race each other in the driveway, then down the sidewalk, and his heart broke to think of those sunny days, now consigned to Before.

"All right, down, all right, you win," Jake heard himself say, shaking his head. "We'll see the lawyer. We'll get your questions answered and we'll see what he says. But we won't let him make any decisions for us, and we'll do it my way."

"What's that mean?"

"You'll see."

Chapter Thirteen

Jake sat at the head of the polished conference-room table with Ryan to his right, waiting for the buzzer that would signal the arrival of Morris Hubbard. Jake had decided it would be safer to have Hubbard meet them at his office, because if they were spotted at Hubbard's office, it would be obvious that they were consulting a criminal lawyer. Here, they were unlikely to be seen by anyone, and even if they were, it would look as if Hubbard were consulting Jake, and there was nothing suspicious about that. Jake met plenty of clients after hours, and, presumably, even a sleazeball DUI lawyer needed financial planning.

Ryan looked over. "Dad, you look worried."

"I'm not," Jake answered, modulating his tone. "How are you? You okay?"

"No." Ryan sipped water from his white styrofoam cup. "I talked to Janine Mae. I told her I was too sick to go out, but she was too upset anyway."

"Oh no." Jake felt a deep stab of pain, thinking about Kathleen. Her death would traumatize everyone she loved, her friends at school and her parents at home. Suddenly the buzzer sounded, and Jake came out of his reverie. He rose, stiffly. "I'll get it, and remember, let me do the talking."

"You said I can ask questions."

"Yes, but we're not hiring anybody tonight." Jake went to the door of the conference room, then stopped. "This is a consultation and discussion only, agreed?"

"Right," Ryan answered, and Jake left the room, strode down the hall, and crossed the reception area to the front door, which he opened.

"Come in," he said, ushering Hubbard quickly inside. "I'm Jake Buckman."

"Mo Hubbard." Hubbard extended a hand, and Jake shook it. Hubbard looked to be in his early thirties, on the short side, with a bulky build in a black fleece pullover and baggy jeans. His gold wire-rimmed glasses, a head of frizzy brown hair, and a thick beard and mustache made him seem like a throwback hippie.

"This way," Jake said, gesturing, and they strode down the hall.

"Nice offices," Hubbard said pleasantly.

"Thanks." Jake opened the door to the conference room, and at the end of the long mahogany table his own beloved son rose, standing to meet his lawyer, like an adult.

"Hi Morris, I'm Ryan Buckman. I'm the one who wrote you the emails."

"Oh, you used an alias. Very clever." Hubbard smiled as he entered the room and shook Ryan's hand. "Call me Mo."

Jake gestured Hubbard to a chair opposite Ryan. "Please, sit, Mo. You want some water or anything? Coffee?"

"No thanks." Hubbard unbuttoned the top few buttons of his fleece to reveal an old-school blue work shirt, then sat down heavily. "How can I help you?"

"Well," Jake said, sitting down at the head of the table, "before I explain the situation—"

"Excuse me, I thought it was your son who contacted me," Hubbard interrupted, turning to Ryan. "Who am I here for, you or your father?"

"Both of us," Jake answered quickly. "My son Ryan is a minor, sixteen years old, and I can explain why we wanted to meet with you."

"Fair enough." Hubbard folded his pudgy hands in front of him on the table. He made no move to take notes or reach for one of the fresh pads and pens from the center of the table.

"First," Jake began, "am I correct in assuming that anything we tell you in this consultation is privileged and confidential?"

Hubbard nodded. "Yes."

"Does that mean, if you were to hear information from us that might be incriminating in some way, you couldn't go to the authorities and tell them what you heard. Is that right?"

"Correct. Not only am I not obligated to do so, I am obligated *not* to do so. Let me explain something." Hubbard cocked his curly head, seeming to address Ryan, mainly. "The way I think about this is simple. My job is to help you. There are rules about how far I can go in helping you. For example, I can't ethically assist you in covering up wrongdoing, and I wouldn't. But the way the American system works is that the prosecution has to prove that somebody did something wrong. That person, called the defendant, doesn't ever have to help them do that. You get to remain silent, just like they say on TV. That right is guaranteed to you by the Constitution. Understand?"

"Yes," Ryan answered, his tone quiet.

"I represent people accused of crimes. My job is to represent my clients fully and zealously, to the best of my ability. I don't involve myself with their guilt or innocence. I don't even ask my clients if they're guilty. You understand?"

"Not really." Ryan frowned. "Doesn't it matter to you if they're guilty or not?"

Listening, Jake felt secretly proud of his son. Ryan didn't

understand because he expected the law to lead to justice, not thwart it.

Hubbard nodded, acknowledging the question. "It doesn't matter to me because I'm not the judge. I'm the defense lawyer. My job is to represent you. I make sure that you have the array of protections the law affords you. The Commonwealth has a lot of resources at its disposal that you'll never have, no matter who your father is. Or your mother."

Ryan blinked, and so did Jake, both of them getting the message. Hubbard was telling them he knew who Pam was, and he had probably already guessed that they had called him about the hit-and-run on Pike Road. And Hubbard's subliminal message—whether Ryan was getting it or not, Jake couldn't tell—was that he distinctly did *not* want to be told who was driving the car that night, so he could maintain deniability. In fact, Jake realized that Hubbard could be assuming Ryan was alone in the car.

Hubbard turned and faced Jake, his eyes small and dark blue behind his glasses. "Now, would you like to fill me in?"

"Certainly." Jake chose his words carefully. "To make a long story short, we left the scene of a car accident, without calling the police or 911, after we had ascertained that the pedestrian was dead and unresponsive to CPR. We were wondering what our legal obligation was, at this point."

"Are you asking me if you have a legal obligation to turn your-selves in?"

"Yes."

"No, you do not. You have no such legal obligation."

"I see." Jake shot Ryan a glance. He had guessed correctly that there was no legal obligation, only a moral one, which para-doxically, wasn't the same thing.

"As your lawyer, I would be under no obligation to counsel you to go to the police. My sole inquiry would be, what can I do for you, legally. I would begin by asking if you had an alibi—"

Ryan interrupted, "But what if we *wanted* to go to the police and tell them everything? What would the police do? Can we explain what happened?"

"Ryan—" Jake started to say, but Hubbard waved him off.

"Ryan, that's a good question. I'm happy to answer it. You're always free to go to the police. But, if that was something that you both decided you wanted to do, I would make sure that before you did it, we arranged a plea bargain." Hubbard spoke slowly, without judgment. "Let me explain what a plea bargain would be in this case. Under 75 Pennsylvania Code Section 3744, an adult who strikes and kills someone with a car, and does not remain at the scene, call the police, and give information, is guilty of vehicular homicide and leaving the scene of an accident. That's a felony of the second degree, carrying a five-year prison sentence—"

"It wasn't an adult who killed someone, it was me," Ryan interrupted again, and Hubbard pursed his lips in his dense beard.

Jake felt his heart sink, but he didn't want to upset Ryan by telling him that he'd just said the exact wrong thing. "Ryan, let Mr. Hubbard continue, then you can ask questions later."

Hubbard nodded. "Ryan, let me finish. I think I'll be answering your question."

"Dad, no." Ryan shook his head. "I don't want him to think you did anything wrong. You were just in the car. I want him to know *I* was driving and *I* was the one who hit her."

"It's okay, buddy." Jake turned to Hubbard, and the two men locked eyes, both of them tacitly understanding that Jake's cover story, in which he was the driver, was now blown. "Mr. Hubbard, you were saying?"

Hubbard relinked his short fingers. "So in the case where the driver is unlicensed and—"

"I have a learner's permit," Ryan broke in.

"Okay," Hubbard continued, "the driver has a learner's permit. But he's driving outside of the restricted hours, yes?"

"Yes."

"Dad is in the passenger seat, presumably having permitted son to drive, correct?"

"Yes," Ryan answered, but Hubbard turned to Jake.

"Jake, are you aware of the doctrine of negligent entrustment?"

"No," Jake answered, but he could figure out the gist. "I'm at fault because I let him drive, right?"

"Correct, but it's more serious than that, in the event of a fatality. It's criminal."

Jake swallowed hard. "I didn't know that."

"Most people don't, and I can see that you've been more worried about your son's legal responsibility, than your own." Hubbard's expression softened. "I understand, I have a son, myself. You thought of him first."

"What's my legal responsibility?" Jake asked, feeling his heartbeat quicken.

"You would be charged with permitting violation of title, in breach of 75 Pennsylvania Code Section 1575, and you would be charged as an accomplice to involuntary manslaughter for negligently entrusting an underage driver to drive. The penalty can be up to five years in prison."

Ryan gasped. "*What?* My dad would go to jail? But he didn't *do* anything!"

"He would be charged with an F2, a felony of the second degree."

Jake absorbed the information, momentarily speechless. He had known it was wrong to let Ryan drive, but he never would have expected it had legal implications, much less a prison sentence.

"*No!*" Ryan started shaking his head, agitated. "Mr. Hubbard, really, my dad just *sat* there, in the passenger seat! He didn't do anything *wrong*!"

Hubbard nodded calmly, in Jake's direction. "Yes, he did. He let you drive. You're an underage driver. As such, if your father permits you to drive and you have a fatal accident, your father is legally more culpable than you. He is a person in a position of authority over you and he was supervising you. The law views him as running the show, not you."

"That's not fair, I was *driving*!" Ryan cried out, and Jake reached over and put a hand on his arm.

"Ryan, let him tell us the law and we'll sort it out later."

"No!" Ryan shook his head vehemently. "Mr. Hubbard, let me just ask you this, if we went to the police right now, and we told them I was driving and my dad was in the passenger seat, what would they do?"

"Without a plea bargain?"

"Yes, without a plea bargain, if we just went and told them the truth, *everything,* even that I smoked up before the movie, because that's why my dad didn't call the cops. He wanted to call 911, he told me to, but he knew they'd test me. Are you telling me they'd put him in *jail*?"

"Yes, they would," Hubbard answered. "To reiterate, your father would be charged with involuntary manslaughter and sentenced to five years in prison. You, as the driver, would probably be charged as a juvenile and enter the juvenile system."

Jake heard that one glimmer of hope. "So Ryan wouldn't be tried as an adult?"

"Probably not, if they had you. If he were charged as an adult, which is always possible, I would move to decertify and have him tried as a juvenile. Still I couldn't guarantee I would prevail. He's so big and well-spoken. He doesn't come off like a child. He comes off like an adult."

"But he's sixteen. That's young."

"It's in between, these days. He *looks* like an adult. I call it 'the falsehood of physicality,' but it hurts him in court. I know from bitter experience." Hubbard inhaled briefly. "Let me explain the differences between the juvenile system and the adult system."

Ryan fell back in his chair, his hand covering his mouth, and Jake said nothing, needing to understand the law.

Hubbard continued, "The purpose of the prison system for an adult is punishment. But in the juvenile system, the purpose is rehabilitation. If you were to tell the D.A. that Ryan was driving, he would be sent to what is called 'placement,' a euphemism for juvenile prison."

Jake began to understand the implications, with a growing sense of dread. If he and Ryan turned themselves in, they would *both* be sent to prison. Even if they got some sort of plea deal, they would both serve some length of time in prison. Their legal position was even worse than he'd thought, and he'd thought it was awful.

"Most of these placements are up in the mountains, in facilities like Northwestern or Glen Mills. You, Ryan, would live and go to school there with other juvenile offenders. If you told the D.A. that you were driving under the influence, you would be evaluated and treated for substance abuse."

Ryan recoiled. "I'm not a *drug addict*. I barely smoke. You can check it, they test us on the team."

"Nevertheless, in three to six months, Ryan, your case would be reviewed. You would go before a judge, and you would have to show that you're making good progress. You could conceivably be free in two years, but the system retains supervision of you until age twenty-one. You will have a criminal record."

Jake tried to imagine the implications. Ryan's life would be ruined, and Pam would be devastated. She couldn't even deal with Ryan going to college, how would she deal with him going to prison? She would lose them both at once. She would never forgive Jake for ruining Ryan's life and for destroying their family. She would divorce him. She would step down from the bench.

Hubbard raised his finger again. "One last point. The DUI. Even if they tested Ryan's blood for marijuana, or THC metabolites, the D.A. couldn't prove that he was under the influence at the time of the accident, or that his level was above the statutory minimum, which is .5 nanograms per liter of blood. The DUI charge drops out, which reduces the sentence from ten years to five."

Jake tried to understand what he was being told. "So by leaving the scene, we evaded the DUI charge."

"Correct, but they'll offer you a worse deal. You don't win, either way. I would advise you, in the strongest possible terms, to enter into a plea deal." Hubbard glanced at Ryan, who looked numb with shock, pressed back in his chair, his eyes glistening. "If you decide to turn yourself in, that is."

"What is the best deal you could get us, if we were to turn ourselves in?" Jake asked, reaching out to touch Ryan's arm.

"The best, I think, is four years for you, and two for your son, with him sentenced as a juvenile."

"So Ryan would be considered a juvenile?"

"If he goes in with you, there's a better chance. If he goes in alone, probably not."

Jake didn't try to process the information, just to gather more. "Who makes the decision about whether he's tried as a juvenile or as an adult?"

"The first assistant district attorney, usually. In this case, given the circumstances, the D.A. may weigh in, too."

"Which way does that cut?"

"My sense is, against you. They would want to avoid any appearance of favoritism."

"And if I went to the police alone, without Ryan, saying that I was the driver?"

"No, Dad!" Ryan blurted out, stricken. "You can't, I won't let you. I'll go, I'll call them, I'll tell them the truth. You won't be able to stop me. I'll tell them you lied and I was driving."

Hubbard answered as if Ryan hadn't spoken, "Mr. Buckman, your going in alone may not be tenable, if Ryan isn't going to let you, and in that event, I can't represent you. I can't suborn perjury, that is, I can't ethically sit there and remain quiet while I know you're lying to the court."

"Understood." Jake was about to ask his last question, but Ryan leaned over across the table to Hubbard.

"Mr. Hubbard, what if I went to the police, and let's say, like, I told them that I borrowed my dad's car and took it out by myself? In other words, like, that I was alone in the car, and I hit Kathleen. My dad wasn't in the picture at all. What would they do?"

Jake recoiled, looking over at Ryan. "I wouldn't let you do that in a million years."

Hubbard glanced from father to son. "Ryan, your father would have to support the story, and it looks as if he wouldn't support your story, just as you wouldn't support his—"

"I absolutely wouldn't," Jake shot back. "It wouldn't work anyway, not with the facts."

Ryan groaned. "Why not, Dad?"

"Son, the timing wouldn't work, and the police would be able to figure that out. The accident happened after I picked you up from the movie, which you went to with your friends. The police could figure out that there wasn't enough time for us to get home and for you to go back out again."

"But how would the police even know I was with my friends?"

"They'd investigate, Ryan—"

"Even after I go in and tell them what happened?"

"Of course, they don't just take your word for it."

Ryan turned to Hubbard for verification. "Is that right? Would the police go talk to my friends, even after I say what happened?"

"Yes, they would."

"Ugh!" Ryan smacked the table, in frustration.

Jake had a final question, so he addressed Hubbard. "One last thing, of a more practical nature."

"Certainly." Hubbard nodded.

"If we didn't turn ourselves in, what are the odds?"

"What are the odds that you'd get away with it?"

Jake winced at his bluntness. "Yes."

"I can't counsel wrongdoing, and I'm not, and I cannot advise you or help you make a decision. I'll tell you the relevant facts so you can make your own decision. Do you understand the distinction?"

"Yes."

"The police in this county investigate thoroughly. They have accident-reconstruction specialists work up the scene, check for debris and tire marks, and physical evidence, like DNA."

Jake felt relieved that Hubbard didn't go into gory detail, because he could see Ryan fidget in his chair.

"They also knock on doors, talk to the local businesses, check local body shops and auto parts stores. I don't know if you read the case, but a man was arrested in Upper Darby last week for a hit-and-run, eight months after the fact. Delaware County police tracked him down via a headlamp he ordered to repair the Toyota 4Runner he was driving when he struck the victim."

Jake didn't interrupt him, running over a grim checklist in his mind. Burned parka, check. Crashed car, check.

"They also visit local hospitals and doctors. They examine red-light and convenience-store tapes. They post it online and solicit tips. Tips are a major factor in hit-and-runs. In all crime, really. People have a tendency to tell their friends."

Jake didn't dare look over at Ryan.

"These things happen rarely in this township, and the local police have expertise, but not experience, unlike places like Coatesville."

Hubbard paused, in thought. "In addition, it was raining last night, and water on the road prevents skidmarks from forming. Also the accident scene is out of the way. There are no street cameras in its vicinity, only in the corporate center."

Jake hadn't told Hubbard that the accident happened on Pike Road, but nobody was kidding anybody at this point.

"By the way, the statute of limitations on leaving the scene is seven years."

Jake blinked, surprised. "I assumed there was no statute of limitations."

"No, that's only for murder. This would be manslaughter, not murder. Do you have any other questions?"

"No, thanks." Jake understood. Hubbard was telling them that the odds were they wouldn't get caught.

"No, thank you," Ryan answered miserably, looking up.

"Well then." Hubbard pushed back his chair and rose. "I'm sorry for your trouble. Please feel free to call me."

"Will do, and please do bill me for this time." Jake began to stand up, but Hubbard waved him back into his seat, heading for the door.

"Please, stay here. I can show myself out. There's no charge for a consultation. Best of luck to you both."

"Thanks." Jake eased down into the chair and patted Ryan's hand, after Hubbard left the conference room. "You okay?"

Ryan hung his head, then looked up with anguished eyes. "I don't want you to go to jail."

"I'm not going to jail."

"But you would, if we go to the police." Ryan rubbed his face, leaving a welt on his fair skin. "I never should have asked to drive. I never thought anything like this could happen."

"Neither did I." Jake got up, went to Ryan, put his arms around him, and gave him a long hug, then held on, as if to support them both. "It's on me. I'm the adult, like he said. I ran the show, not you."

"But you didn't know about the weed. I should'nt've had the

weed." They clung to each other, sad and resigned. "I hardly ever smoke, I swear, Dad."

"I know. It really is my fault, not yours." Jake gave him a final hug, then released him. "I took it too lightly. I didn't think it through. I underestimated the downside risk."

"What?" Ryan looked at him, bewildered, and Jake straightened, standing in the conference room as he had so many times before, explaining to his clients.

"It means that whenever you do something, you have to understand that the worst-case scenario happens, even to good people." Jake hoped Ryan accepted that explanation, even as he realized that that was only part of what had gone wrong. He'd wanted to be Fun Dad, so he hadn't said no. He'd wanted to be closer to his son, so he'd been a buddy, not a parent. It was a mistake he would regret the rest of his life.

Ryan rose slowly. "At least we know what to do. I never would've thought *you'd* have to go to jail, I thought it was just me. If I go forward and turn myself in, they'll get you." He met Jake's gaze directly. "So I won't turn myself in. I won't say a word. I'll shut up."

"Oh no," Jake said, but it came out like a moan. "That's not a given, Ryan."

"Yes it is, no doubt." Ryan's tone grew determined, and he stood up straighter. "There's no other way. I'll never tell, *ever.*"

Jake felt sick to his stomach, even though he was getting what he wished for, or maybe because he was getting what he wished for. "We can talk this out at home."

"Dad, there's nothing to talk about. Like you said, it's a done deal. I can't let *you* go to jail, just like you couldn't let *me* go to jail." Ryan smiled sadly, cocking his head. "You protected *me,* now I'm going to protect *you.* Guess I'm my father's son, huh?"

Jake felt his heart lurch, at the irony. "But it's my job to protect you. It's not your job to protect me."

"That made sense when I was a kid, but not now. I told you

I'm not a baby anymore." Ryan's forehead eased, and his expression turned oddly accepting, almost peaceful. "I wanted an answer and I got one. I'm not going to let anybody else be punished for something I did, least of all, you. I love you, Dad."

"I love you, too," Jake said, and they faced each other, eyeball to eyeball, but not as they had before, in his bedroom. There was no confrontation now, and nobody was spoiling for a fight. Ryan wasn't trying to declare his independence, and Jake wasn't trying to hold on to any primacy he used to have as a parent.

They were both exhausted, trapped, and full of remorse. They were bound together not only by blood and love, but by guilt and lies. They were father and son, but they were also partners in crime.

Ironically, they had never been closer.

Chapter Fourteen

It wasn't until he got home that Jake had a chance to eat something. He stood at the granite counter and spread lumpy strawberry preserves onto semi-frozen Ezekiel bread, glancing up at the television. A cop show was on, so he looked away and finished making his sandwich. He checked the over-the-counter clock. It was 10:58 P.M., and the local news would be on any minute.

"Mrfh!" Moose barked, his round brown eyes looking hopeful, the way they did whenever peanut butter was in the vicinity.

"Here, buddy." Jake slid his index finger along the butter knife, swiped off some peanut butter and jelly, and offered it to the dog. Moose licked it happily, his tail swishing back and forth on the floor like a windshield wiper, reminding him of last night in his car.

I love how these wipers go on automatically! Dad, this car is sick!

Jake wished to God he had said no. If he had, none of this would have happened, Kathleen would be alive, and his son would be happy and carefree. As it was, Ryan was upstairs hiding in his room and getting ready for bed, so he'd be asleep by the time Pam got home. It was the only way he could avoid her cross-examination about the flu, his homework, or how he'd spent the evening.

Suddenly there was a commotion at the front door, and Moose scampered off, barking toward the entrance hall. Jake worried that it could be the police and hurried from the kitchen.

"Honey!" Pam burst through the front door, alive with excitement. She tossed her car keys, little purse, and black shawl on the console table, and Moose wagged his tail frantically.

"Hey, hi!" Jake tried to recover. "You're home early."

"Why didn't you answer your phone?" Pam closed the door behind her. "I've been calling and calling!"

"I didn't hear it, sorry." Jake must have forgotten about his phone in the rental car. "What's up? How come you didn't park in the garage?"

"I didn't bother, I'm in a rush! Where's Ryan?" Pam was already heading for the stairwell, her high heels clacking on the hardwood. "Ryan, come down! Come downstairs!"

Jake didn't like what was going on. This wasn't the way he planned it at all. "He might be asleep, honey. He wasn't feeling well—"

"Oh please. He's been on the phone for the past hour." Pam took off her high heels and placed them on one of the steps, to be taken upstairs. "Enough with the shoes. Showtime's over."

"Mom, what do you want?" Ryan called from his room upstairs.

"Come down, right now!"

"I'm in bed!"

"Come down, this is important!" Pam rolled her eyes and looked at Jake with a knowing smile. "He must be talking to the girl. I checked online and he's on G-chat, too. Did he do his homework?"

"Some of it, I think." Jake began to worry, wondering who Ryan was talking to on the phone and online. "He didn't feel well."

"He has a French vocab test on Tuesday, so he has to study in advance because of the playoffs."

"Aw, cut him a break. He's sick. He slept most of the evening." Jake marveled that his wife always had Ryan's schedule in the back of her mind, running on a parallel track with her own.

"Were you born yesterday?" Pam snorted good-naturedly. "He may have been in his room, but if he was on the phone and G-chatting, he wasn't studying or sleeping."

"It's hard to focus when you don't feel well."

"Mom, what's going on?" Ryan appeared at the top of the stairway and walked down slowly, running his hand along the banister and blinking against the bright lights of the hanging fixture in the entrance hall. His hair was messy, and he was dressed for bed in a maroon Chasers Nation T-shirt and pajama pants.

"Come down, I want to talk to you and your dad." Pam beamed up at him, but Ryan avoided her eye as he descended the stairs, and Jake wanted to give him the heads-up.

"Ryan, Mom says you've been on the phone, but I thought you were asleep. You playing possum, buddy?"

"Nah, sorry." Ryan looked away, and Pam threw open her arms when he reached the floor and gave him a big hug.

"I'm sorry you don't feel well, honey. But humor me and come into the kitchen. I really need to talk to you and your dad."

"What about?" Ryan asked, his tone offhand, as Pam released him from her embrace, took him by the arm, and led him into the kitchen in her stocking feet, with Jake and Moose behind.

"I have amazing news, truly amazing."

"Great, Mom," Ryan said, but Jake looked past his son's shoulder to the TV on the counter, where the local news had just begun and the top story was being reported. STUDENT

KILLED IN HIT-AND-RUN, read a lurid red banner across the screen, and an attractive African-American anchorwoman was saying, "A tragic story is first up tonight. A teenage jogger identified as Kathleen Lindstrom was struck and killed in Concord Chase last night, while running on Pike Road. Police believe the vehicle struck the jogger, then fled the scene . . ."

Jake crossed the kitchen to turn off the TV, but Pam grabbed his arm, beaming.

"Honey, sit down. Ryan, you, too. You have to hear this."

"I was just about to turn off the TV—"

"I can't wait another minute!" Pam motioned them into their tall stools at the granite countertop and hustled around the other side, standing in front of the oven and the television. Jake and Ryan sat down in their seats and faced a delighted Pam, against the backdrop of the news report of the heinous crime they had committed together.

The anchorwoman continued, "Lindstrom was a junior at Concord Chase High and she had just moved here from Seattle with her mother, Grace, but the duo had already made fast friends with neighbors like Dylan Paolucci, who lives next door." The screen switched to footage of an older man standing in his threshold, saying, "I'm still shocked. I just finished talking to her. She was a good kid. Her mom is a doll. I cannot believe somebody would hit her and not even stop the car."

Pam took a deep breath, barely able to contain her excitement as she looked from Jake to Ryan, and back again. "Guess what?"

"What?" Jake asked, but Ryan's attention was riveted to the TV screen, which had returned to the anchorwoman, who was saying, "Police have no suspects at the present time, but they are looking for the vehicle, which is likely to have damage to its passenger-side fender and undercarriage . . ."

"Ryan!" Pam barked, with a mock frown. "May I have your attention? What does it take! Sheesh!"

"Sorry." Ryan straightened up, and the TV screen changed to a remote report by a male reporter in a logo ball cap and windbreaker, standing on an otherwise darkened Pike Road, at the blind curve. He was saying, "The heartbreaking death of young Kathleen Lindstrom has brought new attention to this deadly blind curve on Pike Road, which residents have been complaining about to the Township Board of Supervisors for years. Traffic accidents happen routinely here, usually involving walkers, cyclists, and joggers, but last night's was the first fatality . . ."

"Boys." Pam made a drumroll sound, her blue eyes shining with happiness. "Tonight at the dinner, I found out that there's about to be a new vacancy on the federal district court!"

"Really." Jake could see in his peripheral vision that the TV screen had returned to the anchorwoman in the studio, but the enlarged photo behind her grabbed him by the throat. It showed Pike Road as a crime scene, with yellow plastic tape, red flares, and a black body bag being lifted on a gurney. The voiceover said, "If you have any information on the crash or the location of the alleged hit-and-run vehicle please call Concord Chase police at . . ."

"Guys, what?" Pam scowled, hurt. "Why are you being so rude? What's so damn interesting?"

"Nothing, honey," Jake answered, and Ryan swallowed visibly, but Pam whirled around to face the television, then watched the end of the news report, shaking her head.

"Oh. That *is* sad. Everybody was talking about it tonight. What's the matter with people?"

"God knows." Jake put an arm around Ryan, while Pam turned back to face them.

"Ryan, are you okay? You don't look good. Do you have a fever?" She reached across the table and put her hand on his forehead sideways. She always had an uncanny ability to tell if he had a fever, so they called her The Ther-MOM-eter.

KEEP QUIET | 105

"No, Mom, I'm fine." Ryan pressed her hand away. "Tell us your news. Please."

Pam brightened again, nodding energetically. "Okay, anyway. Judge Medova is going to step down and become managing partner at Ringman Tesher."

"Oh, interesting." Jake didn't know where her story was going, but he was finally able to listen, since the TV news had moved on to a dorm arsonist at Temple.

"And guess who's the front runner to fill the vacancy?" Pam's eyes lit up. "Me!"

"Wow," Jake said, astounded.

"Can you believe it?" Pam squealed in delight.

"What's this mean?" Ryan blinked dully, and Pam reached across the island and took his face in both of her hands.

"It means your mother is going to be a *federal judge!*"

"Great!" Ryan said, mustering up the requisite enthusiasm.

"Oh my God, honey." Jake felt happy for her, went around the island, and hugged her hard. "Congratulations, I'm so happy for you, babe."

"Thank you, thank you, thank you!" Pam hugged him back. "Can you believe it? Can you even believe it?"

"Sure, I can. You deserve it."

Pam giggled delightedly. "The state court judges are always overlooked for the federal bench, except for Judge Spaeth, who was even considered for the Supremes. But since him, I don't think there's been anybody. Isn't it amazing?"

"Absolutely amazing," Jake said, meaning it. He leaned over and turned off the TV.

Ryan rose, placing a hand on the counter. "Can somebody explain to me what this is all about?"

"Sure." Jake's heart went out to his son, trying to rise above the circumstances for his mother. "Pam, tell your son what a big deal you're about to become."

Pam smiled, pleased. "There are two systems of justice in the country. There's a state system, which I'm a part of, and it rules on questions of state law. State judges are appointed for a term of years, and they're elected, which you've heard me say is totally ridiculous. Pennsylvania is one of the few states in the country that still elects judges, instead of having them appointed based on their qualifications and merits. It's like a judicial popularity contest, and a corruption of the law—"

"Mom." Ryan rolled his eyes. "Please don't start with that again."

Pam burst into laughter. "Okay, but as I was saying, the other system of the judiciary is federal, which decides questions of federal law."

"Is one better than the other?" Ryan asked, sitting back down.

"Well, more important matters come before the federal bench. Questions of antitrust law, banking law, constitutional law, and First Amendment law, all sorts of big, complex questions." Pam grinned. "Really cool stuff."

"So it's a big deal," Ryan said, with a shaky smile.

"Yes," Pam answered, beaming. "And another cool thing about it is that federal judges are appointed under the Constitution, for *life*. I never have to run for election again. That means no more county fairs, no more funnel cakes and hot dogs, no dairy and goat shows, no more sucking up to every petty potentate so I can do some good in this Commonwealth."

Jake felt happy for her, but it was still hard to smile. He kept thinking of that news photo, with the body bag. Inside was Kathleen, whom they had killed. He tried to get his act together.

"But guess what, there's no pay raise. On the contrary, I have to take a pay *cut*." Pam snorted. "You know how you've heard me say Pennsylvania judges are among the top paid in the country? Believe it or not, a federal district judge makes fifteen grand *less* than I make now."

"Really?" Jake was surprised. Pam made good money as a Superior Court Judge, but they didn't talk salary in front of Ryan, so he didn't ask her for an exact number. He didn't care anyway, not really, not anymore. He was a financial planner who was learning that money wasn't as important as he'd always thought. "So what happens now?"

Pam smiled up at him. "They nominate me, then I have to go before a Senate committee."

"Mom, you mean like in *Washington, D.C.*?" Ryan asked, surprised. "That's baller, G."

"Yes, exactly." Pam chuckled. "It's a federal appointment, and it has to go through the Senate. It's a long process, like years, and it's very political, but in the end, I'll be there forever." She leaned over the counter to Ryan. "But listen, honey, you can't tell anyone. It's confidential. Don't say anything to any of your friends, the team, or your teachers."

Jake cringed at the irony. Ryan was keeping a wonderful secret to protect his mother and an awful secret to protect his father.

Pam continued, "Monday or Tuesday, they'll press-release that Judge Medova is stepping down, but they won't announce that I'm on deck until the preliminaries are wrapped up. The FBI has to come interview me and you guys, too. They do an in-depth background check of the family."

Jake felt his heart stop. He had no idea what that would involve, but he was instantly worried about Ryan and he could see the blood draining from his son's face.

"Mom, the *FBI*? Why do they have to interview *me*?"

Pam chuckled again. "Don't worry, honey. It's just procedure. You'll do fine."

Ryan's lips parted. "But why do they have to investigate us? And what do they do, like, exactly?"

"Honey, don't sweat it. It's more for Dad and me. The FBI

wants to find out if we do anything illegal, like hire illegal aliens or pay the cleaning lady under the table. But we don't do that, and we never would."

"But what do they do?"

"They talk to you, is all." Pam waved him off, airily. "They do it for security reasons, and to avoid any surprises that might come up during the confirmation process, embarrassing everyone and putting a kibosh on my nomination."

Jake put on his best reassuring smile. "Ryan, there's nothing to worry about."

Pam bubbled over, beaming. "Of course there isn't, honey. I say we celebrate! Your father and I are having champagne, and you can have a ginger ale."

"Great idea." Jake winked at Ryan, trying vainly to lighten his mood. "I'll get the champagne."

"I'll get the ginger ale." Pam crossed to the refrigerator, glancing back at Ryan. "Don't be such a nervous Nellie. We'll pass with flying colors. After all, it's not like we have anything to hide."

Chapter Fifteen

Jake locked the front door, turned off the entrance-hall light, and walked to the staircase in darkness, heading up to bed. It was after midnight, and Pam had already gone upstairs, after Ryan and Moose. He and Pam had polished off a bottle of champagne, but it had only depressed his mood further. He started to climb the stairs, almost tripped over her high heels, then grabbed them on the fly and went up, leaning heavily on the banister.

He reached the second floor and bypassed the closed door to Ryan's bedroom. His son needed sleep, and so did he. He made his way to his bedroom, slipped inside, and closed the door behind him. The room was empty, and he knew Pam was in the bathroom by the faint buzzing of her electric toothbrush. He brought her shoes to her closet, where he dropped them on the rug, catching a glimpse of her at her sink.

Pam's back was to him, and she was bent over, rinsing her mouth, in a lacy black bra and tan bikini panties. His eyes traveled her shapely body, from the exposed nape of her neck to the cleft of her back, taking in the dimples above the lacy edge of her panties and coming to rest on her ass, which was perfect. In any other mood, Jake would have been turned on, but tonight he felt like the lowest of the low. Only hours ago, he'd met with a criminal lawyer and made a corrupt bargain with their son.

What are the odds that you'd get away with it?

Pam dried her face, spotting him in the mirror when she replaced the towel. "Caught you looking, honey."

"Oops." Jake faked a smile. He felt like an intruder in his own bedroom, a pervert peeking at his own wife. He had become a stranger to himself.

"Like what you see?"

"You're amazing," Jake answered, meaning it. She was too good for him. He was unworthy.

"Hold that thought." Pam walked to him, raising her arms and reaching up for him. She had that cool look in her eye, and he knew she wanted to make love. He couldn't refuse her, he never had, and he leaned down and embraced her, on Husband Autopilot. She parted her lips to kiss him, covering his mouth, tasting sexy and familiar, like champagne and Colgate. Her body was soft and warm in his arms, and he found himself kissing her deeply. He felt a vague stirring in his pants and wanted oblivion. He didn't want to think about Ryan, Mo Hubbard, or Kathleen, anymore. He didn't want to think at all.

He slipped his free hand into the back of her panties, cupped her cheek, and lifted her onto him, pressing himself between her legs. She kissed him back with a soft, throaty moan and wrapped her thighs around his waist, pushing herself against his zipper, holding on to his T-shirt in back as he carried her to the sitting area by the fireplace. He stopped kissing her only to lower her onto the chair, where she sat, eyes closed, arching her back, her breasts straining against the dark lace of her bra cup. Her arms fell to her sides, her legs parted, and he knelt between them to yank his T-shirt off over his head.

Do you guys ever even use these chairs?

Ryan's voice popped into his consciousness, unwanted and unbidden, and Jake froze. He didn't even know why he'd taken Pam here, and not the bed. They'd never made love here.

You protected me, now I'm going to protect you. Guess I'm my father's son, huh?

Pam's eyes fluttered open after a moment, in muzzy confusion. She whispered, "Jake?"

No, he thought, deflating. He wasn't Jake. He didn't know who he was anymore. He was the man who left a young girl dead by the side of the road. He was the man who ruined his own family. He was the man who destroyed their wonderful son.

"You okay, honey?"

"No, sorry, I'm just tired." Jake sighed. "It's the booze. It must be."

"So . . . you don't want to?" Pam frowned, blinking.

"Let's just call it a day," Jake answered, leaning down to kiss her, one last time.

Chapter Sixteen

Jake opened his eyes, vaguely aware that Pam was trying to wake him up. He squinted against sunlight pouring into the bedroom, because they had forgotten to pull down the blackout shades last night. His wife's face came into focus, and Jake could see that she was back to business, already made up and ponytailed, in her contacts, maroon Chasers Nation sweatshirt, and jeans. She smelled like face wash and things-to-do lists.

"Honey, wake up." Pam stroked his arm. "The game's at one o'clock. You're coming, right?"

"Yes, right." Jake's head was pounding, and he had a major hangover. He'd been hoping he could keep reality at bay, but it came rushing back to him, leaving a bitter taste in his mouth that had nothing to do with alcohol. "Is Ryan up?"

"Of course. He's already out shooting."

"Is he sick or okay?" Jake heard the rhythmic bouncing of the ball outside on the driveway, the sound of rubber hitting cold asphalt, echoing in the quiet Sunday morning.

"He seems better. Get up and shower, please. I thought it would be nice if we all had pancakes together."

"Pancakes? Ugh." Jake felt his stomach turn over. "How can you eat?"

"I'm fine, and Ryan likes pancakes on game day. Can you be down in half an hour? We have to leave by ten o'clock."

Jake glanced at the clock, which read 8:07. "Why ten, if the game isn't until one?"

"The team has to be there early, and I have carpool, so we're picking up Jerome and Baird, so that adds forty-five minutes. Plus it's an away game, at North Mayfield, and that will take another forty-five minutes extra . . ."

Jake closed his eyes against the familiar rat-a-tat of the schedule, his wife expertly counting backwards. She'd timed everything so they wouldn't be late, because she still lived in the world where the worst thing that anyone in their family could do was to mess up the schedules of the other overscheduled families.

"Now get up and I'll see you downstairs." Pam ruffled up his hair, rose, and left the room, while Jake threw off the comforter, eased himself into a sitting position, and rubbed his face, as if that would ease the pain in his head, or his heart. He got up and walked around the bed, pausing to glance out the window, which offered a parallax view of the basketball hoop, in the driveway in front of the garage.

There was a cold sun in the sky, and Ryan was shooting a foul shot in his black parka and team sweatpants, wearing his earphones, his hair ruffling in the wind. The ball *thwapped* loudly on the grimy white backboard, spun into the basket, and tumbled through its frayed rope netting. Ryan rebounded without missing a beat and shot a layup, which he missed, but he retrieved the ball, again without missing a beat, his iPhone wire jumping around as if electrified. He pivoted perfectly on the ball of his sneakers then hopped into the air to shoot the three-pointer, his right arm high, his long fingers spread, releasing at just the right moment, and the ball swished through the net.

Yes! Jake cheered for the kid silently, though Ryan didn't stop. He went after the ball as he had before and took another shot. He wasn't smiling, and his forehead knitted, focused, and as Jake watched him, he sensed that his son was losing himself in the drill, using it to black out what had happened on Pike Road, like Jake himself had tried to last night, in the booze and sex. He realized that basketball had become a coping mechanism for his son, as well as being part of his identity; Ryan was the quiet kid who was famous as being a shooter, most comfortable on the court, where action substituted for conversation.

Jake watched him, thinking that he'd never been able to decide if Ryan was having fun when he played basketball, even when the boy was younger. Jake had never played basketball, even as a teen, because he had to work after school, as a bagger at the Giant. He'd never pushed Ryan into basketball just because he was tall; Jake had grown up with everybody asking him, *Why don't you play basketball,* and it was Ryan who had taken to the sport himself.

Jake eyed Ryan and could remember him as a little boy, shooting baskets on the driveway, no matter the season or temperature. Everybody in Chasers Nation said basketball was a passion, and they were right, but Jake knew that as soon as Pam saw the passion in their son, she had nurtured it with characteristic drive. She got him into the neighborhood leagues in elementary school, then the school and traveling teams in middle school, and the right basketball camps by the summer of seventh grade. They were called "exposure" or "showcase" camps, run by professional players or people with connections to recruiters, and the most talented players went there to be seen.

Jake remembered what a scene that had been, when he and Pam visited a summer tournament on one weekend. The kids were in ninth grade, still in orthodonture, but a lineup of Division III and even Division I coaches had sat in the front row, notebooks in hand, and by Sunday, the "impact players" had been identified. Ryan had been one. College basketball was big business, but recruiting started before puberty.

Ryan made another three-pointer, and Jake projected forward into his son's future. He didn't know if the boy would be happy at a Division I school, where he'd have to live the game, twenty-four/seven. Jake doubted that he was good enough to play professionally, and Ryan was more than just a basketball player. He had a real interest in environmental sciences, and Pam would rather have Ryan use his basketball prowess to get into a better school academically, in Division III. Jake felt the same way, although now he would settle for Ryan going to any college at all, outside of a juvenile detention home.

Suddenly, Jake noticed that Ryan stopped shooting and was looking toward the garage. Pam was coming out, talking to him, and hugging herself to keep warm. Jake couldn't hear what they were saying but he left the window to get ready. He didn't want to leave Ryan alone with Pam any longer than necessary.

Later, Jake found himself sitting on the hard bleachers at North Mayfield High School gym, which reverberated with the talking, laughing, and shouting of several hundred high-school students, teachers, and families. Little kids ran up and down the stairs between the bleachers, and cheerleaders practiced their splits and dance moves on the sidelines. School bands ran through their fight songs, complete with tubas, trumpets, and drum solos. Student booster groups—the Chasers Nation for Concord Chase and the Cardinal's Nest for North Mayfield, dressed in matching T-shirts and face paint—tried to drown each other out, cheering from opposite ends of the gym. Jennifer Lopez sang "Let's Get Loud" over the loudspeaker, and its throbbing bass ricocheted off the corrugated-metal ceiling.

Jake sat alone on the row, which was still mostly empty. Pam had gone to the ladies' room with some other Chasers' moms, leaving their parkas, scarves, and knit hats in a perfumed clump.

He exhaled a relieved sigh at having gotten Ryan through the morning. Over breakfast, they'd talked about his English homework, and though Ryan had seemed subdued, it was nothing that couldn't be chalked up to normal stress levels before a league playoff. Once they'd picked up his teammates, the boys plopped their game sneakers in their laps, plugged into their iPhones, and chattered away, reliving the plays from their last victory, a sixty-one to thirty-five drubbing of Great Valley. Ryan hadn't contributed much to the conversation even when he was its subject, and the others crowed about his twelve buckets, eight rebounds, and five blocks, with a dunk in heavy traffic. The consensus was that they would win today against North Mayfield, and the only time Ryan spoke was to remind them not to take anything for granted.

Game time was getting closer, and families started to fill in the remaining seats in the bleachers, mixing the Chasers' and North Mayfield fans. A heavyset woman in a hooded parka gestured to Jake. "Sir, are you saving this seat?" she asked, before entering the row.

"No, it's all yours."

"Thanks." The woman sat down at the aisle seat and took off her parka, revealing an I Heart My Corgi sweatshirt, then a short man came up behind her, a Sunday newspaper tucked under his arm.

"Sir, excuse me, is that seat taken?"

"No, you can sit down," Jake answered, gesturing, and the man sat down next to the woman and put his newspaper in his lap. A folded crossword puzzle was on top, and Jake spotted the headline that read, **NO SUSPECTS IN CONCORD CHASE HIT-AND-RUN.**

"I'm Lewis Deaner. My son plays for North Mayfield." The man extended a hand, and Jake shook it. "Are you from Concord Chase? You don't look familiar."

"Yes. Jake Buckman."

"Nice to meet you. I don't go crazy at games, even in the playoffs. I tell my son, I make up for the fathers who sit in the anger-management section." Deaner smiled tightly behind his wire-rimmed glasses, his thin lips stretching like a rubber band. His hair was light brown, thinning at the crown, and he was on the slight side, barely filling out his blue parka and baggy jeans.

"What position does your son play?"

"He's a guard, a sophomore. He's only a substitute, so I doubt he'll see any minutes today. But I come anyway." Deaner slid a ballpoint pen from his parka, uncapped it, and looked down at his crossword puzzle, which was half-completed. "I'm divorced, so I make the effort. That's the lay of the land."

Suddenly the crowd noise surged, and the Chasers trotted onto the glistening wood floor, a moving phalanx of maroon long-sleeved shirts and sweat suits. The coaches jogged along-side them in order of rank; Head Coach Ronald Marsh and his uniformed assistants, then Dr. Dave running next to Ryan.

Deaner looked up from his crossword. "That's my son, on the sideline, about to come on the court. The short one with the glasses. Number 16. Steve."

Jake spotted who he meant, in a pair of plastic wraparound glasses. "Good-looking boy."

"Which one's yours?"

"The one toward the back, number 22." Jake watched Dr. Dave put a hand on Ryan's shoulder and felt a flare of jealousy, even though it was his own fault that Ryan was closer to his coaches than his father. The crowd noise surged again, and the Cardinals hustled onto the floor in their bright red warm-ups. The Cardinal's Nest cheering section rose as one, flapping its arms, and singing a fight song that was unintelligible.

Jake looked around for Pam and her friends, but didn't see them. Ryan fell in line behind his teammates, and they ran a drill, jogging up and down the half-court with their knees high. The Cardinals did the same thing at their end of the court, and the crowd yelled, cheered, and called the players' names, getting more excited. One of the North Mayfield moms on the other side of the aisle produced tiaras from a white Dollar Tree bag and gave them out to her girlfriends. The music over the loudspeaker segued into "I've Got a Feeling."

Deaner watched the Chasers' warm-up session. "Your team came to play, eh?"

"Yours, too." Jake spotted Pam and her friends on the floor, hurrying toward him.

"What do you do for a living, Jake?"

"Financial planner." Jake leaned over, slid out his wallet, extracted a business card, and handed it over, reflexively. "How about you?"

"Technical writer, freelance." Deaner glanced at the card, then slipped it inside his parka. "I can't afford you, I can tell. I bet you drive a nice car, like an Audi."

"Ha! Does it show?" Jake forced a smile. It was a lucky guess, but it rattled him.

Deaner capped his pen and tucked it inside his parka. "You know, my apartment's not around here, it's in Concord Chase. Not far from Pike Road, where that hit-and-run was. You probably read about it. A junior from the high school was killed. A girl."

"Oh, yes." Jake kept his eyes on the court, where Ryan and the Chasers had started a new drill, lining up on both sides of the half-court, taking shots and rebounding for each other.

"I'll come by your office tomorrow morning, and we can have a talk."

"What about?" Jake asked, his tone casual.

"I think you know. I think you know exactly. Make sure you're there." Deaner rose. "Enjoy the game, Jake."

Chapter Seventeen

Jake watched, stunned, as Deaner made his way down the stairs, reached the floor, and vanished into the crowd. His thoughts raced. It had been such a bizarre conversation.

I bet you drive a nice car, like an Audi.

Jake felt a bolt of panic. It was too much of a coincidence. The Audi, the mention of the hit-and-run, even the newspaper headline. What if it was all intentional? What if Deaner *knew*?

Jake told himself not to jump to conclusions. He had to stay calm. He spotted Pam and her friends, climbing the steps and heading toward him. There had been no one else around that night on Pike Road. The corporate center had been empty, there were no houses. But if Deaner didn't know anything, why was he coming to Jake's office? Was Deaner still at the game?

Jake scanned the crowd, but didn't see Deaner. Was he coming back? Why did he leave? What had just happened? Who the hell was this guy? Jake slid his smartphone from his pocket, got online, and typed in **Lewis Deaner freelance technical writer**. Instantly a group of links came onto the tiny screen, and he clicked the first, but it was from a man in Huntsville, Alabama.

Jake reformulated his search request and typed in **Lewis Deaner freelance technical writer PA,** but he got no responses. So either Lewis Deaner wasn't Deaner's real name or the man wasn't a technical writer. He plugged in **Lewis Deaner Concord Chase PA,** but it came back no responses. He tried to compose himself.

"Don't work so hard, honey." Pam was sitting down, handing him a bottle of water and a soft pretzel wrapped in transparent paper. "Want a snack?"

"No, thanks." Jake slipped his smartphone back into his pocket.

"How's he doing?" Pam craned her neck at the court and watched Ryan, who was in line to shoot.

"Fine," Jake answered, though he didn't know. His attention went to the kid with the glasses on the Cardinals, Number 16. The kid took a jumper, and Jake wondered if Number 16 was really Deaner's son. The Cardinals didn't have their last names on the back of their jerseys, neither did the Chasers. Jake could have IDed Number 16 from the Cardinals website, but not in front of Pam, who was introducing two moms in Chasers Nation hoodies, filing in behind her and sitting down.

"Honey, meet Melissa and her sister Gwen. Melissa is Baird's mom. You know him, he's a forward, a senior. He's going to Princeton next year and he'll be playing for them."

"Oh, great, right. Hi." Jake couldn't focus, replaying his conversation with Deaner.

"Nice to meet you," answered Melissa and her sister Gwen, in unfortunate unison, then they laughed. They both had short strawberry blond hair and their smiles were similar, though Gwen looked older, with reading glasses on a multicolored lanyard.

Chasers Nation parents started to find seats in this section, mixing in with the red-shirted North Mayfield parents. He masked his thoughts, which were in overdrive. Maybe Deaner really wasn't a team father? What if he was a cop, digging for information? Working undercover?

"Jake, look, here come Katie and Sean, and Chris and Vanessa with the kids." Pam motioned to a Chasers-clad group, and they waved back, grinning. The moms had maroon basketballs painted on their cheeks, like forty-year-old Raggedy Anns, but Jake found himself eyeing the Cardinal moms with the tiaras, at the end of the row.

"Hello, ladies. Pam, excuse me a minute." Jake rose, setting his water bottle and soft pretzel on the bleacher. "I'm going to the men's room before the game starts."

"Okay, hurry back." Pam patted his leg, but Jake was already walking down the row, returning the smiles that everyone flashed at him and waving back to the other Concord Chase parents.

"Excuse me, sorry," he said, moving down the row, stepping over sneakers and handbags, and finally reaching the aisle, where the tiara moms sat in a rowdy row. "Ladies, can I ask you a question about the Cardinals?"

"Sure," answered the first tiara mom.

"Do you know Number 16, that player with the glasses?" Jake gestured to their half-court, where the team had finished its warm-up and were stripping off their jerseys and sweatpants and handing them to their manager, who stowed them in a red laundry bag.

"Sure, that's Mikey."

"Mikey." Jake's heart began to thump in his chest. Deaner had said his son's name was Steve. "What's Mikey's last name?"

"Murcio, why?" shouted a stocky man from the row behind them, in a Cardinals T-shirt and glasses so thick that Jake took a calculated guess.

"Are you Mikey's father?"

"Yeah. Mike Sr." The man rose, extending a beefy hand. "Why?"

Jake shook his hand, introduced himself. "I think your son

came to the job fair last year and talked to me. I wanted to know if he followed up with the financial planning firm I told him about."

"I don't think so." Mike Sr. looked at the woman sitting next to him, a short redhead. "Babe, did Mike go to some job fair last year and see a financial planner?"

The wife shrugged, with a smile. "Who remembers? I don't even remember yesterday. Don't ask me where I put my car keys."

Mike Sr. chuckled, facing Jake. "Sorry."

"No worries, he's a nice kid." Jake had gotten the answer he needed, which only worried him more. He didn't know who Deaner really was. He kicked himself for giving him a business card.

"Good luck, bro." Mike Sr. lowered himself onto the bleachers, and the tiara moms started to cheer.

"Go, Cardinals, go! Go, Cardinals, go!"

Jake hurried down the bleacher steps, reached the gym floor, and threaded his way through the crowds hurrying to get to their seats before the game. He looked for Deaner on the floor and in the stands, but didn't see him. He followed the signs to the men's room and hurried inside.

The room was empty, and he hustled to the sink, stuck his hands under the automatic faucet, and splashed cold water on his face. His heart raced, his head pounded. He felt like he was having a panic attack.

I bet you drive a nice car, like an Audi.

Jake leaned over, bracing himself on the sink. He had to get it together. Pam would begin to wonder if he was gone too long. He could hear the crowd outside surging again, and the announcer's over-amplified voice welcoming everyone to the game.

He reached for a paper towel and dried his face, barely recognizing the expression on his face, one he'd never seen on himself. It was a mixture of bewilderment and dread, as if he were permanently aghast.

The crowd started cheering wildly, and it brought Jake back. He hurried to the door and pushed it open, only to find Dr. Dave in the hallway. "Oh, hi, excuse me."

"Jake, I don't know if you remember me. I'm Dave Tolliver, Ryan's shooting coach? We met last year at the championship dinner?" Dr. Dave smiled quickly, showing even teeth. He was of average height, much thinner than Jake, and his jet-black hair was cut close to his head, with sideburns too long for anyone not in a rock band.

"Right. Yes. Of course. I knew that. Dr. Dave." Jake extended a hand, which Dr. Dave shook.

"Right." Dr. Dave grinned, looking ready for *GQ* in a charcoal suit jacket of some sleek Italian cut, which somehow coordinated with his hip, graphite glasses.

"Thanks for your help with Ryan."

"It's my pleasure." Dr. Dave's eyes were dark brown, and for some reason, oddly serious. "I was looking for you, and Pam said I might find you here."

"Oh?" Jake said, taken aback.

"Got a minute? It's about Ryan."

Chapter Eighteen

"Sure, but the game's about to start." Jake gestured to the gym, where the announcer was introducing the Cardinals cheerleaders. The crowd responded with cheering that echoed harshly in the corridor, painted white cinderblock with a wide red stripe.

"This won't take long." Dr. Dave slipped his hands inside his pants pockets. "I'm concerned that Ryan seems off tonight. He's going to have a rough game."

Oh no. "He's been sick." Jake felt his chest tighten. "But he wanted to play, and don't sell him short. He'll have a good game."

"He didn't warm up well. I'm concerned that something's wrong with him, and it's not physical."

"Of course it is." Jake tried to shrug it off. "He was throwing up all day Saturday. He had some bad nachos. He's only playing today because he'd never let the team down."

"Jake." Dr. Dave paused, lifting his eyebrows slightly. "I'm a practicing child and adolescent psychologist, for twenty-five years. I know the difference between a teenager who's got food poisoning and one who's got something on his mind."

"No he doesn't. He's just sick."

"Seriously, it's more than that."

"How do you know this?" Jake tried not to sound skeptical, just interested.

"He's *off*."

"Off?"

"Yes, off. He's not focusing. He's out of sync. He didn't walk in the way he always does, the way he did last week. He's a shooter, and a shooter is a creature of habit. Basketball grounds him. It keeps him centered—"

"I know that." Jake was in no mood to be lectured about his own son.

"Then you know he has a system that works for him. He keeps his warm-up exercises and his warm-up routine the same. He takes the same number of shots, in the same way. His work in the gym is always focused and purposeful—"

"I know. He's my son."

"—but tonight he's shooting flat. He's not getting enough lift on the ball. He's not releasing it high enough, so he's pushing it instead of throwing it—"

"He'll be fine."

"No, he won't, you'll see. We'll win, but Ryan's an impact player and he won't help the team today."

"Why are you telling me this?" Jake asked, unable to keep the impatience from his tone. "What do you want me to do about it?"

"Fine, I'll come to my point." Dr. Dave pursed his lips. "I get the impression that you're riding him, and I'm asking you to back off during the playoffs. Ryan's hard enough on himself, and it's a critical time."

"I'm not riding him," Jake blurted out, surprised. The crowd had started hollering again, and the announcer called the Cardinal cheerleaders onto their floor, to their music, "Brick House."

"Jake, please don't be defensive."

"Then don't make me defend myself. Don't tell me I'm riding my son when I'm not."

Dr. Dave put up a hand like a Zen traffic cop. "I should explain. I spend a lot of time with Ryan. I know him very well. He tends to tighten up when you come to a game—"

"So what am I supposed to do, not come to my son's game?" Jake felt his anger overcome his worry, bollixing him up. "I don't need to stand here and listen to you tell me about my own son."

Dr. Dave emitted a sigh. "When I asked Ryan, he said nothing was wrong. But Pam told me that you and he had some sort of fight on Friday night—"

"*What?* Why are you talking to my wife about our son?" Jake felt panicky. Pam couldn't be so open with Dr. Dave about their family business. It was too dangerous, after Pike Road.

"I talk to Pam all the time about Ryan. That's my job."

"What job?" Jake heard his tone sharpen. "You're a volunteer. What are your qualifications?"

"You're angry, so you're challenging me." Dr. Dave exuded a professional calm. "You don't really want to know my qualifications."

"Try me." Jake hated being told how he really felt, especially by people who had no idea how he really felt.

"As I said, I'm a child and adolescent psychologist. I have a small but growing specialty in adolescent sports psychology—"

"What does that have to do with basketball? You're talking about 'impact players' and 'lift on the ball,' but you're supposed to be a shooting coach."

"I played varsity basketball for three years at Penn, then I played professionally in Italy and Brazil before I got my degree." Dr. Dave emitted another small sigh. "But, this isn't about you and me. This is about you and Ryan. Pam said that you fought, because you didn't like something he said—"

"It wasn't that big a deal." Jake had a story, and he had to stick with it. "It was about texting."

"You asked him to stop texting?"

"Yes, and what parent hasn't?"

"The fight wasn't really about texting. You asserted your authority, and Ryan was unwilling to recognize or credit that authority, which you can understand, given the history of your relationship."

Jake bristled. "You're out of line."

"I'm trying to help."

"I don't need your help."

"What if Ryan does?"

"He doesn't."

"Jake, you needn't feel threatened by me. I'm not trying to replace or supplant you. There's room for us both."

"No, there isn't. Butt out." Jake turned away, strode down the corridor, and turned the corner into the noisy gym just as the Chasers were being introduced. Ryan was second in line, shifting his weight from one sneaker to the other and eyeing the bleachers where they'd told him they'd be sitting. Jake waved at him, but Ryan didn't see, so he hurried down the sidelines behind the team benches, which were separated from each other by a long metal table that held reporters sitting in front of open laptops.

He reached their bleacher section, which had filled in completely, with parents, kids, and students sitting shoulder-to-shoulder. He scanned the crowd for Deaner, and made his way to Pam, who was standing up with everybody else, clapping. He took his place to stand beside her, and she gave him a kiss on the cheek.

"Perfect timing!"

"Yes, right." Jake had to put a stop to her talking to Dr. Dave, game or no game. It was too risky, especially today. "Honey, Dr. Dave found me."

"Good. Did you talk to him?"

"Why did you tell him that Ryan and I had a fight?"

"He's worried about Ryan." Pam kept her eyes on the court, but leaned over and answered, to be heard over the crowd noise.

"Ryan's sick, that's all. There's nothing to worry about."

"Dr. Dave thinks it's more. He asked me if there was anything that happened recently that could have bothered him, and I told him about the big fight you guys had."

"It wasn't that big a fight."

Pam scoffed, keeping her attention on the court. "You made him cry, Jake. He never cries. So it was a big fight."

Jake couldn't believe the irony. He was getting in trouble over a fight he didn't even have. "Don't you think that's something that should be kept between us?"

"No, why?" Pam glanced over, puzzled, then turned back to the court. The Cardinals had been introduced, and the announcer was asking everyone to face the flag for the national anthem.

"It's our business, not his."

"Don't be silly. It doesn't matter if he knows. Parents fight with kids all the time." Pam put her hand over her heart when the anthem started playing, and she began to sing loudly, in her characteristically pretty soprano.

"It matters to me." Jake put his hand on his chest, sang the national anthem, and when everybody burst into applause, he leaned over to Pam. "Honey, do me a favor. Don't encourage Dr. Dave's snooping into our personal life."

"He's not snooping." Pam looked at him like he was crazy, then faced the court, where the team captains, referees, and coaches were gathering at the center.

"These things aren't any of his business."

"He's a friend of ours, a friend of our family's." Pam stopped clapping, and Jake could see he was getting her attention.

"Please, let's keep the conversation with him to basketball, not our family life. We already had therapy. We don't need more."

Pam frowned. "What did you say to him?"

"I told him Ryan was fine and I could handle it."

"What does that mean?"

"I told him to butt out."

"You *did*?" Pam's lips parted in dismay. "You said that? Jake, how could you? Why?"

"He's telling me that Ryan gets tense when I come to games. That's out of line."

"Ryan wants your approval, you know that. He wants to play well when you come. He doesn't need you to get him in bad with the coaches. God, they talk to the recruiters all the time. You want to queer it for him? What were you thinking?" Pam shook her head, missing the jump ball that started the game.

"Pam, I'm his father—" Jake noticed the Chasers' moms sneaking a glance at them, so he kept his voice low. "And I don't want you talking to any third party about something as personal as my relationship to my own son—"

"Oh, please." Pam rolled her eyes. "Don't be such a control freak."

"It's our business, my business—"

"You're just *jealous,* and you have absolutely no right to be. Nature abhors a vacuum, Jake, and Dr. Dave stepped in to fill a void that was created by *you*. He didn't go looking for Ryan, Ryan went looking for *him*." Pam's fair skin flushed with resentment. "Now you've decided to step back in, and good for you, but don't expect everything to be just the way you want it, right away. It takes time. You have to *earn* your way in."

Jake regretted bringing up the subject here. Chasers' and Cardinals' families were eyeing them, even though the game was in full swing. "Pam, relax—"

"No. You can't just snap your fingers and make people do what you say, or feel what you want them to feel. I hope you didn't piss Dr. Dave off." Pam craned her neck, scanning the sidelines of the court. "You should go see him right now and apologize. He usually sits in the front row behind the bench. Do you see him?"

"I have nothing to apologize for, Pam."

"Then I will." Pam pointed. "There he is, by Coach Marsh."

"Pam, really?"

"Absolutely." Pam rose and made her way down the row, then the stairs, toward the court.

Jake lost sight of her, then gave up. He felt eyes boring into his back, but he had bigger problems than being the subject of gossip. He had Lewis Deaner on the brain. He didn't know who the man was and if he knew something or was bluffing. Jake felt his gut clench and tried to get into the basketball game. The lighted scoreboard read **Home 10, Away 4.** The Chasers were behind. There were nine minutes left in the first quarter, so there was plenty of time to catch up. Ryan stole the ball and dribbled it down the court, his hair flying.

"Go, Ryan," Jake shouted, making a megaphone of his hands.

"Ryan, Ryan, Ryan!" chanted the Chasers' student section.

"Shoot, Ryan! Shoot!" called a Chasers' mom in back.

"DEFENSE!" bellowed one of the Cardinals' dads.

Ryan stopped with the ball, his sneakers squealing, faced the basket, and took a jumper from the outside, like he had in the driveway this morning. The crowd shrieked as the ball hit the transparent backboard, bounced onto the rim, and dropped outside the hoop, missing the basket. Ryan seemed to stall, as if rooted to the shiny wooden floor.

"Follow your shot, Ryan!" somebody shouted in back.

And Jake's heart sank, because he knew what he was seeing.

He's off.

Chapter Nineteen

Pam drove home because they'd taken her car, and Jake rode in the passenger seat, in suburban exile. They'd barely spoken for the remainder of the game, and he didn't know if she'd talked to Dr. Dave, though he assumed she had because she'd been on the warpath. Jake's thoughts kept circling to Lewis Deaner, and he'd spent the rest of the game looking for him in the crowd. He'd even checked the parking lot after the game let out, but no luck.

Pam braked when they came to a red light and glanced in the rearview mirror at Ryan, who sat in the backseat, plugged into his iPhone, listening to music. The Chasers won, forty-five to thirty-eight, but Ryan had been benched for the second half, unprecedented in his basketball career. He'd scored six points instead of his usual fifteen or so, and missed every three-pointer. He hadn't played good defense either, and the ball had been stolen from him twice. After the game, he'd come out of the locker room with his head down, stone-faced and atypically apart from his teammates, who'd emerged laughing, talking, and slapping five after the victory.

"How are you feeling, honey?" Pam asked, to the rearview mirror. The sky around them was gray-bright, thick with a winter cloud. The air smelled damp and chilled, like snow was coming.

Ryan didn't reply. Jake glanced back, but he couldn't see Ryan, who was sitting behind him.

"Ryan? You okay?" Pam repeated, louder, though it was obvious that Ryan was avoiding conversation. He knew Ryan had to be dying inside, the least of his worries being the way he'd played.

"Ryan!" Pam said, more sharply, because she knew when she was being avoided, too.

"I'm fine, Mom."

"Honey, don't beat yourself up. Everybody's entitled to a bad day, and you've been sick. Your body can't recover that fast. You're probably dehydrated." Pam squinted into the rearview. The traffic light was still red. "Don't you have any water with you?"

"No."

"We could stop at McDonald's or Dunkin' and get you some. You want to?"

"No thanks."

"But they're on the way home, and you must be hungry. Don't you want to stop and get something to eat? It might perk you up."

"I don't want anything."

"What did Coach Marsh say?"

"Not much."

"But what?"

"He said, next time to tell him if I'm not feeling good."

Pam frowned. "Okay. But what would he have done differently?"

Ryan shrugged.

"He didn't say?"

"No."

"He would have played you, no matter what. You've never not started."

Ryan said nothing.

"Did you talk to Dr. Dave?" Pam glanced sideways at Jake, who knew that she wanted to know if Dr. Dave had said anything about their argument.

Ryan didn't reply.

The traffic light turned green, and Pam hit the gas. "Ryan, did you talk to Dr. Dave?"

"Yeah."

"What did he say?"

"Nothing."

"Ryan, he didn't say *nothing*," Pam shot back, her tone exasperated. "Can't you fill me in? Do I have to pull teeth here?"

"Mom, watch your driving!"

Jake cringed. "Ryan, please don't talk to your mother that way."

Ryan gestured to the road. "Dad, she's not looking where she's going. She didn't even see that Subaru, turning left."

Pam frowned in annoyance. "I saw it, Ryan. It wasn't anywhere near us."

Jake didn't know what Subaru he was talking about, but anxiety was plain in his son's voice. "I'm sure she did, Ryan. Just watch your tone."

Pam's head snapped toward Jake. "Thanks, but I can talk to my son myself. I don't need you to intervene."

Jake let it go. He knew she was only blowing off steam and he wasn't about to fight with her. Instead he looked out the window, and his gaze flitted restlessly over the strip mall with its CVS, Subway, and Rita's Water Ice, a sight he found oddly comforting. He'd heard people complain that the country had become so homogeneous, with the same chain stores everywhere, but he didn't have a problem with that. The chains were a part of his daily routine: he got his coffee at the Wawa, his turkey hoagies at the Subway near his office, and his chocolate-covered doughnut at Dunkin' Donuts drive-thru, right before he hit the on-ramp. The sameness of the stores and their food implicitly reassured him that everything would always be the same in his life, at least until recently.

I bet you drive a nice car, like an Audi.

Pam straightened up. "Ryan, I know you feel disappointed about the game, but you don't have to sulk like Achilles in his tent. I'm trying to talk to you because I love you. It's a good problem to have, that you have a parent who cares enough about you to ask you how you're feeling, okay?"

Ryan groaned. "Mom. You're not asking, you're nagging."

Jake kept his face turned to the window, feeling a pang. He knew that Pam would be hurt by that dig and that Ryan was hurting inside, too, which was why he'd made it. Jake didn't say anything because he'd been warned off, so he kept his own counsel. Pam defaulted to silence, but she fed the SUV some gas. He felt the lurch of its angry acceleration and watched the scenery go by faster; the Acme, the Cold Stone Creamery, the Walgreens, and the Pottery Barn blurring into one neon streak of commercialism with convenient parking, open on Sundays and taking all major credit cards.

They traveled in silence, then crossed into Concord Chase, and Pam steered onto Concordia Boulevard. They passed another Wawa and a massive Wegman's, then she put on her left blinker and moved into the left lane. Jake realized with dismay that she was going to take the shortcut home, via Pike Road. They'd go around the same curve on which they'd struck and killed Kathleen Lindstrom.

Jake had to do something. He couldn't put Ryan through the pain or take the chance that the boy would throw up, cry, or react involuntarily, showing their hand.

Jake waved her off. "Honey, don't take Pike. Why don't you just go straight?"

"Why?" Pam glanced over, frowning. A truck was barreling down the oncoming lane toward them, and she stopped before she turned onto Pike to let it pass.

"This is where that girl was killed. Let's not go this way."

"Since when are you such a sensitive flower?"

"Pam, really." Jake knew that she was punishing him for fighting with Dr. Dave, but she didn't know she was punishing her son as well.

"Don't be silly."

Jake turned away. He didn't have anything left to say that wouldn't tip her off and he was suddenly tired of the bitterness between them, the back-and-forth. He missed the Pam of last night, the one who wasn't keeping score. The truck rumbled past, its big muddy tires spraying gravel, and Pam took the left turn, driving onto Pike.

Jake kept his face to his window, to avoid looking down the road and reliving everything that happened before the curve. Ryan remained silent in the backseat. The car grew so quiet that Jake could hear the tinny beat of the music through Ryan's earbuds and wondered how he could listen to such loud music, then realized the boy must've cranked up the volume. He prayed Ryan could keep it together when they reached the blind curve.

"It's just that it's so much faster to take Pike," Pam said, her tone gentler. "Plus I want to get Ryan home. He's not feeling well."

Ryan said from the backseat, "I'm fine, Mom."

"Well, good," Pam said, lightly. "Glad to hear that, honey."

Jake looked out his window. He wondered if Ryan was sending him a message, saying he was fine and telling him not to worry. The SUV cruised forward, and he started wondering about Lewis Deaner again when they approached the Concordia

Corporate Center sign, with a sign that listed businesses in the B section: Marble Fabricators, Lee Security, Ltd., Tropical Technologies, Inc., Cryotechnics, and a few others.

Jake considered it. Lewis Deaner could have been employed by any one of those companies, in any capacity. The closest office building in section B wasn't far from Pike Road, maybe a hundred feet to the left, due north, and someone could have been working late on Friday night, in any one of those buildings. Jake hadn't seen any cars in the lots along Pike Road that night, but there was a large interior parking lot in the corporate center. Deaner could've parked there and all he would have had to do to see the accident was to look out the back window of one of the offices.

Jake felt his gut clench, trying to guess how much Deaner knew, if anything. Jake thought back to the accident; he had gotten out of the car first, and Ryan had come later, from the driver's seat. They were both tall and they looked alike. It would be hard to tell who was driving, from a distance. Maybe Deaner didn't know who had been driving, whether it was him or Ryan.

Dad . . . I killed . . . that lady . . . I killed . . . that lady.

The SUV traveled down Pike Road, and Jake remembered what Deaner had said about having an apartment near Pike. He surveyed the woods to the right, and to his surprise, he spotted some buildings through the trees, in the distance. There were a series of red brick low-rises of an older, boxy design, and they looked like an apartment complex, situated on the other side of the woods. Jake hadn't known they were there, but he used Pike Road only as a conduit, and the apartments wouldn't have been visible from Pike during most of the year, when the trees were in full leaf.

The SUV closed in on the blind curve, and Jake tried not to think about what had happened that night. Instead he eyeballed the distance from Pike to the apartment buildings and estimated it to be about the length of three basketball courts. That would be too far away for Deaner to see any details of the accident unless he had been using binoculars, which made no sense. But it wasn't impossible that Deaner had seen the Audi or could identify it at that distance, because the car's frowny headlights were a well-known design feature, recognizable to anyone who knew anything about cars and easily visible at night, even in the fog.

Pam slowed as they approached the blind curve, and Jake mulled over the possibility that Deaner could have seen the accident from his apartment and could identify the Audi. Still, how could Deaner have identified Jake, much less found him? Had he seen the Audi's license plate? How? Or if Deaner was an undercover cop, maybe someone else had seen it and called it in as a tip.

Pam reached the blind curve, and Jake reached for the door handle, reflexively bracing himself for a collision that had happened days ago. A forlorn memorial had been set up by the roadside—a motley clump of plush teddy bears, grocery-store flowers, thick Yankee candles, and sympathy cards, next to a maroon singlet from the track team and a handmade sign that read **Chasers Pride! We miss you, Kathleen! Xoxoxo**

Pam cleared her throat. "I guess this is where the hit-and-run was."

Jake didn't say anything, and neither did Ryan.

"It's a dangerous curve, so I could see how it could happen. But how could he not stop?" Pam *tsked-tsked.*

Jake didn't answer, and he prayed Ryan stayed quiet.

Pam steered around the curve, staying in her lane. "Sorry we came this way," she said softly.

"S'okay." Jake felt his anger ebb away, if not his shame. The SUV powered forward as Pam accelerated, and he scanned the dirt shoulder of the road, checking. There was no shard of glass, no piece of heavy plastic, not even a skidmark to incriminate them.

Dad . . . I killed . . . that lady . . . I killed . . . that lady.

Jake found himself sending up a silent prayer, asking forgiveness for himself and Ryan. And yet, at the same time, he watched the apartment buildings recede in the distance, wondering what Deaner really knew about the accident, who Deaner was, and what he wanted. If Deaner was a cop, then he wanted Jake and Ryan, truth and justice. But if he wasn't, Jake had a good guess what he wanted. He'd find out tomorrow, for sure.

Chapter Twenty

Jake stood in the doorway to Pam's home office, where she was at her desk on the cell phone. She motioned him inside, and he entered and sat down in the pink flowered chair opposite her. They had achieved an uneasy truce during dinnertime, then Ryan had gone to his bedroom to do homework and she had retreated to her home office to make calls to the powers-that-be about her judicial nomination. He'd come in to see her to find out any details about the FBI interviews, so he could prepare Ryan. Lewis Deaner had to settle for the backburner, for now.

Pam held up an index finger, flashing him the one minute sign, and Jake looked idly around her office. It was smaller than his, but it had a cozy feel, which was why she always called it her nest. The two windows on the wall had a sunny southern exposure, but they were dark now, and red oriental-type lamps gave off a soft, homey glow. He liked her office, but it was very feminine, with pink walls, a maroon, red, and pink Heriz rug, and pink-and-red curtains in a pattern that had colonial people standing in front of thatched huts.

Toile, Pam had said, of the curtain pattern. *It's called toile.*

How do you spell that?

T-O-I-L-E.

Like toilet?

Pam had laughed. *You're useless, completely useless.*

Jake tried to relax in the chair, but couldn't. He was facing an entire wall of her framed diplomas, admission certificates to the Pennsylvania and New Jersey bars, and documents that admitted her to practice law in the Supreme Court of Pennsylvania and the Third Circuit Court of Appeals. They stared him in the face, setting into stark relief the paradox of their different positions. His wife was sitting behind a cluttered desk, trying to become a federal judge, one of the highest positions in the country in which to make and to enforce civil and criminal law. He sat opposite her, as if diametrically opposed, having committed the worst crime imaginable and concealed it from her and the authorities, in a conspiracy with her own son.

"Sorry if I was testy today." Pam hung up the phone, excited and happy.

"No worries. I'm sorry too. How's it going? Anything new?"

"Actually, yes." Pam leaned excitedly over the messy papers. "This is really happening fast. They're going to make it public later I think. My name is definitely going up the ladder to the White House, to be nominated."

"Honey, that's amazing! Congratulations!"

"I know! Isn't it so great?" Pam's eyes lit up, then she seemed to check herself. "But I can't count my chickens before they're hatched. There's a lot that has to happen between now and then, and you know these vacancies can be open for years."

Jake liked the sound of that. Ryan needed a few years to get past the accident. "So then they're not going to investigate you for a few years?"

"No, you misunderstand me. They do the investigation now and the nomination happens, then there's the Senate hearings, but you have to wait to be confirmed. That's the part that takes years."

"Oh, too bad." Jake hid his alarm.

"Patty Shwartz still hasn't gotten on the Third Circuit and she was nominated over two years ago, for a seat that was vacated two years *prior*. She had her hearing and she *still* hasn't been confirmed." Pam shook her head. "It's classic hurry-up-and-wait."

"So when does the investigation start?"

"Right now."

"But your nomination isn't public yet—"

"No, to be precise, I haven't been nominated yet. It's the president who does the nominating." Pam's voice turned professorial. "There's a questionnaire I have to answer and hand in next week, so if that goes smoothly, then it becomes public and starts officially."

Jake tried not to panic. It was too short a time for Ryan to have any emotional distance from the hit-and-run.

"The way it works is first, I get nominated by the president, then I have to submit the answers to the questionnaire to the Senate Judiciary Committee within five days from the date of the nomination."

"Five days? Wow."

"They make my answers public for three weeks and the hearing is scheduled anytime after that."

"So this is all happening this month?" Jake masked his dread.

"They emailed me all the questionnaires and information, and I printed it out. I ran out of paper, you believe that?" Pam gestured happily to the stacks on her desk. "I have to answer all of it *this week*. I can't believe how extensive it is." Pam flipped through a thick packet of papers, bolted at the top with a heavy metal clip. "This is only one of the questionnaires. It's sixty pages long!"

"Let me see." Jake held out his hand, and Pam gave him the packet, which he began to flip through. He passed headings for Education, Employment, Bar and Court Admissions, Public Statements, and Published Writings. He didn't see the part about the FBI. "It's a lot of work here."

"I know, right? And you see where it says I have to give the names of the counsel in these cases? They contact them, all of them. They interview them."

"Who does? The FBI?"

"No, the FBI investigates me and you, personally. The Department of Justice, the ABA, and the Senate Judiciary Committee investigate my career and finances. But they do overlap, not surprisingly. It's a bureaucracy. There's multiple questions that basically cover my judicial career, with an emphasis on any personal wrongdoing."

Jake shuddered. "Wrongdoing? You? How absurd."

"Obviously, but they have to ask. There's tons of questions that require disclosure of any violations of the law since I was eighteen years old. It even asks whether I've been accused of violating any county or even municipal regulations or ordinances." Pam snorted. "The only criminal questions that aren't covered are traffic violations for which a fine of fifty dollars or less was imposed."

Jake managed a smile. "You don't even have that."

"I know. I'm such a good girl. They ask about tax liens, collection procedures, or any kind of civil-law violations or state-bar proceedings. It's all public, except our financial records. The financial stuff will take forever." Pam rolled her eyes. "Will you do that part for me?"

"Of course. Is that for the FBI, too?"

"No. Those questions come from the Justice Department and the office of the Attorney General. They want to make sure there's no financial conflicts of interests, and they want our tax returns, for God-knows-how-many years."

"That's okay, I can deal." Jake wasn't getting anywhere beating around the bush. "Tell me about the FBI. How does that work?"

"They assign a special agent, or sometimes two, to investigate us. I was on the phone with Michael Rizzo just now, and he told me that over a three-week period, he had twenty-four hours of face-to-face interviews with the FBI."

"Really?" Jake's mouth went dry. "That's a lot longer than I thought."

"You and me both." Pam cringed. "Worst job interview ever."

"How long did they question his family for, did he say?"

"He said they spent an entire day with his wife, because she had a lot of financial ups and downs they had to sort out. But we don't have that. Anymore."

Jake knew what she was referring to. "How about his kids?"

"They don't have any. And they asked him for phone records, old passports, case files, and even some old school records."

"Do you think they'll ask for Ryan's school records?"

"I don't know."

"Will they interview Ryan alone or with us?"

"I don't know that either. He has nothing to worry about, but I bet they'll spend a lot of time with you and ask questions about your finances. But we don't have anything to worry about though. We do everything by the book."

"How about Ryan? What could they possibly ask him?"

"I have no idea. We're as clean as a whistle, really." Pam shrugged. "And they really do talk to the neighbors. Rizzo told me that the FBI contacted twenty of his friends and classmates all over the country, even the world. He said they really do go up and knock on the neighbors' doors. They asked his neighbors if he and his wife got along well with everyone, fought excessively, drank excessively, or were ever seen doing anything suspicious or unusual. Can you imagine that?"

"Sheesh." Jake had a sick feeling in the pit of his stomach, praying that no one had seen him burn the parka the other day.

Pam plucked some papers off the desk and handed them over. "Here, can you take a look at this? It's the financial part. Go to page fifty-nine."

"Sure." Jake flipped to the page, which was headed **Deferred Income/Future Benefits.** He skimmed the question. **List all the sources, amounts and dates of all anticipated receipts from deferred income payments, stock, options, uncompleted contracts and other future benefits** . . . "Boy, they aren't kidding."

"No, they're not. And go down to item number 22, which is source of income."

Jake read down to the paragraph. **List sources and amounts of all income received during the calendar year preceding your nomination and for the current calendar year, including all salaries, fees, dividends, interest, gifts, rents, royalties, licensee's fees** . . . "I get the idea."

"It's a nightmare."

Jake didn't bother to correct her. He knew exactly what a nightmare was and he was living it. "I can answer this for you. I'll do it tomorrow at the office."

"Thank you, thank you, thank you." Pam picked up another set of papers and handed them over the desk. "They also need a complete and detailed statement of our net worth, which goes back before the nomination, and the worst part is, since there's always a delay between the nomination and the hearing, sometimes three and four years, we have to keep updating the information, on a quarterly basis." Pam threw up her hands. "It's like doing your taxes every quarter for the next five years!"

Jake smiled. He wished he were living in Before, too, back when the only thing he had to worry about was paperwork. "Don't worry, we'll get through it."

"I wonder if I'll even make it." Pam flopped back in her cushy chair. "They said one of the reasons my name came to the front

was because I'm a registered Independent. I'm the most apoliti-
cal, but that's not always the best thing."

"Sure it is. You're about the job, not about the politics."

"Ha! Well, of course, it being the federal government, there
is a document that actually gives you the precise qualifications
for the job." Pam searched around her desk, located some papers, and held them up. "Here we have a form. Presto!" She
read aloud. "I'm paraphrasing, but the first requirement is, I
have to be a citizen."

"Check."

"I have to have a reputation for integrity and good character."

"Check," Jake said, but that would disqualify her if anything
about the accident came to light.

"I have to be fair and unbiased."

"You are."

"I have to be of sound mental and physical health."

Jake smiled. "Mental health? You can't win them all."

"Very funny." Pam grinned and returned to her document.
"I have to be committed to equal justice under the law, have an
outstanding legal ability, and competence and a willingness to
manage trial proceedings."

"You have all that. You'll get it."

"But the fact that I'm not political means that nobody really
backs me from either party."

"Or conversely, it means that neither party opposes you and
your nomination sails through."

"Thanks. I try to do the right thing, every case. I try to follow the law." Pam raised her hand like the Statue of Liberty. "I
stand for the law!"

"That's my girl!" Jake masked his emotions, feeling like a
total fraud.

"I'm also supposed to think about why I really want to be a
federal judge." Pam paused. "Let me remember how Rizzo put
it. He told me I'm supposed to engage in 'critical self-reflection.'

I told him don't worry about that, I'm a woman. I wake up in critical self-reflection."

Jake smiled. "You want it, right?"

"More than anything."

Jake got up, walked around the desk, and gave her a big hug. "Then you shall have it, my love."

Chapter Twenty-one

Jake was at work the next morning by six o'clock, watching the parking lot through the floor-to-ceiling windows of his office and wondering if Lewis Deaner was going to pull up. Jake would be the first to see Deaner enter the building, whether or not Deaner parked in the spaces designated for Gardenia visitors. His office was three floors up, on the corner of the rectangular building, the corporate equivalent of the castle built on high ground. But it was still dark outside, and the lot was almost empty, so all Jake could see in the window was his own troubled reflection.

Still he kept an eye out, ignoring the flop sweat under his shirt. His tie felt like a noose. He'd barely slept last night, but he'd come to the office on time, always the first one in. He'd kept his door closed to signal no interruptions, but he still hadn't gotten anything done. He couldn't focus. He'd tried to do the things he had to do—check his email, then the markets in Japan, London, and New York—but all the while, in the back of his mind, he'd been worried about Lewis Deaner.

Jake caught sight of the treeline beyond the parking lot, and the jagged branches looked like so many hunting knives, cutting into the sky. He wondered for the umpteenth time if Deaner lived in the apartment building near Pike Road or worked in one of the businesses in the Concordia Corporate Center—or if he really knew anything about the accident, at all. Last night, Jake had searched online for information about Deaner or the accident, but found nothing new. He'd told Ryan not to confide in Dr. Dave, and Ryan had agreed, still shaken from driving down Pike Road again. When Jake had left him, Ryan was beginning to tackle his homework, his *American Pageant* textbook open next to his laptop. He was studying the American Dream, and Jake ignored the irony.

He saw his own troubled reflection ghosted in the window, but checked the parking lot again. Cars began to enter, but no sign of Deaner. In time a frigid sun climbed the sky, and cars arrived one by one, first among them his ace office administrator, Amy Carlino, who parked her maroon Acura next to his rental Toyota. She got out, gathered up her big purse, and eyed his car, undoubtedly worried about why Jake had a rental. He felt touched, wondering how disillusioned she would be if she knew about Pike Road.

Jake watched the Gardenia lot fill up, and his employees emerged from their Nissans, Jettas, and SUVs, their phones to their ears, juggling travel mugs, cigarettes, purses, and tote bags. None of the spaces was officially reserved or assigned, but the employees knew where each other parked, like seats at a dinner table. So far, no sign of Deaner.

His attention turned to the farther sections of the lot, scanning it for an unfamiliar car. The lot accommodated five other companies, all of them bigger than Gardenia, so any car could have belonged to Deaner. He checked out the drivers, but none was Deaner. In the meantime, he could hear the noises outside his door as Gardenia filled up with all sixteen employees, which included five portfolio managers that reported to him, as well as specialists in banking, fixed income, research, sales, and marketing.

"Jake?" said a voice behind him, and Jake startled, then swiveled his chair around. Amy stood in the open doorway, puzzled. "I knocked, but you didn't hear me."

"Amy, sorry." Jake tried to get his head in the game. A cold sunlight filled his office, which had a side wall of light wood shelves, and a beige leather couch and matching chairs across his desk. His desk had a glass top that matched the one on a round conference table. Mullioned panels flanked his doorway.

"Mrs. LeMenile is out in reception. A new client, remember? She's on your calendar for ten o'clock. You ready for her?"

"Sure. Yes."

"You okay?" Amy searched his face with large, espresso-brown eyes. "You don't look well."

"I'm fine, thanks." Jake couldn't remember the last time he'd lied to Amy, except for her surprise birthday parties, which he lied to her about routinely. "By the way, I had a fender bender over the weekend, so expect the insurance company to call."

"I was wondering." Amy frowned with concern. "Meanwhile, did you hear about that hit-and-run on Friday night? The girl went to Concord Chase? Did Ryan know her?"

"No." Jake forced himself not to show any reaction. "Also, we may get a visit from a guy I know, named Lewis Deaner."

"Okay, I'll go get Mrs. LeMenile. Be right back." Amy left and returned a few minutes later with a handsome older woman. "Jake, this is Mrs. Guinevere LeMenile," Amy said, before she slipped out, closing the door.

"Hello, Mrs. LeMenile." Jake rose to greet her, extending a hand, which Mrs. LeMenile shook, her grip surprisingly strong. She had sleek silvery hair, which was clipped back off of her lined face, and she was tall, weathered, and lean in a camelhair jacket, jeans, with brown boots that lent her a horsey air. Her hooded eyes were a lively gray-green, alert and sharp, set off by a green silk scarf.

"Jake, call me Guinevere. Wonderful to meet you."

"Please, sit down." Jake gestured to his conference table and sat down opposite her. "Can I get you some coffee or tea?"

"No, thanks, I haven't much time." Guinevere set her leather bag on the floor and plunked down in the chair, crossing her legs. "I'm here because my friend Helen Weissman recommended you. She can't say enough good things about you and you made her a significant amount of money."

"Thank you, and I think the world of Helen."

"I'm a widow, and my husband died two years ago, leaving me with an estate of $5 million." Guinevere's manner was authoritative, and she didn't pull out any bank statements, notes, or scraps of paper like many of his first-time clients. "Two million of that are the proceeds from his life-insurance policy, one is our combined savings, 401(k), and pension fund. I live in our home, which is worth two. My money is currently in short-term Treasury bills and I'm making nothing, but I've become very dissatisfied with the fees I'm paying my current financial planner. Even though I negotiated them down from 1 percent to .5 percent, it still seems utterly ridiculous for what is essentially a liquid asset, don't you agree?"

"Yes," Jake answered, because she was absolutely right. Suddenly his attention was drawn away by activity at Amy's desk, but he could only see part of what was going on through the mullioned windows.

"I think I'm ready to put that money to work for me, so I've come to you. Why don't we begin by your telling me about Gardenia?"

"Sure. Right." Jake wondered if it was Deaner at Amy's desk, which would be odd. Guests had to wait in reception before being sent back. "We have almost a hundred . . . million dollars under our management." Jake felt himself falter, distracted.

"We look for high-quality stocks from established companies, ones that pay dividends, and—"

"I read that on your website." Guinevere waved him into silence with a wrinkled hand. "I'd rather you explain how you make your investment decisions, exactly."

"I would be your portfolio manager, but here we make our investment decisions as a group." Jake tried to look past Guinevere to see what was going on, but couldn't. "The investment committee, which I head, uh . . . meets three times a week and we share our expertise. We invest only in quality growth stocks, er, and there are only approximately thirty to forty of those."

"Like which ones, for example?"

Jake had to think a minute, though he'd picked the stocks himself. "Disney, IBM, Eaton Corporation, Qualcomm, Exxon-Mobil, Johnson & Johnson, and Chevron, to name a few."

"That list could use some tweaking, don't you think?" Guinevere sniffed. "It doesn't include the biotech companies, which are a very good buy right now."

Jake could tell he was losing her, by a new distance in her demeanor. He tried to get his head in the game. "That brings me to an important point about Gardenia. We don't follow trends or crazes. If you read the biotech companies are hot, that doesn't cause us to rebalance your portfolio."

"Why not? You'll miss out. Rather, *I* will."

"Our view is long-term." Jake felt his mouth go dry when he saw Amy getting up. He caught a glimpse of her talking to someone, but couldn't see whom. "A bubble can burst and a fad stock . . . can turn out to be a dog, and we don't want you in that position. We diversify where appropriate to lower your risk."

"Well, obviously."

Jake couldn't get back on track. He couldn't have Deaner out there, on the loose, saying God knows that. "Nor do we . . . churn your portfolio. Our turnover average . . . is 15 to 25 percent over a year, much lower than the typical 75 percent."

"But your fees are higher than a place like Vanguard."

"That's true, but . . . we charge nothing to manage Treasury bills or similarly liquid assets, and we charge 1.5 percent on stocks and 1 percent on—"

"That's not insubstantial." Guinevere lifted a graying eyebrow. "It's higher than Vanguard, which is essentially offering its services at cost."

"You're comparing apples with oranges. They administer index funds, which are—"

"I know what an index fund is." Guinevere frowned, a fissure deepening between her bright eyes. "Please don't condescend to me."

"I'm sorry, I didn't mean to." Jake swallowed hard. Amy left her desk, and people were milling around in the area. "Vanguard has $2 trillion under management . . . and 28 million clients—"

"What difference does that make?" Guinevere's eyes narrowed. "They told me that at my asset level, they would assign me to an asset manager, just like you."

"But we have a more personalized approach . . . not only in the stocks we select, but in the . . . uh . . . ancillary services we offer." Jake couldn't focus. He didn't know where Amy was. "We view your portfolio . . . er, as merely one part of the whole that we will provide for you or your loved ones—"

"My husband and I had no children. There's just me. When I die, my money goes to Thorncroft Equestrian Center."

"Okay, then we can help you find an accountant and an estate lawyer—"

"I have an estate lawyer, and my will is in place, as is my living will and power of attorney."

"Good, well, then." Jake was kicking himself. He knew she'd have her ducks in a row. He reached onto the middle of the table, picked up a Gardenia promotional folder, and offered it to her. "This sets forth all of our ancillary services. For example, in the event of your incapacity or illness, we will step in and liaise with your estate lawyer. We can even pay your household bills for you—"

"In other words, you do a lot of hand-holding." Guinevere set the Gardenia folder aside. "But I don't need my hand held. I have a horse and a pony and I'm perfectly capable of taking care of both. In fact, they're provided for in my will. So why do I need Gardenia?"

Jake found himself shifting in his chair, to see the hallway better. Amy still wasn't back, and for a second, he felt a bolt of fear that Deaner could have done her harm. Anything was possible.

"Jake, that's it! Am I *boring* you? Because you keep looking over my shoulder. Hmph!" Guinevere reached down and grabbed her bag. "You know, I had been worried that I was a rather low-net-worth individual for Gardenia. I saw on your website that many of your clients have assets of $10 million and up, and I'm concerned that my account wouldn't get the attention I deserve."

"Guinevere, wait, I assure you that $5 million is a lot of money by any measure, and it's a lot of money to—"

"I'm sorry, but I've just made my decision." Guinevere stood up and tucked her bag under her arm. "Thank you for your time. I'll be on my way."

"No, wait." Jake jumped to his feet. "Hold on, please reconsider. I can assure you that here, you would get kid-glove, personalized treatment."

"I'd rather save the fees." Guinevere charged for the door, with Jake on her heels.

"But if you would—" Jake followed her out, only to find Lewis Deaner standing with Amy, in front of her desk.

"Jake?" Amy turned to him, in confusion. "Mr. Deaner says

you asked him to stop by this morning, but I told him you were in with Mrs. LeMenile. I asked him to wait in reception, but he doesn't seem to want to—"

"Hello, Jake." Deaner's eyes bored into Jake, from behind his wire-rimmed glasses. "Did you forget about our appointment?"

"Hmph!" Guinevere said, striding past the desk. "Just as I suspected. You double-booked the appointment. You're worse than my gynecologist!"

Chapter Twenty-two

"What the hell is this about?" Jake folded his arms, standing against the windows while Deaner's light blue eyes flitted around, taking in the glass desktops, watercolors pressed between glass panes, and crystal awards. It struck Jake for the first time that almost everything in his office was breakable.

"Jake, you should ask me to sit down." Deaner met his gaze coolly. "Isn't that what you do with clients?"

"You're not a client. Tell me why you're here."

"Then what am I? Or more accurately, what are we going to tell your employees I am?" Deaner spoke quietly, and his tone was reasonable. He had several fine lines in his forehead, so he must have been older than Jake had thought at the game, maybe in his fifties. "Because if Amy doesn't think I'm a client, you're going to have to explain who I am and why I'm here. Unless you want me to."

"Sit down, then." Jake hated that Deaner knew Amy's name. He must have gotten it off the website.

"You should sit opposite me, shouldn't you? Play your part,

Mr. Financial Planner." Deaner unzipped his parka, and lowered himself into the chair.

"Tell me what's this all about." Jake stood his ground, behind the chair.

"Shouldn't I look like I'm taking notes? That's what clients do when you talk, isn't it, Jake? They write down what you say?" Deaner slid a pad and pen from the center of the table, wrote something, and flipped it around to show it to Jake. It read, **Go, Ryan, go!**

Jake's heart thudded in his chest. "Why are you here? Who are you? What's your real name?"

Deaner didn't reply, but set down the pad and picked up the Gardenia promotional folder. He slid out a brochure, which had a photo of Jake in shirtsleeves, smiling confidently. "Nice tie."

"Answer my question."

"Slick materials. Very upmarket." Deaner waved the brochure. "No one would ever guess where you and Ryan were Friday night."

Jake froze. He forced himself to stay in control. Not to confirm or deny. Deaner could be bluffing, or he could be an undercover cop or a private investigator, even wearing a wire.

"Now, sit down. You'll need to."

Jake lowered himself into the chair. His chest tight, his mouth dry.

"I figure you make almost a million bucks a year." Deaner set the Gardenia folder aside. "Your house is probably worth about $550K, and I bet it's paid off. You're not a flashy guy. You live below your means. You're cheap, which means you have a ton of dough in savings, pension plan, 401(k), college fund for Ryan. I'm guessing almost a million, and you trade your own account. You're trying to grow it. How'm I doing?"

"Get to the point."

"Fine. I know what happened Friday night." Deaner pushed

up his glasses with a finger that had a bitten-off nail. "Ryan was driving your car and he hit the jogger. You both got out of the car. You switched seats with him and drove away."

Jake felt his world explode around him. The glass tops, the crystal awards, the massive windows. Shards of glass flew everywhere. He didn't know how he could put it back together again. It was all gone, falling away, shooting through space.

"Yes, I know it all. I saw it. You threw yourself on the sword for your son, good for you. *Dad.*"

Jake struggled for self-control. The worst-case scenario had just gotten worse.

"What was it that Ryan had in his hand? You were about to call the cops, after all. I heard you yelling."

Jake reeled. He had no idea how Deaner had seen or heard them. The apartment complex, the corporate center. Somewhere, somehow.

"You gave her CPR. Was she dead when you left her, or did you leave her to die?" Deaner shook his head. "You're not a monster, right? You're basically a decent guy, but you slipped up. Hey, it happens."

Jake didn't reply. He couldn't. Emotion churned in his gut. Inwardly he raged at Deaner, then at himself. It was his own actions that brought him to this point. But he had to shift into damage control or all was lost.

"You're wondering if I have proof, and I do. Take a look-see." Deaner reached inside his parka, pulled out an iPhone, hit a few buttons, and showed the screen.

Jake almost gasped. The photo was an enlargement of Ryan and him at the accident scene, in front of the headlights, their faces grainy but visible. The photo was dark, but Deaner must have enhanced it somehow.

"But wait, there's more, as they say." Deaner took the phone back, then swiped the screen a few times. "Let me show you the video. The parting shot, as it were. Here." Deaner held the phone up, and the video started.

Jake watched himself kneeling in front of the body, then running to Ryan and saying something, and the both of them hustling to the car.

Deaner half-smiled. "The audio isn't great but I can fix that, and I will, if I have to. So can the cops. Wait for the last shot. It's priceless."

Jake watched the last shot, which was a close-up of his own license plate, taken as the Audi receded down Pike Road. The video ended, the screen froze, and a white arrow ghosted over the darkness of night.

"The End." Deaner emitted a dry laugh.

"Where did you get that?" Jake asked, finding his voice. He had a million questions.

"None of your business."

"Do you live in those apartments near Pike Road? Or do you work at the corporate center?"

"None of your business."

"Who are you? What do you do?" Jake's face felt hot and damp. He told himself to get a grip but couldn't.

"I told you."

"You lied. Why were you there that night? What were you doing?"

"Who said I was there?"

Jake recoiled, confused. "You said. You said you saw what happened."

"I meant on the video."

"So if you didn't take the video or the photos, who did? How did you get them? Who gave them to you?"

"Also not your business."

"How did you find me? Did you follow me that night? Was it from the license plate?"

"Now to my point, as you put it." Deaner put the iPhone back into his pocket. "I'll go to the police tomorrow unless you wire $250,000 to this account by eleven o'clock."

"So you're blackmailing me." Jake felt the blood drain from his face. He didn't know what to do. He couldn't believe this was happening.

"Obviously." Deaner slipped his hand into his other pocket and extracted a yellow Post-it packet, then tore one off the top and pressed it onto the glass tabletop. "This is the bank you wire it to."

"You want me to wire blackmail money to a *bank* account?"

"It's offshore, a numbered account. Not that hard to set up, interestingly. When I get the confirmation that the wire transfer went through, I'll send you the video and pictures."

Jake's mind raced. He didn't know how to react. He couldn't process it fast enough. "You won't go to the police."

"Try me."

"I'll bring you down with me." Jake knew the best defense was a good offense.

"No you won't. You'll have no credibility. You'll only make it worse for your wife and son. Bigger news, bigger headlines. Scandal. Yikes."

Jake's stomach turned over. Deaner knew about Pam, too. He had no leverage, not a card to play. "How do I know that if I pay you, this is where it ends? Or that whoever took the video won't want to get paid, too?"

"You don't."

"Plus it's a digital file. You have other copies. How do I know you'll give me all of them?"

"Again, you don't. You don't know anything." Deaner shifted back his chair, getting ready to leave. "You only know what happens if I don't get paid. A world of pain for your son."

"But I can't get that much money that fast."

"We both know you can. You have the dough. Liquidate stocks in no time. Cash one of those client's checks you must have lying around. You're a financial planner, so plan some *finances*." Deaner stood up and crossed to the door. "You have until eleven o'clock tomorrow."

"I can't do that." Jake felt his blood pressure rise, pounding at his temples. "I'd never do that. I never have. It doesn't work that way, anyway."

"I don't think you're taking me seriously, Jake. Good-bye." Deaner opened the door and said loudly, "Thanks so much for the meeting. I'll be in touch."

Jake watched him walk down the hall and nod good-bye to Amy, who got up from her chair and came over.

"Who was that guy?" she asked, blinking.

"A possible new client. I met him at Ryan's game."

"Did you sign him? Should I send him some papers and open up a file?"

"Not yet."

"Don't look so worried, Jake. You'll reel him in, sooner or later. You always do." Amy smiled under her headful of curls, and Jake could barely manage to smile back.

"Thanks."

"Funny, I never would've pegged that guy for having money, and my paydar is pretty good."

"Paydar?"

"Yeah. Like gaydar, only with dough. I can usually pick 'em, even when they dress down. But that guy fooled me."

"Gotta get back to work." Jake went back into his office, where he closed the door and hurried to his desk. He got on-line, went to the website for his bank, and signed in to check his accounts. **Interest Checking, Savings,** and **Money Market,** read the blue virtual folders, and he thought back to what Pam had said last night, about the financial disclosure required for her nomination.

It's like doing your taxes, every quarter for the next five years!

Jake leaned over to get his messenger bag, tugged out the

forms that Pam had given him, and flipped through them frantically. The questionnaire asked for the "**sources and amounts
of all income received during the calendar year preceding your
nomination and for the current calendar year, including all
salaries, fees, dividends, interest, gifts, rents, royalties, licensee's fees . . .**"

Jake couldn't see any way around the questionnaire. Even if he
wanted to pay the blackmail, he couldn't take $250K out of their
accounts without its showing, and if the money didn't appear in
another account, canceled check, or trade receipt, the FBI
would find out. They would get caught. It would scuttle Pam's
nomination, if not send them both to jail.

Jake tried to think, his temples throbbing. Even before the
FBI would find it, he knew Pam would. She was always going
online and checking their household balances. She might not
check the money market, but he couldn't take the risk.

Cash one of those client's checks you must have lying around.

Jake's gaze traveled the office and came to rest on the crystal
awards. He'd gotten a check for $321K from one of his longtime
clients last week. It was still in the company safe, waiting to be
deposited because it had come in too late on Friday. It was due
to be deposited today. He racked his brain to think of a way
he could use the check, borrow the $250K, and replace it later,
somehow, after the FBI interviews were over and Pam's judgeship was in the clear.

Jake stopped his thinking in its tracks. Was he seriously
thinking about stealing? He couldn't, ever. He loved his clients,
and he loved Gardenia. It was his baby, he'd raised it from in-
fancy. He had personal integrity; he had morals and pride. He'd
worked hard to gain the trust of his clients, and he had a spot-
less, unimpeachable record. He was a Good Guy, so when had
he turned bad? Then he knew the answer, on Pike Road.

Jake considered another option. He could try to stall Deaner
until after the FBI interviews. Then he could take the money

from his personal money market and replace it before Pam realized it had gone missing, or he could sell some stock, which she checked far less often. Suddenly his cell phone started ringing on his desk, vibrating next to his keyboard.

Jake looked over, and the call was from Ryan. The screen showed a candid photo of his son, grinning on their driveway with a basketball tucked in the crook of his elbow. Jake reached for his phone and hit ANSWER. "Hey, pal, what's up?" he asked, keeping his tone casual.

"Dad!" Ryan sounded hysterical. "Dad! You need to come get me at school, now!"

Chapter Twenty-three

Jake pulled up around the back of the school, outside the cafeteria, which faced the student parking lot. He spotted Ryan hurrying toward him without a coat, hunching his shoulders against the cold. Jake leaned over in alarm and opened the passenger-side door. "Ryan, what's the matter?"

"Dad, drive." Ryan jumped into the car, pulled up his long legs, and slammed the door closed. "Hurry. Just go."

"Where? Why? What happened?" Jake hit the gas, glancing over. Ryan looked distraught, but hadn't wanted to tell him why on the phone.

"Drive away. Where nobody can see us. Please." Ryan gestured quickly, pitched forward on the seat, and Jake drove through the lot, past cars with **Go Chasers** painted in maroon on the windows.

"What about school? Did you cut class?"

"No, they don't know I'm gone yet. It's A Lunch." Ryan raked his bangs in agitation. "Dad, for real, class is the least of my worries right now. Something really scary is going on. Really scary."

"Okay, calm down. Relax. Whatever it is, we can handle it." Jake steered out of the student lot and on to the winding road that led to Lincoln Avenue, where he made the green light, then took the left fork and entered the Stone Hills neighborhood, so named because the homes were made of an indigenous tan-and-brown fieldstone.

"Is anybody following us, can you tell?" Ryan peered at the mirror outside the car.

"No, of course not," Jake answered, but he checked the rearview mirror anyway. There was nobody behind him except a FedEx truck. "Why would somebody be following us? Ryan, what's going on?"

"Pull over." Ryan stayed glued to the outside mirror.

"Okay, relax." Jake heard his phone ringing inside the breast pocket of his suit jacket, but he'd get it later.

"I don't know." Ryan scanned the street, shifting in his seat. "Do you see anything random? Is anybody following us?"

"No. Relax, I'll park." Jake pulled over at the corner and put the car in park, leaving the engine running for the heat.

"Do you think it's safe here?"

"Of course it is." Jake looked around, and the street was quiet and still. A young mother pushed a stroller, her ponytail caught on the hood of her parka.

"I'm scared shitless. I went to my locker and checked my phone before lunch. Look." Ryan slid his iPhone out of his pocket, opened the text function, and showed Jake the text in its bright pink bubble.

i am crazy 4 u

"What, Ryan? Some girl has a crush on you." Jake exhaled, relieved.

"Right, that's what I thought. At first I thought it was from Janine Mae, but it isn't." Ryan started talking fast, running his words together. "She's in my phone and if it were from her, it would come up with her name. I don't know that number. It's not in my Contacts. See?"

Jake looked at the phone number from the text, which had a 999 area code. "So? Somebody has a crush on you. Somebody you don't have in your phone already."

"Totally, that's what I thought, too. I got stoked, thinking some girl liked me. I'm so stupid." Ryan scrolled to the next text. "Look at this."

Jake read, **ur an awesome player**

"Wait." Ryan scrolled down to the next pink bubble, which had been delivered a minute later. "It gets worse, a lot worse."

Jake read the text, beginning to get a bad feeling. **i watch u all the time** "Okay, kinda creepy."

"That's nothing, compared to the end. You look at the rest. I can't. It makes me want to hurl." Ryan thrust the phone at him. "My phone number's not that easy to get. It's not on Facebook, and anyway, I have all my privacy settings on. The school has it, so it could be someone who works in the office. It's on the team portal, but only the team can get in. You'd have to hack it. I don't think I have it anywhere else."

Jake scrolled down through the line of pink bubbles, reading: **i wish i cld b w u**

ur soo sexy

ur soo cute

ur soo tall

ur shredded

i love ur hair

u have gr8t eyes

I love ur smile

i think of u all the time

i dream abt u

i see u

i watch u

"How many are there?" Jake asked angrily. It had to be Deaner. Deaner must have gotten Ryan's cell-phone number. Or the texts were from whoever made the video, if it wasn't Deaner.

"Like fifty or so, I stopped counting. They came one after the other, like seconds apart." Ryan kept shaking his head, his fair skin mottled. "Keep reading. It gets worse. *Way* worse."

Jake seethed, reading.

i kno everything about u
i follow u everywhere
u can't get away from me

Jake scrolled up and checked the time of the first text, delivered at 11:02. That would have been minutes after Deaner had left his office. Jake had thought that Deaner would go after him, but he'd gone after Ryan instead. Jake scrolled down again and read more texts, delivered only seconds apart.

we shld b 2gether
we belong 2gether

"Oh no." Jake reminded himself to stay in control. He had to keep calm for Ryan, who was almost hyperventilating.

"Do you see this? Do you *see*? Keep reading to the end!"

Jake read on: **we r meant to be**
i am ur destiny
i see u at lunch
i see u in algebra
i see u in english
i see u in western civ
i see u in French
i see u in chemistry

"Dad, she knows my schedule! She knows everything! Or it might not even be a girl, who knows? They musta hacked the student portal, too. Whoever this is, a boy, girl, or whatever, they're crazy!"

"I know, I can tell." Jake felt his temples pounding again. He wanted to get ahold of Deaner and beat the living hell out of him. He kept reading. **i see ur games**

i see u at practice
u cant get away frm me
no one loves u like me
u have 2 be w me
u will be w me
u cant get away
u killed me
u deserve 2 die
dont u feel guilty?
dont u feel bad?
dont u feel sad?
kill urself
kill urself
kill urself

"Oh my God." Jake gritted his teeth, enraged.

"Keep going. You're almost there."

Jake scrolled down.

kill urself on pike rd
die & join me
you know who i am

"Bastard!" Jake exploded. "I'm going to kill this guy!"

"What guy? How do you know it's a guy, and do you understand what this means?" Ryan grabbed his arm. "Whoever sent this knows what happened. They know it's *me*. What are we going to do? They *know*. Look at the next one, it's a picture."

"Okay, try and stay calm." Jake looked at the screen, which showed a thumbnail photo of a young girl. He tapped it to enlarge it, though he could guess who it was. A school photo of a beautiful young girl popped onto the screen, and she had long, dark hair with large, dark brown eyes, and a wide, sweet smile. The caption read, **I'm Kathleen Lindstrom.**

"That's the last one." Ryan twisted around in his seat, frantic.

"Dad, whoever sent this, they *know*. This *is not* a lucky guess. This is *not* a troll. Somebody *knows* I did it. Somebody is *stalking* me. He could be watching us *right now*."

"No, not really." Jake had to cool him down. He patted Ryan on the knee, which was drawn up to fit his long legs into the cramped Toyota. "He's just trying to scare you. Don't give him the satisfaction."

"Who? Why? Why's he trying to scare me?"

"You have to let me handle this." Jake looked over, and Ryan's eyes went wide with disbelief and fear.

"What are you *talking* about? Do you know who this is? What's going on?"

"Please, let me handle this." Jake would have to come up with the money for Deaner. There was no other way. "You have to go back to school. What time is lunch over?"

"Dad, I can't go back to school. What if it's somebody at school? Is it somebody at school?" Ryan went wild-eyed with bewilderment. "How do they know I play basketball? *What's going on?*"

"Trust me, it's better if you don't know."

"You have to tell me." Ryan shouted, jabbing the air with his index finger. "It's *me* they're after. It's *me* they want. I'm the one who did it! I have a right to know. It's *my* life!"

"We're not going to discuss this now. You have to get back to school." Jake checked the dashboard clock, which read 11:50. His phone rang again, but he'd have to get it later. "Tell me what time lunch is over."

"12:10. I'm supposed to be in Western Civ at 12:15, but Dad, I'm not going. I'm done for the day! Tell me what's happening!"

"Listen to me. You have to let me handle this." Jake disengaged the emergency brake. "The only way to deal with this is if you do what you're supposed to do. Go to class, then practice, then come home. I'll explain everything."

"Dad, *get real*!" Ryan exploded, distraught. "I can't go to class!

What do you think, I can sit there and listen? Take notes like nothing's wrong? You don't know what it's like at school today! All the girls are crying, all the teachers are upset. They're going to do a memorial for her tonight. They're planting a tree out front. The girls track team went around the homerooms to collect money for a scholarship fund." Ryan gestured, his arms flailing wildly. "*Janine Mae* was tight with her, she was *popular*! You saw, she was supercute, Dad. She had tons of dates. I killed her, and this *guy* knows it. *Who is he?*"

"Ryan, work with me. We can talk about this at home tonight. Nothing's going to change between now and then. You give me your phone and I'll get you a new number." Jake put the car in gear and was about to give it some gas when Ryan's phone signaled an incoming text. They both looked down at the screen.

"Oh my God! It's another picture!" Ryan tapped the thumbnail on the touch screen, and it opened to the photograph that Deaner had shown Jake this morning, of Ryan and him arguing in the headlights, next to Kathleen Lindstrom's fallen form. "Oh no! No!"

"Ryan, don't panic. I have this under control—"

"Oh my God!" Ryan dropped the phone. His hands flew to his head. "He has a picture! There's a picture! Oh my God, what are we going to do? He has *proof*! That's *proof*! Dad, I don't want you to go to jail!"

"Ryan, you have to keep your wits about you. I have this in control. I saw that photo already. I know what to do about it." Jake started to put a hand on Ryan's arm, but he batted it away, angry.

"What are you *talking* about? You *knew* about this? Why didn't you *tell me*?"

"Take it easy, I just found out this morning." Jake kept his tone reassuring and put the car back in park. "But you don't have to think about it anymore. It's going to go away."

"What do you mean? How did you see that picture? It can send you to jail! Tell me everything!"

"Okay, relax. I'll tell you but you have to be calm. I'm handling it." Jake had no choice but to level with him. "Bottom line, a man came to my office today and he's blackmailing us."

"*What?*" Ryan's hands flew to his face and stayed there, cupping his own cheeks. "Are you *kidding* me? Are you *kidding* me right now, Dad?"

"You have to calm down. It's as simple as that."

"You mean we're getting *blackmailed* like on *TV*? Like *a movie*? Did he have *a gun*? In your office—"

"I'm not telling you another thing unless you calm down, and you have to go to class after this."

"Oh my God! What are you talking about? Are you crazy?" Ryan threw up his hands, bursting into mirthless laughter. "Are you blackmailing *me* now?"

"Stop." Jake felt his temper begin to give way, his anger at Deaner and himself spilling onto Ryan, scattershot. "You said you weren't a baby, so stop acting like one. You need to rise above this, Ryan. You need to ask more of yourself."

"How?" Ryan dropped his hands. "What?"

"Calm down. Get a grip."

"But I'm *scared*! I'm scared for *you*!"

Jake felt a deep pang of guilt. "I know that, but the best way to help me—to help us both—is to stay in control. In charge."

"Okay, okay. Okay, I'm calm." Ryan took a breath. He picked up his phone and held it in his hand. "Okay, I hear you. I'm calm. Just tell me what the guy said, and I'll go to class. Who is he?"

"I don't know who he is. I don't know any more than I'm telling you." Jake put the car in gear again, fed it some gas, and pulled away from the curb. "All you need to know is that the man is asking for money. Luckily, we have money, and I'm going to give it to him. After I give him the money, it's done. Period. Do you hear me? It ends."

"How do you know he won't go to the police anyway?"

"Because it's not in his interest. If he goes to the police, he goes down, too."

"Why?"

"Because blackmail and extortion is illegal," Jake answered, off the top of his head. He had no idea if that was the proper name for the crime and he didn't care. He had to end this conversation. He drove past the lovely houses of Stone Hills and the young mother pushing the stroller, feeling surreal talking about blackmail and thugs.

"So you're going to pay him? How do you know he won't try asking for more money? That's what they do in the movies."

"I don't, but you don't have to worry about that because I have plenty of money. If he asks for more money, I'll give him more money."

"But where does it end?"

"We have the money, Ryan. It's not an issue. We live within our means, you know that. We all say I'm cheap, and it's paying off."

"How much money did he ask for?"

"Ryan, why do you have to know the details?" Jake turned left, heading back toward the high school. "The details don't matter. It's really better if you don't know everything."

"Please, just tell me."

"He asked for $25,000."

"Oh my God. Oh my God. That's, like, a *year* of college tuition."

"Don't even worry about it. I have it in savings. It's worth the money to me."

"But what will Mom say? She'll notice that, for sure."

"No, she won't know." Jake got ready to tell another lie. He kept his face forward, looking through the windshield as they were approaching Lincoln Avenue, heavily trafficked during the noon rush. "We have separate checking and savings accounts, in addition to the joint account that we use to pay our bills. I don't ask her questions about hers, and she doesn't ask about mine."

"Why do you do that?"

"Have separate accounts? You've heard her say that she thinks every woman should have her own money. She likes it, too, because when she buys me a present, I don't see how much it costs. I feel the same way." Jake was making it up as he went along, getting away with it only because he'd never talked to Ryan about their family finances. Maybe Ryan had been right, that Jake treated him like a baby. "Plus when I trade some stocks, I don't like her to see the losses. I want her to think I'm smart." Jake looked over and flashed a smile, trying to cheer him up, but it wasn't working. "Trust me, everything is going to be all right. This has turned into a business deal, no more and no less. I do these every day. I got this."

"Oh man, I can't believe this happened." Ryan moaned, his forehead dropping into his hands. "I'm so sorry, Dad. I screwed this up so badly."

"No you didn't. I did."

"Get real. It's on me." Ryan's tone had softened, and his shock and anger had gone, but Jake wasn't sure it was an improvement.

"Stop, son. Let it go. We're almost out of the woods." Jake drove across Lincoln Avenue, entered the Concord Chase campus, and headed for the road that led to the student parking lot. He glanced at the dashboard clock, which read 12:05. "Good, we're right on time. Where should I take you? Around the front or the back?"

"The front. It's closer to Western Civ."

"Okay." Jake drove on the road, bypassing the student parking lot and leading to the main entrance. "Just stay cool for the rest of the day, and I'll fill you in tonight. Try to put this out of your mind."

"I'll try," Ryan said, just as his phone signaled an incoming text, and they both jumped.

"Don't look at it," Jake said quickly. "It'll upset you. He's trying to upset you. Give me the phone."

"No, *I* got *this.*" Suddenly, Ryan raised his phone and slammed it down on the dashboard, again and again, until it went silent.

Chapter Twenty-four

GARDENIA TRUST, read the polished plaque on their wooden door, and Jake powered through into the office. He tried to look and act the way he always did, but he was sweating under his suit jacket. He was on fire after reading those texts and he knew it had to show. He strode through the empty reception area, with its sky-blue patterned couch, walnut end tables, and brass lamps, and it was the first time in his career he'd been happy there were no clients.

Jake plastered on a smile as he approached the reception desk. Debbie Tarkington had been with him since she graduated from community college, and her unflappable nature made her the perfect choice for the front desk. Not all of Jake's clients were easy to get along with, and he knew that money didn't guarantee good judgment, starting with the man in the mirror.

"Jake, hi." Debbie smiled, a welcoming grin that creased her pretty face. She was African-American and had large eyes and short hair, which she wore natural. She handed him a packet of pink phone messages. "Here's your calls. Everything go okay?"

"Yes, thanks." Jake thumbed through his phone messages, to avoid meeting her eye. He hadn't explained where he was going when he'd left, which he knew was unusual. "Sorry I ran out. I had to take care of a few things for Ryan. He was sick this weekend, but he went to school today."

"I hope he feels better. By the way, Martin wants to see you and so does Ramon. They both said it was important, so you can pick your poison."

"Okay, thanks." Jake didn't have time to talk to either of them. Martin Niemeyer and Ramon Ramirez were two of his best portfolio managers, but they would have to wait. "I'm not taking calls this afternoon. I don't need interruptions."

"Gotcha. Also there's leftover pizza in the coffee room."

"Thanks." Jake walked down the hall just as Martin popped out of his office and came striding down the long hallway toward him. A bright young refugee from Lehman Brothers, Martin still looked very Wall Street, with his moussed brown hair, frameless Swiss glasses, and charcoal pinstriped suit.

"Jake," Martin called out, in his characteristic bark. "We need to talk about Disney. I'd like to buy a block for Bob Cadison and I need to—"

"Martin, do whatever you think is right." Jake patted him on the shoulder and kept walking down the long hall, which ended in his office. "I can't talk now."

"But you know how he is. He second-guesses every pick, even Disney."

"Then call and explain it to him."

"I know, I know," Martin called after him, wearily. "Like you always say, 'It's his money, not mine.'"

"Right." Jake cringed, inwardly. He kept going toward his office when he saw Ramon lumbering down the hallway on the right, an unmistakable figure because the man was built like a refrigerator. Ramon had played right tackle at Harvard and still managed to graduate at the top of his class, the antithesis of the dumb jock.

"Boss man!" Ramon called out, with a broad smile. His silk tie flew as he walked and his white shirt and dark suit pants strained at the seams because he was so supersized. "You didn't answer my email."

"Sorry, but I can't talk now." Jake couldn't remember the last time he checked his email. He reached Amy's desk at the same time that Ramon did.

"I know, but I need your okay on the Shamir trust. Remember, for the kids? I sent you an email about it."

"Ramon, sorry, I didn't get a chance to look at it. You decide. I'm wall-to-wall this afternoon."

"Appreciate the confidence." Ramon clapped him on the back, then went back down the hall, and Amy looked up worriedly.

"Jake, how's Ryan? Is he feeling better?"

"Yes." Jake had mumbled something before he left about Ryan's not feeling well. "He thought he might want to come home from school, but he decided to stick it out."

"Good, Pam was worried."

Jake hid his surprise. "Pam?"

"Yes, she called here. She said she called your cell, but you didn't answer and she needed to talk to you."

"Oh damn." Jake remembered the phone calls that had come in when he was with Ryan. He had forgotten about them, completely preoccupied on the way back to the office. He reached into his breast pocket, slid out his phone, and saw the screen banner that showed two missed calls from Pam.

Amy blinked under her dark curls. "She said call her back as soon as you get a chance."

Jake was in real trouble, because he'd have to explain what

was going on with Ryan. "I'll call her right back. Will you hold my calls for the afternoon? I really need to focus."

"But you and Ramon have an appointment at 3:30 with the Marchman Group, remember?"

"Oh, right." Jake had forgotten that, too. The Marchman Group was one of his corporate clients, and he needed to see them, but this was no time to meet with anybody. "Do me a favor and cancel it. Apologize profusely. I have a ton of work and I didn't get enough done this weekend."

"Gotcha." Amy picked up the phone, and Jake hurried into his office and closed the door behind him. He hustled to his desk, woke up his computer, and logged onto his bank program, then he called Pam, multitasking.

"Honey?" Pam said when the call connected. "What's going on? You went to school? Is Ryan okay?"

"Yes. Sorry I missed your call." Jake watched their accounts pop onto the computer screen.

"So what's going on?"

"He was queasy again after lunch and he thought he might want to come home." Jake knew that Pam's real question was why Ryan had called him, not her. It was unprecedented in their family history, so Jake knew he had to address it up front. "He didn't want to bother you, so he called me."

"He could have called me. It's no bother, he knows that."

Jake had to think of something to help the story. "He heard us talking in your office last night, about your nomination and all the work you have to do, the questionnaires and everything. He tried to cut you a break."

Pam moaned. "I want him to feel like he can still call me, though. He's my priority, no matter what. I mean, how much longer do I even have with him? I'll call him after school and tell him—"

"Don't honey. This is the way we want it to be, right?" Jake fell back on his default, best-defense is a good offense. "Ryan is learning that he can lean on me sometimes, too. Like we said in therapy, you want him to know he can turn to me. Don't call him and make him feel like it's strange. You're relegating me to the junior varsity."

"Sorry, I know, you're right." Pam sounded convinced, if miserable. "So what did you two decide? Is he at home or at school?"

"We decided together that he was feeling well enough to finish school and go to practice."

"So did he miss class?"

"No, we met during lunch, we talked, and he went to Western Civ on time."

"Well, aren't you guys so smart?" Pam still sounded unhappy. "He has a test today, and it's a bitch to make them up. He'll never have the time, and the makeup tests are always harder. Well done."

"Thanks," Jake said, as if he could take pleasure in any decision he'd made recently.

"I tried to call him but he doesn't answer his phone. I know it's probably in his locker, but I wanted to leave him a message telling him that I was thinking of him. But he hasn't called me back yet."

"I'm sure he will when he can." Jake flashed on Ryan breaking his phone on the dashboard. "In the meantime, we handled it together, just fine. Now. What did you call me about?"

"Bad news. My questionnaire has to be finished by Wednesday now, because we have to get an accountant to look it over before I turn it in. I already have a call in to Ellen."

"Why can't I do it?" Jake had to buy time and the last thing he needed was their accountant Ellen poking around. "I'm an accountant, we don't need another one."

"Michael thinks we need to have an independent accountant review everything. He thinks it would help if Ellen wrote us a letter, too."

"A letter saying what?"

"That our finances are in order, like an official stamp of approval."

"There's no such thing."

"Jake, it's just window dressing."

"We don't need it. I'm as official as it comes, I do our taxes. All Ellen has to do is sign her name to the return."

"Don't get all bent out of shape, honey. We might be gilding the lily, but if it helps me get nominated, why not? The issue isn't the accuracy of our record-keeping, but whether we're up to shenanigans."

Jake shuddered.

"You can't give a stamp of approval to your own bookkeeping or tax returns. It has to come from someone independent. If it's too much work, Ellen can do everything. Is that better for you?"

"No, I want to do it," Jake answered quickly. "Don't worry about it, I'll get the papers together and have them FedExed to Ellen for Wednesday morning. All she'll have to do is write her phony-baloney letter, okay?"

"That would be great, thanks. I love you."

"I love you, too."

"Talk later. I'll be home late tonight. The powers-that-be want to powwow about the nomination. Can you deal with dinner for Ryan?"

"Sure, take care," Jake said, hanging up. He found himself staring at their online bank account, which had logged him out. He had to pay the blackmail or Deaner would keep torturing Ryan.

Jake sweated under his jacket, thinking about that check in the safe.

Chapter Twenty-five

Jake clicked through the Gardenia Trust spreadsheet on his computer, trying to figure out how to get the money from company or client funds, but he couldn't find a way. The check in the safe couldn't be used because it was made out to Gardenia, and even as the company's principal and sole owner, he couldn't cash it or deposit it into his own account. It could only be deposited into Gardenia's holding account, and from there, it couldn't be wired to any personal account, much less offshore. Gardenia's bank, Pennsylvania National Bank, would simply refuse to do it, because it would run afoul of FDIC regulations, which was only one of the layers of rules and regulations. Gardenia was also a state-chartered trust company, so they were also governed by FNRA and the SEC, because they were also an RIA, an alphabet soup of laws.

Jake rubbed his face, trying to understand his position. He couldn't use his personal funds because the FBI would see, and he couldn't use Gardenia money because he couldn't get it. The problem was that the FBI would be able to see the balances in any existing accounts, but that gave him an idea, because it meant that they couldn't see the balances in any accounts that didn't exist right now.

Jake reached for his phone and scrolled down to Harold Ackerman, his banker at Pennsylvania National, in charge of all of Jake's personal accounts, as well as Gardenia business accounts. He pressed in the number and Harold picked it up after the first ring. "Harold, I need a favor. Confidentially."

"You got it. How can I help?"

"I need a personal line of credit for $250 grand to be opened today."

"No problem, Jake. You have the balances to back that up. You want it in your name, or yours and Pam's?"

"Just mine, and I need it wired to an offshore account by eleven o'clock tomorrow morning, at the absolute latest." Jake knew it would be an unusual request, but he also knew that Harold wouldn't ask any questions. Anybody who dealt regularly with high-net-worth individuals knew that they had expensive secrets like gambling debts, mistresses in fancy apartments, and the occasional cocaine habit. Jake hated the thought that Harold would believe one of those things were true about him, but his reputation didn't mean more to him than Ryan's life.

"I can do that. A wire transfer takes fifteen minutes, if I set it up now. The money's not the problem, the paperwork is. You know how it goes."

"Tell me about it." Jake understood. It would've sounded topsy-turvy to anybody who didn't know how banking worked, but he knew better. Harold could put his hand on $250,000 faster than he could get the stack of forms through the bank bureaucracy.

"I'll set it up, and get it out first thing tomorrow morning. Wire room's open at nine. It'll be done by nine fifteen."

"Okay. Thanks much." Jake pressed END, relieved. It was a good plan and he thought it would work, at least in the short run. Since the personal line of credit didn't exist until now, it wouldn't show on his and Pam's current bank statement, which they would be disclosing to the FBI. Jake would have to replace it by their next quarterly tax return, but he could do that with some gains from stock dividends or other trading. It would take fancy footwork, but he wasn't a financial planner for nothing.

Jake's phone started ringing in his hand, and he looked at the screen. It showed a picture of Pam again, the photo taken on Myrtle Beach, in happier times. He picked up and pressed AN-SWER. "Hi, honey. You forget something?"

"I'm worried." Pam sounded tense. "I thought you told me that Ryan went to Western Civ today."

"He did."

"No, he didn't."

"How do you know that?" Jake asked, dismayed.

"I checked the Parent Portal."

Jake cursed the Parent Portal, which was an online program by which Concord Chase parents could log in and check on their kids' daily assignments, tests and paper grades. Pam checked it as often as she checked their bank balances or her carbohydrate count.

"Jake, he was absent from class. He missed his test."

"Are you sure?"

"Of course. The Portal doesn't lie."

"It could be a mistake."

"No it couldn't. The information comes from the teachers themselves. Mr. Nelson even made a note on the Portal that Ryan has to contact him to schedule a makeup exam."

"Mr. Nelson might've made a mistake." Jake knew it was lame the minute he said it. He couldn't think of something better to say. It was exhausting, all this lying, putting out fires.

"Jake, come on. If Ryan's not in class, you notice. He could be really sick." Pam's voice sounded thin with anxiety. "I called the school nurse, but she's at another school on Mondays. I called the office, but they don't answer after four o'clock."

"Don't get all worked up, honey." Jake logged out of the Gardenia accounts and cleared his Internet history, just in case. "Did he go to the class after Western Civ?"

"He doesn't have class after that. He has Study Hall, last period of the day on Monday."

Jake didn't know Ryan's class schedule, but Pam had it memorized, every year. "I'm sure he's fine."

"Don't minimize it, Jake. He could be really sick."

"I'm not minimizing it," Jake said, though that was exactly what he was doing. "He's not a hundred percent, but I'm sure he's fine. He was fine when I left him."

"How do you know that? You didn't feel his forehead, did you?"

"No, but he looked fine." Jake got up from his desk and went to get his coat from the back of the door. He had to find Ryan, either at practice or at home, and see what happened.

"How he looks doesn't mean anything. You're taking this too lightly. You never think anything can go wrong, but it can."

"I'm not taking it lightly." Jake couldn't believe the irony. No one knew better than he that things could go wrong. He opened his office door and hurried into the hallway.

"I called his phone again but he still doesn't answer, and I know he usually checks it after school, before practice. That means he didn't return my first phone call."

"He told me he broke his phone, I should have mentioned that." Jake looked around but Amy wasn't at her desk. He didn't leave her a note because he didn't want her to blow his cover again.

"I assume he went to practice. But what's he up to? It's not like him to cut class. If he's not sick, something went wrong with your plan."

"I understand, and I'll take it up with him as soon as I get home." Jake hurried down the hall toward reception.

"Good. I'm not going to be home 'til ten or so, maybe later, but you should be the one to get to the bottom of this, anyway."

"I agree. I'll take care of it."

"Jake, remember, if he's not sick, he lied to you. You have to call him out on that, even though you're Fun Dad."

Jake couldn't remember ever wanting to be Fun Dad, much less having any fun. He passed Debbie and he pointed to his phone, so he had an excuse for not telling her where he was going. "Got it. Don't worry about it. Good luck with your meeting, and I'll see you when you get home."

"Text me and let me know how he is."

"I will. Love you." Jake flew out of the office, bypassing the elevator and jogging toward the stairwell.

"Love you, too. See you later. Bye."

"Bye." Jake hung up on the fly, banging through the exit doors, off to go find his son.

Chapter Twenty-six

"Ryan?" Jake opened the bedroom door to find his son asleep on top of the comforter in his practice sweat suit, his hoodie pulled over his head and his ears plugged with his earbuds. His arm was flopped over Moose, who was asleep, amid an open laptop, textbooks, and school papers.

"Ryan!" Jake said, louder. He was still in his suit jacket, breathless. He'd raced home, but traffic had been terrible. He approached the bed, but only Moose woke up, thumping his tail on the comforter and raising his head slightly.

Jake sat down on the edge of the bed, gave the dog a quick pat, and tugged one of the earbuds from Ryan's ear. "Ryan, wake up."

"Dad?" Ryan's eyelids fluttered, and Jake rubbed his arm, in the cottony sweatshirt.

"How are you doing, pal? Are you okay?"

"Yeah," Ryan answered, weakly.

"Why don't you wake up? We need to talk."

"Leave me alone. Can't I sleep?" Ryan's eyes closed again.

"No, we need to talk." Jake rubbed his arm again, to get him going. "Why didn't you go to Western Civ? Your mom found out from the Parent Portal that you missed your test."

"Don't worry about it, Dad. I'll tell her that I was throwing up again."

"No, you can't do that. Because I told her that I saw you during lunch and you seemed fine."

"What?" Ryan frowned, opening his eyes. He rose sleepily and propped himself on his elbow. "Why did you do that? She never had to know."

"I didn't tell her. Amy did. Mom called my office."

"Oh no." Ryan rubbed his face, leaving reddish streaks, and sat up.

"Why didn't you go to class? You said you were going to."

"I *was* going to." Ryan met Jake's eye, pained. "I went to my locker and got my books, and I was about to go in, but I just couldn't stop thinking about the pictures and that night, and now someone's *blackmailing* us. It's just so bad. It just keeps getting worse and worse."

"I know, I'm sorry." Jake squeezed him on the shoulder. "I know, it's a lot to deal with, but that's why you have to let me deal with it."

"What happened with the blackmailer guy?"

"It's all in order. I have the money and I'm giving it to him tomorrow."

Ryan's eyes flared in alarm. "Dad, be careful. Are you meeting him somewhere? He could have a gun."

"He's coming to my office, and I'm in no personal danger." Jake squeezed his arm again. "Don't worry about me. Worry about yourself. You have to do your thing at school. You can't be missing these classes. It's not good for you and it's too hard to explain. You went to practice, didn't you?"

"Yes, but I screwed up there, too." Ryan shook his head. "I sucked so bad. It's like I forgot how to shoot."

"Oh no." Jake's heart went out to him. It killed him to think that his son was getting so derailed. "It'll come back. You're just upset now, is all."

"I don't know. I don't even know if I'm going to start next game. It's a shit show."

"Watch your language," Jake heard himself saying, out of an impulse to control something, somewhere, to hold a line against chaos, but misplaced. "It's okay."

"No, you're right." Ryan slipped off his hood and rubbed his hair front and back. "I gotta man up. Coach is starting to look at me funny, and Dr. Dave's all up in my grille."

"Dr. Dave? What does he have to say?"

"He thinks I'm depressed."

"Did he say that?"

"No, but I can tell. He hints around."

"You're not depressed."

"I know that. I told him that." Ryan shook his head. "If he knew what was going on, believe me, he'd understand."

"Yes he would. But he can't know what's going on."

"I know that, Dad." Ryan hit a key on his open laptop and the screen came to life, showing the front page of the local newspaper. "I was reading about Kathleen and her mom. The mom got her a job at this IT company where she's a web designer, and they seem really close." Ryan scrolled down, so a photo of Kathleen appeared next to one of her mother. "They're both really pretty, aren't they? They have the same smiles and eyes, like the shape is the same." Ryan pointed at the photos. "See what I mean? I think they had a hard life. Janine Mae told me Kathleen's mom and dad got divorced last year, and there was a big custody trial over her, that's why the mom moved here from Seattle."

"Ryan, I don't think it's a good idea to be thinking about her, so much."

"This is the company where they worked." Ryan scrolled down to a group photo. "So many people liked her and her mom.

They interviewed them in the paper, you should see the stuff they said. They were super tight and they were always laughing, and the people they work with put up their own money for the reward and the company matched it, even this little company of, like twenty-five people, they put in their own money—"

"Ryan, stop." Jake glanced at the laptop. "I don't want you to keep researching her online."

"I know, but I can't help it, Dad. I try not to, but I just can't help it. It's all anybody at school's talking about." Tears brimmed in Ryan's eyes, which were bloodshot. "Janine Mae was crying in school, Dad. She was crying about her best friend from the track team, who I killed. What if she found out it was me? She would hate me, *I* hate me—" Ryan's voice broke, and Jake leaned over and gave him a hug.

"Ryan, no, don't. I know it's hard now, but it's going to be okay. We're going to get through this together."

"Dad, I don't know, it's like she's always on my mind. I keep thinking about her, like that blackmailer said, like she's my destiny or something."

"No, no, don't think that way. She's not your destiny." Jake felt his chest seize. "That guy was just making up those texts. He was trying to get to you. Don't let him get to you."

"No, but some of the stuff he said, it's *true*." Ryan pulled away, his expression anguished. "Like when he said that you can't get away from me, I *feel* like that. I feel like I can't get away from her."

Jake felt terrified for him. "No, you just feel guilty. You're a good person and you feel guilty. But that feeling will diminish in time."

"No, no, I don't think it will. It's only getting worse, Dad."

"Don't say that!" Jake said, urgent. "If you keep saying things like that, you'll make it true, and it doesn't have to be true, not at all."

"But I'm obsessed with her, *obsessed.*" Ryan shook his head in bewilderment. "Like no matter what, I'm thinking about her, and like, we're studying that if you tell yourself not to think about something, the more it makes you think about it. That's why I couldn't go to Western Civ. I was walking to the door and I started to get so freaked, and I saw Caleb, and, he said, 'What's the matter with you, dude?' He knew right away. I mean, I couldn't get in control."

"Caleb?" Jake asked, worried. "You didn't tell him anything, did you? Wasn't he the guy who sold you the dope?"

"The weed? Yes, right." Ryan's expression changed suddenly, as if a mask came over his unguarded features and he seemed to catch himself.

"Ryan? Did you tell him?"

"No, no, no way." Ryan shook his head in a newly jittery way, and Jake could see he was hiding something.

"What? What happened? You're a terrible liar, Ryan. I can see it all over your face. Did you tell him something? Anything?" Jake tried to control his fear, but it was impossible. "If you did, tell me now and we can deal with it. Don't hide it from me. We're in this together."

"I didn't tell him anything."

"I don't believe you."

"I didn't say anything, not a word!" Ryan raised his voice, but Jake could see that he was protesting too much.

"Then what is it? What's bothering you?"

"We smoked up, that's all, Dad. I'm sorry—"

"You got *high* at *school*?" Jake asked, appalled.

"Yes, I'm sorry." Ryan raked his hair back with a shaking hand. "Caleb told me it would help me mellow out for practice, and it really did. It did. It got me back in control."

"No!" Jake practically cried out, feeling suddenly like everything was circling the drain. "Ryan, I did this to help you. It defeats the whole purpose if you start to fall apart. If you start to cut classes. If you start getting high. That's not you. That never was and never *can be*—"

"I know, Dad, I know, I'm sorry—"

"You can't do this to yourself, you *can't*." Jake found himself grabbing the open *American Pageant* textbook and smacking the page, so loudly that Moose woke up, blinking. "Ryan, *this* is what you need to think about. *This* is what you need to focus on. Your *schoolwork*. Your *game*. Your*self*." Jake picked up the laptop. "Not this. Not Kathleen Lindstrom. Not her mother. Not how nice they were." Jake was about to put down the laptop when he glanced at the screen, and did a double-take. The group photo that had been on the screen was larger, because he must have hit a button when he picked up the laptop. The enlargement enabled him to see something in the company photo he hadn't seen before. He looked closer and couldn't believe his eyes.

"Dad? What is it?"

"Nothing," Jake answered, but he was lying through his teeth. He set the laptop on the bed and struggled for emotional control. In the back row of the group photo stood a line of employees, and on the end, half-hidden by the row in front of him, was a face that Jake recognized instantly.

It was Lewis Deaner.

Chapter Twenty-seven

Jake left Ryan in his bedroom, then hurried into his home office and closed the door, stricken. He felt the situation ebbing away from him. He flashed-forward on Ryan's becoming depressed, obsessed with Kathleen, spiraling downward, letting his grades and the team fall by the wayside. It could end in suicide, as if Ryan was doomed by the very actions set in motion to save him. Jake wasn't about to let that happen without a fight.

He hustled to his desk, logged onto the Internet, sat down, and typed in the name of the company he had seen on Ryan's laptop. The company website popped onto the screen, and it read GreenTech Enterprises in kelly-green letters. Directly below that was a candid photo of Kathleen Lindstrom, sitting at a laptop on a desk, evidently at the GreenTech office. The photo was framed by a black memorial border, and next to it was a paragraph:

GreenTech mourns the passing of Kathleen Lindstrom, who was the victim of a hit-and-run accident last Friday on Pike Road in Concord

Chase. Kathleen was the beloved daughter of web designer Grace Lindstrom, and Kathleen worked for us part-time, impressing our entire office with her intelligence, charm, and beauty. She even started us running at lunchtime and we lost a total of 76 pounds combined! She will be profoundly missed, most especially by her devoted mother, but by all of us whose lives she touched. GreenTech and its employees are posting a $10,000 reward for information leading to the arrest of the person responsible for her death, and if you have any such information, please call the authorities . . .

Jake looked away, because he didn't want to focus on Kathleen now. He wanted to focus on Deaner and understand how Deaner was connected to her. Jake hadn't realized that they could have known each other. He scanned the left side of the website, which listed categories for several different pages; IT Support, Web Design, GreenTech Web Hosting, GreenTech Consultancy, About Us, and Contact Us.

Jake skipped to About Us and clicked the link. Onto the screen appeared the group photo that had been on Ryan's laptop. It showed about thirteen employees lined up in three rows, and the last person in the last row on the left was Deaner. Jake clicked on the picture to enlarge it, double-checking, and it was definitely him: a short, slight, and bespectacled man, his appearance as nondescript as blackmailers ever got. It must've been a recent picture because he had the same thinning hair, wire-rimmed glasses, and oddly controlled expression.

Jake hit a button to return the picture to normal size, then read the caption below, which contained the employees' names. He scanned them quickly to reach the name of the man he knew as Lewis Deaner, but the first name on the row wasn't Lewis Deaner, but Andrew Voloshin. Jake blinked, absorbing the information. So Deaner's real name was Voloshin and he wasn't a freelance writer, but worked at an IT company.

Jake returned his attention to the photograph and spotted

Kathleen Lindstrom in the second row, only two people away from Deaner/Voloshin. Kathleen was standing next to her mother Grace, an attractive woman with curly brown hair. They had their arms around each other, the both of them smiling happily at the camera, wearing almost identical outfits, an artsy T-shirt and skinny jeans.

The photo stopped Jake in his tracks. He could see how close Kathleen and Grace were from their body language; they looked like a mother and daughter who were best friends. Tears brimmed in his eyes, and he felt the deepest ache welling up in his heart. He couldn't imagine how grief-stricken Grace would be, bereft over a beloved daughter that had been taken from her, so young and so violently. Jake was the one who had taken her young life, as surely as if he had been at the wheel himself, and he felt the full weight and agony of his guilt. He knew how much he had compounded his sin, by lying about it every day since then and by compelling Ryan to lie, too. He'd traded Kathleen's life for Ryan's future, and he would never, ever forgive himself. He'd played God, so he couldn't even ask God himself to forgive him.

He wiped his eyes with his arm, and tried to swallow, but couldn't. He refocused on the screen, trying to get his thoughts back on Deaner. It was obvious from the photo that Deaner knew Kathleen and her mother. It was a small company, so it couldn't have been otherwise. Jake wanted to know what they did for GreenTech, so he scrolled down and scanned the company description, which read:

Our offices are in Shakertown, and we're one of the few companies in the Delaware Valley who offer greener computer services—including solar-power, low-power and low-material-use computer systems, IT support, and green-web-design services. We've been in business over ten years and we're growing! Call us anytime for an estimate to meet your IT needs, in a way that helps you, your business, and our planet!

Jake considered it, vis-à-vis Andrew Voloshin. It seemed consistent with Voloshin's manner and appearance that he was some kind of IT guy. He logged back into the search engine, then went to White Pages, and plugged in the name Andrew Voloshin and Concord Chase PA, because Deaner had said he lived in an apartment in Concord Chase. The screen changed and read, **your search has yielded no results,** so Jake tried again. Voloshin worked in Shakertown, so Jake plugged in Andrew Voloshin and Shakertown PA. The screen changed, showing the question, **Did you mean this Andrew Voloshin?** Underneath was an address with the phone number:

> Meadowbrook Mews
> 37 Meadowbrook Lane
> Apartment 2C
> Shakertown, PA

Jake grabbed his phone from his pocket and dialed Voloshin's number. He felt a darkness come over him, a sheer malevolence he'd never felt in his life. He was about to talk to the man who had terrified Ryan. The man who could drive his son crazy, even to suicide. Jake felt in his heart, for the first time ever, that he was capable of committing murder. If he were ever in the same room with Voloshin again, the little man wouldn't get out alive.

"Jake?" Voloshin answered, his tone surprised, but Jake didn't let him get out another word.

"Who the hell do you think you are, scaring my son? I'll kill you for that. Do you hear me? You leave my boy alone!"

"You weren't taking me seriously." Voloshin seemed to recover. "I had to show you that I—"

"We made a deal. You'll get your money. It'll be there by eleven, and you better send me the copies of that video and photos. The deal is between me and you. You leave my family out of this or you'll get nothing. *Nothing!*"

"Oh, I don't know about that—"

"Don't test me. It's killing my kid to keep this secret, so if it's not going to help him, I'll blow it wide open. I'll go to the police myself. We both will. I'd rather have my son sane and in jail than crazy and outside of it." Jake heard himself yelling and realized that what he was saying was true. "So don't press me. Don't test me. You don't know me."

"Now who's the tough guy?"

"I am," Jake growled, and this time he meant it. He could feel it, a bile and fury inside, bubbling. "If you ever, *ever* contact my son again, I'll come after you. I know where you live. I have your phone number. I know where you work. You'll never get away from me. I'll find you *wherever* you go." Jake heard himself threatening Voloshin, an eerie echo of the very texts that Voloshin had sent to Ryan. Suddenly Jake started to wonder about something. He'd just learned that Voloshin knew Kathleen, so maybe the way Voloshin had gotten the photos of the hit-and-run wasn't because he lived or worked close by, at all. "Wait. You live on Meadowbrook Lane, but that isn't anywhere near Pike Road. GreenTech isn't in the corporate center, either. It's in Shakertown, three towns over. You didn't happen upon the accident scene and take that video. You didn't see it from a neighboring office or an apartment complex. I'm onto you. I have your number. You were on Pike Road yourself. You were there *already*. You were *stalking* her."

"What? No, that's—"

"Don't bullshit me. It all makes sense. Kathleen was a young, beautiful girl who works in your office. Her mother gets her a summer job there. You're a lonely, single nerd, the dweeby IT guy who codes all day."

"You don't know what you're talking about. I'm friends with her mother. Kathleen was the daughter of my good friend, that's all."

"Oh, please. You started out friends with the mother, but

you're not blind. A beautiful young high-school girl comes into your world, and you fall head over heels. You think about her all the time." Jake sensed he was right, even as he said it. "You took those pictures and that video, no one else. That's how you got the pictures. That's why you were so close. That's how you got such a great video, even in the fog. You found out where she runs, where the track team runs. What were you doing? Hiding in the bushes? In the woods? Waiting for her to run by? Did you know her running schedule? Her route?"

"We were just friends. She was my friend's daughter. I was a friend of the family—"

"Give me a break!" Jake burst into laughter, but it wasn't mirthful, just a release of pressure. "You were *friends*? A man your age is *friends* with a gorgeous sixteen-year-old girl? Who're you kidding? Did you hit on her or just fantasize? You're a sick freak! You're a *predator*!"

"It's not true—"

"If you were such good *friends,* then why are you capitalizing on her death?" Jake realized it was true the moment he said it. "You're such great *friends* with her that when she gets killed by a car, which you witness, you don't go to the police? You don't say to them, these people killed my *friend*? You don't even give your other good friend—her *mother*—the information?" Jake could hear Voloshin had gone silent. "Instead, you sneak around and try to blackmail my son, who had an accident? You try and make money from the girl's death, the daughter of your very good friend? You *disgust* me!"

"I don't need to listen to this."

"Neither do I," Jake shot back. He pressed END, hanging up. Suddenly he heard some noise downstairs, the slamming of the front door, then someone coming upstairs.

"Jake! Ryan!" It was Pam, and she sounded furious.

Chapter Twenty-eight

"I'm up in my office!" Jake got off the computer, erased his Internet history, and got up just as his door flew open.

"Jake, we have a problem." Pam stood frowning in the doorway, still with her trenchcoat over her suit. She hadn't even kicked off her black pumps. "Where's Ryan?"

"In his room, resting."

"Resting! Very good!" Pam spun around on her heel and stalked down the hall toward Ryan's room, her coat billowing behind her. "I'm getting to the bottom of this, once and for all."

Oh no. Jake hustled after her. "What's going on?"

"Wait until you hear this," Pam called over her shoulder.

"Why are you home so early?"

"Because no meeting is as important as this." Pam flung open Ryan's door and entered his bedroom, which was empty except for Moose. The golden retriever stood up in the bed unsteadily, wagging his tail, but Pam crossed the room and knocked on the bathroom door. "Ryan? Ryan, come out of the bathroom."

"Mom?" Ryan called from inside the bathroom. "I'll be out in a little bit. I'm about to take a shower."

"Honey, give him a break." Jake tried to calm the waters. "I already discussed it with him. He wasn't feeling well, and that's why he didn't go to class. He made it to practice though."

"Ryan!" Pam tried the doorknob, but it was locked, then she banged on the door. "Come out of the bathroom, right this instant!"

"Honey, relax." Jake had never seen her this upset. He started to worry about what she knew, or what she thought she knew.

"Don't tell me to relax! I was right, all along. I knew it. I knew something was going on." Pam banged on the door again, and from inside the bathroom came the sound of a toilet flushing.

"Mom, chill." Ryan opened the door and came out of the bathroom, looking more put together than before, with his hair combed back and his hood off his head.

"Don't you tell me to chill!" Pam grabbed his arm, pulled him toward the bed, and made him sit down. Moose licked Ryan's face and wagged his tail harder, thinking this was some new game. "Where were you during Western Civ?"

Jake stepped in. "Pam, I already discussed this with him. You don't have to—"

"The hell I don't!" Pam put her hands on her hips. "Ryan, I asked you a fact question, as the lawyers say. Where were you during Western Civ?"

"I didn't feel well—"

"I didn't ask you how you felt. I asked you where you were."

"I was with Caleb," Ryan answered, not meeting his mother's eye. "I didn't feel well, and he had a study hall, so we hung out."

"And what did you do?"

Jake couldn't take seeing Ryan twist in the wind. "Honey, don't yell at him. He doesn't deserve to be yelled at."

"Yes, he does." Pam ignored him, still glaring at Ryan. "He deserves that and more. You don't know what he's done."

Jake shuddered inwardly. He went over and put his hand on his son's shoulder, to steady him. "Pam, whatever it is, yelling at him won't help. Why don't you talk to him and we'll sort it out in a civilized fashion, instead of screaming questions at him?"

Pam folded her arms, pursing her lips tightly. Suddenly she became very still, searching Ryan with her eyes and not saying anything. The room fell abruptly silent, except for the dog's excited panting. Jake told himself to stay calm while Ryan glanced up at his mother, then looked down, hanging his head. Somehow the ferocity of Pam's angry, loving gaze seemed to break Ryan down, and his strong shoulders slumped. His hands fell to his sides, and Moose nudged his nose under Ryan's palm, which was the dog's favorite bid for attention.

"Pam," Jake said, trying to get control of the situation. "Why don't you tell us what's on your mind, and Ryan can respond?"

"No," Pam answered, almost sadly. She kept her eyes on Ryan's bowed head and folded her arms in the bunchy trenchcoat. "I don't want to tell Ryan what I know. I want Ryan to tell me what he and Caleb were doing, because I want to find out if I raised a liar."

"Pam." Jake was still trying to defuse the situation. "He's already told you the truth. He admitted he cut class and hung out with Caleb."

"Ryan?" Pam looked down at Ryan, still ignoring Moose on the bed. "Did I raise a liar?"

Jake swallowed hard. "Pam, don't call him a name. You know we're not supposed to do that."

"Oh, Jake, shut up. You hate that crap as much as I do." Pam returned her attention to Ryan, who had hunched over, resting his elbows on his knees, in collapse. "Ryan, did I raise a liar?"

"Yes," Ryan whispered, almost inaudibly, without looking up. "It's not your fault, but I am a liar."

Jake felt his heart break, rubbing his son's back. He didn't want Ryan to think of himself as a liar. "Buddy, that's not true."

"Yes, it is, Dad."

"No, no that's not true." Jake squeezed Ryan hard, avoiding Pam's gaze. He could feel his son shaking just the slightest, as if the truth had a pressure of its own and was trying to force its way out of his very body. Jake couldn't let that happen, because if Ryan spilled his guts now, Pam would make them go to the cops for sure. It would ruin them all. Suddenly, he got another idea. "Ryan, why don't you tell your mother what you told me, that you and Caleb were smoking during class." Jake looked up at Pam, whose lovely features were fixed so grimly that they could have been etched in marble. "Pam, Ryan told me the truth. So if that's what you're talking about, you didn't raise a liar."

"Really." Pam heaved a quiet sigh, and her blue-eyed gaze shifted from Jake to Ryan and back again. "So he told you the truth."

Jake nodded, relieved. "He told me everything. He told me that he's never going to smoke again, and he knows it's bad for him and illegal."

Pam sucked in her cheeks, unplacated. "Was he going to tell me?"

"We both decided it might put you in an awkward position, being a judge. It's enough that he told me, isn't it?" Jake didn't press his luck. "How did you find out?"

"Dr. Dave told me that he suspected it today at practice." Pam kept her eyes on Ryan, even though all she could see was his crown. "So I called Caleb's mother. She found marijuana in his drawer, a fair amount of it. It turns out he's been selling it, too."

"That's terrible," Jake said, keeping his arm on Ryan, who was still trembling.

"Ryan?" Pam asked, her tone gentler. "I was so disappointed to think that you would do something unlawful, not to mention stupid. I don't care if everybody else does it, I disapprove completely of smoking marijuana. I told you already, everybody I know who smoked dope in college just got dumber and dumber. And that's only the ones that didn't go on to worse drugs."

Jake didn't interrupt her, because he could see that they had dodged a bullet. He kept his arm around Ryan, praying that the trembling would subside.

"Ryan, I know you feel stressed and bad about what happened at the game, but your reaction to negative emotion can't be to reach for a drug. Or alcohol. Or anything else. Do you understand?"

Ryan didn't answer or even move, except to tremble.

"Ryan?" Pam paused. "I hope you don't need me to tell you what could happen if any of the coaches from these college programs found out that you were smoking, especially during school hours. Division I is too competitive, and they want players who not only make an impact, but who are assets to the program."

Jake kept his mouth shut, but all this talk of impact players made him sick to his stomach.

"If you get a bad reputation with these recruiters, you can jeopardize not only any scholarship possibility, but your entire future. I don't mean to sound like that D.A.R.E. program in elementary school, but it's true, and they never should have discontinued it. The choices you make now have huge implications for the rest of your life—"

"Mom, I know," Ryan said hoarsely, staring at the ground, and Moose beat his tail on the bed at the sound.

"He knows," Jake added, hugging Ryan closer and jostling him just the slightest, to signal that they were about to end the conversation. "Pam, I gave him that lecture, times ten. You don't have to worry about that. I worked him over, and he gets it. Really."

"Good." Pam cocked her head, trying to see Ryan's face. "Ryan? Tell me that your dad's right and I don't have to worry about it.

Tell me that you'll always tell me the truth and that you'll do the right thing, no matter what anybody else says is right. Only you know what's right, and you have to answer for that, always."

Ryan kept his head down. Moose thumped his tail on the bed.

Jake jostled Ryan again, feeling the tension build in his son. "He knows."

"Jake, don't answer for him. I'd like to hear him tell me himself." Pam frowned, her head still cocked as she tried to see Ryan's face. "Ryan?"

"Ryan, answer your mom." Jake looked over, then held his breath.

Ryan looked up at Pam, his eyes filmed and his expression agonized. After a moment, he cleared his throat. "Mom, I killed Kathleen Lindstrom on Pike Road."

Chapter Twenty-nine

The next few hours were pure agony, and if Jake expected the truth to be cathartic, it didn't turn out that way. Ryan became too upset to tell the story, and Jake took over and told her every detail, including their meeting with the lawyer Morris Hubbard, the blackmailer texts, opening of the line of credit to pay the blackmail, the transfer to be delivered by eleven o'clock, his phone conversation with Andrew Voloshin, and his suspicion that Voloshin had been stalking Kathleen Lindstrom. Pam had listened in horrified silence, easing herself into Ryan's wooden desk chair, still wrapped in the cocoon of her trenchcoat. She kept her pumps on her feet, like a soldier who wanted to die with his boots on. She had said nothing except to ask questions, and Jake felt more and more tense, waiting for the proverbial sword to fall.

"So that's it," Jake said, when he had finished. "I'm sorry, honey. I feel horrible about this, and so does Ryan. You know that, you can see that. And I'm so sorry for what this does to you, that it puts you in an awful, awful position—"

"Hold on a second." Pam raised a hand, weakly, and her voice was pained. "I'm trying to understand how the man I married would leave a young girl dead on the road."

Jake took it on the chin. "It's like I explained, honey. I made the best decision I could at the time. I only had a second, I had to react. I've replayed it over and over, I know it was wrong. I didn't know what to do, I just reacted, to protect Ryan."

"Mom." Ryan sniffled, sitting next to Jake on the bed. "He thought he was helping me, and he was. He was about to call 911 when I told him about the weed. He woulda called if I hadn't smoked up. It's not his fault, it's mine."

Jake patted Ryan's leg, touched. "It's okay, I can take it. Your mom is right, it was a terrible decision. I knew it was when I made it, the moment I made it."

Ryan shook his head, distraught. "But Dad, would you make it differently if you had to do over again? You saved us both from prison." He whipped around to Pam, who was slumped sideways in his desk chair, leaning on his desk. Behind her was a lineup of plastic *South Park* figurines and a Funny or Die poster of Will Ferrell. "Mom, what would you have done? Don't be a judge, be a person."

"I'm not being a judge," Pam shot back, shaking her head.

"Then what would you have done, if you were Dad?" Ryan raised his voice, his nose still stuffy from crying, so he sounded oddly like himself as a young boy. "Let's say you were the one that night on Pike Road. Would you have called the cops and sent me to jail?"

"*I* never would've been in that position!" Pam shouted, suddenly. "*I* never would've let you drive!"

"Mom, I can get my license in a month. What difference does it make? It's arbitrary!"

Pam's eyes flashed with anger. "All time limits are arbitrary, but that doesn't mean they're not limits. The law is made up of time limits. I've thrown people out of court because they missed a month-long time limit to file an appeal. And when you get older, try to file your tax return on April 16! It's not acceptable under the law. You shouldn't have been driving, and your father shouldn't have let you drive. He admitted as much. This is *all his fault*!"

"Agree, I agree." Jake nodded, dry-mouthed. Pam sounded so angry that she'd passed through the heat of that emotion into a cooler disgust, or worse, disrespect. He wondered if they'd be able to keep their marriage together, but then again, after she went to the police, he'd be in prison and they wouldn't be a family anymore, anyway.

"No, Dad! Don't let her put it on you! She's acting like a judge, and nobody has a right to judge us, even her! Nobody was there but us! Nobody knows what it was like but us!"

"Ryan, are you crazy?" Pam rose, her eyes flashing with anger. "What you did was unlawful and morally wrong. You should know that, and so should your father. I fault him more than you. He's the adult. He's the one who's culpable, not you—"

"Mom, no!" Ryan shouted at her, and Jake put a restraining hand on Ryan's arm, because he could see the hurt cross Pam's face. She'd wanted father and son to become closer, but not allied against her, especially in these circumstances.

Pam faced Ryan, agitated. "Ryan, you're naïve. You don't know what you're talking about. The fact is, the law judges you. A court will judge you. A judge will judge you. I'm just the sneak preview."

Ryan threw up his hands. "You think I don't know that? You think I don't know that I'm sending my own father to jail? That I'm going to jail? But right now I don't need a judge, I need a *mother*."

Pam gasped, then shut her mouth, stricken. Her fair skin looked suddenly tinged with pink, as if she'd been slapped in the face. Ryan was watching her, his eyes glistening, and before

Jake could realize what was happening, Pam had come forward and opened her arms to her son, and Ryan had gotten off the bed to meet her.

"I'm so sorry, Mom. I'm sorry, I'm really sorry. I feel so bad about everything, and about her. Everybody at school is so upset, they have grief counselors and everything—"

"I understand, I'm here. No matter what, I'm here for you and I love you." Pam held him close even though she was so much shorter, and Ryan found a way to lean his head sideways on top of hers. She hugged him, then rocked him, just the slightest. "We'll figure this out together."

"Just don't blame Dad. It's not his fault, please."

"Okay, enough fighting for now." Pam released Ryan from her embrace, walked him over to the foot of the bed, and sat down beside him, putting her arm around him.

Jake caught Pam's eye, and he knew his wife well enough to know that she was only tabling the discussion. She hadn't forgiven him. She would never forgive him. She would blame him always, and he deserved it. He would blame himself forever, too.

Pam sighed heavily. "Well. I know what we have to do next, like it or not."

Jake looked past Ryan to Pam. "Pam, listen, please. I know you want to go to the police, but let me just explain why we shouldn't."

"Before we get to that, hold on." Pam held up a hand, without meeting Jake's eye. "I know a way to make this easier, immediately. First I'm going to withdraw my name from consideration for the judgeship."

Ryan moaned. "Mom, no. I'll get my act together when the FBI talks to us, I promise. I can do it. I'll just answer the questions. I know how to put it out of my mind, if I have to."

Jake realized Pam was saying that because she'd never get nominated or appointed, after he and Jake had been convicted. "Pam, please, don't withdraw. Don't give up. We can get through the investigation. The line of credit will be paid back by next quarter, if not next month. Voloshin will be paid off, which buys me some time to think about how I will explain the transaction later."

Pam shook her head, her lips pursed. "No, it's all right, I'm fine with it. We have bigger problems right now."

"Mom—"

"Pam, please. Why?"

"It's too much to deal with right now. Enough said." Pam waved them both into silence, her expression stern. "We're in a crisis, and we have to get through it. Jake, call off the line of credit, or take it back, or do whatever you have to do. Will you do that, first thing tomorrow morning, or better yet, call Harold tonight?" Pam spoke without even looking at him. "Tell me you'll do that for me. It's the very least you can do."

"I will," Jake agreed, reluctantly. "But Pam, as for what to do about going to the police, just hear me out—"

"No, my mind is made up," Pam said firmly.

"Listen," Jake said anyway. "I hate keeping this secret, and I hate that Ryan has to keep it, too. I know you're a judge and you believe in the law. I know that." Jake tried to make his argument as logically and rationally as possible, as if he were a litigant before her bench. "But Hubbard was right on the legalities, wasn't he? If you go to the police and tell them the truth, Ryan will be convicted of vehicular homicide and sent to a juvenile detention center. No college, no basketball, no future. Even if you're mad at me, if you go to the police, you'll be punishing him. Neither of us wants that."

"Mom, here's what I think," Ryan started to say, but Pam cut him off with a chop.

"Hush. I don't want to know what you think, because I don't want you to have any responsibility in this. This situation wasn't created by you, and you're not going to weigh in on it, one way or the other."

"Mom, no," Ryan shot back. "That's treating me like a baby."

"Oh please." Pam waved him off. "That crap may work with your father, but he didn't give birth to you. You may think you're large and in charge, but I see through that. You may not be a baby, but you're still a kid. You leave wet towels on the bed. You don't know how to fill out a check. You'd wear clothes with *mold* if I let you. I'm not going to let you have a say in decisions that are this important. I wouldn't let you make a decision about whether or not to go to college, would I? You're going to college, whether you like it or not, because that's what's best for you. So I'm not going to let you make a decision about whether or not to go to prison. It's simply not your decision. It's a decision I make for you. Because *I'm your mother.*"

Jake saw his opening. "But, Pam, what if we disagree? You shouldn't trump me. I'm his father, and I have an equal say. I will not stand by and see him go to prison for this. Not for something that was my doing."

Pam met Jake's eye, for the first time, but there was no love there, only controlled fury. "Jake, at this point, you're right. We have no choice now. You made sure of that when you left the scene. You turned an accident into a crime."

"I know, I'm sorry, but—"

"So Jake, you pay that blackmailer from our savings or money market. I'm not going to the police, and my son isn't going to jail."

Jake couldn't believe his ears.

"This is a secret we're going to keep, as a family."

Chapter Thirty

Jake went into his home office while Ryan took a shower and Pam escaped to her office down the hall, to make the phone calls that would end her becoming a federal judge. He flopped miserably into his desk chair and buried his face in his hands. He couldn't think, he could only feel, and what he felt was abject misery. He didn't see any way out of the situation, of his own making. He had wanted Pam to agree to keep their secret, and he'd gotten what he wished for, but it was only the lesser of two evils. He felt a creeping dread that it had only increased the pressure on all of them, tying their family together in a corrupt bargain, each one tethered to the other in a way that doomed them not to survive, but to sink.

Jake straightened up and tried to shake it off. He could hear Pam talking through their common wall, but he couldn't make out the words she was saying, and he felt awful for her. She'd stormed out of Ryan's room right after she announced her decision, and he hadn't had a chance to talk to her alone or to say how sorry he was, again. He knew she'd unload on him later, saying all the things she couldn't say in front of Ryan, and he hated being betwixt and between, living in that hell reserved for married people, who had to postpone their fights for not-in-front-of-the-kids. But no couples fought about things like this, ever.

Jake tried to focus and make himself do things, so he called Harold and instructed him to stop the line of credit and wire the $250K from their money market and savings account. Harold agreed, no questions asked, of course. Then Jake went online, plugged **Andrew Voloshin** into the search engine, and tried to find out more about him, but couldn't. Voloshin wasn't on Facebook or any of the other social-networking sites and belonged to no professional organizations or alumni groups. Jake felt too distracted to keep looking, much less to answer any emails from work, and when he heard Pam finally get off the phone, he rose, left his office, and went down the hall to hers, knocking gently on the door.

"Pam, can I come in?"

"Yes," she answered, and Jake opened the door, not surprised to see her teary-eyed at her desk. Her eyes were puffy, her hair undone, and she held a crumpled Kleenex in her hand. She slumped in her chair, framed by the soft pink walls and the red-and-pink toile curtains. All the feminine appointments of her office reminded him there was still a girl inside his wife, and he knew her heart was broken.

"I'm so sorry, honey." Jake started to come around the desk, but Pam stopped him with a hand, her soft features hardening.

"Don't even think about it."

"I'm sorry, I really am." Jake stopped in front of her desk. "Are you okay?"

"Do I look okay?" Pam tossed the Kleenex in the wastebasket.

"What did you tell them?"

"That I wanted to spend more time with my family." Pam chuckled, but it was without mirth. "I don't know how you could do it, Jake, I really don't. You've ruined everything, you know. You've ruined our lives. Above all, you've ruined Ryan's life. He's never going to be the same, ever. This secret, it will ruin him."

"I'm sorry," Jake said again, because she was right and it was all he could say.

"It's such a joke," Pam said, disgusted without batting an eye, though she never cursed. "You finally decide to pay attention to your family. You want to step back in and reestablish a relationship with your own son, your only son. So I say, like an idiot, go pick him up at the movie. And what do you do? You decide it would be a great idea if he drove the car!" Pam raised her voice, throwing up her hands. "What a great decision! Wasn't that a *great* decision? Wasn't that one of your greatest, all-time decisions *ever*?"

Jake didn't reply. She needed to blow off steam, and he deserved every word.

"Fun Dad evidently is the last one to know that a father is supposed to be a parent, not a friend. It's Parenting 101, but you didn't get the memo. It's every magazine article, or on every Dr. Phil or Oprah episode *ever*." Pam scoffed. "That's right, she went off the air, so it's her fault. It's *Oprah's* fault! Because it's not your fault, right, Jake? It can't be! I have a son blaming himself, but really it's *your fault*."

"I admit it's my fault. I know it's my fault."

"I know that, too, but that doesn't do us any good, because Ryan doesn't know it's true. Ryan was properly brought up, by me I might add, which means that he has a conscience. He knows the difference between right and wrong, as do I. Only *you* don't know the difference between right and wrong."

Jake didn't say anything. She was right, and there was nothing to say.

"You'll never convince him of anything else, ever," Pam said, louder. "Even though the law would apportion the lion's share of the guilt to you, he'll still feel guilty. And now he feels guilty because you would be the one to go to jail and not him. The kid can't win!"

"I tried to explain it to him—"

"I don't know who you are, frankly!" Pam jumped to her feet. "You leave a young girl on the road, *dead*? You crash your own car? You burn evidence? You lie to the police? You lie to Amy, and to Harold? You lie to *me*!" Pam snorted. "What a bunch of bull! You made me feel bad because I questioned you with Ryan! You made me feel like I was hurting your getting close to him! You backed me down, you manipulated me, and you lied to me every step of the way! I didn't raise a liar, but I sure as hell *married one*!"

"Pam, I know, I'm sorry—" Jake said, then fell abruptly silent when the door opened and Ryan was standing there, his hair wet from the shower, dressed in his gray T-shirt and sweats.

"Mom." Ryan stood in the threshold, his hand on the doorknob. His eyes were dry, and his forehead smooth and untroubled under bangs so wet they dripped on his shoulders, like raindrops. "You need to let it go now. Dad said he was sorry, and you need to get off his back."

Jake's mouth went dry. He knew Ryan was trying to help, but it would only upset Pam more if Ryan intervened and took Jake's side. "Ryan, it's okay—"

"Ryan, please, go." Pam waved him out, agitated. "This is between your father and me. I'm sorry if you heard, but this is between us."

"I disagree." Ryan looked from her to Jake, oddly calm. "You were talking about the hit-and-run, and that's not just between you guys."

"Ryan, I—" Jake started to say, but Pam cut him off with a chop of her hand.

"Jake, why don't you let *me* answer our son? Ryan was speaking to me and questioning what I was doing, and he deserves an answer from me, not you."

"Fine," Jake said, tense.

Pam continued sternly, "Ryan, in point of fact, we weren't talking about the hit-and-run. We were talking about our relationship, about the importance of honesty in our relationship, in our marriage. So you see, it wasn't something that includes you. It's not the same issue."

Ryan blinked, unusually unfazed. "Mom, you sound so much like a judge tonight. Why don't you let it go? I think you've ridden Dad long enough."

"I don't."

"I do."

"Oh really?" Pam shot back, her tone sharpening. "Ryan, it's not your place to tell me how to talk to my husband, even if he's your father."

"I can have an opinion."

"No, actually, you can't."

"I can't have an opinion?" Ryan snorted. "Are you serious right now?"

"Okay, you can have an opinion, but it's not one I need to heed or even hear. You have no standing."

Ryan pursed his lips. "Mom, why are you being such a hypocrite to Dad?"

"I'm not being a hypocrite!" Pam glared at Ryan. "How dare you say such a thing to me!"

"Mom, if you think honesty is so important in a marriage, then why don't you tell Dad about Dr. Dave?"

Jake wasn't sure he heard Ryan correctly, for a second.

"Ryan!" Pam barked, angry. "What are you talking about?"

Jake held his breath, betwixt and between again, knowing and not knowing.

Ryan gestured, grandly, toward Jake. "Go ahead, Mom. Tell

Dad about Dr. Dave. Tell him the truth. I could tell him, but I want you to. I want to know if I was raised by a liar."

Jake felt something give way inside his chest. He kept his eyes on Ryan, who stood motionless, because he couldn't bring himself to look back at Pam. He didn't want to know what she looked like right now, being confronted with an accusation. He didn't want to see her deny it, or admit it. It had never occurred to him before, but as soon as it was given voice, he realized it couldn't be otherwise. Because Ryan never lied, not until Jake had taught him to.

"Mom." Ryan hesitated, evidently waiting for Pam to say something, but she didn't. "Honesty is important in any relationship, isn't it? What about your relationship to me? Why don't you tell *me* what happened with Dr. Dave?"

"Nothing!" Pam said, but her tone didn't sound as strong.

Jake still didn't look at her.

"Nothing? Really, Mom?" Ryan grew preternaturally still. "Dr. Dave's married, too, you know. So tell me, do you know the difference between right and wrong? Does he? Because I heard you on the phone with him, when you came to pick me up after practice. It was sophomore year, I forgot my French book and I had to go back inside, to my locker. Then I realized I had it with me, so I came around the corner and I heard you on the phone with Dr. Dave. I think it was Dr. Dave, but it was definitely somebody named Dave. Because you said, 'I miss you, Dave. I love you.'"

Pam gasped.

Jake didn't turn around. His body felt suddenly stiff, as if he were getting ready to absorb a blow, his muscles bracing for impact in a collision that had already occurred. It was his own personal hit-and-run, taking place not on Pike Road, but in his very home.

Ryan's face fell, and he looked suddenly sad, but he didn't cry. "Mom, you're right. It isn't my business. It's more important that you explain it to Dad than to me." Ryan faced Jake, with a heavy sigh. "Dad. I'm sorry. I thought you should know. Good night." Ryan closed the door, leaving Jake facing the door, turned away from Pam.

"Jake," Pam said hoarsely. "I can explain."

Jake found himself walking stiffly to the door. He didn't know why. He didn't want to leave but he couldn't stay.

"Jake," Pam said, louder. "It's over, it's history. I ended it last year, before we went to counseling. It didn't last that long, only six months. It was a symptom, and I knew it—"

Jake opened the door and walked out, not sure what came next. For the first time in his life, he didn't have a plan.

Chapter Thirty-one

Jake found himself stopped at a red light, sitting at the wheel of the rental Toyota, without even remembering getting in. He came into the moment as if he'd been pulled into the present from his own subconscious, a black void that matched the darkness around him. He didn't have his coat on but was still in his shirt and tie from work. He was stopped at an intersection, and there were no other cars on the street. The dashboard clock read 9:28 P.M. He'd been driving for two hours.

He checked the street sign on the corner to his right, but he couldn't read it. His eyes were blurry and his nose leaking; he realized he'd been crying. He wiped his nose on his shirt-sleeve, looked around, and saw only the spiky black trunks and branches of trees, silhouetted in the light from the windows and front-door fixtures of the large houses, whose peaked roofs and massive entrances hulked shadowy in the night.

He didn't recognize the neighborhood. He felt dislocated, disoriented, generally out of place. He glanced at the dashboard and determined that the car had a no-frills GPS, but he didn't bother to turn it on. He didn't know where he wanted to go. He had no destination, so he didn't need a route.

When the light turned green, he was in no hurry to hit the gas, but he did anyway, proceeding straight through the inter-section without knowing whether he was heading north or south, toward home or away. It didn't matter. It was all uncharted terrain. He didn't know how he had gotten here, not only liter-ally, but to the point where he'd become a suburban husband and father who was driving around aimlessly, in a car that wasn't even his own. He'd worked hard his whole life and followed all the rules. He had risen out of the ashes. He was a self-made man; he had made himself and his business. But the other things he had made were a son who was self-destructing and a wife who had fallen in love with a better suit.

Jake cruised down the dark street, hollow and aching in-side, thinking of Pam. He wanted to know when her affair had started, and why. He wanted to know where they did it, how they did it, how many times they did it. Where they did it, which house, which car. If she liked it better with him, if he was a bet-ter lover. Who started it, and exactly how it ended. If it ended, why he was still calling her.

The darkness seemed to envelop Jake, swallowing him whole, but still he drove forward into the void. He didn't know what Pam saw in Dr. Dave, other than the fact that he was so frig-ging helpful with Ryan. Jake kicked himself for not guessing that something was going on between them. There were too many phone calls, too many times she quoted Dr. Dave. Jake began to doubt the whole shooting-coach thing, questioning whether Dr. Dave became Ryan's shooting coach in order to get close to Pam, in the first place.

Jake had never felt so stupid in his life, ashamed that he hadn't realized she was cheating. He'd never cheated on her and had never really been tempted. His sin had been that he worked too hard, not that he ever dreamed of straying. He saw himself in her; they were so much alike that he never imagined she'd break the rules, or break her word, ever. That was why he'd been so surprised tonight, when she'd agreed to keep the secret about Pike Road. He always thought of Pam as the good girl to his good boy, and it was more her style to do what she had eventually done—nag him until he finally went to a marriage counselor. He didn't want to think about her sleeping with another man, underneath another man, with her legs wrapped around him.

Jake spotted another car on the road, driving toward him in the oncoming lane, its high beams on. It was the kind of thing that usually made him nuts, and he would normally blink his lights to signal the other driver to lower his high beams. If that didn't work, he'd been known to turn on his own high beams out of spite. But tonight he didn't do either of these things. On the contrary, he fed his car some gas, and a different idea popped into his head:

He considered crossing the yellow line and driving straight into the lights.

He drove forward and so did the oncoming car, about a hundred yards apart, then ninety, then eighty. He thought of how easy it could be, just to jerk the steering wheel to the left at the last moment. He wouldn't have to think about it, time it, or work very hard to make it happen. It would be just like when he hit the Dumpster. Easy, peasy.

He looked directly into the high beams, and they seared into his eyes. The cars were seventy feet apart, then sixty, then fifty. He hit the gas and stared into the light, forcing himself not to squint or look away, flooding his brain with a brightness that obliterated the houses, driveways, and recycling bins, like the white-hot blast of an atomic bomb.

The other car raced toward him, its unseen driver unaware of what he was thinking, and Jake knew all he had to do to achieve the desired result was to aim his left bumper at the left bumper of the oncoming car and the impact would do the rest.

The oncoming car barreled toward him, its headlamps double-barreled beams of light, and he wondered what the driver's face would look like, just before they crashed. Shock. Horror. Surprise.

The cars were thirty feet apart, then twenty. He gritted his teeth, squinting against the high beams. The cars were ten feet apart, and he squeezed his eyes shut, grimacing, waiting to see what would happen, and when the other car was almost upon him, he realized he couldn't do it.

He opened his eyes and drove straight. He couldn't kill another human being. He couldn't be responsible for the death of anyone else, ever, in the time he had left on earth.

The other car whooshed past him, the driver not knowing what could have happened, and Jake exhaled loudly, emitting a breath he didn't even know he'd been holding. It struck him that he hadn't driven into the other car not only because he didn't want to kill anyone else, but also because he didn't want to die. He wanted to live. He wanted to redeem himself. For Kathleen Lindstrom's tragic death. For Pam's infidelity. For Ryan's depression.

Jake steered down the darkened street, past the windows that looked into family rooms containing happier families. He didn't have a plan, any longer. The time for plans was over. He didn't believe in them anymore, anyway. Pam didn't plan on cheating on him. Ryan didn't plan on killing Kathleen Lindstrom. Nobody planned on the worst, but they got it just the same and had to deal. He knew the saying that "Man plans and God laughs," but he'd learned the truth was exactly the opposite—Man plans and God cries.

His thoughts returned to Pam, without pain. He knew in his heart why she had strayed, but he loved her still. He didn't want to give up on their marriage, no matter what. He didn't know how she felt; he didn't know if he was ready to find out. He hoped they could put back the pieces of their new life, one that they would make together, with Ryan. Their son needed the both of them now, more than ever, and the three of them had to go forward and hang together in a way they hadn't before.

He pulled over to the side of the street, braked, and plugged his home address in the GPS, then pressed START. **Calibrating Route**, said the GPS, with an arrow pointing behind him. He hit the gas, pulled away from the curb, and started to head home, his mind running free. He wanted to go home, talk to Pam, and work everything out, even if it took all night. He wanted her to know that he was sorry she felt abandoned by him; that he hadn't realized it had gotten so bad. He would tell her that he was sorry, and he flashed-forward to a heart-to-heart in their bedroom, that ended with her coming into his arms, crying and asking him to forgive her.

He wound his way through the quiet suburban streets; the GPS had been set on the shortest route, not the fastest, but he didn't bother to reset it. The lighted blue GPS screen showed a right turn, but he'd been too preoccupied and missed it, so he went straight and the GPS screen switched to **Recalibrating Route**. Jake read the screen, realizing that's exactly what he was doing too, in his life. He would be recalibrating a new route, for himself, Pam, and Ryan, too.

He stopped at a traffic light, which bathed the car's interior in a blood-red glow. He flashed on Friday night after the crash, wiping the blood from his hands, then finding it etched in the lines of his palm. He tried to push it from his mind, to recalibrate again. He reminded himself that he was going to go home and try to move forward, with Pam and him putting their marriage back together for their own sakes, and for Ryan's. They wouldn't be able to get through this together unless they acted as a family. Their house, divided, could not stand. He hoped she'd be happy that he still loved her and was willing to forgive her.

So it came as a shock to Jake when he finally got home and pulled into the garage, only to find that Pam's car was gone. Pasted on the garage door was a sheet of legal pad that read:

I will not be back tonight. Don't call or text me. Ryan is asleep. Tomorrow, go to work your usual time. I will come home and take him to school. Leave me alone. Goodnight.

Chapter Thirty-two

The next morning, Jake was in his office as early as usual, showered, shaved, and stiff in a cutaway collar and fresh suit. He looked out his window into the dawn of a new day, another frigid one under a cloudy pewter sky. He ignored the overseas markets, his voicemail, email, a stack of tri-fold correspondence, and pink phone messages on his desk. He wouldn't think of working until the wire transfer went through this morning, and maybe not even then.

Last night he'd hardly slept for thinking of Pam, though he'd followed her directions, not texting or calling her and leaving the house early, so they hadn't run into each other. He prayed she hadn't run to Dr. Dave. He'd thought of calling him, but she would be too angry. He did call the Marriott Courtyard Suites near the house, but they wouldn't tell him if she was there. He'd even called the local hospital, in case she had an accident.

Jake racked his brain, thinking where Pam would have slept. Her best friend had moved to Singapore last year, and though she was close to all of the Chasers' moms, she wouldn't confide in them, given Dr. Dave's status with the team. She was in a book club, but she wouldn't want them to know, and as a judge, she wasn't close with anyone in the bar. She had a secretary, Christine, who was a stodgy sort, and otherwise in her chambers, there were her three law clerks, in their twenties. Pam had no one else but him and Dr. Dave, which worried him.

Jake heard noises beyond his closed door as Gardenia came to life, but he kept his eyes to the window, idly watching as his employees filled in the spaces in the parking lot. Amy parked her car next to his rental, and he took his receiver off the hook, so she'd think he was on the phone and wouldn't interrupt him. She knew him well enough to know that something was really wrong.

Jake's cell phone rang. The screen read **Harold**, and he grabbed it, knowing it would be about the wire transfer. "Hey, everything okay? I was just about to call you."

"Not exactly. We have a glitch, but I trust it won't be a problem."

"What glitch?" Jake asked, his gut churning. "There can be no glitches."

"The woman who usually does our wires, Barbara, called in sick this morning. I just found out. I'm out of the office and I won't be in until later."

"So what does this mean? You can still transfer the money by eleven, can't you?"

"No. I can do it by noon, but not eleven."

"*What?*" Jake exploded. If the money wasn't there on time, Voloshin would go to the police.

"I won't be in. I'm out of the office at a meeting. I stepped out to call you."

"I need it by eleven!" Jake shouted. "I have to have it by eleven! You said you could do it!"

"I know, sorry. It'll just be an hour later—"

"That's too late!" Jake checked his watch—9:02. Voloshin would take the photos and video right to the police. It would ruin Ryan and him, and now, even Pam. She'd kept their secret, a judge who kept quiet about her son's hit-and-run.

"Harold, leave the damn meeting! Where are you, Timbuktu?"

"North Jersey. It's too important, and if I did, it would raise questions."

"But this *matters more*! Leave!"

"Jake. I would leave if I could, but I can't make it back in time anyway."

"Make somebody else wire the money!"

"No. We have another woman in the wire room but it wouldn't be prudent to use her."

"Why not?" Jake heard himself panicking. "All she has to do is push a button!"

"But it's going to an offshore account."

"Harold, don't tell me I'm your only client to wire to an offshore account!" Jake found himself on his feet. "I wasn't born yesterday!"

"I'm not saying that." Harold's voice stiffened. "What I'm saying is that only Barbara handles such transactions. I can't ask anyone else to do it. I'll do it myself as soon as I get back to the office."

"There's *nobody* else? Not even one of your other bankers?"

"No, not possible."

"You can't trust one of your other bankers to send a wire for one of your best clients? Are you kidding? You have all my personal accounts, all of my business accounts, and Gardenia's!"

"Jake, that would be imprudent. Trust me, I have only your interests at heart. I'll be in by noon—"

"Can't *I* go over and do it? I know how to do a wire transfer—"

"Hold on, I got a better idea. Let me go to Plan B. I may have a way to get it done ASAP, but I can't be sure."

"What way?"

"Let me hang up and see if I can make it happen. I'll call you as soon as it's done."

"Call me as soon as you fix it!"

"I will. Talk soon."

Jake pressed END, sat down in front of his computer, and got online and plugged in GreenTech. Blood pounded in his temples. His mouth tasted dry. He had to go to his own Plan B. He couldn't take the risk that Voloshin would go to the cops. The GreenTech site came on the screen, and he clicked to the Contact Us page, found the main number, and pressed the link to make the call.

"GreenTech," answered a woman. "How can I help you?"

"I'm calling for Andrew Voloshin."

"I don't see him. May I tell him you called?"

"Do you know where I can reach him? Is he out of the office?" Jake's heart throbbed in his chest. Voloshin could be on his way to the Caymans. Or sitting outside the police station.

"I don't know. Our receptionist isn't at the desk, and I just happened to be passing by."

Jake felt frantic. "Is there anyone else there who would know where he is? It's really important that I speak to him."

"Why don't you call him on his cell?"

"I wish I could, but I forgot the number. I have it in my business phone, but I left that in the car. I'm calling you from my personal phone."

"I don't have his cell. Hold on a minute. Let me see if anybody knows where he is."

"Thanks." Jake checked the clock while he waited—9:35, then 9:36.

"Hello, sir?"

"Yes. Were you able to find where he is?"

"Sorry, nobody knows. Sometimes he comes in late, if he's been up coding. You can try him at home if you want."

"Fine, thanks." Jake hung up, went online for the White Pages, got Voloshin's home number, and pressed it into his phone.

"Hello?" a man answered, but his voice sounded raspy, unlike Voloshin's.

"I'm looking for Andrew Voloshin. Is he there?" Jake double-checked to see if he'd dialed the correct number, which he had.

"Who's calling?"

"I'm an . . . associate of his." Jake didn't know who he was talking to, so he chose his words carefully.

"What's your name? What's this in reference to?"

Jake decided to stick with the story. "I'm a financial planner that Mr. Voloshin contacted. I need to speak with him."

"What did you say your name was?"

Jake hadn't said. He glanced at the clock—9:42. "Jake Buckman of Gardenia Trust. Is Mr. Voloshin in?"

"Mr. Buckman, I'm Detective Zwerling with the Shakertown police. I'm sorry to inform you, but Mr. Voloshin is dead."

Chapter Thirty-three

"My God!" Jake couldn't process it quickly enough. It should be good news, but it didn't feel that way. His blackmailer was dead. His troubles should be over. Relief flooded his system, but it left him shocked. He was stunned. "But he wasn't old. How did he—"

"Actually, Mr. Buckman, he was murdered. We've notified next of kin, and it should be public."

"When did this happen?"

"Last night. Mr. Buckman, what company did you say you were with?"

"Gardenia Trust." Jake forced his brain to function. The police were at Voloshin's apartment. Photos of him and Ryan on Pike Road were in Voloshin's phone and undoubtedly his computer. The police might have seen them. If so, the police had proof that Ryan was guilty of the hit-and-run. Fear crackled through Jake's body like electricity.

"Gardenia Trust? Is that local?"

"Yes, in Concord Chase." Jake tried to sound normal. He told himself maybe the cops hadn't seen the photo and videos yet.

"Where?"

"In the Bates Mill Corporate Center."

"We'd like to see you, Mr. Buckman. Would you be available in half an hour?"

"Sure, yes," Jake answered, because anything else would be suspicious. Why would the cops want to meet with him, if they hadn't found the photos and video? Would they arrest him in the office? Would they take Ryan at school?

"Mr. Buckman, we'll see you then."

"Okay, thanks." Jake hung up, stricken. His heart thudded in his chest. His first thought was of Pam. He had to tell her about Voloshin. He scrolled to her cell number and pressed CALL, but it rang, then went to voicemail. He left a message, "Honey, call me as soon as you can. It's very important. I love you." He hit END and considered calling her chambers, but remembered the court was sitting this week and she would be on the bench.

He rose and began pacing, trying to collect his thoughts. He told himself he was jumping to conclusions. Maybe the police hadn't collected the phone and laptop for evidence yet. Or maybe Voloshin had password-protected his phone and computer, and the police hadn't looked through them yet. He didn't know what time Voloshin's body had been found or when the police had started investigating.

He paced back and forth. His temples throbbed. He considered calling a lawyer to represent him when the cops came, but it would only make him look guilty. Still it made sense to get some legal advice. He thumbed through his phone log, found Hubbard's phone number, and pressed CALL. The phone rang, then went to voicemail, but Jake hung up, telling himself to remain calm. He had seen enough TV shows to know he shouldn't volunteer any information.

He resumed pacing. He remembered that he had called Voloshin last night from the house. He'd have to make sure to mention that to the police, before they got Voloshin's phone records.

Suddenly Jake stopped stock still, his pacing ceased. If the police had found the photos and the video, then discovered the wire transfer, they could figure out that Voloshin was black-mailing Jake. The police might even suspect Jake of murdering Voloshin. His mouth went dry. His thoughts raced, threatening to run away with him. The blackmail gave Jake a perfect motive for wanting Voloshin dead, and Jake's only alibi was that he was home with Ryan, who was implicated in the same crime. The police could be coming to question him in connection with Voloshin's *murder*.

Jake realized he had to stop the wire transfer. His gaze flew to the desk clock—9:59. The police would be here in no time. He had to get ahold of Harold and reverse the instructions. He raised his phone and pressed Harold's cell number. The call rang once, twice, then three times and went to voicemail.

Jake heard the beep and left the message, "Harold! Change of plans. *Don't* send the money to the account. Do you under-stand? Call me as soon as you get this message, but in *no* event should you send the money to the account." Jake wanted to make sure Harold got the message, so he scrolled to the text function and typed: **Harold, Major change of plans. Do NOT send the wire transfer. Call me ASAP.** He hit SEND, but still wasn't satis-fied. He pressed the number for Harold's office at the bank.

The call was answered, "Hello, this is Pennsylvania Nation-al's Wealth Management Group. I'm Marie DiTizio, how can I help you?"

"Hi Marie, it's Jake, and I have a problem." Jake knew Marie but he didn't know if she had been told about the transfer. "I need to reach Harold. He called me this morning, and I know he's in a meeting. You know where he is?"

"Yes, of course, but our clients are confidential, as you know—"

"I don't care who the client is. Call him for me. Not on his cell, but at the client. Somebody has to put a note in front of him right away and tell him to call me. It's very important."

"Interrupt his meeting?"

"Yes, Marie, I wouldn't ask you if it weren't an emergency."

"May I help you instead?"

Jake hesitated. "Did Harold discuss anything with you about one of my accounts yesterday or this morning?"

"No, but if you update me, I'm sure I can help—"

"Then no, thanks. I need you to call Harold, get a note in front of him, and tell him to call me immediately. Have them write on the note that he should *not* do what we discussed. You understand?"

"I suppose I could do that," Marie said uncertainly. "That he should *not* do what you discussed."

"Yes, exactly." Jake glanced at the clock, feeling time slipping away. The police would be here soon. "Call me right back after you've made the phone call."

"Of course. I'll attend to it right now."

"Thanks, good-bye." Jake pressed END on the phone and checked the clock—10:06. The police were on their way. Phone in hand, he hurried to his office door, flung it open, and hustled to Amy's desk. "Hey, we had some terrible news this morning."

"What's going on?" Amy focused her warm brown eyes on his face, her concern immediate. She had on a funky multicolored scarf and dangling silver earrings with bright red stones.

"Amy, do you remember that prospective who dropped in yesterday morning? Lewis Deaner?" Jake leaned over, lowering his voice, even though the closest desk wasn't within earshot. "I just got a call from the police, and he was found murdered in his apartment."

"Oh my God." Amy's hand flew to her mouth. "That's terrible."

"I know, and the police are going to be here in about twenty minutes."

"Here? Why?"

"I assume they want to investigate and ask what we met about yesterday." Jake tried to remain composed. Over Amy's shoulder, he spotted Ramon heading his way.

"How did they know that you met with him? Is that who you were on the phone with?"

"Yes." Jake saw Ramon, trying to flag him down. "I called Deaner at home to follow up with him, and the police were there. They're on the way over now."

"So what do we do?"

"Will you make sure the big conference room is available? Obviously, we'll keep this between us."

"Sure thing." Amy nodded quickly, so her curls bounced and her earrings swung. "Ramon has the Janoviches coming in this morning, but I'll move them into the small conference room."

"Good, thanks. Also please meet the police in reception when they come in and take them into the conference room. I don't want them identifying themselves at the desk, in front of the clients."

"I'll be smooth." Amy smiled, but Jake couldn't.

"I'm expecting an important call from Harold at Pennsylvania National." Jake glanced at her desk clock, a comical plastic cat—10:08. "I'm hoping he'll call on my cell before they get here, but if he doesn't, I want you to put him through to me immediately, even if I'm in with the police. Okay?"

"Gotcha."

"Jake!" Ramon called out, reaching the desk. "Can we sit down and go over the Brady trust—"

"No, sorry," Jake interrupted him. "I don't have time right now."

"But I can't set up this trust without your approval and I can't meet with them without the trust being set up. I sent the documents to you Friday, remember? I followed up on Sunday, when I didn't hear from you."

"Ramon, I'm busy," Jake snapped, tense.

"But they're coming in this afternoon to review the documents and sign the papers."

"Then put them off."

Amy pursed her lips, looking from Jake to Ramon like a child in a custody battle.

"I can't do that." Ramon shook his head, bewildered. "Brady is impossible to get a meeting with. He's a surgeon, and you know how they are with schedules. If I don't have the papers ready, he'll be pissed."

"Then he'll be pissed!" Jake exploded. "I'm busy, how many times do I have to say it? I'm busy! Don't you get it?"

Ramon's dark eyes flared, and Jake stalled momentarily, taking in Amy's tight expression, and the other assistants, frowning in surprise. They'd never seen conduct like it from Jake, and he edged away. He realized that what he was seeing in their faces wasn't even a fraction of their reaction if they knew what he had done. That the police could arrest him for a hit-and-run, maybe even for murder. They could take him away in handcuffs this very morning.

Jake felt himself edge backwards. Gardenia would have to close. Some of his employees had been with him since the beginning. He would do to them what his old company had done to him. They would lose their jobs, this very morning. Their lives would turn on a dime, and so would the lives of their spouses, their kids, and the people who depended on them.

Jake turned on his heel and fled down the hall to the conference room, checking his watch on the fly. He'd prayed Harold or Marie called before the cops got here. He couldn't take the call in front of them. That would take nerves of steel, which he was fresh out of at the moment. His cell phone waited in his breast pocket like a bomb ready to explode.

Jake hustled through the reception area and into the conference room, hiding from everyone.

Even himself.

Chapter Thirty-four

Jake turned to see the conference-room door opening and Amy ushering in two men, one middle-aged and the other in his early thirties, both dressed in dark suit jackets and slacks.

"Jake," Amy said, calmly. If she was upset with Jake from his outburst, she was too professional to let it show. "This is Detectives Zwerling and Woo, from Shakertown."

"Thanks. Welcome, gentlemen. I'm Jake Buckman." Jake approached them with a false smile and an outstretched hand. He couldn't tell from their impassive expressions whether they had seen the photos and videos, much less suspected him of Voloshin's murder.

Amy returned to the door, then paused. "Jake, they didn't want coffee or anything, so I'll go."

"Thanks." Jake nodded, and Amy slipped out, closing the door behind her.

"I'm Bill Zwerling," said the middle-aged detective, who had a raspy voice and smelled vaguely of cigarette smoke. He was a chubby five foot seven, with wavy gray hair, slack jaws, and a bulbous nose. His paunch popped through his unbuttoned jacket as he gestured to the younger detective. "This is my partner, Rich Woo. We showed our ID to your secretary, I mean, assistant. But if you want to see—"

"No, that's okay. Hello, Detective Woo." Jake extended his hand to Detective Woo, who was tall and lanky, and his grayish suit fit him perfectly at the waist, as if he worked out.

"Good to meet you." Detective Woo flicked back his glossy black bangs, which flopped longish over his forehead and ears. "My father always says I should see a financial planner. Invest what I've saved."

"Your father's right. Detectives, please sit down." Jake gestured them into chairs, giving them the view facing the window. "I'd be happy to advise you, Detective Woo. It's never too early to start saving for retirement."

"Problem is, you have no idea what my pay grade is. There's not a lot left over, if you follow."

"I hear that, but you have to start somewhere. You're young, and I wish I knew then what I know now." Jake met Detective Woo's gaze, but still couldn't tell what the police knew or if they suspected him of Voloshin's murder. He sat down at the head of the conference table, which he hoped would reinforce his credibility.

"How much money do I have to have to use your services, Mr. Buckman? Do you have a minimum?"

"Please call me Jake, and no, not at all. We'd be happy to put you in our Gardenia mutual fund, which contains the same blue-chip stocks that we put high-net-worth individuals in." Jake checked the walnut clock on the credenza against the far wall. It read 10:28. That transfer had to be stopped or he was dead meat.

"What's the cutoff, money-wise, between me and high-net worth?"

"Those with assets over $500,000. I'd be happy to meet with you, anytime."

Detective Zwerling cleared his throat, as he pulled a slim spiral notepad from inside his breast pocket and flipped open its cardboard cover. "Let's get this show on the road, shall we? We have a busy day ahead of us."

"Fine." Jake forced himself to stop checking the clock so often. He didn't want to show his hand to the cops, like he had Guinevere LeMenile. "I'm very sorry to hear about Mr. Voloshin's murder. That came as a shock. We don't have many of those in Concord Chase."

"He lived in Shakertown, the north end. Trust me, it happens." Detective Zwerling shifted in the chair, his belly lipping the table.

"How was he killed?" Jake wanted to make sure he asked any questions that seemed appropriate.

"He was stabbed to death. Another tenant found him in his apartment, because he left his laundry in the washer."

"Ugh, that's terrible." Jake didn't have to feign repugnance. "Do you have any suspects or is it too soon?"

"*Way* too soon. It's not like TV, where the body hits the floor and they already cleared the case." Detective Zwerling curled his lip in a way that suggested he'd given the lecture before. "Me, I'm a big *Dexter* fan. They get at least a few episodes to solve the crime."

"I wonder why somebody would kill him. He seemed like a nice, harmless guy."

"The details of our investigation are confidential, but his valuables appear to be missing. Wallet, laptop, phone, like that."

"How sad." Jake clucked unhappily, though relief surged through him. If Voloshin's laptop and phone had been stolen, the police probably didn't know about the video and photos incriminating him and Ryan. Still he couldn't be certain, and if the wire transfer wasn't stopped, it could blow everything. He checked the credenza clock as discreetly as possible—10:34.

"Mr. Buckman, Jake, you don't mind if we tape this, do you?"

Detective Woo slid a handheld tape recorder from inside his pocket, pressed a button on the side, and set it down on the table between them.

"No, I don't mind at all. So how can I help you?" Jake hadn't anticipated the meeting would be recorded, but his answer appeared to be moot anyway.

"We have a few questions." Detective Zwerling clicked the back of his pen with a chubby thumb. "Jake, just tell us something about yourself. Family? Residence?"

"I'm married, and we have one son, in high school." Jake didn't supply any names, to keep them out of it. "I live in Concord Chase."

"For how long?"

"Twenty years, and I've had the business the past five."

"You own it?"

"Yes."

"Good enough." Detective Zwerling took notes. "Tell me how you came to meet with Mr. Voloshin."

"I was at my son's basketball game at North Mayfield, last Sunday afternoon. He sat next to me."

"You're a big guy, Jake. Did you play hoops in high school?"

"No."

"College?"

"No. I worked."

"Okay." Detective Zwerling took notes. "Why was Voloshin at the game, do you know?"

"Yes. He was with North Mayfield and was watching his kid, a sophomore." Jake decided to stick with the story Voloshin told him, because it was too risky to improvise. He didn't want the detectives to know that he knew Voloshin had lied about his name, family, job or anything else. He doubted the police had asked Amy any questions, because she knew Voloshin as Deaner, and he doubted the police would go find the tiara moms.

"Did Voloshin tell you what he did for a living, at the game?"

"He was a freelance writer."

"How long did you speak with him?"

"About five minutes."

"That's all?"

"You know how these games are. You end up sitting with people, trying to make conversation or drum up business. Network. I told him I was a financial planner, I gave him a business card, and he said he'd come see me." Jake heard himself volunteering too much, out of nervousness. "To make a long story short, he came by my office Monday morning and we met."

"Where, here?" Detective Zwerling took more notes on his pad.

"Yes, but not in the conference room. In my office."

"For how long did you meet?"

"Fifteen minutes."

"So, short?" Detective Zwerling took another note.

"Yes."

"Is that typical?"

"No."

"Why did it end so soon?"

"He seemed like he'd heard enough." Jake swallowed hard. "He ended it."

"Did you make notes during the meeting?"

"No."

"Do you, usually?"

"No." Jake sneaked a look at the credenza clock—10:40. He could hear it ticking in his brain.

"What did you talk about?"

"I told him about the company and our investment philosophy, like I do with any new client."

"You were hoping to get his business?"

"Yes, I was hoping to sign him." Jake kept his answers short. He wasn't about to take any chances, in case the detectives had somehow seen the photos or video.

"What do you mean, sign him?"

"We have an agreement that new clients sign, called an Investment Advisory Agreement."

"Did he sign it?"

"No, I didn't offer it to him. We didn't get that far." Jake remembered that he ought to mention his phone call to Voloshin, to preempt any suspicion when the police found Voloshin's phone records. "By the way, I called him on Monday night, to see if he had any questions or if I could help him further, but he said no."

Detective Zwerling made a note. "What time did you call him?"

"About nine o'clock or so."

"After business hours?"

"Yes." Jake tried not to look at the clock and to keep his focus on Detective Zwerling, in a natural way.

"Is that typical for you to call a client, a prospective client, outside of business hours?"

"Sure, especially if I want his business." Jake wasn't lying. "I'm self-employed, so I work all the time."

"But he turned you down, so why did you call him?"

"To follow up, to make sure."

"What did he say?"

"That he was thinking it over."

"I see." Detective Zwerling made another note. "So then why were you calling him at home, this morning?"

Oops. "I'm persistent."

"Did he tell you how much money he had?"

"No."

"But you still tried to sign him, as you say?"

"Yes."

"You tried that hard to sign him, but you didn't even know how much money he had?"

"Yes." Jake could see he wasn't buying it.

"You must really have wanted his business." Detective Zwerling frowned so deeply, three lines creased his brow.

"I really want everybody's business." Jake could see he had to convince him. "To be frank, five years ago, I lost my job. It turned out okay, I founded Gardenia, but I never want to go back there again. It's a mentality."

Detective Zwerling blinked. "How typical is it that a client doesn't tell you how much money he has?"

"Very typical."

"How so?"

"Clients like him, who aren't referred to us by an accountant, estates lawyer, or a banker, aren't well-versed in what we do. Like Detective Woo." Jake gestured casually at the younger man. "Not everybody in that situation wants to disclose their assets. They're concerned about confidentiality. They don't understand, or really trust, that all of their financial information is confidential. We're very careful about that here."

Detective Zwerling made another note, then looked up at Jake, cocking his head. "Did Mr. Voloshin tell you where he worked as a freelancer?"

"No."

"You didn't ask?"

"No."

"Did he tell you his salary or anything about his finances?"

"No."

"Again, you didn't ask?"

"No. I don't want to come off as prying, too early in the relationship. I never begin a relationship with a new client by asking them about their assets, because as I say, they regard it as prying. I give them my sales pitch and explain how we can tailor their portfolio to meet their investment goals." Jake gestured at Detective Woo again. "As I told you, the truth is, it doesn't matter how much money someone may have. I know I can grow it over time, no matter how much it is, and that's the point I make at the outset."

Detective Zwerling didn't seem impressed. "Did he tell you where he kept his money? What his bank was?"

"No."

"You didn't ask him that either?"

"No."

"Why not?"

"Same deal."

Detective Zwerling lifted an unruly eyebrow. "Let me get this straight. When you talked to Mr. Voloshin, you had no idea if he even had the money to invest?"

"Yes that's right." Jake stole a glance at the credenza clock—10:54. He began to sweat under his starched shirt.

"How do you know he wasn't wasting your time?"

"I don't, but most people don't come in if they don't have the money or close to it. In any event, I think long-term. They may not have it now, but they could someday."

"Did Voloshin seem wealthy, to you?"

"I never make an assumption about how much money anyone has by their appearance or their manner. My assistant Amy calls it paydar, and my paydar is terrible." Jake smiled when Detective Woo did, though Detective Zwerling didn't. "Mr. Voloshin wasn't an ostentatious man, but I know from experience that someone like that could have a fortune socked away, or they could be a waiter."

Detective Zwerling frowned again. "You mean a waiter, like in a restaurant?"

"No," Jake answered, grasping for purchase on the terra firma of shop talk. "In my profession, a waiter is somebody who's waiting for an inheritance. They live on the interest of trusts during most of their adult life and many of them live very frugally. They tend to look and act like Mr. Voloshin."

Detective Woo clapped his hands together, smiling. "You mean they're *waiting* for their parents to die? Oh, that's *cold*."

Jake flushed. The clock read 10:56. "I didn't make up the term. We all use it. I guess it is harsh."

"*Waiters!*" Detective Woo laughed.

"Enough, Richie." Detective Zwerling pursed his lips. "To get back on track, Jake, did Voloshin tell you that he expected to be coming into money?"

"No, he didn't."

"Did he ask you about setting up an offshore account for him?"

"No, he didn't. In point of fact, we're not a bank, so we don't set up any bank accounts, offshore or otherwise. We're an investment company and we invest our clients' money in stocks, bonds, and the like."

Detective Zwerling hesitated. "We did find evidence that would suggest Voloshin had set up an offshore account, himself. We're trying to understand where the money to fund it would be coming from. Do you have any information about where Voloshin was getting the money?"

"No."

"None at all?"

"None."

"Where do your clients usually get money from?"

"What about inheritance?" Jake shrugged, casually.

"Don't think so. He has a mother and we notified her as NOK, or next-of-kin. But she's upstate in a nursing facility, with insurance footing the bills. Did he mention anything to you about a girlfriend?"

"No."

Detective Zwerling frowned. "He didn't mention a girlfriend?"

"No." Jake wondered if Voloshin had a girlfriend, because the detective's tone sounded surprised.

"There was no talk of providing for anyone?"

"No, no beneficiary or anything like that."

"Didn't you think that was strange, since he had told you he had a son, and an ex-wife?"

"No, because as I say, he didn't give me much information at all. He played it close to the vest, and I pitched him."

Detective Zwerling pursed his lips as he took notes. "So he didn't say anything to you about a woman."

"No."

"Did you see what kind of car he drove?"

"No."

Detective Woo shrugged, glancing again at Detective Zwerling. "Give it up. I'm telling you, I'm right."

"Give what up?" Jake sneaked a glimpse of the credenza clock—10:59.

Detective Woo answered, "One of the tenants heard Voloshin arguing with a woman last night and saw a brunette leaving his—"

"Richie," Detective Zwerling interrupted. "Enough."

Detective Woo fell silent, and Jake remembered that Kathleen's mother was a brunette. Maybe she had found out that Voloshin was stalking her daughter. But he didn't know why she would kill him.

Detective Zwerling returned his attention to Jake. "To move on, Voloshin was never married. He had no ex-wife. No kids either. This isn't confidential, it'll be in the newspapers."

Jake faked a confused frown. "But he said he was watching his son at the basketball game."

"That wasn't true."

"So he's not a dad? He doesn't have a kid on the team?" Jake recoiled in fraudulent shock. The clock read 11:00. Either the transfer was stopped, or he was dead. The realization stressed him to the max. His heart beat wildly, throwing itself against the inside of his chest, as if it were trying to escape his very body.

"You say that financial planners don't set up offshore accounts?" Detective Zwerling set down his notebook, laying his pen on top.

Jake tried to recover. "No."

"So why did he want to meet you?"

"I don't know. Maybe he thought we did, mistakenly."

Detective Zwerling narrowed his eyes, making his crow's-feet look even deeper. "But you said he didn't ask you if you did."

Jake felt his mouth go dry. "Maybe he decided against it, after he saw the offices or something."

"But why did he come to you, in particular?"

"Because we met at the game." Jake struggled not to choke on his words. "I pitched him. I wanted him to come in."

"Then why would he lie to you about the son, and the ex-wife? It doesn't make sense."

"I don't know. Maybe to fit in, to make himself seem more normal, more like one of my clients?"

"But why? Why you? Did he go to the game to meet you?"

"I don't know. I am one of the top ten independent financial planners in the region, rated by *Barron's.* The other top guys are in Philly and Pittsburgh."

"So why not just come to your office, like any other client? Why make up some story and meet you at the game?" Detective Zwerling shook his head, his dissatisfaction evident.

"Maybe he didn't want to wait until Monday."

"But how does he even know you'll be at the game?"

"My son's a well-known high-school basketball player, in the newspapers all the time. It's a logical assumption I'd be there." Jake didn't elaborate. He wanted to keep Ryan's name out of it altogether.

"Do you go to his games?"

"Not all of them, but this was the playoffs. I go then." Jake saw a way out. "So maybe Voloshin made it a point to run into me. Maybe he thought he'd feel me out at the game, then he listened to my pitch and decided to come in, but saw that we don't do the kind of thing he was interested in."

"Why didn't he ask you about it then?"

"An offshore account? Would you, if you saw this place?" Jake gestured at the conference room. "We're obviously not the kind of place that deals in shady offshore accounts. We don't even breathe that word around here."

"Hmph." Detective Zwerling paused. "Anyway, so he expected to come into money. But I don't know where he expected to get it from. Do you have any idea?"

"No."

"In your practice, or whatever you call it, how do clients generally come into money?"

"Inheritance, gift, stock windfall. He could've even won the lottery. I have two lottery winners among my clients."

Detective Woo's face came alive. "The *lottery*? Whoa! That's incredible! What's it like to win the lottery?"

Detective Zwerling snorted. "It ruins your life, right?"

Detective Woo laughed. "Come on, Bill! Only *you* could find something wrong with free money! It's the best thing *ever*!"

Detective Zwerling snorted again. "Be careful what you wish, grasshopper."

"Winning the lottery can be a wonderful thing," Jake jumped in, relieved to change the subject. "I've seen it change lives for the better."

"Tell me!" Detective Woo leaned forward. "What do they do when they win? Give a party? Buy a Lamborghini? If I won, I'd take all of my buddies to Cabo!"

"Not on my watch." Jake managed a smile. "We'd discuss it, but I'd invest you consistent with your goals, and I'd refer you to an accountant, a private bank, and an estates lawyer."

Detective Zwerling scowled. "And a shrink, because you'll need one."

Jake let it go, and the clock ticked to 11:02. Suddenly his phone signaled that a text had come in. He rose and reached for his pocket, looking for an excuse to end the meeting. It had to be Harold or Marie, calling with the best or worst news of his life.

"Detectives, excuse me, I was waiting for that text and I need to make a call. We're finished here, aren't we?"

"Well, yes, I suppose we're done." Detective Zwerling flipped his pad closed. "For now."

For now. Jake fled for the door, glancing at his phone screen. The text wasn't from Harold or Marie, but from Pam, and it read:

Don't worry. I took care of Voloshin.

Chapter Thirty-five

Jake pressed in Pam's cell-phone number, hurrying back through the reception area to his office. He'd been expecting to hear from Harold, not his wife. What did she have to do with Voloshin? And last night? It struck him suddenly that Pam could be the brunette that the detectives were talking about, who had been spotted at Voloshin's apartment complex.

Oh my God.

Jake hustled down the hall and caught Amy's eye. Pam wouldn't have *killed* Voloshin, would she? It was almost unthinkable, but she was the best mother on the planet. Would she have killed Voloshin to protect Ryan?

Jake waited for the call to connect while he motioned to Amy that he was finished with the detectives and she should see them out. He slipped into his office and closed the door behind him. "Babe?" he said, as soon as Pam picked up. "What did you—"

"I *told* you not to call me." Pam's voice sounded thick with frost. "If I wanted to speak with you, I would've called you. I spent last night and this morning cleaning up after your mess.

Plus I stopped by the mall, bought Ryan a new phone, then dropped it off at school. Now I have to get to work and I can't take the time—"

"Pam, what did you mean by that text?" Jake hurried across his office to his window, so that he could see when the police left the building. His heart was pounding in his chest. His shirt was damp with flop sweat. "We have to talk—"

"The hell we do, and I'm driving. The traffic is terrible and I'm not about to get killed because you want to kiss and make up—"

"It's not about us, it's about your text. What did you do to Voloshin?"

"I handled the situation. I don't think it's wise to talk about it over the phone."

"Why not? Pam, what did you do?"

"Trust me. Not over the phone and not now." Suddenly Pam gasped. "*Damn* you! I almost hit that truck! Haven't you caused enough trouble? I'm hanging up—"

"No, don't! Pam, the police were just here." Jake was about to explain when he heard his phone signal that another call was coming in. He prayed it was Harold or Marie. He glanced at the screen, which showed Harold's cell-phone number. He had to find out whether the transfer had been stopped. "Pam, where are you?"

"In Fraser, about to get onto 202."

"Meet me at the quarry, there won't be anyone around. I'll be there in fifteen minutes."

"The quarry? What quarry?"

"Where we used to go, you know, when Ryan was little. Go in the entrance we used to use."

"Why? What's going on?"

"See you there. Good-bye." Jake pressed END and picked up Harold's call, breathless. "Harold, did you stop the transfer?"

"Yes, but what the hell is going on—"

"Thank God!" Jake almost shouted with relief. He leaned for support against the large glass window, leaving a sweaty handprint. Outside, the police hadn't yet appeared, leaving the building. "Harold, you're *sure* you were able to stop the transfer?"

"I'm positive."

"*Absolutely* sure?"

"It's done."

"Does it leave any trace that it was attempted, electronically?"

"No, but this isn't like you. First it's top priority that it goes through, then it's top priority that it doesn't? Are you okay?" Harold's tone softened. "I'm asking you as your friend, not as your banker. We've known each other ten years, through thick and thin, you remember. We go back."

Jake remembered. "No, I'm fine," he answered, firmly. "Thanks."

"So where do we go from here? What do you want me to do?"

"Forget the whole thing. I'm fine, and I appreciate your jumping on it when I needed you to."

"No problem." Harold's voice snapped back to business. "Then I'd better go. I left the meeting to call you."

"Thanks again. See you." Jake pressed END just as the two detectives emerged from the building entrance below. He couldn't leave the building until they were out of sight, so he watched them walk toward the front row of parking, reserved for Gardenia visitors. Two of the spaces were filled by a Volvo and a Jaguar, which Jake figured belonged to the Janoviches and the Warners, but next to them was a Crown Victoria, an older model in a dull navy blue. He assumed it belonged to the detectives, confirmed when they made a beeline for the sedan. But then they stopped suddenly, turned around in unison, and looked back at the building.

Detective Zwerling shielded his eyes, and they both squinted up at the building's façade, their heads together in conversation. Evidently, they were trying to locate his office window.

Jake edged away from view, shuddering. He didn't know why they were looking back at him, if they didn't suspect him of something. He realized that they hadn't asked him where he was last night, to see if he had an alibi, so maybe they didn't suspect him at all. Or maybe they didn't want to tip him off. Maybe they were playing games with him, doling out their questions as they continued their investigation. What was it that Detective Zwerling had said?

I suppose we're done . . . for now.

But it was Pam he was worried about. Had she killed Voloshin? It seemed unthinkable. She was a sitting judge. Jake knew Pam to the marrow and he never would have believed her capable of murder. But then again, he never would have believed she would cheat on him, either. Or that she would keep the secret about the hit-and-run. Or give up a federal judgeship that she had wanted forever. What other sacrifices would she make for Ryan? Where did she draw the line?

Still, he couldn't wait to see her.

The simple fact was, Jake loved his wife.

No matter what.

Chapter Thirty-six

Jake arrived at the quarry, the gravel popping under his tires. He cut the ignition and parked, but he didn't see Pam. He got out of the car and checked around to make sure, but she wasn't there. The only activity was on the far side of the immense quarry, at the construction site. Workers walked this way and that, backhoes toed the ground, and oversized trucks dumped loads of soil. The rumble of the equipment echoed off the rock walls of the crater.

Jake found himself worrying briefly if the construction workers could see him and checked around for security cameras. He knew he was being paranoid but he couldn't help himself. He'd driven here with an eye on the rearview mirror, checking to make sure that the detectives weren't following him.

Jake breathed in deeply, trying to relax. The air carried the familiar grit he remembered from his childhood, making it hard to breathe, but that could have been his memories. He glanced inside the enormous crater at the greenish brown water below, slightly choppy in the wind off the surface of the deep cliffs. A jagged vein of darker rock ran around the circumference of the quarry, a high watermark like the dirty rim of a bathtub, and his gaze traveled upward, over the strata of the limestone, its streaks of gray, tan, and brown formed over centuries.

It struck him that he was looking at a cross-section of time itself, if not his own personal history. His childhood would've started somewhere in the grayish streaks near the top, forty-odd years ago, and his father's and mother's would have started an inch below that, almost a century into the past, as if the layers of the limestone were the pencil lines they used to draw on the kitchen doorjamb when he was growing up, to chart his height. He and Pam drew the same lines on their kitchen doorjamb to mark Ryan's height, the only tradition of his family's worth keeping.

Jake realized with a deep pang that his mother would weep if she knew that her son had just been questioned by the police, after he'd left a young girl dead on the road. He also knew what his father would say.

Just my luck.

Jake swallowed hard, eyeing the strata of rock in the sun, which spilled into the countless crevices on the face of the cliff, illuminating even the tiniest of crevices, indentations, and faults, making shadows everywhere. The quarry kept no secrets, hiding nothing, but lay bare every buried sin, exposing it to light and air. Jake sensed he was looking at his own history, in which his decision on the night of the hit-and-run would become the blackest vein, a fault line that would render him and his family unstable, forever.

Story of my life.

There was a noise behind him, and Jake turned to see Pam driving up, on the phone. He wondered if she was talking to Dr. Dave, which brought him a stab of pain. He couldn't read her expression because she had designer sunglasses on and she was dressed for work in one of those jackets-over-a-dress combinations that she favored. She turned off the engine, hanging up, then threw open the car door, jumped out, and let it slam behind her.

"Pam." Jake walked toward her, raising his arms to embrace her, but she stiffed-armed him.

"Why am I here?"

"What happened with Voloshin last night?"

"I told you, I took care of it." Pam slipped the phone into her blazer pocket and folded her arms. Her tone was cold, and her hair blew in the wind off the quarry. "I cleaned up your mess."

"You didn't kill him, did you?" Jake had thought of nothing but that question on the drive here.

"*What?*"

"Andrew Voloshin is dead. He was found stabbed in his apartment last night. Two detectives were just at my office questioning me. They said one of the tenants saw a brunette leaving the complex last night. He was also heard arguing with a woman. Kathleen's mother is brunette, but so are you. It wasn't you, was it?"

"Are you serious?" Pam asked, sounding for the first time like herself. She tore off her sunglasses, revealing a horrified expression.

"You would never kill anybody, even for Ryan, would you?"

"Of course not." Pam's eyes flared in disbelief. "I don't know what you're talking about! Voloshin's not dead, he can't be. I just saw him."

"He is dead. Murdered." Jake's thoughts raced ahead. "If you didn't kill him, who did? And why?"

"I just saw him," Pam repeated, shaking her head.

"What time? Where did you see him?"

"Around ten o'clock, at his apartment."

"You went to his apartment?" Jake asked, dumbfounded. "Why? What were you doing? How do you even know where he lives—"

"If you let me explain, I will," Pam snapped, her eyelids

fluttering briefly. "I looked him up online, like you did, and I found his address. I decided to go over there."

"Why?"

"Why not?" Pam shot back. "You drove us straight into a ditch. You kept everything from me and you instructed Ryan to keep everything from me, so I had no say in what was going on. But once I found out, did you think I was going to sit around and do nothing?"

Jake didn't interrupt because she was on the warpath.

"I used to be a pretty good litigator, remember? I still have sharp teeth and I'm not without resources. I decided to go over there and give him a piece of my mind. I wanted him to back off of Ryan and I wanted him to know that he wasn't getting any more money after this initial payment. I wanted him to know that I wasn't about to be blackmailed into bankruptcy." Pam paused. "Wait, what about the transfer? Did you pay him?"

"I stopped it in time. It never went through."

"Good." Pam rubbed her forehead irritably, leaving pinkish welts with her nails. "So I drove over and knocked on his door. The apartment complex is one of those with townhomes stuck together, only two stories. Duplexes, and it's kind of run down. His apartment is on the second floor of one of the townhouses. His name was on the mailbox. I went in the downstairs door behind the first-floor tenant—"

"The tenant let you in? Just like that?"

"Please, he's an old man and I gave him a big smile."

"Did you tell him that you were there to see Voloshin?"

"What's the difference?"

"I'm thinking about the police. I'm wondering if you're the brunette that they were referring to or if the old man can identify you—"

"Of course he can't. It was dark. He could barely see me through his trifocals, and anyway, I didn't explain anything to him. I just walked in behind him, smiled, then went upstairs."

Pam threw up her hands, with the sunglasses looped around her thumb. "Honestly, Jake! What are you so worried about?"

Jake let it go. He didn't want to tell her what he was so worried about, not yet.

"Anyway, I went upstairs, and Voloshin's apartment door was open partway. I knocked and called for him, but it swung open all the way."

"He leaves his door open?"

"It was the only apartment on the floor, so I assume he wasn't worried about it. I went in. He came up later with a basket of laundry. I guess he'd been in the laundry room, wherever that was."

"So he came into his apartment and found you there?" Jake was trying to imagine the chronology.

"Yes, but not before I did some snooping."

"What did you do? What did you see?"

"Hold on. When he came in, I explained to him who I was and why I was there."

"What did you say?"

"I told him that I was Ryan's mother and a judge, and that he was the lowest form of life on the planet. I told him that if he ever breathed a word of what he knew or bothered us again, then I'd go to the police myself."

"Did you raise your voice?"

"Of course. That's my forte."

"Did he?"

"Not really. He asked me to leave, but I wasn't about to go until I said my piece. Then I left."

Jake couldn't hide his dismay. "The police said one of the tenants overheard a woman arguing with him."

"That would be me. That little bastard, he's the worst kind of bully. A coward." Pam paused. "It's too bad he's dead, murdered that way, even if it means he can't blackmail us anymore. I mean, I wouldn't wish that on anybody."

"The killer made it look like a burglary, or it was an actual burglary. But Voloshin was alive when you left him?"

"Of course. He threw me out. Walked me to the apartment door."

"And you went downstairs. Did you see anybody on your way out?"

"No."

"What about the old man? The first-floor tenant?"

"No. I didn't see anybody. Why are you asking me all these questions?"

"I want to know. Then what did you do?"

"I went to the car and left."

"Were you wearing your sunglasses?"

"Of course not. It was nighttime."

Jake tried to imagine it. "Did the place have a security guard, like a gatehouse at the front?"

"No, you just drive in."

"Did you see any security cameras around or any security guards?"

"There was no security guard, and it was too shabby to have any surveillance cameras."

"How long would you say you were there?"

"Talking with him? Five minutes. Before that, snooping around? About ten minutes. I took pictures."

"You took pictures inside his apartment?"

"You're not going to believe what I saw." Pam looked at her iPhone, and Jake came over as she thumbed through to her camera roll, a multicolored grid like an electronic mosaic. She looked over at him, then edged backwards again. "Forget it. I don't have time to look at them. I have to get to work."

"You're not even going to stand next to me now?"

"You think everything is fine, just like that?"

"No, of course not, but—"

"Nothing's fine, nothing. You got us into this mess. You ruined our lives. You ruined our *son*."

"Honey—"

"Don't 'honey' me. I don't want to talk about it now. I have to get to work. If I get in any later, people will start asking questions."

"Can I see the pictures?"

"You can't see them in the sun, anyway." Pam waved the iPhone at him. "He keeps a bulletin board over his desk and it has lots of pictures of Kathleen. He was stalking her. You were right, okay? Is that what you need to hear?"

"So you took pictures of his desk." Jake wondered if her fingerprints would show up anywhere. "Was his computer there?"

"Yes, a laptop. I took a picture."

"The police said that whoever killed him took his laptop and phone. Did you see a phone anywhere?"

"No, I assume he had it with him. Maybe it will show up in the photos. You can look for yourself." Pam hit a few buttons on her iPhone. "I'll email—"

"No, don't email—"

"Why not? I just did."

"Pam, think about this." Jake realized that she hadn't thought it through, probably because she'd been so upset. "The police are looking for a brunette who had an argument with Voloshin right before he was murdered. They suspect he had a girlfriend, but we know that woman is you, unless another brunette came by later, like maybe Kathleen's mother, but still, I don't know why she would—"

"So what?" Pam checked her watch. "Could you speed it up?"

"So after you leave Voloshin's apartment, sometime during last night, he turns up dead. If the police figure out that you were the brunette, they could suspect you of his murder. They could come question you, like they did me, at your chambers or at home."

Pam stood stunned, blinking. Behind her, a shadow crossed the quarry from a passing cloud.

"You were the last person to see Voloshin alive, and the photos you took are proof that you were in his apartment last night. Now that you sent them to me, and even if you delete them from your phone, we can't delete them from the email server." Jake could see her withdrawing, recoiling as it dawned on her. "Your picture is in the newspaper from time to time, so one of the tenants could have recognized you. Or even if you hadn't been seen, a security camera or even a traffic-light camera could've taken your picture. If the police come to question you, you're done for, and so are we all."

Pam's lips parted, but she still didn't speak.

"Honey, are you okay?" Jake asked gently, reaching for her arm, but she jerked it away, dropping her sunglasses and iPhone. They both bent down to retrieve the items, but she reached them first and snatched them up from the gravel and dirt, then held them to her chest in an oddly protective way.

"Jake. That's not possible, what you're saying." Pam frowned, shaking her head and backing away, her voice softer. "That's impossible. Nobody would think that of me. The police would never think that."

"They could, honey. They came to my office today because I called Voloshin this morning, telling him the transfer would be late. His murder hadn't hit the news by then, but it probably has now—"

"That's why the police came to you? What did you tell them?"

"I told them that Voloshin came to me as a prospective client but that I didn't sign him. I did the best I could, but I couldn't really explain why he sought me out at the basketball game." Jake could see she was getting more upset, backing away from him and shaking her head. "If they get his phone records, the police will see that I was the last person to talk to him last night, but I think I explained that. They didn't ask me if I had an alibi, but they still could. And you, what's your alibi?" Jake didn't ask because she was so distraught, but what he wanted to ask was, *Is Dr. Dave your alibi?*

"Oh no. Oh no." Pam closed her eyes, still clutching her phone and sunglasses. "I put myself on the hook, didn't I? I went over there. I argued with him, loudly. I didn't try to hide. I didn't wear sunglasses or anything. Anyone could have seen me. Anyone could've heard us arguing. Anyone could've seen my car or my license plate. I didn't know someone would *kill* him. Who would *kill* him—"

"Honey, don't worry. We'll figure this out, together." Jake took a step toward her.

"No, leave me alone, I have to go." Pam turned away, hurrying toward her car.

"Pam, please!" Jake hustled after her and caught her arm, but she wrenched it back, tears filling her eyes.

"Don't touch me! Leave me alone! I hate you! You ruined everything, everything, everything!"

"Pam, no—"

"Stay away from me! Stay away from our house!" Pam reached her car and flung open the door. "I'm going home tonight, not you! You won't live there, ever again! It's over, Jake! *We're over!*"

Chapter Thirty-seven

Jake sped away from the quarry, as if his guts had been kicked out of him. He turned onto Concordia Boulevard, its four lanes of traffic beginning to congest with the coming noontime rush, and he steered the car toward home. He wasn't going back to the office and he wanted to look at the pictures from Voloshin's apartment, then figure out if he could delete them from his email server.

We're over!

Jake tried to put Pam's voice out of his mind, but couldn't. He looked through the windshield at the traffic light, but all he saw was her tears. His fingers curled around the plastic steering wheel, but all he could feel was the warmth of her hand under his palm. He had taken that touch for granted. He was trying to wrap his mind around the fact that she had cheated on him, but now it was beginning to sink in that she could really be in love with Dave, and that he had lost his wife forever.

A horn blared behind him, and Jake came out of his reverie, checking the rearview mirror. A massive construction truck was flashing its lights for him to move out of the fast lane. He hit the gas, powered through a yellow light, and reached for his phone, pressing the buttons on-the-fly to call the office.

"Hey, how are you doing?" Amy picked up instantly.

"I'm fine, thanks. Amy, I'm not going to be back to the office for a couple of hours. Can you deal?"

"Totally." Amy paused. "But what's going on? You seem so—"

"I thought I'd work at home. I got nothing done this morning and I don't need any more interruptions."

"Is there anything I can do?"

"Hold the fort and I'll give you a call as soon as I know what my schedule is. Take care."

Jake turned left off of Concordia Boulevard, got home in no time, and hit the house running, letting the door slam closed behind him. Moose waddled out of the kitchen, his fluffy tail wagging slowly.

"Hey buddy," Jake called to the dog, then hurried up the stairs, taking them two at a time, his tie flying. He reached the second-floor landing, slid out of his jacket, and hurried into his home office, where he tossed his jacket onto the couch, plopped down in his desk chair, and hit the mouse to power up his computer.

He opened his email, watched his incoming pile onto the screen, and scanned the countless client emails for Pam's name. Moose trundled into the office, panting from the effort of going up the stairs, in his characteristic *huh-huh-huh.* The golden lumbered over to the desk, and Jake palmed his big head before the dog could start his nudging routine.

Jake found Pam's email, scrolled to the attachments, and clicked OPEN. There was a list of ten photos and he opened the first one. The photo must have been taken from the door to the apartment, and it showed scenes of a tiny galley kitchen next to a small living room, with an old black futon and a wooden coffee table. There was no other furniture in the room, nor were there any books or newspapers. Two windows on the far wall had broken blinds and between them, oddly, was a poster series of tennis player Anna Kornikova.

Jake opened the next few photos, scenes of Voloshin's apartment, messy and nondescript. The following few photos were of a massive black monitor affixed to the wall and surrounded by a floor-to-ceiling entertainment center, also in black, with plastic video games shoved every which way in its crammed shelves. There was a photo of large black speakers and consoles that lined the top shelf, mixed with an array of weird pornographic figurines.

Jake shuddered. He opened the next photo, which was of a black laminate desk cluttered with Red Bull cans, cellophane Tastykake wrappers, and bags with multicolored Skittles strewn amid a dark tangle of joysticks, headsets with microphones, controllers, wires, a mouse, and a large silver laptop.

Jake eyed the laptop, wondering if it had contained the pictures of him and Ryan on Pike Road. Either way, he assumed the killer had taken the laptop. The right edge of the photograph showed a doorjamb that must have led to a bedroom, but that wasn't what caught Jake's eye. What he noticed was the brownish cork edge of a bulletin board on the wall, which must've been the one that Pam mentioned.

Jake clicked open the next photograph and sat back in his seat, trying to absorb the shock. It showed the bulletin board full of curling photos of Kathleen, which looked like they had been printed from the computer; Kathleen at work, company picnics, and softball games, hitting the ball, eating a chili hot dog, or smiling with her arm around her mother, who sported an identical grin. Jake cringed at one of the mother-daughter photos, in which both Kathleen and her mother were wearing matching bunny ears.

"I'm so sorry," he heard himself say, realizing he said it aloud only because Moose nudged his leg. Jake could never begin to imagine the depths of that mother's pain at losing her daughter, and he knew he could never forgive himself for his responsibility for Kathleen's death. Everything that had happened since the hit-and-run followed as inevitably as one domino knocking down another, except that the dominoes were the people he loved the most in the world and the mess was their life as a family.

Jake told himself to get a grip. He scanned the photos again to see if he'd missed anything, but he hadn't. It only confirmed that Voloshin had a crush on Kathleen and that both mother and daughter trusted him as a friend, or they never would've posed for the pictures.

Jake clicked on the last attachment and opened the photo. It showed the left-hand side of the bulletin board, and oddly, it was different from the right-hand side. The pictures were darker, printouts of photos taken at night, and they showed Kathleen running alone or with the track team down Pike Road. In the background was the corporate center and the road that came off of Pike, Dolomite Road. A few of them had thumbtacks in the corner and photos underneath, as if they were a series. One of the photos was taken at twilight in the summertime, with the girls running back toward the school in sweaty Chasers singlets and skimpy shorts, a sight that must've given Voloshin quite a thrill.

Jake noticed two photos on the far right, mostly hidden under the others. They had also been taken at nightfall, but there were no runners in the foreground; one had a woman with a ponytail getting into the passenger side of a dark car parked along the brush on Dolomite Road, its back bumper facing out. The second photo showed two figures sitting in the same car, the driver taller than the woman with the ponytail, more the height of a man. Their heads bent together as if they were kissing, indistinct silhouettes in the front seat.

Jake didn't get it. He moved the mouse and clicked on the photo to enlarge it, but couldn't see the people in the car, whose backs were to him. He squinted at the license plate, which was a Pennsylvania plate, and he could make out only the first three letters, HKE, and none of the digits. A red plastic thumbtack in the corner of the photo suggested, as before, that it was one of the series, but it got Jake wondering.

Who were the people in the photo?

He thought about it, and tried to reason it out. This was a bulletin board about Kathleen, so if Kathleen wasn't one of the people in the car, that would be the only photo *not* of her. So did it mean that Kathleen was meeting a man in a car? Jake enlarged the photo on the screen, trying to read the rest of the license plate, but he couldn't. He scrutinized the silhouette of the man, but couldn't see anything other than he was in the driver's seat and seemed to be of average height and build.

Jake squinted at the car, which looked long enough to be a four-door sedan of some type, and it was navy blue or black because it blended with the background. He enlarged it further, and after a few clicks, was able to read some chrome lettering on the upper left side of its trunk—535.

It was a BMW.

Jake thought about deleting the photos, but hesitated. He was already planning his next move.

Chapter Thirty-eight

Jake turned left onto Pike Road, approaching it from the opposite direction than he had the night of the hit-and-run, when Ryan was driving. There was no car on the street, which ran single lanes in both directions, and no police, runners, or dog-walkers were in sight. His dashboard clock read 1:30, so he was assuming that most of the employees at the corporate center had already gone back to work, and there were no students out yet because school was still in session.

Jake decreased his speed short of the blind curve ahead, with its makeshift memorial. The flowers, candles, and sympathy cards sat in a forlorn pile by the side of the road, and he felt a familiar tightness in his chest at the sight, but he pressed his emotions away. It was strange and risky to return to the scene of the crime, but he wanted to see if he could figure out what Voloshin had been up to, as well as the identity of the people in the BMW sedan.

Jake braked, getting the lay of the land. The blind curve was probably five hundred feet up ahead, then Pike Road jogged to the right, then the left and continued straight. Dolomite Road ran perpendicular to Pike Road, about a hundred feet down from the blind curve, and from where he sat, he could see the corner of Dolomite and Pike Roads. He couldn't see beyond that, farther down on Dolomite Road, because he was at too oblique an angle.

He picked up his iPhone from the passenger seat, scrolled to the camera roll, and retrieved the photo of the sedan from the bulletin board, which he'd enlarged before he left the house. The picture was too dark and unfocused to reveal anything going on inside the sedan, but it did show the sedan's location and orientation on Dolomite Road, which was all Jake needed.

He drew an imaginary line from the back of the sedan, across Pike Road, and into the brush on the left side of the road, working on the assumption that its trajectory would point to Voloshin's location when he took the photo. The only thing on the left side of the road was overgrowth and trees, but he had a theory to test and there was only one way to find out if he was right.

Jake took one last quick look around, turned off the engine, slid the keys out of the ignition, and got out of the car. He reached the undergrowth in four feet, then started making his way through the brush, using his arms to shove aside branches and tangled vines. He worked as quickly as possible because he didn't want to draw any attention to himself. He began to sweat, wishing he'd brought pruning shears.

Jake powered steadily forward, walking a straight line by orienting himself by one of the apartment buildings in the distance, a sandstone low-rise that he kept ahead of him, like the North Star. Twigs snapped under his shoes, and nettles clung to his pants. He consulted the iPhone picture and the sandstone apartments as he kept moving through a grove of evergreens that had grown together in natural tangle.

He passed one tree and behind it found a large area where the grass had been flattened, but it was a large circle, made by resting deer. He kept going, sensing that if he didn't find any-thing soon, he'd missed his guess. He fought his way around ivy that clung to one of the evergreens, and suddenly came upon another flat area, but this one had clearly been man-made. Tree limbs had been pruned back, and sucker vines had been cut. The undergrowth had been flattened but the area wasn't a large circle like deer made. He stood in the middle of the flat area, turned around with his back to the sandstone building, and faced Dolomite Road.

Bingo.

Jake felt his heartbeat quicken. There was a raggedy break through the trees, all the way to the blind curve and to a sec-tion of Dolomite Road. If Voloshin had stood in this spot, he would have had a perfect view—the same view as the photos of Ryan and him that had been taken, exactly where the hit-and-run accident occurred.

Jake's stomach twisted. Voloshin had aimed his camera as if it were a rifle and he'd managed to catch Ryan, Jake, and now, Pam in his crosshairs. And the evergreens would have screened Voloshin from view, and the little pervert would also have been free to spy on Kathleen and photograph her whenever he wanted, especially if he knew her schedule and worked from home often enough that he didn't have to account to the office for his time. Voloshin had set himself up like a hunter in a blind, wait-ing for the girls to run by.

Jake looked down, and a few white berries caught his eye, oddly bright in the brownish underbrush. He bent down, moved the undergrowth aside, and picked up the berries, examining them. They weren't berries at all. He flashed on the photo of Voloshin's desk, with its bags of Skittles. The white berries were candy, their coating washed away by the rain, probably dropped by Voloshin during one of his stalker sessions.

Jake hurried back the same way he came, keeping the sand-stone apartment building directly behind him, moving tree limbs and vines out of his path until he reached the edge of the woods. He stalked through the grass at the edge of Pike Road, hustled to his car, jumped inside, and started the engine. Luckily, there was still no one on the street.

He hit the gas and cruised forward, approaching the blind curve. He glanced over at the memorial as he passed it, sending up a silent prayer for Kathleen, then took a right. His destination was Dolomite Road and it lay just ahead, at a ninety degree angle to Pike. He turned right onto Dolomite, orienting himself, slowing his speed and taking in the surroundings.

The street was quiet and still, with no cars or foot traffic. On its left side was the parking lot that surrounded Concordia Corporate Center, which was screened from the street by thick landscaped hedges and zigzagging evergreens. On the right side of the street were more overgrown woods and trees, the parcel evidently unused.

Jake drove down the street and noticed that the left side of the street stayed the same, with the thick landscaped greenery that screened the corporate center, but on the right side, the woods stooped for a clearing of a few homes, newish clapboard colonials, one of which had a FOR SALE sign out front. He drove to the end of the street, which veered left and led to one of the remote parking lots of the corporate center, where a group of black Goren's Janitorial vans were parked.

Jake turned around and cruised back up Dolomite Road, heading toward Pike Road. He passed the houses on his left and slowed his speed when he got to the place where he thought the BMW sedan had been parked. He braked, cut the ignition, and got out of the car.

"Sir!" said a man's voice. "Stop right there! Sir!"

Jake froze. It had to be the police or security for the corporate center. He didn't see anyone. The voice came from beyond the hedges.

"What are you doing, sir? You hold on! Right there!"

"Okay, sure." Jake's mouth went dry, and there was a rustling in the evergreens and movement of the limbs as an older man emerged, dressed in an insulated purplish-blue jumpsuit, with a white patch that read CONCORDIA CORPORATE CENTER. His face was a network of wrinkles, his bifocals slid down his bony nose, and he was as lean and worn as the rake he carried.

"Where do you work, sir? You got the bulletin, didn't you? I was told all the tenants got the bulletin!"

"I don't work here." Jake crossed to his car door, but the old man held up a gnarled hand.

"There's no more parking back here! I don't know when you people are going to learn!"

"I wasn't parking here." Jake thought fast. "I was thinking about buying that house at the end of the street. Do people park here a lot? Is that a problem? If it is, I don't want to buy the house."

"Oh, beg pardon." The old man seemed to stand down, leaning on the rake. "You don't want to buy a house on this street, not unless you like a peep show. This is a lovers' lane, that's what we used to call it. Everybody comes here to park 'n spark."

"You mean from the high school?" Jake's ears perked up.

"Hell, no! I mean our tenants! From these businesses." The old man gestured back to the corporate center. "They got so many women working here now, and there's all kinda tomfoolery goes on here at lunch. You'd be surprised what I find in these bushes this time o' day! Cigarette butts, beer cans, *rubbers*! Disgusting! They have a *damn* good time in these cars! Every morning, too, from partyin' that goes on after work!"

"I bet." Jake opened his car door. "I'll be going now. I appreciate your giving me the information. It doesn't sound like a great place for the kids."

"No sir, no way! Nice talking to you. Bye now."

"Take care." Jake started the engine, steered down Dolomite, and turned right on Pike Road. He felt like he was getting closer to something, but he didn't know what. He assumed for a minute that it was Kathleen in the photograph of the BMW sedan, because if it hadn't been, Voloshin would have no reason to put it on his bulletin board with the other photographs of her. If Voloshin had been in his duck blind, watching Kathleen on one of her nighttime runs, he could have discovered that she wasn't running, but meeting someone on Dolomite Road.

Jake took a right turn, preoccupied. His theory made sense because it answered some of the questions he'd had earlier, like why was Kathleen running alone so late at night? Maybe it wasn't unusual for the track team, but what if Kathleen was using running as a pretense to get out of the house at night? What if she was going to Dolomite Road to meet someone, in a car? But who was she meeting? Someone whom Kathleen was keeping a secret, probably from her mother, if she was meeting him in a car.

Jake turned right and joined the traffic on Concordia Boulevard. Ahead lay the manicured main entrance to the corporate center, with its varietal grasses in mulched beds, around the brown sign that read CONCORDIA CORPORATE CENTER, HOME TO AMERICAN BUSINESS! Underneath that was a listing of corporate tenants; Brej Construction Management, Moxico, LLC, Valley Tech, SMS, Goren's Janitorial, Branson Hospitality Services, with a subhead that read FORTUNE'S 100 BEST COMPANIES TO WORK FOR! He scanned the list as he approached, thinking that the most likely person to know about the lovers' lane on Dolomite Road was someone who worked at one of these businesses. He reached the entrance and on impulse, turned right into its campus.

If he got lucky, he'd spot a dark BMW with an HKE license plate.

Chapter Thirty-nine

Jake cruised the parking lot and scanned a row that held a gray Toyota, a lemony VW Beetle, a white Acura, and an older brown Honda, his thoughts churning. If Voloshin had discovered that Kathleen was meeting a lover, he could have become jealous, even angry. What if Voloshin had tried to blackmail her lover, the way he tried to blackmail Jake? Voloshin could have threatened to tell the man's wife, if the man was married, or to tell Kathleen's mother, or even the authorities, because Kathleen was underage. The lover would be guilty of statutory rape if it came to light that he'd had sex with Kathleen.

Jake surveyed the parked cars, cruising past the bumper stickers and decals. MY CAT CAN BEAT UP YOUR HONOR STUDENT, a navy blue Nittany Lion, a white circle for Academy of Notre Dame de Namur, an oval 13.1 decal, and a puzzle piece for Autism Awareness. He didn't see the BMW yet, and his head was full of questions. What if Voloshin had tried to blackmail the BMW driver, but unlike Jake, the man hadn't come up with blackmail money? Or what if the man in the BMW had been the one who murdered Voloshin?

Jake's fingers clenched around the steering wheel, and he drove down one line of parked cars, then the other. The police would have seen the bulletin board in Voloshin's apartment, unless the killer took it. He assumed for a moment that the killer took the bulletin board, along with the laptop and phone, then he rejected that as highly unlikely. If the killer were a burglar, no burglar would take a bulletin board, and it would attract attention to be hurrying from the apartment with a large, unwieldy bulletin board.

Jake spotted BMWs, but they were the wrong color, too, so he drove on, mentally testing his theory. The killer could have gotten away with taking only the photo of the sedan parked on Dolomite Road, but that was unlikely too. The photo was half-hidden and someone who committed murder would be in a hurry to escape. Jake drove preoccupied past USPS mailboxes, FedEx, DHL, and UPS drop-offs, and the endless signage that replaced trees; THIS IS A TOBACCO FREE WORKPLACE, SPEED LIMIT 10, UNAUTHORIZED VEHICLES TOWED AT OWNER'S EXPENSE, ADDITIONAL PARKING ON OTHER SIDE OF BUILDING, ALL VISITORS PLEASE CHECK IN AT 200 CONCORDIA PARKWAY.

Jake navigated to another section of the parking lot and surveyed the cars, but they seemed to recede into the background as he realized something awful. If the killer looked inside Voloshin's computer and phone, then he would know what actually happened the night of the accident on Pike Road, that he and Ryan were responsible for Kathleen's death. And the killer would also know that Jake was being blackmailed, too. The police had said that they had seen evidence that Voloshin was setting up an offshore account.

Jake felt a new tingle of fear, and another set of questions rushed at him. If the killer had feelings for Kathleen, he could want revenge on those responsible for her death. What if the killer decided to come after Ryan? Or him, or Pam? Jake had to find out who killed Voloshin, so he could protect his family.

His troubles weren't over with Voloshin's death, they were just beginning. Whoever the killer was, he was a lot more dangerous than Voloshin.

Jake headed down another aisle of cars and checked each one, redoubling his efforts. Who was the killer? How did Kathleen find him? If her mother didn't know about him, did any of her friends? How could such a nice young girl be mixed up with somebody ruthless enough to stab a man to death? Suddenly his phone started ringing, and he checked the screen. It was Pam calling, and he picked up. "Yes?"

"Listen, I don't have much time. We're on break during oral arguments." Pam's tone was clipped and professional. "I just spoke with Ryan. He called me."

"Okay, what's up?" Jake sensed Pam was telling him that Ryan called her, not him, as if they still were playing tug-of-war with their son.

"There's a memorial program tonight at school for Kathleen. The team is going, and he has to go with them."

"Oh no." Jake pulled over and parked, so he could focus. "That'll be tough for him. Can't he get out of it? Can't we say he got sick again?"

"No. He has to go. We have to go, too. He'll need the support. You have to leave work early. The program starts at six thirty."

"Okay, fine." Jake didn't bother explaining that he wasn't at work. "But honey, listen, we have to settle this. I can't move out now. You have to let me stay home."

"No I don't. Get a hotel room. No one has to know. We'll keep it a secret. You're good at that."

"Pam, I don't think you and Ryan should be alone in the house right now. It's not safe."

"You're just saying that because you don't want to break up."

"That's not true. I'm saying it because you could be in danger. So could we all. The more I think about it, the more I worry that whoever killed Voloshin could come after us—"

"I thought you were worried about the police. Now a murderer's coming after me? What is this, scare tactics?"

"No. It could happen, babe. I looked at those pictures you took and I figured out that Kathleen was meeting someone in secret. I'm thinking he's the guy who killed Voloshin—"

"So what are you saying? I need a bodyguard?"

Jake hadn't gotten that far in his thinking. "You might—"

"Oh, great! Of course we can't go to the police, or Ryan goes to jail. My son goes to jail!"

"That won't happen."

"What do we do then? Got any ideas?"

"We can talk about it tonight. I need you to be careful. Keep an eye out when you're driving or when you—"

"Jake, if you're trying to scare me into staying in this marriage, it won't work. You don't understand the damage you've done. You don't get it."

"We can fix it. I can fix it."

"No we can't," Pam shot back. "I didn't go outside the marriage because I wanted to, I went out because I had to. I'm not proud of it, but it is what it is. And we gave it a shot, which you totally destroyed. I'm making myself crazy, going over it and over it in my head. If we had broken up, you wouldn't have been in the car Friday night with Ryan. None of this would have happened."

"You can't think that way. You don't know that—"

"Yes, I do. Get your head out of the sand, Jake. It's over. It has to be. We can't go back, we just can't. I can't. I'm *done*. I can't forgive you, ever. I want a divorce."

"Babe, listen, I love you, and no matter what problems we're having, we have to get through this together. Even tonight, we have to put up a united front, for Ryan's sake."

"You're saying that for you, not for him."

"No, I'm not. You know this is killing him, and we have to

make sure he keeps it together. He's cutting classes, getting high, messing up in basketball. God knows what he could do next. He needs us both—"

"You're shameless! Since when are you so sensitive to our son? Since he started taking your side? Since he decided *I'm* the bad guy?"

Jake told himself to remain calm. "Pam, you said you don't have time to talk, so let's not waste time fighting."

"It's so unfair to me, Jake!" Pam raised her voice. "This is unfair to me *and* him! You're the one who put us in this impossible situation! You're the one who told him it was okay to drive in the first place!"

"We've been over this—"

"But somehow, I'm the one who's a murder suspect, and now, a *target*! That girl would be alive if not for you!"

Jake felt the truth in her words, and her contempt for him, like a knife to the chest. "I know that, believe me, I know that every minute. But as far as we go, you and me, please just let me live at home, at least for the foreseeable future."

"Damn you! Damn you for doing this! You're putting me in a corner!"

"No, I'm trying to make the best of it. We have to stay together. You want to kick me out later, fine, but for right now, let's agree to disagree."

"I'll be *damned* if I'll pretend that everything is fine!"

"You don't have to."

"You're damn right I don't! This is awful, Jake, all the way down—"

"I know that—"

"It's awful and it's all your fault. Now you're telling me we're in *danger* and all of it is *your fault*!"

"Honey, I'm sorry, I've said it a thousand times, and I mean it—"

"Wait, hold on." Pam lowered her voice, as if someone had come into the room. "See you at home by six fifteen. Don't be late."

"Okay, bye," Jake said, but Pam had already hung up.

Chapter Forty

The sky was beginning to darken, and an early chill came on. Jake had searched the parking lot at the corporate center over an hour, with no luck. He'd found three black BMWs, but one had a New Jersey license plate and none had a plate with HKE. It was still his theory that the killer worked at the corporate center, though he kept it open as a possibility that the killer worked elsewhere and used Dolomite Road to park, finding it on his own.

Jake parked in his driveway and walked to his front door, glancing over his shoulder to make sure he hadn't been followed by the detectives or anyone else. Nothing on their street was amiss, and there were no cars he didn't recognize. The houses stood quiet because nobody was home from work yet.

Jake unlocked the door and let himself in, but Moose didn't greet him. He stopped, feeling a glimmer of worry, but heard voices talking in the kitchen and one of them was Ryan's. "Ryan?" Jake called out, puzzled. "You're home?"

"Hey, Dad! We're in the kitchen!"

We? "Hi! Be right in." Jake tossed his keys on the console table and slid out of his jacket, noting that his sleeve had tiny tears from the thornbushes. He set the jacket on the chair and walked to the kitchen, where Ryan was sitting at the table with a girl Jake didn't know. Soda cans, an open bag of hard pretzels, and crumpled napkins covered the table, next to an open laptop and two stuffed backpacks. Moose sat next to Ryan's chair, sniffing the pretzel bag, his tongue lolling out of his mouth.

"Dad, this is Sabrina, from the track team." Ryan flushed, gesturing at the girl, who looked tall and wiry, and her long, dark red hair was tied back in a floppy double ponytail. She had on a gray dress, whose short sleeves showed the ripped arms of a runner. Her eyes were grayish, and tiny freckles dotted her largish nose and cheekbones, which were pronounced, even a little gaunt, like someone with zero body fat.

"Hey, Mr. Buckman." Sabrina half-smiled, showing a row of Invisalign braces. "Nice to meet you."

"Hi, Sabrina." Jake crossed to the refrigerator, opened the door, and slid out a can of Diet Coke. He wished he could talk to Ryan alone and see how he was doing, because he seemed subdued and disheveled, with his bangs in his eyes and his blue polo shirt wrinkled.

"Dad, did Mom tell you about the memorial assembly tonight for Kathleen Lindstrom?"

"Yes, that's why I'm home early. How was school?" Jake avoided Ryan's eye while the awkward moment passed. He had no idea how his son would get through such a difficult evening, knowing what they had done and having to put on a false face for all of his classmates.

"Fine, good." Ryan met his eye briefly, then looked away.

"What happened to practice?" Jake leaned against the counter. He didn't like the fact that Ryan was alone in the house, with God-knows-who watching.

"They canceled it because of the assembly tonight. The whole athletic department's going."

"I see. How did you get home?"

"Sabrina's mom dropped us off. We can take her to school with us, after Mom gets home. That's okay, right?" Ryan's expression looked guarded, and Jake knew he was giving him the heads-up.

"Sure, great. So what are you guys doing? Homework?"

"No," Ryan answered. "Sabrina has to give a speech tonight at the assembly, and I'm helping her. Rather, I'm supposed to be helping her, but we're not doing so great."

"I'm sure you're helping." Jake cringed inwardly, on Ryan's behalf.

Sabrina frowned at the laptop, tucking a strand of long red hair behind her ear. "I suck at writing. I freeze up. Ryan's one of the best writers in the class, that's why I asked him to help me. I don't know how to do this, especially this, like, a eulogy. It's too hard."

Jake felt a stab of guilt. "I'm sorry about your loss. Was Kathleen a good friend of yours?"

"Not really, because she just came this year, so it wasn't like I had that much time to get to know her. I'm team captain, and Coach wants me to do it . . ." Sabrina faltered. "I just can't believe Kathleen's really gone. It's so . . . weird."

Ryan looked away.

Jake nodded, pained. "I'm sure it's difficult. I know."

Sabrina kept shaking her head. "I'm supposed to give this speech, but I don't know what to say and I don't want to say the wrong thing. I can't speak in front of all of those people. Kathleen's mom is going to be there and her father, and my parents and everybody in the school will be there, waiting for me to say something, and I mean, *everything* I write sounds lame." Sabrina deflated, and her gaze returned to the laptop. "But I still have to write this speech, and I don't know what to say. I don't have that much time left and what I wrote so far really sucks."

"No, it doesn't." Ryan motioned at the laptop. "You have a good start."

"Argh." Sabrina moaned. "No I don't, and Coach said it has to be, like, three hundred words. I only have forty words so far, and I worked on it the entire study hall. I can't do it. Mr. Buckman, can you help?"

"Sure." Jake faked an encouraging smile.

"I'll read you what I have so far." Sabrina hunched over the laptop. "First, and this doesn't count for the words, I have to introduce myself and say thank you to everyone for coming, like to the faculty and families. Right?"

"Right."

"Okay. Then, I say," Sabrina read from the laptop, " 'The Lady Chasers and Concord Chase High School in general suffered an extremely tragic loss when Kathleen Lindstrom was killed last Friday night in a horrible hit-and-run accident. Everybody loved Kathleen, who was friendly, outgoing, an asset to our team, a great hurdler, and fun to be with.'" She looked up. "Mr. Buckman, what do you think?"

"That's a great start." Jake was trying to say something helpful, but the words practically lodged in his throat. "Keep going."

"But I don't know what to write next. I'm sucking. I can't do this." Sabrina buckled her lower lip. "It's so horrible that she died and it's even worse that the guy didn't even stop and see if she was okay. People like that should be *shot*. I should say that, I should give a speech about *that*."

"No, just keep going. You can do it. Write what you feel."

"I *can't* write what I feel. I feel sad and weirded out, that's all. We all are, so *sad*. I don't know how we'll run without her. We'll lose to Methacton for sure. Nobody wants to run. I think we should cancel the meet. We just cry, like, all the time. Her wake is tomorrow, and we're going in uniform, like a tribute to her."

Jake felt terrible and he knew Ryan did, too. "Then write about Kathleen. Write about what she was like, as a person."

"That's what I tried to do, but I can't." Sabrina sighed again. "That's why I said she was friendly and nice and everything, but I didn't know her that well, and we weren't that friendly, then she got tight with Courtney and Sarah and Janine Mae. I'm not good at giving speeches, anyway. I can't do this. I should've told Coach that I can't do it and it's really too important and I'm failing at it, epically."

Ryan shook his head. "No, you're not. You're doing fine."

"I'm not, I *suck out loud*! I'm going to let everyone *down*!"

Ryan shrugged. "Why don't you tell a story about her? Sometimes if you tell a story about somebody, that tells the audience something about them. Like we studied about in *The Great Gatsby*. People tell stories about Gatsby before you even meet him."

"Great idea," Jake said, grateful. "It will cheer them up, too."

"Och." Sabrina dropped her chin into her palm. "There's a lot of stories about her, but I don't know if they're good enough to tell."

"Like what?" Ryan asked, swallowing visibly.

"Like she really liked to sing on the bus, and she had a good voice, but that's not good enough." Sabrina cocked her head. "Well, also, she was superhot and all the guys on the boys' team really liked her, but that's not a good story to tell at something like this, either. Right, Ryan?" Sabrina turned to him, knitting her forehead. "Like remember when Sam and Caleb, they both asked her to the Halloween dance? That's not a good story, is it?"

"No." Ryan flushed.

Jake stepped in to rescue him. "Sabrina, I think Ryan means you should tell a story about her, about something she did."

"Oh, right. Totally." Sabrina thought a moment. "She was really good with computer graphics, and she made an awesome website for the travel track team. It had animated gifs and everything." Sabrina brightened, straightening in her chair. "In fact, oh, I have a good story, a better one. There was the time she raised the money to buy shirts for the travel team, that's a good story. We all had the same singlets, but our gym bags and

T-shirts didn't match. We never looked as good as the other travel teams, like Great Valley always looked awesome. They even had matching scrunchies, blue-and-white."

Ryan nodded, with a shaky smile. "Good. Then tell that."

"But that's not the story. Your dad said tell a story about her, like something she did. That doesn't tell what she did. I didn't get to that part yet."

"Okay." Ryan pursed his lips, and Jake could see that was the last thing he wanted to know. He prayed Ryan could get through tonight and the next few weeks. Jake would never forgive himself if Ryan tried to hurt himself. He'd quit Gardenia and go on twenty-four-hour suicide watch, if that's what it took.

"Anyway, Kathleen got everybody together and she got this idea where we would stuff envelopes for free to get the money for the T-shirts, and we all worked together and we had the money in, like, four weekends, all because of her." Sabrina brightened. "And the coolest thing was that we all had fun, like we weren't doing another stupid bake sale or standing out in front of the Acme, begging for money in front of an oaktag sign, like we were Brownies or something. It was like we worked for our T-shirts, all of us together, the way a team should be. It was a really different idea and she thought it up herself." Sabrina stopped abruptly, her smile fading. "Except she won't even get to see the gym bags. They didn't come in yet. We got the T-shirts and the scrunchies, but the gym bags take longer. She'll never get to see them . . . now."

Ryan paled. He didn't say anything, and neither did Jake. The only sound in the kitchen was the *huh-huh-huh* of Moose's panting.

Sabrina looked over at Ryan, her eyes shining. "Ryan, what do you think? Is that a good enough story?"

Ryan sighed heavily, but couldn't even muster up a smile. "It's great, Sabrina. Just great."

Chapter Forty-one

Night fell hard and cold, and White Springs Road was congested with stop-and-go traffic, heading to the high school for the memorial service. Jake sat in the passenger seat, tense, while Pam drove them in silence. They'd exchanged pleasantries for show at home, putting up a false front for the kids, and she'd freshened up, drained a cup of coffee, and changed her shoes. She drove without looking at him, sitting ramrod-straight, her eyes fixed on the road.

We can't go back, we just can't. I can't. I'm done. I can't forgive you, ever.

It hurt Jake to be so close to her, in the familiar intimacy of her car, while she walled him off. He knew that she had to be dreading going to the service tonight, and she felt all the guilt and shame he did, but with an overlay of anger and resentment. He wished he could comfort her, but he was the cause of her pain. Their coats touched, but they couldn't. He could smell her perfume, but he couldn't kiss her. He was married to her, but she wanted a divorce. She had slept with someone else, maybe even last night. He felt heartbroken and furious, both at once.

The kids rode in the backseat, their heads bent over their iPhones and their ears plugged with earbuds. Ryan didn't text at all, but listened to music, and Sabrina rehearsed her speech, whispering to herself like a nightmare voiceover, ". . . a tragic loss for the track team and the Concord Chase High School community as a whole . . ."

They stopped behind a long line of cars, plumes of exhaust floating into the air like ghosts. Jake tried to tune Sabrina out, but wasn't succeeding. She was whispering, ". . . and she had so many talents and hobbies, for example, she was excellent with computer graphics and made a super-professional website for . . ."

They were almost at the high school, which was just around the corner. A dark van inched beside them in the right lane, and Jake looked over. Inside the van was a couple just like them, except the man was driving. A younger kid played a handheld video game in the backseat, his face wreathed in eerie green-blue light. Jake had checked every passing car to make sure it wasn't the dark BMW, the detectives, or otherwise suspicious.

The traffic eased, and Pam steered right around the corner onto Racton Hill Road. Flashing police lights sliced through the black night, from cruisers out in force, parked on the curb. Cops grouped on the sidewalk, and Jake realized that they were just directing traffic to the high school. One motioned the cars to keep moving, waving a flashlight with an orange cone.

Jake thought of the detectives and worried if they would interview him again. Would they just drop in or call first? Did he need a lawyer? Did Ryan? Should he call Hubbard? Jake hadn't gotten a chance to talk to Pam alone yet. She would get a lawyer, probably a separate one from him and Ryan. And she'd get a divorce lawyer, too.

"We're late," Pam muttered under her breath.

They were only at the middle school, and Jake could see the high school ahead on the left, a long, two-story box of red brick, its continuous panels of windows ablaze with light. "Not very."

"That's not the point. Late is late."

"So will everybody else be, in this traffic."

"Again. Not the point."

Jake let it go. He was trying to make it better, but that was impossible. They were going to the memorial service for a young girl they had killed, and they were ruined, guilty, and afraid. A corrupt family, bound by a secret crime. Bankrupt, despite the money they had. Nothing could be made better.

The traffic eased, and the car began to move forward. Pam exhaled. "Finally."

Jake didn't say anything. He could hear Sabrina whispering, like a prayer, ". . . Kathleen was an extreme loss for the Concord Chase High School community in its entirety . . ."

"How'd your Western Civ make-up go, Ryan?" Pam asked, tilting her mouth up as if she were talking to the rearview mirror.

"Fine," Ryan answered, after a moment.

"How do you think you did?"

"Fine."

"Really?" Pam arched an eyebrow, edging up in the driver's seat.

"What, did you look on the Parent Portal?"

"Yes. Did you?"

"No. He graded my test already?"

"Yes."

"What did I get, Mom?"

"Don't worry about it. You'll do better next time."

Ryan didn't reply.

Sabrina whispered, ". . . Speaking as the captain of the track team, I can assure you that Kathleen will be sorely missed by every . . ."

Jake turned to Ryan, who looked crestfallen. "Don't sweat it, buddy."

Ryan didn't say anything to him, either.

Jake turned back around, pained. He didn't want to think about what would happen to Ryan if he and Pam divorced. His son was already depressed and guilt-ridden. It wouldn't help that he'd ping-pong back and forth between their houses. Jake would become a weekend father, if that. Everything had gone to shit because of his decision on Pike Road. In trying to be a good father, he'd been a terrible father. In trying to save his son, he'd destroyed him. He'd driven his wife away. He'd lost everything.

Story of my life.

Sabrina said, ". . . there are so many cool stories about Kathleen, like that she sang the loudest on the bus, and that everyone on the guys team wanted to take her out, but there is one main story I know that will tell the audience about her . . ."

Jake felt his chest tighten as they reached the lighted brick CONCORD CHASE HIGH SCHOOL sign and turned into the entrance, where another cop directed them to keep moving toward the back, behind the school.

"Damn." Pam sighed. "They're sending us to the lot by the tennis courts. It'll be a long walk." She shifted up to the rearview mirror, slowing the car. "Ryan, Sabrina? You guys want to get out here, since we're running late?"

"No," Ryan answered, after a moment.

"But honey, you won't get a seat."

"The team will save me one."

Sabrina said, "I'll stay. I'm good."

"Okay." Pam fed the car some gas, and they approached the entrance doors on the right, then they stopped again in the line of traffic. A thick crowd thronged under the lighted canopy that covered the entrance doors, and at the perimeter, a TV news crew filmed a pretty anchorwoman raising a bubble microphone to a tall, well-dressed man with dark hair, talking in the bright white klieglights.

Pam snorted. "I can't believe TV people are here. They're

vultures. Have they no shame? Does the world really need another man-on-the-street interview?"

Jake felt his heart sink, on Ryan's behalf. He could see for himself that Kathleen's death shocked the entire school community, and he had underestimated how difficult this would be for Ryan. His son lived in this world and he'd have to deal with it, every day, all day at school. Jake glanced back to check on him again, but Ryan was looking pointedly away from the TV cameras.

Sabrina leaned forward. "Mrs. Buckman, the guy they're interviewing is Kathleen's dad. I saw his picture online, asking if the community could help him find who killed Kathleen."

"Poor man," Pam said quietly, and Jake realized that the only thing they shared tonight was guilt. He eyed Kathleen's father talking in the klieglights and realized he was just another father like him. Jake had taken that man's child, in trade for his own.

Pam drove along the road, which continued between the school on the right and the main parking lot on the left. She seemed distracted by something in the parking lot, and Jake craned his neck to see. It was Dr. Dave, getting out of a white Prius and chirping it locked. A woman in a black down coat stood with him, presumably his wife.

Jake gritted his teeth. She had a pretty face and a sweet smile, and her short brown hair ruffled in the wind. He wondered if she knew that she had been cheated on, or if she was as naïve as he had been. The couple left the parking lot and crossed the road with the crowd, right in front of their headlights.

Jake itched to get out and beat Dr. Dave to a pulp, but Dr. Dave walked straight ahead, acting as if he didn't recognize Pam's car. Jake looked over to see Pam's reaction, but she stared straight ahead, too. Just then he noticed a car in the parking lot, sitting a few rows back, to the right—it was a black BMW sedan, with an HKE license plate.

My God. "Pam, hold on, be right back," Jake blurted out, reaching for the door handle.

"No, Jake, please don't." Pam turned to him in alarm.

"It's not what you think." Jake flung open the door. "I see a client I need to talk to. See you inside."

"Wait a sec, there's a space," Pam said, but Jake was out the door, hitting the ground running.

Chapter Forty-two

Jake hurried through the parking lot, going against the crowd heading toward the school entrance. One of the mothers looked over at him curiously, so he slowed his pace as he made a beeline for the BMW. He didn't want to draw attention to himself. He hadn't thought about the possibility he'd see the BMW here, but he'd been focused on Ryan and Pam.

Jake threaded his way through the crowd, squeezed sideways between parked cars, and finally reached the BMW. It was the correct model, a 535, and its Pennsylvania plate read HKE-7553. It had to be the same car as the one in the photograph. His heartbeat quickened. So Voloshin's killer was at Kathleen's memorial service. It seemed risky, unless the killer was someone who would have been conspicuous by his absence, the way Ryan would have been if he hadn't come.

Jake glanced around and ascertained that no one was watching him, so he walked to the driver's side of the car and tried the door handle, but it was locked. He peeked inside the front seat. The car had a black interior and it was hard to see in the dark, but it looked empty and gave no clue as to the driver's identity. He peered in the backseat, but it was also empty. He walked around the trunk and checked for the car dealership, or anything to give him more information about the driver, but there wasn't one listed. The license plate had a chrome surround, but it read BMW, with no dealership.

Jake slipped his hand in his pocket, took out his phone, and snapped a picture of the car's license plate, then turned away and hurried back to the school entrance, adrenalized. So the BMW driver would be at the service tonight, and the more Jake thought about it, the more credibility it lent to his theory. The driver had known Kathleen, maybe even loved her, and he could have killed Voloshin because Voloshin was blackmailing him about their relationship—or maybe in a fit of rage, when he went to Voloshin's apartment and saw that Voloshin was stalking her.

Jake joined the crowd going into the entrance, turning his head away from the TV cameras and scrutinizing the people around him. The killer could be any one of the dads, who looked just like him—a moving mass of crow's-feet, expensive haircuts, and Patagonia jackets slipped over shirts and ties, because nobody had time to change after work. They tossed away forbidden cigarettes, checked their email, or talked on the phone, making their last calls.

Jake caught snippets of their conversations—*you have to be kidding me, Tom, you didn't file it yet?*—or with their wives—*I don't have time to call the roofer, can you?*—or their kids—*so how was school, buddy?* None of them sounded or seemed like a killer, which made Jake suspect all of them, everyone around him. Then he realized he wouldn't have to play guessing games anymore. He could leave the memorial service, stake-out the BMW, and see whoever came to claim the car.

Jake's heartbeat picked up, and he thought of a new plan. He would confront the killer and warn him to stay away from Ryan and Pam—or risk exposure to the police. It would be piling one corrupt bargain on top of another, but it would keep Pam and Ryan safe. He reached the entrance doors, went through, and crossed the threshold into a large, tiled entrance area leading to the administrative offices and the auditorium.

CHASER PRIDE, read a poster-painted banner, and the crowd flowed in two messy lines to the auditorium doors, which had been propped open. Suddenly it struck him that Pam and Ryan were here, unprotected. The killer would know who they were, but they wouldn't know who he was. The killer could be following Ryan or taking a seat next to Pam, this very minute.

Jake pressed forward, looking for Pam or Ryan, but he didn't see them anywhere. He didn't know if they'd gone inside, but assumed they had, knowing that Pam was in a hurry and she'd seen that parking space. He shifted to the right, went around a large family, and joined the other line into the auditorium, which was moving faster. Still, no Pam or Ryan.

Jake finally got inside the auditorium, which was standing room only in back, and wedged his way through the standees to find Pam and Ryan, but they weren't there. He scanned the audience for Pam and Ryan, but there were so many people it was impossible to see them. Faculty, staff, parents, and younger kids filled the seats, walked down rows, tilted their heads together in conversation, checked smartphones, opened programs, or hoisted toddlers onto their laps. Many of the female students were crying, their arms around each other. Mothers wiped tears from their eyes, and fathers craned their necks toward the front, where the program was beginning.

Jake defaulted to looking for Ryan because he was so tall and would be sitting with a very tall group, the basketball team. He began methodically, noticing that two aisles ran the length of the auditorium, dividing the seats into three sections. He checked the leftmost section for the basketball team, but no luck. He checked the middle section, but didn't see them there. He shifted to the rightmost section and finally spotted a tall bunch of scruffy boys on the far right section, at the middle.

He edged forward and looked for Ryan, but he wasn't sitting with the team and there was an empty seat at the end of the row. Jake swallowed hard, beginning to be afraid. What if Ryan and Pam were still outside? What if the killer had intercepted them on the way in? He didn't want to leave and go see until he was sure they weren't in the auditorium.

The crowd quieted, and Jake sensed the program was about to start. He glanced at the stage, a sleek maple curve framed by maroon curtains, and a middle-aged woman tapped a microphone on the lectern. Next to her were the flags of the United States and the Commonwealth of Pennsylvania, then a row of brown folding chairs with some students and school-administration types, and finally, an easel that held an enlarged photograph of Kathleen, framed in black.

Jake's throat caught, but he looked away. Then it struck him that the speakers were supposed to be seated on the stage and that Sabrina was slated to be a speaker. He looked again at the folding chairs, but Sabrina wasn't there. And one folding chair remained empty.

"Welcome, ladies and gentlemen, faculty, students and family. I am Pamela Coleridge, principal of Concord Chase High School, and I thank you for coming this evening to celebrate the life of Kathleen Lindstrom, a lovely young woman who was taken from us cruelly, and too soon . . ."

Jake tuned the speaker out, his heart thudding in his chest. The empty chair on stage was proof that Ryan and Pam must still be in the parking lot, unless Sabrina was sitting with her team.

". . . this program will be brief, and time won't permit us to acknowledge all of the special people here tonight, except that I would like to take a moment to acknowledge Kathleen's mother Grace and her father William, both of whom are with us, at this impossibly difficult time. They're seated in the front row . . ."

Heads turned this way and that as everybody tried to see Kathleen's parents, and murmurs and sniffles rippled through the crowd. Jake tried to find the girls track team, but there was nothing to distinguish them from any other female students.

". . . our first speaker will be Ms. Talia Kelso, who teaches computer science and runs our computer lab, which, as you may know, was Kathleen's home away from home. Ms. Kelso, please come up . . ."

Jake noticed on the stage that one of the teachers, a petite African-American woman with a thick braid, was getting up from the folding chair and crossing to the lectern. He had to find Ryan and Pam, or Sabrina, so he kept scanning the crowd. He surveyed the rows for them, getting more worried by the minute, as the speaker continued her speech.

". . . Kathleen had a remarkable aptitude with computers, but it was her happy, upbeat way that all of us loved. I will never forget Kathleen and neither will any of my teaching assistants in the computer lab. Thank you, and now I would like to introduce our next speaker, Janine Mae Lamb, a junior who was a very good friend of Kathleen. Janine Mae?"

Jake paused, recognizing the name of the girl that Ryan had wanted to date before the accident. He watched as a pretty, petite girl in a black dress rose uncertainly on stage and walked to the lectern with her head downcast, her long blonde hair obscuring her face. Ms. Kelso hovered behind the lectern as Janine Mae reached it and grasped its edges for support. When the young girl raised her eyes to the audience, Jake could tell, even from a distance, that she was crestfallen and already teary.

"Hi, everyone," Janine Mae said, her voice shaking, her drawl pained. "Kathleen's mom and dad, Mr. and Mrs. Lindstrom . . . I know how much you loved Kathleen . . . and I'm so sorry about your loss . . . and I wanted to, uh, speak about her tonight . . . I don't know if I can, but . . . I'll try . . . for her."

Jake swallowed hard, and the audience fell into an anguished silence, holding its collective breath at the rawness of the girl's grief.

"I'm up here because I just really want everyone to know Kathleen . . . the way I did." Janine Mae wiped her eyes with a small hand. "We met, uh, the first day of track, and since we were both new to Concord Chase . . . and, uh, neither of us knew anybody . . . we bonded, like, uh, instantly." Janine Mae sniffled, and her shoulders began to shake. "You never would have known that Kathleen was new . . . she was so friendly and open-hearted . . . and she trusted everyone. We only knew each other for a few months . . . but we really got super close . . . and . . . we told each other . . . everything." Janine burst into a sob, making a heartrending hiccup into the microphone. "Kathleen was my best friend . . . and now she's . . . she's gone . . . and I can't believe it . . ." Janine Mae broke down, and Ms. Kelso stepped forward, cradled the girl, and walked her offstage while the crowd murmured and sniffled anew.

Principal Coleridge hurried to the lectern, adjusting the microphone. "Thank you, Janine Mae, for your very heartfelt words. You said all that you needed to, and I know we all agree. Our next speaker is Christopher Slater, who is president of the Concord Chase Chamber of Commerce . . ."

A tall man in a suit rose and strode to the lectern, but Jake resumed looking for Pam, Ryan, or Sabrina. He migrated to the left to change his angle on the audience and get a view of the rightmost section, in front.

". . . I'm honored to be here tonight to speak about Kathleen," the speaker was saying. "I was so impressed with Kathleen when she came to my office on behalf of the travel track team. She was trying to raise money for new uniforms, but she didn't simply ask . . ."

Jake realized the speaker was telling the same story that Sabrina had told them, and tuned him out. He wedged his way through the crowd, excusing himself, and managed to get to the left side of the auditorium, which gave him a better view of the rightmost section. Still no luck.

". . . Kathleen proposed that the track team would work on the weekends, stuffing envelopes for the Chamber of Commerce, and donate their pay to the team itself. Kathleen further proposed that the Chamber should match the funds and sponsor the team . . ."

Jake couldn't wait another minute. Pam and Ryan weren't in the auditorium, and anything was possible. He made his way to the exit, squeezing through the standees.

". . . in a world where too many people expect things to be given to them, Kathleen was willing to sing for her supper. My wife and I have three young daughters, and we hope that they grow up to be as exemplary as she . . ."

Jake had reached the exit door when he noticed movement on the left side of the auditorium. A side door opened in the wall, and Pam ducked inside, followed by an obviously flustered Sabrina, then Ryan, who hung his head.

". . . I must say, I agreed with Kathleen on the spot, and my fellow Chamber members and I are proud to sponsor the team. My colleagues on the board and I are thrilled to see our name and logo on the team shirts, hats, and the gym bags . . ."

Jake exhaled with relief, feeling his every muscle relax. Pam and Ryan stopped and stood by the side door, leaning against the wall, and he knew they would be there for the program, safe and sound in plain view. Sabrina hurried down the aisle, climbed the steps to the stage, and scooted behind the speaker, who kept talking.

". . . I will never forget the times that Kathleen and her merry band of runners invaded my offices, to stuff envelopes for the Chamber of Commerce. We keep a very professional atmosphere, even on the weekends, but Kathleen brought her own brand of youthful energy to the place. She shook up even the staid Concordia Corporate Center . . ."

Jake's ears pricked up at the mention of Concordia Corporate Center, and he took a second look at the speaker, who was a handsome man, probably in his forties, with lanky blond hair. He wore a stylish dark suit, and his smooth, confident manner bespoke a born salesman. Jake wondered who he was and glanced at the open program of a woman near him. The program read, CHRIS SLATER, PRESIDENT, CONCORD CHASE CHAMBER OF COMMERCE; PRINCIPAL SHAREHOLDER, CS REAL ESTATE DEVELOPMENT, LLC.

". . . Kathleen came to the office many times, to get the job done, and I came to know her well. Of course, being a budding graphic designer, she told us what was wrong with our Chamber website, which you can imagine, didn't please my conservative old board very much . . ."

The audience smiled and sniffled, and Jake began to put two and two together. Slater was a charming, attractive, and successful man who knew Kathleen well, had met with her several times, and helped her find corporate sponsorship for the travel track team. A man like Slater would be catnip for a young girl, especially one who needed a father figure. And Slater's offices were in the Concordia Corporate Center, so he knew about Dolomite Road.

". . . I've gone on long enough, although in my own defense, I had been asked to stall to give our final speaker, Sabrina Moravia, a chance to arrive. So thank you for your attention tonight, and again, my wife and I, together with the Chamber of Commerce, offer our deepest sympathies to Kathleen's mother and father. We share your grief. Now, I will yield the floor . . ."

Slater flashed a charming smile, strode from the lectern, and sat down. Kathleen was a gorgeous young girl who could have tempted even the most married of men, and Jake got a hunch.

Maybe the killer wasn't in the audience, at all. Maybe the killer was on the stage.

Meanwhile, Sabrina took the lectern, gripped the sides, and cleared her throat. "I am the captain of the Concord Chase girls' track team, the Lady Chasers, and I thank you all for coming tonight . . ."

Jake tuned out her speech and mulled it over. Voloshin could have been stalking Kathleen, seen her and Slater together in the BMW when it was parked on Dolomite, then tried to blackmail Slater the same way he tried to blackmail Jake. Slater had a wife and kids, so he would have wanted to keep any relationship he had with Kathleen quiet, which made him a good target for blackmail. Plus Slater was obviously successful, so he had the money to pay. And Slater's motivation for killing Voloshin could have been that either he didn't want to pay the blackmail or he didn't trust Voloshin.

Sabrina was saying, "Mr. Slater told the same story about Kathleen that I was going to, but I can tell it from a different view, *her* view, which will tell you more about her. We were all so worried about going to his offices and meeting this important businessman, but Kathleen told us not to worry, that he was a normal guy and we should believe in ourselves . . ."

Jake began to feel as if his hunch was sound. All he had to do to verify it was get to the BMW before Slater did. He focused again on the stage, where Sabrina was finishing her speech. The principal was getting up from her seat to conclude the service, so it was time for Jake to go. He made his way to the back door, slipped into the empty entrance hall, and made a beeline for the exit.

"Jake, that you?" a voice called out behind him.

Jake turned around, and his mouth went dry. Standing in front of a display case with sports trophies was the last person he wanted to see.

Chapter Forty-three

"Jake!" It was Detective Zwerling, standing alone. He was in his dark suit with no overcoat. "What's your hurry? Trying to beat the traffic?"

Jake slowed his pace, busted. "No, I have to make a phone call."

"Good, I'll walk you out." Detective Zwerling hustled toward him, sliding his leather shoes on the tiled floor, then he fell into step, and they walked to the doors together. "So what brings you here?"

"You know, the memorial service." Jake told himself to remain calm. The service must have ended, because the crowd filed out of the auditorium doors and surged into the entrance hall, wiping tears, checking phones, and zipping coats.

"Did Ryan know Kathleen Lindstrom?"

"Pardon?" Jake asked, blindsided. He didn't remember mentioning Ryan's name to Detective Zwerling. "Uh, no, he didn't. He came with the basketball team."

"You came alone, with your son?"

"No, my wife came, too," Jake answered, hating to bring up

Pam. He didn't know if Detective Zwerling was making conversation or interrogating him, but it felt like the latter. They reached the doors, left the school, and stepped into the cold night air. Jake glanced toward the parking lot, but the BMW was too far away to see in the dark. The crowd flowed noisily around them, and he looked for Slater, but didn't see him. It would take longer for Slater to get out, since he'd been on the stage. At the fringe of the crowd, the TV klieglights flicked on and cast a pool of light onto the pretty reporter, who raised her microphone and started saying something that Jake couldn't hear.

"I'd like to meet your wife." Detective Zwerling half-smiled, his slack jowls draping the corners of his mouth like fleshy curtains. Close-up, his skin looked slightly greasy and he had a five o'clock shadow. "I understand she's a judge. Where is she?"

"She's still inside, undoubtedly talking. I wouldn't wait if I were you." Jake hadn't mentioned that Pam was a judge, so they *had* been investigating him. He prayed it would take her a while to get out of the auditorium, so Detective Zwerling couldn't see she was a brunette, much less *the* brunette. Then he wondered if Detective Zwerling knew that already.

"It's nice you both came."

"We wanted to show our respect for the family."

"How do you know them?"

"We don't. We came because of the school, the community. To show respect, generally." Jake tried not to sound nervous, but he kept saying the wrong things. The crowd filled the sidewalk, crossed the road to the parking lots, and scattered to their cars. He sneaked a glance at the lot for the BMW and at the crowd for Slater, but no luck. The TV reporter collared a passing mom for an interview, positioning her in the klieglights that filled the area under the canopy with artificial light.

"Sad case, isn't it?" Detective Zwerling reached into his breast pocket and pulled out a pack of Merits, with a blue Bic lighter stuck in the cellophane. "I hate to see those girls crying. They're just kids."

"Yes, it's very sad." Jake slid his phone from his pocket. "Excuse me, I'd better make that call—"

"You can't take a minute to talk? I'm starting to think you don't like me." Detective Zwerling made a mock-wounded face as he shook out a cigarette and palmed the lighter. "You like my partner better, don't you?"

"No, not at all." Jake forced a smile.

"Come on. Now I *know* you're a liar. Everybody likes Woohoo better." Detective Zwerling laughed abruptly, then plugged his mouth with the cigarette, which flopped around while he spoke. "Hell, so do I."

Jake forced another smile, tense. He scanned the crowd for Slater, who would be easy to spot, tall and blond. The BMW seemed to be in the same parking space, a dark line in the far section of the lot.

"I can't figure it, can you? What kind of person hits a young girl and doesn't even stop?"

"I have no idea." Jake felt guilt-stricken, but told himself not to let emotions get the better of him. The night echoed with the hoarse noise of engines starting, and white and red taillights flashed as cars left spaces in all sections of the lot.

"At first I thought the driver was a drunk." Detective Zwerling lit his cigarette and blew out a cone of acrid smoke. "Usually is."

"I bet." Jake had to shake Detective Zwerling but didn't know how.

"They turn themselves in after they sober up. First thing Monday morning, we get a call. They're lawyered up by then."

"Really." Jake glanced again at the section of the parking lot with the BMW, but still couldn't see it. Cars were leaving the lot where the BMW was parked, but he thought it was still there, in its dark line. Slater wasn't among the crowd, which kept spilling out of the school, so Jake still had a chance.

"We can't prove anything that late and they know it. Standard operating procedure for degenerates."

"That's terrible."

"But we didn't get any call yesterday morning. Still haven't. I checked. Lindstrom's not my case, but we're a small department." Detective Zwerling's hooded eyes watched Jake through the cigarette smoke. "Concord Chase is a small community. I didn't realize how small until today. After we saw you, we went to Mr. Voloshin's place of employment. He worked at a company called GreenTech. Did he mention that to you?"

"No." Jake felt a bolt of panic, but tried not to betray himself. More engines started, and headlights sliced through the darkness as cars swung onto the road leading to the exit.

"It turns out that Kathleen Lindstrom worked at Green-Tech, too. Part-time. Her mother got her the job. She's the web designer there. Are you sure Voloshin didn't mention it to you?"

"No, not at all." Jake swallowed hard. The crowd kept flowing to the parking lots, and the TV reporter moved closer and collared another parent to interview. The klieglights followed her, casting a bright halo that Jake couldn't see around. If Slater left the building and walked behind the lights, Jake could miss him.

"What's up, Jake? You looking for someone?"

"My wife and son, when they come out."

"Oh. As I was saying, the employees at GreenTech were all upset. It's like a one-two punch, if you think about it. Last week they lost Kathleen in the hit-and-run. Last night they lost Voloshin in the murder." Detective Zwerling spoke casually, as if he were thinking aloud. Cigarette smoke leaked from between his thin lips. "Quite a coincidence, don't you think? It's a small company, and they lost two employees in a matter of days. What're the odds, eh?"

"God knows." Jake masked his panic. If Detective Zwerling was making a connection between Kathleen's death and Voloshin's murder, he could have been here scanning the crowd for Voloshin's killer. And the trail could lead to Slater, or to Pam. Maybe even to Ryan.

"Kathleen's mother is very upset about Voloshin's murder." Detective Zwerling took another drag of his Merit. "She considered him a friend of the family. He took a real interest in Kathleen. Taught her coding, Flash, animated gifs. Whatever that is. I'm no techie expert."

"Me, neither." Jake couldn't see the crowd beyond the TV klieglights. Cars were leaving the lot where the BMW was parked, and he couldn't tell if the BMW was still there. He felt his chances slipping away and he couldn't let that happen.

"I'm a detective twenty-two years. That's my expertise and—"

"Excuse me." Jake brandished his phone like a weapon. "I really have to make that call."

"Right." Detective Zwerling cocked his head, blowing smoke out to the side. "Why don't we reconvene tomorrow morning? You free at nine? I'll come by the office with Woohoo."

"No, I'm busy."

"When are you free? I'll work around."

"I'm not sure." Jake knew he needed a lawyer. He'd call Hubbard ASAP. "Tomorrow's not good for me, but I can give you a call, maybe Thursday."

"Too late." Detective Zwerling pursed his lips, his cigarette forgotten. "Jake, I gotta say, I believe you know more than you're letting on."

"No, not at all." Jake felt his mask start to slip. He remembered the photo of the BMW's license plate he had in his phone. It would be so easy to show it to Detective Zwerling and tell him everything. It was Jake's last chance to do the right thing.

They could catch Voloshin's killer together, whether it was Slater or not.

"Really?" Detective Zwerling eyed him through the flimsy curtain of smoke. "You sure? You're jumpy."

"Don't be ridiculous," Jake answered, getting a grip. He couldn't come clean without exposing Ryan, himself, and Pam. He used to care about justice, but now he cared only about his family. He used to know the difference between right and wrong, but all he knew now was that he loved Pam and Ryan, above all else. And he had to get to the BMW before its driver did.

"I'll call you tomorrow."

"Fine," Jake told him, turning away. He walked toward the BMW parking lot and got close enough to see that the BMW was still there, though cars on either side of it were gone. He pressed a button on his phone for show and held it to his ear, as if he were talking. Detective Zwerling would still be watching him, though for all the detective knew, Jake could have been walking toward his own car. Suddenly red taillights went on in the back of the BMW, and the sedan began to pull away.

"No!" Jake heard himself say, holding the phone to his ear. He couldn't run after the car. He couldn't do anything that looked suspicious. He must have missed Slater or whoever it was when they passed on the far side of the TV klieglights. Then he realized he could still get a glimpse of the driver, when the BMW turned around and joined the line of traffic to the main exit.

But it didn't.

Jake gritted his teeth as the BMW drove away, straight across the emptying parking lot toward the exit at the middle school, one of a slew of other drivers who wanted to get out faster.

"Damn it! Damn, damn, damn!" Jake turned around to see Detective Zwerling, standing alone under the canopy among the crowd of families. The TV klieglights reflected off the cigarette smoke that wreathed him, reducing him to a blurry silhouette.

Jake didn't see Slater in the crowd, but he couldn't wait any longer. His plan was blown, and he needed damage control. Detective Zwerling would be wondering what he was doing. Pam's car was parked nearby, and he walked to it casually, while he scrolled to the text function on his phone and texted Pam:

I'm at ur car. Take Ryan out back door. Cops out front. Talk to no one! BE CAREFUL!

Chapter Forty-four

"Ryan, how are you doing?" Jake asked, as soon as Sabrina had gotten out of the car and closed the door behind her. Pam reversed slowly out of the driveway, stalling until Sabrina got inside her house safely, but Jake was really worried about Ryan. The ride had been mostly silent, with Pam keeping her eyes on the road, Sabrina texting with her friends, and Ryan looking out the window, plugged into his white earbuds.

Ryan didn't answer, so Jake twisted around in his seat to see if he was texting. He still wasn't, oddly. He had pulled his hoodie on and seemed almost immobile, except for the jostling of the car as it bobbled over the Belgian blocks that marked the end of Sabrina's driveway. His iPhone sat ignored in his lap, and his face remained turned to the window, though there was nothing he hadn't seen before, only older stone Tudor homes that lined Baird Road, in the exclusive Chase Run neighborhood that served as the model for their development.

"Ryan? You okay?" Jake asked again.

"Let it go," Pam snapped, then her lips resealed shut.

"I want to know how he's doing." Jake kept his tone soft.

"How the hell do you think he's doing? Does he have to spell it out?"

"Fine," Jake said after a moment, then faced front in the passenger seat. He didn't want to bug Ryan, and Pam had been looking daggers at him from the moment she met him at her car. He didn't have to ask why. The memorial service must have been awful for them both. He hadn't had a chance to explain why he'd texted her because the kids had been there. He'd have to fill her in when they were alone, assuming she wasn't leaving him.

Just my luck.

Jake tried to shoo his father's voice from his head, but he wasn't succeeding. He turned his face to the window in the silent car, idly watching the beautiful homes passing darkly. Warm, golden light shone from within, through iron lattice on arched windows, illuminating spacious family rooms behind tall leafy oak trees. It was a clear night and the moon was almost full, a jagged hole shot through a black sky, glimmering on the SUVs below.

Pam seemed to accelerate, driving faster than usual through the winding streets, and Jake reached instinctively for the hanger strap, as if it could tether him to the world he knew and loved. He could lose his wife tonight, and his son was too upset to talk to him. His family was slipping through his very fingers and the only thing in his hand was a fake plastic strap.

He couldn't remember when he had felt this low, and the answer was never. Not even when he'd lost his job, because he still had Pam and Ryan. All he had lost then was money, but he still had a family and that was everything, at the end of the day. It struck him then that he really wasn't like his father, after all. Because his father had always had his family, but no money, and thought that was nothing. But Jake knew better. He had seen it from both sides, and he knew what he was losing. Everything.

Jake flashed on Detective Zwerling and felt a new bolt of fear. He would need to get ahold of Hubbard and get some advice right away. He didn't know what to expect from the police or how to react, and he couldn't afford to slip up and arouse suspicion that would up the ante on an investigation. He would have to explain to Pam about the BMW and his suspicions about Slater, as well as how he had blown it when he had a chance to catch the driver.

Jake, Pam, and Ryan made it home, got out of the car, walked to the house and unlocked the door, still without saying a word to each other. They piled into the entrance hall, a tense and sorrowful threesome, tossing jackets and purses onto the chair beside the console table. Only Moose was his usual happy self, trotting from the kitchen to greet them, smiling with his tongue lolling out of his mouth and wagging his feathery tail.

"Ryan, you all right?" Jake tried again, but Ryan lumbered past him to the stairwell, his head still covered by the hoodie and his ears plugged with the earbuds.

Pam interjected, "Jake, please, let me talk to him—"

"Honey, I can talk to my own son. You can't be my proxy, remember?" Jake hurried up the stairway after Ryan. Moose joined the chase, delighted at the new game, his toenails clicking on the hardwood stairs.

"I don't want to talk." Ryan kept walking upstairs. "I want to be alone."

Pam hurried up after Jake. "Jake, stop, you're going about it all wrong."

Jake ignored her. "Ryan, unplug those things from your ears. Please, let's—"

"No." Ryan kept going, and Jake caught up with him, placing a hand on his shoulder as they both reached the landing.

"Ryan, I know you feel bad—"

"Dad, stop, you don't know." Ryan whirled around, yanking the earbuds from his ears. "I'm not blaming you and I'm not mad at you, that's why I don't want to talk right now. But I can promise you one thing for sure—that you do *not* know how I feel, either of you."

Jake's heart broke at the anguish on Ryan's face, but there was a new tone in his voice, stronger.

Pam reached the top of the stairs, her fair skin flushed with emotion. "Ryan, please, just listen—"

"No, Mom. *I* was the one who killed her, not Dad and not you." Ryan stabbed his finger into his chest with conviction. "*I* was the one everybody was hating on tonight, the one who took her from her friends, from Janine Mae and the rest of the team. And from her computer teacher and her *mom,* and her *dad,* and they both loved her so much they were in this big custody fight over her—"

Pam moaned. "Ryan, I know, but I'm worried about you—"

"Mom, it's not about me. It's about her. You want me to be happy, but can Kathleen? Can she? She's not going to prom or the meet against Methacton. She won't be going to college. She won't even see the *gym bags* she wanted so bad. It's not about me, in the end. I'm *alive.* She's not. She's *dead,* and *I killed her.*"

"But not on purpose—" Pam started to say, but Ryan cut her off with a hand chop.

"What difference does that make, Mom? Did you see her picture on the stage? And the one in the program? *I killed that girl.* So I want to feel *horrible,* I deserve to feel *horrible.* That's fair, right? Me feeling *horrible forever,* because she's dead forever." Ryan paused, dry-eyed, seeming to gather strength from his own words. He backed toward the door of his bedroom, and Moose trotted beside him, his tail still wagging merrily. "You always tell me to take responsibility for my actions, and I am. I'm trying to. I can't do it in public without Dad going to jail, but I can do it privately. So don't freak out because I'm not happy. I'm *not supposed* to be happy. I'm supposed to feel exactly how I feel. It's the least I can do. For *her.*"

Jake felt frightened. He had never seen Ryan this way, determined to self-destruct.

Pam sagged against the banister, stricken. "But Ryan, Caleb's mom said that you were saying something about dying, that sometimes you felt so bad that you wanted to die."

Jake turned to Ryan, horrified. "Is that true? Did you say that?"

"Of course." Ryan almost smiled. "*Of course.* Honestly, I wish I were dead, not her. I wish I could give up my life for hers, right now. Maybe I can. Maybe I will. Nobody gets away with murder. *Nobody.*"

Pam gasped. "Ryan, no. It wasn't murder—"

Ryan snorted. "How is it different, Mom? I'm not talking about some stupid legal definition. She's dead, and I killed her. I deserve to die. I wish I were dead."

"No, Ryan!" Jake cried out. "Don't say that. Don't ever say that!"

"Leave me alone, go away." Ryan reached his bedroom door, fumbled with the knob, and then turned back to face them. "Also Mom, tell your boyfriend to leave me the hell alone." Ryan turned back, went inside his room with the dog, and closed the door behind him.

Jake faced Pam, angry. "What is he talking about, 'your boyfriend'?"

"Jake, not now." Pam raked her manicured hand through her hair.

"Yes, now. Tell me."

Pam sighed, weary. She couldn't meet his eye. "Dave wants to start seeing Ryan, professionally. Caleb told him what Ryan said, too. Dave thinks Ryan is becoming depressed and it would help to talk to him, as a therapist—"

"Are you *kidding* me?" Jake exploded. "Dave said that to Ryan?"

"To both of us, before the service. He's only trying to help him—"

"Doesn't that violate some ethical code? He was *sleeping* with you! Or *is*!"

"No, it's over, I told you."

"Then where were you last night? Did you go to him?"

"No, I stayed in a hotel—"

"Thank God for small favors!" Jake charged down the stairs. "The *balls* on this guy! *Enough!* I've had enough of Dr. Dave! I want him out of my life! Out of my family!"

"Jake, what are you doing?" Pam called after him. "Don't go over there. You can't. His wife is in town."

"So what?" Jake hit the entrance hall and grabbed the car keys from the console table. "It's between me and him!"

"Jake, don't do anything crazy!"

Jake flung open the door and rushed outside.

Chapter Forty-five

Jake's blood boiled as he drove along Dr. Dave's street, a single lane that snaked through dark woods, filled with towering evergreens and oak trees. There were no other houses on the street, much less painted mailboxes, holiday flags, or recycle bins that had to be rolled away by nightfall. Of course Dr. Dave lived in the Pendleton Tract, a beautiful hundred wooded acres under easement to the county, never to be developed. Jake hated that the man who cuckolded him had evergreens that weren't planted in a zigzag pattern.

He turned onto Dr. Dave's driveway and parked behind his Prius, in front of a house that was predictably spectacular, an ultramodern series of glass-walled boxes with concrete edges and flat rooflines, situated on at least six wooded acres. Jake cut the ignition, blood pounding in his ears. He'd had only a single second thought on the drive over, which was about Dr. Dave's wife. He didn't want to tell her that her jerk of a husband was cheating on her. That would hurt her the way he'd been hurt, so he'd have to make sure she was out of the way, to avoid collateral damage.

He got out of his car and slammed the door behind him, which echoed in the woods. He stalked up a flagstone path, bordered with tiny lights to show the way through the trees. The air smelled fresh and clean, which infuriated him all the more. His enemy even had better oxygen.

He glanced at the floor-to-ceiling window on the left of the house, which looked into a showplace living room, with black leather sofas and chairs. A set of gauzy curtains muted the view, but the living room was empty. He reached the front door, also of glass panels, and he was about to pound on one hard enough to break it when the door opened.

Dr. Dave stood in the threshold, blinking calmly behind his hip graphite glasses, and Jake realized that Pam must have warned him that he was coming, which felt like a body blow.

"Dr. Dave, tell your wife to get lost. She's not going to like this conversation."

"She left for the airport. Come in." Dr. Dave opened the door, standing aside politely. Classical music played in the background, from a crystal-clear sound system. "So what are you going to do, Jake? Punch me in the noggin? Go ahead. You're bigger than I am. Displace all the anger you want."

Jake stepped inside. "Hold the jargon. I'm not impressed."

"I was in the kitchen, having dinner. Would you like something?"

"Are you out of your mind, shrink?"

"Suit yourself." Dr. Dave turned neatly away on his thin black loafers and sauntered down a short hall to the back of the house.

"Oh I get it. This is the psychology part. You act very cool when the raging husband comes over." Jake stalked after him into a modern kitchen. Stainless steel appliances lined the back wall, under a large window that was as black as night, reflecting the two men like a dark mirror.

"Not at all, Jake. I'm a therapist, and so I understand the power of a good conversation." Dr. Dave crossed to an island with tall cherrywood stools and a black granite countertop, which held a complete place setting, a plate with a chicken breast and wild rice, next to a glass of wine and an open bottle. Suddenly a little Siamese cat jumped onto the countertop, but Dr. Dave pushed it roughly to the floor, where it landed on its feet.

"You preyed on my wife and now you're preying on my son. I want you to leave my family alone."

"How do you feel about Lambrusco? It's coming back, you know, and this Lini Vineyard produces such a special grape." Dr. Dave lifted the bottle of wine, showing off the label.

"Stick your wine up your ass and listen, I'm talking to you." Jake collected his thoughts. "I'm not going to hit you. I'm not a bully, a thug, or a badass. But I'm not a pushover either."

"I take it that's a no on the Lambrusco." Dr. Dave picked up his glass, swirled the wine around, then took a sip. Meanwhile, the cat walked to the back door, meowed, and sat down, curling its brownish tail around its delicate brown feet.

"I came here to say that I'm trying to save my marriage and my family, and if you can't respect that, then I don't know what kind of a man you are." Jake couldn't hold back his temper. "Put another way, if I catch you anywhere around my wife or my son again, I will beat you to death with my bare hands."

"My." Dr. Dave took another sip of wine, which darkened his teeth. "These are two separate issues, your wife and your son. As for Pam, if your marriage were a happy one, your wife wouldn't have come to me, and I assure you, she came to me."

Jake swallowed hard, suppressing a deep stab of sexual jealousy.

"As for Ryan, I'm his shooting coach, whether you think I'm qualified or not, so it would be quite impossible to comply with your demand."

"Take care of the other kids. Leave him alone." Jake's phone rang in his pocket, but he let it go, guessing it was Pam.

"Are you sure you have Ryan's best interests in mind?" Dr. Dave seemed to be warming up, wanting to spar. He leaned against the counter, palming his glass. "In my professional opinion, Ryan is experiencing situational depression brought on by several factors, such as the conflict between you and Pam, his schoolwork, and the championship. He's been making statements to his teammates that suggest he's having suicidal ideation, which is—"

"I know the term, and you're not qualified to be Ryan's therapist. You were sleeping with his mother."

"I know Ryan very well, and we could work together and have a very good outcome. I'm sure that Ryan would love to work with me. We're very close." Dr. Dave set down his wine, and the cat meowed again, loudly this time.

"I *said,* leave my son alone." Jake didn't tell Dr. Dave that Ryan knew about his affair with Pam, because he didn't want Dr. Dave to know more about his family than he already did.

"Jake, you're making decisions for Ryan that he's perfectly capable of making for himself. Excuse me, this cat won't shut up." Dr. Dave crossed to the back door, twisted the deadbolt, and opened the door. The cat slipped outside, and in the next moment, a motion-detector light went on in the backyard, illuminating a fancy two-car garage.

In front of it was parked a gleaming black BMW 535.

And its license plate read HKE-7553.

Chapter Forty-six

Jake almost gasped in shock, looking out the window. It was *the* BMW. It didn't belong to Dr. Dave, so it must have been his wife's. They must've driven separately to the memorial service.

Jake's thoughts raced. He didn't realize Dr. Dave had known Kathleen, but he must have. Dr. Dave must have been the one who had an affair with Kathleen, not Slater. Dr. Dave would've known about Dolomite Road because that's where the athletic teams ran. Dr. Dave must have killed Voloshin.

Jake turned around just in time to see Dr. Dave pull a handgun from a cabinet drawer, aim it at his chest, and start firing.

CRAK! CRAK! CRAK! went the gunshots. Flames burst from the gun barrel.

Jake dove out of the way, too late. He doubled over reflexively and hit the tile floor. His stomach exploded in searing pain, like his gut caught fire. He curled into the fetal position, gripping his belly. Warm red blood spurted from between his fingers. He tried to get up. Intense pain felled him. He couldn't move for the agony. He tried to scream but could only whisper, "No."

"Wow, you're still alive?" Dr. Dave set the gun on the island. "No matter. You won't be for long."

"No, no." Jake felt sheer terror. Blood sprayed from his belly, spattering the tile floor. He tried to stanch the flow, but he couldn't. He shifted to get up again, but agonizing pain seared through his entire body.

"Sorry, Jake. I'd put you out of your misery, but the trajectory of the bullet would be wrong. It has to be level and face-to-face. I saw on TV."

Blood gushed everywhere, spattering the tiles, running in rivulets in the grout. Jake watched it leak from him, helpless. He began to lose consciousness.

"I had to shoot you, in self-defense." Dr. Dave picked up his knife from beside his dinner plate and crossed to him. "You drove here, enraged about Pam and me. She called and said you weren't the violent type, so I didn't call 911. You and I were talking it over, apparently reasonably, but suddenly you became angry and tried to kill me."

Jake felt dizzy and faint. The pain raged in his stomach.

"You grabbed my steak knife and tried to stab me." Dr. Dave knelt down with the knife beside Jake, picked up his hand, placed the knife in his palm, and wrapped his fingers around the handle. "I managed to get to my gun and protect myself. Unfortunately, by the time 911 arrived, you had bled to death."

Jake pulled his hand away, but the knife clattered to the floor. The pain was so intense it immobilized him. He was going to die.

"Are your keys in your pocket?" Dr. Dave plunged his hand into Jake's pocket, fished around, and pulled out his car keys. "Perfect. The police will find Voloshin's laptop and phone in the trunk of your car. They'll figure that you killed him because he was blackmailing you. After all, he had proof that you and Ryan killed Kathleen in the hit-and-run."

Jake looked around wildly. He couldn't save himself. He

couldn't get away. Dr. Dave was framing him for Voloshin's murder.

"Kathleen was one of my favorite clients, and she was incredible in bed. Trust me, the ones with father issues are the best." Dr. Dave straightened up, hurried to a base cabinet, and took out a Whole Foods bag. A gray computer cord hung out of its open mouth. It had to be Voloshin's laptop and phone.

Jake didn't want to die. Pam and Ryan needed him. Blood drenched the floor. He could barely see as Dr. Dave left the kitchen with the bag, then the front door slammed.

Ring! Jake's cell phone rang again. It had to be Pam. His heart fluttered with hope. It was his only chance. His cell phone was in his right back pocket. He didn't have any time to lose. Dr. Dave would return any minute.

Jake moved his arm toward his pocket. He cried out in agony. He froze. He couldn't move. His body began to shake uncontrollably. He couldn't keep his eyes open. His phone stopped ringing. It was over.

Jake heard the front door slam, then footsteps returning to the kitchen. He roused, opening his eyes to see Dr. Dave knock his dinner plate to the floor, scattering the chicken and rice.

"The proverbial signs of a struggle," Dr. Dave said, half to himself. He straight-armed the wineglass and bottle off the counter, and they shattered on the tile. He upended a cherrywood stool, then another. He eyed the kitchen, putting a finger to his mouth, then crossed to the oven, grabbed a metal frying pan from the stovetop and threw it clanging to the floor. He walked over to the toaster and pushed it over, then the coffeemaker. He swept newspapers off one of the stools, then glanced over at Jake.

"What, you're still alive? Get on with it, man. I have to call 911, but you don't look dead enough." Dr. Dave took the gun off the counter and walked to Jake, cocking his head as if he were thinking aloud. "I bet I could get away with another shot."

"No," Jake whispered, in terror.

"I could say I was afraid you could get up, in fear for my life."

Dr. Dave aimed the gun at Jake.

Suddenly, there was a noise from the front door.

Dr. Dave turned away, toward the sound.

And all hell broke loose.

Chapter Forty-seven

"NO!" Ryan bellowed, barreling into the kitchen with Pam at his heels.

"No" was all Jake could whisper, horrified they were in harm's way.

Ryan took a flying leap at Dave and tackled him heavily to the ground. They both yelled and grunted, struggling for the gun. Suddenly a shot fired. Pam screamed.

Tears of fright sprang to Jake's eyes. He didn't know whether Ryan or Dave had been shot. He prayed to God for Ryan's life. Pam burst into tears, covering her head with her hands.

Suddenly Ryan staggered to his feet, supporting himself on the kitchen island. Pam ran to his side, crying with relief. Dr. Dave remained on the floor, moaning and holding his shoulder.

Jake thanked God. He could've died a happy man at that moment, but Ryan and Pam rushed together at him.

"Jake, Jake!" Pam sobbed, throwing herself to the floor beside him. "Honey, the police will be here! I worried you got in a fight, when you didn't answer! An ambulance is on the way! They should be here any minute!"

"Dad, don't die, please don't die!" Ryan bent over him, distraught. "I love you, Dad! I love you!"

Jake looked up at them, feeling weaker by the second. He wanted to tell them he loved them. He wanted to tell them to be happy without him, that nothing else mattered to him as much, on the face of the earth. "Pam," he tried to say, but it came out fainter than a whisper.

"Honey, stay with us!" Pam embraced him, beginning to sob. "The ambulance will be here any minute!"

"Dad, don't die, please, please!"

Jake could barely hear them. He felt himself slipping away. He flashed on the bag that Dr. Dave had put in the trunk of his car, with Voloshin's laptop and phone. It contained the only evidence that connected Ryan to the hit-and-run. If Ryan and Pam disposed of it, nobody would ever know what had happened. If they gave it to the police, they would go to jail. He tried to say, "Ryan . . . trunk . . ."

"What, Dad?" Ryan bent over him, crying. "The *trunk*? Of the *car*?"

Jake managed a smile, closing his eyes. They would figure it out when they opened the trunk. They would decide what to do.

Jake knew what he would do, if he had a second chance. But he couldn't say, and he'd have to leave the decision to them.

Because he was gone.

Chapter Forty-eight

Jake couldn't keep his eyes open. He was bathed in light, warm on his face, and for a minute he didn't know if he was alive or dead. He squinted around him and realized he was lying in a hospital room. Sunshine poured through the window and fell on his bed, in a glowing shaft of gold. He thanked God he was alive.

The room was empty, and he lay there, feeling horrible, exhausted and weak. His stomach throbbed with pain. He could think only slowly, as if his brain didn't work. His throat felt raw and dry, it was hard to swallow. An IV shunt was taped to his hand, a plastic clip covered his index finger. Monitors glowed next to his bed, and the door to the room was open. He became aware that the hallway outside sounded busy. People were talking and carts rattled, a metallic sound. He could smell the faint aroma of coffee and eggs, mingling with institutional disinfectants. He wasn't hungry.

He closed his eyes against the sun. He tried to remember how he had gotten here. He must be snowed under with painkillers. It must've been last night. Dave had shot him in the gut.

322 | Lisa Scottoline

He'd been bleeding, lying on the floor. He remembered Dave pointing the gun down at him, about to fire again. Then Ryan, rushing in. And Pam, crying at his side. His wife and son had saved his life.

Jake thought of something else. The bag of evidence in the trunk of his car. He wondered what Pam and Ryan had done with it, whether they had shown it to the police or gotten rid of it forever. They weren't around, nobody was, so he figured they must have come clean to the cops and gone to prison.

His heart lurched at the thought, but they had done the right thing, in the end. He prayed that Ryan had been charged as a juvenile, not an adult, so Jake would bear the brunt of their punishment. He could accept going to prison, and he understood why it was necessary. He had *lived* why it was necessary. He had to take responsibility for Kathleen's death, and he'd rather live with honesty in prison than live on the outside, in guilt and shame.

Suddenly, there was a commotion at the doorway, and Pam, Ryan, and Detective Zwerling entered the room. Pam closed the curtains against the sunshine, then looked at Jake and did a double-take.

"Babe, are you awake? Thank God!" Pam crossed to his bedside, with Ryan next to her, breaking into a broad grin.

"Dad, how are you?"

"Fine," Jake answered, hoarse. He assumed Pam and Ryan must have been out on bail. They were wearing the same clothes as yesterday, so they hadn't even gone home. Or maybe they were released on Detective Zwerling's recognizance, waiting to see what happened to him. Jake didn't want to jump to the last possibility, which was that Pam and Ryan had hidden the evidence and hadn't told the police, and they were all back at square one.

"Good to see you." Pam smiled down at him, her expression soft, but not completely unguarded.

"You, too," Jake croaked out, but he knew it didn't begin to communicate the power of the emotion he felt for her. He thanked God he was still alive and prayed that Pam would stay married to him, but that was a conversation for another time.

Detective Zwerling was almost smiling. "Buckman, you're tougher than I thought."

Pam took his hand and held it lightly. "How do you feel?"

"Okay."

"Honey, do you want some water, or juice? Are you in pain?"

"No."

"The doctor said you're going to be fine, in time. They did an ex lap, an exploratory laparotomy, and they removed the bullets from your stomach. There was a lot of internal bleeding, because one went through a major blood vessel, the—"

"Wait, first tell me what's going on with . . ." Jake didn't want to finish the sentence in front of Detective Zwerling, but Pam nodded, reading his mind.

"We told the police about the laptop and phone. They found them in the trunk of your car. Ryan and I agreed to go forward, and we figured that's what you'd want to do, too."

"I did, but how did you know?" Jake felt the weight of the world lifted from his shoulders, but he was still confused about what was going on.

"I know you." Pam's expression grew grave. "As for what happened next, I'll leave that to the authorities to explain. Bill?"

"Sure." Detective Zwerling edged closer to the bed, looking down at Jake, and the folds of his face fell into deep lines. "Pam and Ryan gave us a statement about what happened last Friday night. You'll have to give us one, too, when you're feeling well enough. But neither you nor Ryan are being charged with vehicular homicide."

"Why not?" Jake asked, dumbfounded.

"The autopsy determined that the injuries Kathleen sustained as a result of being hit by your car were postmortem."

"What?" Jake didn't understand, struggling through a pharmaceutical fog to think.

"Kathleen was already dead when you hit her. The cause of her death was blunt force trauma to her head. The District Attorney charged Dr. David Tolliver for her murder and the murder of Andrew Voloshin."

"Are you saying that Dr. Dave *killed* Kathleen?" Jake couldn't process it fast enough. All this time, he had thought that he and Ryan were responsible for Kathleen's death.

"Yes, we believe so."

"How? Why?"

"This is confidential, but in the circumstances, I'll fill you in. Kathleen was a patient of Tolliver's, sent by her mother to help cope with the divorce and custody case. Her parents had no knowledge of any relationship between them, outside the client-doctor. Kathleen's friend Janine Mae told us that Kathleen had fallen in love with an older man, in secret. Kathleen didn't tell Janine Mae that the man was Tolliver. She told Janine Mae it was someone she met online."

Jake couldn't believe what he was hearing. His stomach was killing him, but he didn't want to interrupt Detective Zwerling to get more painkillers.

"Janine Mae knew they met sometimes on Dolomite Road, at night. Tolliver probably used his wife's car because the school teams could have recognized his car."

Jake realized he'd been right about that much, but he was too astounded to feel any satisfaction.

"We think that Tolliver wanted to break off the relationship, but Kathleen didn't. We believe that Kathleen threatened to tell her parents if he called it quits, so Tolliver killed her." Detective Zwerling pursed his thin lips. "Tolliver lawyered up and isn't talking, but we have hard evidence against him. Again, confidential, but we have his hair and fiber on Kathleen's body and clothing. We also have her blood in the BMW. We collected

DNA and expect it will be corroborative, but the results aren't back yet. The forensics show that he killed her in the BMW, by slamming her head into the dashboard."

Jake felt a wave of disgust.

"He left her body by the side of Pike Road. He probably thought she'd look like a victim of a hit-and-run, given the blind curve. You and Ryan came by shortly thereafter, maybe even within ten minutes, according to the best estimate of the pathologist."

"Pathologists can figure that out? How?"

"By the location and type of her injuries, during the autopsy. It's about blood loss and so forth."

Jake tried to understand the implications. "Did you know all along that whoever was guilty of the hit-and-run didn't actually kill Kathleen?"

"No, we weren't sure, and the pathologist couldn't be a hundred percent certain. If there had been more time between the time she was actually killed and when her body was hit, he would have been more sure. But it was our theory, and we liked you."

Jake blinked, surprised. "I like you, too, Detective Zwerling."

Pam snorted, with a sly smile. "Jake, in police talk, 'like' means 'suspect.' The police suspected you."

Detective Zwerling permitted himself a tight smile. "We didn't release that information to the newspapers. We were still investigating. Your actions flushed Tolliver out, but we don't sanction citizen involvement. Law enforcement is for professionals, Jake." Detective Zwerling's smile faded, and his jowls deepened with disapproval. "You almost lost your life. You would have, if not for your wife and son."

"I know. Thank God for them." Jake felt a surge of love for his family, and Pam squeezed his hand.

Detective Zwerling straightened up, as if he were becoming official again. "The D.A. will be in to see you, later today. He'll tell you that you'll be charged with leaving the scene of an accident and failing to give information. Those are misdemeanors in the first degree, or M1s. They involve fines and such, but no prison time."

"I'll take whatever punishment I have coming. But what about Ryan?"

"The D.A. exercised his discretion not to charge Ryan as an adult, in view of your efforts in the case. He'll be charged with the same offenses as you, but as a juvenile. He'll get probation and have to perform community service. He'll have no criminal record when he comes of age."

"Thank you, that's wonderful. We're very grateful." Jake felt relief wash over him, momentarily forgetting about his pain.

Ryan said, "Yes, Detective Zwerling, thank you again."

Pam looked from Ryan to Jake with a worried frown. "Even so, there's going to be other repercussions, for all of us. I'm stepping down from the bench."

"Babe, really?" Jake sighed. He could tell from Ryan's resigned expression that it wasn't news to him. "Do you really have to?"

"Yes, of course. My oath is to uphold and defend the Constitution and the laws of the Commonwealth, yet I chose to hide illegality. It's misconduct, and if I stayed, it would damage the reputation of the Court." Pam pursed her lips, but she didn't seem angry at Jake, just regretful. "I already emailed the Chief Judge and my colleagues, so they won't find out from the newspaper. The D.A. plans to hold a press conference at one o'clock. The reporters are already swarming in front of the hospital."

"I'm sorry," Jake told her, meaning it.

"Thanks, but it's not on you, honey." Pam smiled at him, sadly. "It's on me. I made my choice, and I'll take my lumps."

"So you won't be a judge anymore?" Jake felt terrible for her.

"That might be a good thing, huh?" Pam winked, with a crooked smile. "No more Judge Mom."

"But what will you do?"

"I'm not sure yet. Let's not talk about it now." Pam shrugged it off. "Nobody's getting off scot-free. I'm embarrassed and ashamed, so are we all. There'll be gossip and headlines. It won't be easy."

"I know." Ryan nodded, his lips flattened to a grim line. "People are already posting about it on Facebook. I'll lose a lot of friends, I know. Everybody will be talking about it. The big-time recruiters and programs will bounce. Bye-bye, Division I."

"That might be right." Jake appreciated that Ryan was being so realistic. "I guess I'll lose clients. Plus Amy and my employees are going to be disillusioned. But I can deal."

Pam eyed him, her anxiety plain. "What will happen to Gardenia? Do you lose your certification over this?"

"I don't think so. Amy will stay, and I have enough cushion to float the payroll for a while. It's Ryan I'm worried about." Jake turned to his son. "Buddy, can you take the heat?"

"Totally. We both can. Don't worry about it, Dad. We've been through worse, haven't we?" Ryan looked down at Jake, his gaze grown-up. "Here's what I think. It's awful that Kathleen died, the way she died, but I didn't kill her. I didn't kill *anybody*. I don't have that on my conscience anymore. I don't have to lie to anybody or hide anything. I feel, like, so grateful and *free*. Do you see, Dad? I'm *good again*."

Pam's eyes glistened, but she didn't say anything, letting Ryan and Jake have their moment.

"Ryan, you always were good," Jake said, hoarsely, his entire body flooding with peace.

"We'll get through this together."

"Yes, we will." Jake reached for Ryan's hand, and Ryan reached back, and Jake could feel the warmth, strength, and power that flowed between them, palpable in the clasp of their hands, which were large and so much alike.

"I love you, Dad," Ryan said, with feeling.

"I love you, too, boy," Jake told him, and at long last, he could feel the beginning of a reconnection between them, one that had less to do with superficial things like cars and girls, and more to do with something important, natural, and even eternal.

Flesh, and blood.

Epilogue

Six months later, Jake and Pam were sitting on the bleachers at a packed basketball game, watching Ryan. The gym thundered with the clamoring of parents, siblings, and students. Kids ran up and down the aisles. Moms cheered, dads clapped, and Jake felt as if everything was the same as before—except that everything was also different.

The gym was smaller and shabbier, in a tougher part of town. Ryan wasn't playing, but assistant-coaching, and none of the players was very tall, because they were eight-year-old girls. Their ponytails bounced in their matching scrunchies, their purple T-shirts hung to their knobby knees, and their wide-leg shorts flapped when they ran. Jake took a special interest in the kids' gear because he had bought it all. The team was the Gardenia Guardians, named for what was left of his company.

He nudged Pam, pleased. "They look good, huh?"

"What?" Pam kept watching the game, craning her neck.

"They look good!" Jake said, louder, and Pam looked at him like he was crazy, her blue eyes amused behind her glasses.

"What are you talking about? They're losing by seven points."

"The uniforms, I mean."

Pam rolled her eyes. "It still bugs me they're purple. Gardenias aren't purple."

"White is boring, honey."

"Gardenias aren't white, they're ivory, which is a *lovely* color."

"Kids don't want lovely. They want cool, and purple is cool."

"Oh, hush! Watch the game." Pam turned to the court.

Jake half-watched the game, contentedly. Bottom line, he was happy to be alive. His stomach still hurt from time to time, but he'd even started running with Ryan. In fact, he'd already lost two pounds. Well, it was a start.

Jake sensed the worst was over. Dr. Dave had pleaded guilty to both murders and was sentenced to life without parole, thus avoiding the death penalty. The media had moved on almost instantly, though the gossip lingered in their development, at school, in social media, and in the financial-services community. They would forever be the family who had left the scene of a hit-and-run, but they tried to hold their heads high. Jake hadn't lost his certification, and Amy and almost all of his employees stayed with him. His remaining clients were making money, so he hoped that word-of-mouth would attract new ones. If it didn't, he'd stay small or start over. He'd learned there were worse things in life than losing your job.

Pam nudged him, pointing to the court. "Honey, look. Tiffany's going to shoot."

"She'll miss."

"Don't be that way."

"Please. They always miss. The final scores are, like, three to two."

Pam hit his leg playfully. "Aw, but she's so cute. I love that little girl."

"That's true. She's adorable." Jake watched Tiffany shove the basketball two-handed into the air, then it fell to the court, bouncing away.

"Oh well." Pam chuckled, shaking her head. Both teams raced after the ball, tumbling over one another, a rolling mob of flailing arms and outstretched fingers.

"Looks like a shoe sale at Nordstrom's," Jake said, and Pam laughed, which pleased him no end. They were back in therapy, putting their marriage back together, sometimes with Ryan, too. Pam had been depressed for months, but had begun to come around after the headlines died down. The local law firms didn't make her a job offer, so she was working as a contract lawyer, writing briefs for the big, white-shoe firms in Philly. They wouldn't put her name on the papers, but they were happy to have her brainpower. They'd considered moving away from Concord Chase, but decided against it, unanimously. It wouldn't work in the age of Facebook, and they were through with family secrets.

Ryan had gotten through a predictably difficult junior year, with the school and the team in turmoil. The Chasers lost to Lower Merion in the championship, and the basketball recruiters never called Ryan again, though he'd weathered the social storm at school and kept his grades up. The assistant-coaching gig had fulfilled his community service obligation, but he'd already finished the required hours. He'd found a calling in coaching and landed a summer job assistant-coaching in the playground league, for the Concord Chase Rec Department. He was even talking about applying to colleges closer to home. Pam was relieved he wouldn't be leaving the nest completely, and Jake acted like he was happy on her behalf, but he was happy for himself. He loved spending time with Ryan, and it turned out that he didn't have to compete with Call of Duty. On the contrary, he learned to play video games.

Jake watched Ryan calling to the kids on the sidelines, and his heart swelled with pride. He went to all the games, just to watch Ryan, and felt as if he was finally gaining ground with their son. Ryan, Pam, and he spent more time together than ever before, maybe because nobody else would talk to them. Turned out there was nothing like a public shunning to bring a family closer.

The cheering crowd leapt to its feet, and one of the girls on the opposing team blew past a Gardenia Guardian and actually scored a basket. Jake watched as the little Guardian burst into tears, ran off the court, and beelined to Ryan. Ryan bent down, gave her a big hug, then talked to her and sent her back into the game.

Pam let out a sympathetic moan. "Aw, that's Talisa, the poor kid. She feels terrible."

"Yes, but look at our son," Jake said, with a quiet satisfaction. He fast-forwarded into the future, to the time when Ryan became a father to his own child. Jake could see how loving Ryan would be, and how kind. They had both wanted to meet with Kathleen's parents to apologize, but the Lindstroms had declined the meeting, and it had been Ryan's idea to plant a weeping willow in their backyard, as their private memorial to Kathleen. Suddenly Jake's heart lifted, easing a burden that he hadn't realized he was carrying until this very moment. He had made so many mistakes as a father, but in the end, he'd done one thing right. He'd been a better father than his own, and Ryan would be the best father of all.

"Jake." Pam leaned over, excited. "Look!"

"I'm watching, I'm watching." Jake came out of his reverie.

"Not at the game, at the stands." Pam pointed across the court. "Look over there. Do you see what I see? Third row up, in the pink ball cap, with the white tank top. Isn't that Sabrina?"

"Yes." Jake nodded, matter-of-factly.

"What's she doing here? Is something going on between her and Ryan?"

"Well, he was worried she friend-zoned him, but he's taking her out tonight. It's their first date but she texts him constantly from Friends Central camp, where she's a counselor-in-training. She writes funny texts and he likes that—"

"Wait. How do *you* know all this?" Pam looked at him, wide-eyed.

"I'm *baller,* honey. I'm baller *G.*"

"*What?*" Pam burst into laughter, and Jake wrapped his arms around her, kissing her forehead and catching a scent of her gardenia perfume. His wife was the most wonderful woman he had ever known, and he felt so grateful to be her Husband Material.

Just my luck.

Acknowledgments

I usually love to write my acknowledgments, but not this time, because we at St. Martin's Press have just lost our beloved publisher and friend Matthew Shear to cancer. This novel is dedicated to him, because I loved him and owe him so much, in so many ways. Permit me to tell you about him, because he was someone who loved books.

Matthew was simply a warm and wonderful man, with a big heart and an even bigger grin. He was a hugger. If you sat next to him at dinner, you knew you were going to have the best time of anyone at the table. He was honest and real and fun. He had great judgment. He loved life. He was witty, but no snob. He was the smartest guy in the room, but not a show-off. He could talk about books all day long, but he talked more about his wife of thirty-some years, Sabrina, and his two daughters, Hayley and Lindsey. As much as he loved to talk, he was a great listener. He listened intently when you spoke, and anyone who knew him can picture his direct, dark-eyed gaze while he listened as easily as they can recall the distinctive sound of his laugh, which was loud and joyful. It wasn't a musical laugh. Musical is overrated, as far as laughs go.

Matthew was also a brilliant publisher, and if you don't know what a publisher does, the answer is: everything. In my case, when I first came to St. Martin's Press, Matthew took me under his wing and told me that the house would take great care of me, and it has. He read each of my manuscripts and called or emailed to tell me what he liked in each one. He looked at my book covers with new eyes and changed them so they would reach a wider audience. He weighed in on any newspaper ad for my books, tweaking the taglines, and he moved my publication dates around to get my books in stores when it was best. He took me out of mass market paperback, where I had been published for twenty-odd years, and put me into trade paperback, which got a book of mine on the bestseller list for sixteen weeks, a sales record for me. The move was a radical change for a suspense author at the time, but now has become common. Most of all, he treated my daughter Francesca and me with respect and affection, and considered our opinions—as if we were his partners, not merely his authors. He helped develop the careers of so many authors like me, all because he loved our books and us.

Matthew Shear was larger-than-life, and so he will survive death. Those of us who knew him will never forget him. And we will always love him. In time, we will go on, because he'd want us to, and in so doing, we honor him. So I will thank that great group of wonderful people at St. Martin's, all of whom he loved as his office family, most especially, my incredible editor and dear friend, Jennifer Enderlin, as well as our truly fearless leader, John Sargent, the divine Sally Richardson, and the great crew of Matt Baldacci, Jeanne-Marie Hudson, Brian Heller, Steve Kleckner, Steve Cohen, Jeff Dodes, Jeff Capshew, Nancy Trypuc, Kim Ludlam, John Murphy, John Karle, Rob Grom, Paul Hochman, Stephanie Davis, Caitlin Dareff, and all the wonderful sales reps. Thanks to adorable cover designer, Michael

Storrings. Thanks to Mary Beth Roche, Laura Wilson, Esther Bochner, Brant Janeway, and all the great people in audiobooks. I love and appreciate all of you.

Now onto the experts and kind souls who helped me with *Keep Quiet*. Any and all mistakes herein are mine. I'm a former lawyer, but criminal law wasn't my field, and my first thanks go to a supersmart and dedicated public servant, Nicholas Casenta, Esq., Chief Deputy District Attorney of the Chester County District Attorney's Office. Nick has helped me with every book so far, including this one, and I throw hard questions at Nick, at all hours of the day and night, via panicky email. His answers are always spot-on, superbly well-reasoned, and incredibly helpful, and I couldn't be more grateful to him. Thank you so very much, Nick!

Thanks to Binney Weitlisbach, Betty Tafel, and Holly Palermo, of Haverford Trust, who took the time to answer all my dumb questions about financial planning. Thanks to Chief Gene Dooley and Detective Patricia Logic of the West Whiteland Township Police Department, and Chief John M. Narcise, Lieutenant Robert P. Klinger, Detective Stephen Jones, Officer Andrew J. Wahn, and Nancy Shechan of the Willistown Township Police Department, who took their valuable time to answer my dumb questions about police procedure. Thanks to Dr. Nicole Kimze, who took her valuable time to answer my dumb questions about medical procedures. Thanks to Michael Skinner, Esq.

Thanks to Doug Young of the Lower Merion School District, and his lovely staff. Doug is an amazing young man, who took his time to explain the techniques and Zen of basketball and basketball recruiting to me, as well as what life is like on a great basketball team in a great school like my alma mater, Lower Merion High School. Doug played on the same team as Kobe Bryant, and they are both rock stars to me. Thanks to Aces Nation, for being so welcoming to me, and congratulations to the championship-winning Aces!

Thanks and love to my wonderful agent and friend Molly Friedrich, who has guided me for so long now, and to the amazing Lucy Carson and Molly Schulman.

Thanks and love to my dedicated and wonderful assistant and best friend Laura Leonard. She's invaluable in every way and has been for more than twenty years. Thanks, too, to my great assistant and friend Nan Daley, who helped so much with the research on this book and supports me every way she can.

Thank you very much to my family, and to my amazing daughter Francesca, for everything.

But my final thanks, as my first thanks, go to Matthew Shear. I am eternally grateful.